BREATHE

Cover Design: Opulent Swag and Designs

Editor: Editing4Indies

Proofread: Rumi Khan

Format: Opulent Swag and Designs

C.L. MATTHEWS

IN MY LOWEST MOMENTS, THE ONLY
REASON I DIDN'T COMMIT SUICIDE WAS THAT I
KNEW I WOULDN'T BE ABLE TO DRINK
ANY MORE IF I WAS DEAD.

ERIC CLAPTON

C.L. MATTHEWS

DEDICATION

TO THE ONES FIGHTING FOR THEIR LIFE DAILY,
THIS IS FOR YOU.

C.L. MATTHEWS

SPECIAL THANKS TO DIMPLES.

WITHOUT YOU, THIS BOOK WOULD BE TRASH.

...ly a number at £20 ...
... so I r... ...
...ith called at night Joh...
... and told me he had
... — so I asked
...ber ... to you which
...as last ... How you
... German soldier who h...
... asked the Irish prison...
... near ... On the w...
... German's head but
... of the fact ... On ...
... whata the good of h...

PART I
TOXICITY

There's always a *before* and an *after*.
The *before* tends to be the good times.
Everything that occurs before the bad.
The *after* is the shit that's dealt.
Whether it's depression, heartbreak, or losing
everything that mattered to you in the "before."
Both signify a chapter ending.
Both also depict a gnarly picture.
One thing you'll learn, nothing can change the before
like the after, and nothing can change the
after without accepting the before.

- TOBY

PROLOGUE

TOBY

EVERY DAY, IT'S LIKE THIS.

Run.

Sweat.

Weightlifting.

Exhaustion.

To distract myself from my problems, I run until I can't. I work out until my limbs are heavy with exhaustion. I exert myself until my body shuts down. My mind works until it's a heap of nothingness, too, because that's easier than accepting the fate I've been given. The one I single-handedly served myself on a platter full of blood, guts, and bones, hoping for a better outcome than becoming a meal. But that's what happens when you hope. You lose, and until you weigh the loss with the outcome, you're bound to give up more than you bargained for.

My feet stop at the Magic Bean, the shop Lo and I always went to after runs. The craving for a Danish—one I've bought her on many occasions—stabs through my stomach, reminding me how little I eat or indulge anymore. As soon as I walk through the door, the heat outside is replaced by a crisp breeze and the scent of my favorite beverage. Black coffee, no sugar.

The clerk behind the counter isn't someone I recognize, but of course not. A lot has changed in the five years I've been gone. Why not take my favorite barista too?

As soon as it's my turn at the counter, I see Alara. My favorite coffee shop employee comes out from the back, eyeing me almost as if she's not sure it's really me. As soon as her mind connects with my face, she smiles and moves the dude clerk away.

"Tobias Hayes, is that you?" she questions in her usual cheery voice.

I grin back, happy to see a friendly face in Hollow Ridge. "Sure is. Can I get my regular?"

"A black coffee?" she jests and laughs.

She used to joke that only psychopaths drink coffee black. It's not a bad assessment, according to the people around me.

With a nod, I give her my card. As soon as I sign the receipt, giving her a nice tip, I wait for my coffee. Thirty seconds later, I have it gripped in my hand.

When I turn around, my hand slips.

Do you hear that sound? That's my life fracturing at this moment. The room is silent, yet the coffee cup dropping from my grasp, toppling to the ground and spilling is like a large thump, mimicking my heartbeat. Everyone's gaze meets mine, making me more aware of where I'm currently residing. Their expressions range from worry and confusion to annoyed and amused.

I ignore them. In the end, they don't matter.

My eyes go back to what made me drop my coffee, or rather, who.

Years.

It's been several since I've seen her, yet the pain is as fresh as a brutal collision. It's as real as a moment of disaster in a beautiful package. It's as damning as an end before it began.

Her short hair is now long again, the tresses hitting the middle of her back like then. But it's not then. It's now. It's bitterness in a glass of whiskey. It's distaste in a cup of joe with sugar. It's heartbreak in a room of dead people.

She's even more beautiful now.

Radiant.

Delicate.

Fierce.

Her eyes light up, but the glossiness isn't the same. Back then, they were always brimming with tears of heartache, and now, they shine with affection. The vast difference between before and now is stifling.

The affection she offers has everything to do with the russet brown-haired toddler begging for her attention. He can't be older than four, but something about him triggers something in me.

That single night.

The one that changed it all.

My forehead beads with sweat, my stomach concaving with the possibilities. No. She wouldn't keep that from me. Even with our past in the air, our pain on repeat, our friendship gone... she wouldn't keep a child—my child, if that's the case—away from me.

Right?

She feeds little pieces of a bagel to him, her eyes lighting up as he smiles and giggles. Her eyes, the ones I've loved for years, gaze at him as if he created the earth itself. Maybe he did. Maybe he's godly and ethereal. Maybe, by some chance, he's a miracle. Our miracle.

I forget about my coffee on the ground, and my steps become more frantic in my haste to get to her. The breath of coffee I inhale reminds me of all the mornings we spent together, enjoying a cup of joe and pastries for her sweet tooth before we'd go for a run.

Then the memories fade, and the pain returns.

I'm only six feet from her table, five steps tops to get to her, to demand answers, but before I make it, a hand on my chest halts me abruptly. I turn to the person stopping me, and my glare is met with lustrous fiery almond eyes.

My heart drops farther, if possible, striking me in another place that hasn't felt in so long.

"What the fuck are you doing here?"

4

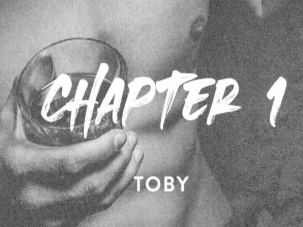

CHAPTER 1

TOBY

MY HEAD RINGS AS MY PHONE'S ALARM CLOCK BLARES *Journey*, waking me up, while also spearing into my skull repeatedly. How much did I drink last night? How did I get home?

Why can't I remember anything? I told myself not to drink again since benders don't benefit me. Change. The six-letter word I've been trying to implement into my life. I want change. What the hell have I done now?

The smell of flowers, fresh linen, and something else invades my nose, only further worsening the pounding in my head. Who even likes this mixture? It smells like an old people's home. You know the floral smell, the one they think old people appreciate but, in reality, hate just as bad as young people?

Is this my house? *Wait.* I no longer have a house. After everything, it ended up on the market and selling within two months. That's what happens when you abandon all hope. You realize items are just that... items. They don't matter and neither does anything else.

My eyes strain to open, forcing my spine erect. My body winces in response, the pain as fresh as the wave of nausea. My gaze scans the white bedroom, the plain walls, the clean white dressers, side tables, and carpet to match. It's like a wedding room, one where innocence goes to die. And a moment later, someone's groaning. *A woman.*

Soft delicate noises are my favorite pastime. They're infiltrating and caressing, giving me the ease only whiskey offers.

Turning slowly, I remain as quiet as possible, and my eyes land onto a contented form. Usually after a night of partying, I don't pay attention to someone after they've fulfilled my needs, but she's somehow different. Her cinnamon spice hair fans out around her, making the room seem vacant and colorless in comparison. She's snuggling her pillow as if it's the source of all happiness. Her eyes are shut, serene, something I haven't experienced in a long-ass time.

Peace.

Sleep.

Someone by my side.

The thought of those necessities, the human touch I've lacked for years, hits me square in the chest. I miss Lo. My Sparkle. My light. She was a driving force in my life. She made me want to get up in the morning and strive for better. She made me better and sober. *She ruined you.* And I welcomed that ruin like the alcohol bottle always gripped in my palm.

When we spent time together, it felt like I could conquer the world. Without her, I proved I'd fall. It's the last thing I wanted, but it's the reality I live with every day. My inability to staunch my alcohol dependence became clear in the first month without her. Two years later, I'm still a slave to my vices.

Waking up in a pool of vomit with an empty bottle and unabated pain only solidifies that my problems are worsening. That's my repeat action—binge. Without her, I'm lost. Without her, I'm a shell. Without her, I'm *worthless*.

I collect my shame, bottling it up in a Mason jar along with my soul.

When will my collection be too much to bear?

My bedmate's light snoring brings my attention to yet another fateful night from the bottle. Why is this stranger in my bed, or rather a bed I don't recognize? What happened last night? I was... *where the hell am I?*

My mind attempts to wrap around last night's events, but I draw many foggy images. One sticks, though. One of this auburn-haired goddess.

"Toby," I mumble, my voice hardened. This was supposed to work out in my best interest, not give me a young twenty-something chef who has never held a job before. A year at a renowned restaurant as an intern chef isn't considered holding a job, even if that's what she's proud of.

"Joey," she responds, her eyes wary. *Like me, she doesn't want to be here either.*

Tough shit, Sous.

I shake my head.

A chef. *My* chef?

Joey.

Who names their female child Joey? If she's my employee, I wonder how fucked I'll be when HR gets ahold of this tidbit. Rubbing the sleep from my eyes, I attempt to shift without waking her, but the bed creaks anyway. She groans as my body finally frees itself from the confines of sheets, feathers, and a comforter.

What did we do last night?

It looks like a cheap remake of that awful *Twilight* scene. As the image infiltrates my mind, I chuckle at the dumbness, unable to hold back the comparison. Lo always loved the books. Not the movies, but she watched them anyway. *Made sure to force me to watch too.* My laughter costs me, and her eyes widen. Unlike me, she is up in a flash. Her face wild with fear and confusion. *Jesus.* She must not remember either.

In the past two years, I've slept with so many women I can't see straight when trying to picture them. But this? Her worried look and uncertainty have me feeling like utter shit. Were we not supposed to sleep together? Did she not want this? Fuck. I'm never this irresponsible. Scratching my head, I try to recall more from last night, scouring my brain for a morsel of truth.

"Never have I ever..." Joey pauses, biting her lip. *"Fucked in*

public." Her face reddens, scrunching in the most adorable way. Almost like she's a young teen and I'm an old pervy man with too much experience. It's not entirely wrong. She loosened up with the drinks she ordered, and it's enticing to see the fiery girl mellow.

All of us, sans her, take a shot. There was that one situation with a teacher my sophomore year... I nearly forgot. Jase gave me hell for that. It didn't stop me from fucking her every chance I got.

Mommy issues and all.

I shake my head at the memory. Did I decide to go pre-teen last night? This is so fucked. Who plays *never have I ever* anymore? *High schoolers that want to get tanked and lucky.*

My head spins as awareness dawns on me. She's young…

The pinching to my head doesn't abate while I try to filter through last night. My memory of her age isn't hitting me at all. Is she even legal? Joey. This woman, she's petite and small, nearly half my height, which is saying a lot since I'm six-five. Bitter indifference mars her face, the grimace making a crumpled-up piece of paper seem smooth.

Should I say something, or just soak in this awkward silence?

"Hey," I mutter lamely, my face feeling hot for some reason. Without meaning to, I reach behind my head, grabbing my neck. Sweat lingers there, perspiring like a welling pond. *What's wrong with me?* Lo always said I did this when discomfort rises inside me. Maybe she's right. Joey's eyes meet mine. The fear is gone, but annoyance has risen in its place.

Maybe what they say about redheads is true…

"Hey," she mocks, her temper flaring, making her cute shortness seem even more adorable.

Adorable.

Cute.

What. The. Hell?

"Want to tell me why you hate me already? It usually takes a lot more than a greeting for that. Usually, after fucking, it's not *hate* they're feeling either."

She scoffs, her nostrils flaring. Narrowed eyes meet me with malice as though I'm a perpetrator. "Of course. You think you were some fucking glorious god in the sack. If a cliché generator could use someone's brain as the artificial intelligence, it'd be yours."

I can't help but laugh. *Damn.* What did I do, and why do I even care?

"So you're saying, I wasn't good?" The taunt leaves my lips before I think better of it.

Her face goes through a barrage of emotions and feelings, but how it pinks her cheeks is answer enough.

"I *was* good then," I murmur, mentally patting my back. Not being able to recall the last time someone didn't enjoy themselves.

Her. She didn't. She hated you after.

I close my eyes at that, the memory, the pain, the melancholy. She's gone. I'm gone. We're nothing anymore.

"Nope, but nice try. Maybe next time, you should use your mouth for more useful things than speaking," she rebuts with a raised brow. Her legs wiggle as she tries to shimmy herself back into her jeans. Her hips are generous and so is her ass. I'm stuck watching her struggle to pull them over her plump curves, appreciating every grunt of frustration. An unstoppable smirk tilts my lips, loving how flushed she is from both embarrassment and irritation, but it's the little growl she lets out as she wiggles that has me chuckling at her expense.

"Need help, Gumby?"

"Gumby? Are you fucking joking? Do I look like a bendy green piece of Play-Doh?" Her voice rises with each word as though it's an accusation and not a fun way to tease her. She's wrong. It's the definition of *fun.* Her hair—wild, fiery, and twisted in every which way—only makes me unable to take her seriously. I'm enjoying this far too much, especially when she's only been hostile since I've woken her up. "And what are you... fifty? Gumby seems a little past your time."

Guess what they say about waking chicks up is true.

Lo was never that way.

She lived for mornings.

I lived for her.

Fuck.

"Well, if I tried moving like that, I'd fall on my ass. Yet here you are, a professional. Green or not, you're bendy," I argue, shoving any and all twinges of pain about *her* out of my mind. It's not the time. It's never the time. She'll never leave me. She's left a stain on my soul, and no cleaner—no matter how potent—will ever be able to erase our memories.

Our past. Our lack of future. "And Gumby is a fucking classic. Don't dog on him."

"Fuck you," she spits, her anger rises along with my amusement.

"I'm sure I've done just that, Gumby. I mean, look at us. Naked. Jovial. *Just fucking dandy.* I'd call that an after fuck fest affair." I wink at her, and the sound of annoyance that slips past her rosy lips has me chuckling. Being an ass shouldn't be this enjoyable, yet I find myself really smiling for the first time in years. A time when alcohol isn't what's making me forget. This, I want to remember. The way she glares, the feel of her hateful words lashing me as a whip would, and the scent of stupid fucking flowers that'll be laced into my memory like a sewing string to fabric. I want it all to stay in my mind.

And that's new.

"You're incorrigible," she hisses. After her last few twists, she's finagled her jeans on and is barely tossing her shirt over her shoulder before storming past me. "Let's pretend this didn't happen."

"Easily," I muse, waving her goodbye. Even as the lie leaves my lips, I'm sure I'll never omit the memory of her.

She stops in her tracks, her back stiffening, probably realizing she's still topless. "Where's my bag?" Her fear mounts, and she hesitates, turning toward me. Confused and scared, she's full of animosity.

Unable to stop myself from taking her in once more, her perky tan nipples stare back at me. They're stiff, reflecting her hardened exterior. My eyes catch on the tiny barbell on the left one, wondering why she only has one. Then my gaze travels to a tattoo curving her right breast, wondering what the simple words mean.

When she catches me gawking, she covers herself, and I find myself getting lost at her toned stomach and the tiny belly button with another silver glinting jewelry piece dangling from it.

Goddamn.

Never thought I'd think piercings were appealing, but here I am.

"Hey, old man. My eyes are up here." She snaps her fingers aggressively. "I asked you a question." Our eyes meet as a challenge both of us seem to be unwilling to lose continues.

"Old man, really?" I finally hiss. I'm not *that* old. But compared to her, I might be. "I haven't seen your purse."

"Bag," she grunts. "Purses are for prissy bitches. As you can tell, that's *not* me." With her last words, she's finally slipping on her cropped top. Her midriff shows beautifully, and her perky little nipples tent the fabric as I look, making me feel like a pervert. I need to stop staring. This could be bad. She could be a teenager. Fuck. No. *I could never...*

"I haven't seen your *bag*," I clarify. "I just fucking woke up for chrissake." If she could narrow her eyes further, they'd be shut. That's what she looks like now, barely seeing, trying to drill every annoyed strand of her displeasure into one expression. I rub my eyes, trying to convince my brain to stop looking at her.

"Definitely needed your beauty sleep," she grumbles, rolling her eyes. "Wrinkles are hot for old people, I guess."

"What's that, Gumby?" I ask, knowing exactly what she said.

"What, can your old man ears not hear?" She smirks, folding her arms across her chest haughtily. Amusement glints in her expression, and it's as charming as a dildo stuck to a ceiling.

"It's called selective hearing, doll. Every grown man learns it."

"*Grown.* That's for sure." She eyes me from head to toe. I've had it with her attitude and sassy mouth. Yeah, patience is a virtue, but it's one that seems to have skipped out on me when Lo did. I inch forward swiftly, uncaring that I might scare her. Just as I thought... her eyes widen a smidgen right before she puts her guard up, testing me. I grip her face, wanting to be gentle, but it tends to lead to memories of *her*, and tenderness is the last thing I can offer. Joey's so tiny below me, her head barely hitting my shoulder. Bending so we're eye to eye, I hold her gaze.

Hers is full of disdain and annoyance.

Mines mirror hers to a fault.

"Only a grown man could fuck you to completion, *Sous.*" She shivers at my words, her body unbending in my hold. It's beautiful, knowing she won't conform to my touch but also realizing she can't hide the excitement in her expression either.

"Obviously, it wasn't to completion if I'm still walking,"

she spits back, jerking her face free of my hold. Her cheeks are flushed, her eyes pure amber fire, and my dick reacts like she's the hottest fucking steak on the grill.

"Guess a redo is in order. Since you seem to question my skills."

"Pass. Have places to go, people to do, things to accomplish… and riding *your* dick isn't on that list," she rebuts, her face lighting up with a win I didn't concede to.

CHAPTER 2

THREE DAYS EARLIER

JOEY

"HEADED HOME ALREADY?" ROBBIE ASKS AS I TAKE off my apron for the last time. Robyn Goode, my tall and slender co-chef, stands opposite of the working counter.

Her hair isn't tucked into her chef toque yet. It's long and russet brown, strikingly straight and thick, but never done up. In the entire year I've known her, she doesn't do anything special to it. Not even when we cater events.

She's the sweetest person in this hellhole, but she's also the softest spoken. One day, I hope she'll flap the wings she tucks into and free herself of the burden of fear.

She doesn't know, but I was fired.

Technically, I'm walking out before he can say it. I'm surprised Lucien didn't make a bigger deal and scream at me like he usually would. Guess it helps that I have leverage.

Like the fact that he's a pervert.

And I have proof.

"Actually," I start, not knowing how to word it without sounding like I'm the bad guy. "Today's my last day. To new adventures and whatnot." Shrugging my shoulders, I act like it's nothing, but really, the knowledge that I'm pretty much jobless weighs heavily on my shoulders.

She eyes me, her face one of confusion. *Believe me, girl. I feel you.*

In an attempt to alleviate the situation, I smile. Throwing my apron in the trash with a full good-fucking-riddance feeling, I finally feel content. While being without a steady income isn't in anyone's best avenue, being tortured by a pig in my own workplace wasn't big on my to-do list either.

I'll overcome it, I always do. Sometimes, we don't have any other option.

"Where will you go?" she asks meekly, her face sinking with actual sadness. Her voice is uncertain, her body closed off and filled with anxiety. It's not a pleasant look, but she'll be fine without me. Maybe she'll flourish without competition. Envy can squander someone's hope, but something tells me her unassumingness isn't from me being the better chef.

In the past year we've worked together, we have grown

close. Well, as close as two chicks can get in a workplace that houses the devil himself.

We bonded through gossip and built each other up when our boss brought us down. It wasn't something to write home about, but it definitely has been more than a hello and goodbye. We aren't *friends* friends. We don't speak outside of work and events surrounding it. I don't have her number, and she doesn't have mine. It's not for lack of trying on either of our parts, but relationships outside of work tend to mess me up.

I'm not loving.

Or lovable.

But we exist and bring some odd comfort in the days of unpleasant menu items and screaming matches.

"I don't know," I finally reply, offering honesty. That much I'll always give. I pride myself in always being up-front. When you're lied to as much as I've been lied to, honesty is the only vital option. "I just need somewhere to go where I'm not the victim anymore. Branch out. Be free..." As I trail off, understanding licks her features. Why does she stay? I know why I have. My dad stopped helping me out, and I had to make a name for myself. But our boss is brutal to her too. Did he proposition her?

"Why do you stay?" It slips free, though I'm sure I already have my answer. She scrunches her face in displeasure, her eyes haunted and full of disdain. It's not directed toward me, though. I can tell it's for whatever makes her stay.

"I don't have a choice," she utters, her voice so small at

the moment.

"If he—" I start, but she places a finger over her lips, her eyes scanning the room to point out the cameras. Her posture and stance tell me to keep quiet.

"Need a smoke? I definitely do," she states, eyeing the back exit. She knows I don't smoke anymore, which means she needs privacy. Lucien is one of those tedious restaurant owners who has cameras everywhere. Every corner. Blind spot. Any place a person would pass or go to hide for a little privacy, he has a camera.

With our luck, the bastard probably has one in the bathroom.

As soon as we leave the back door, she lets out a large breath. "I'm stuck here because he has something on me," she finally speaks, pulling out a smoke at the same moment. After lighting it, she inhales so much in her first drag that I'm sure she'll die from lack of oxygen.

It's sad when you can see the desperation coming off a person in waves, bleeding, suffocating, drowning them with each passing breath.

"Fight it," I say poignantly, knowing that his threats are only words, especially for what he does when he thinks no one's around. "He won't do shit to you. He's too much of a pussy." She shakes her head vehemently as if I know nothing. Maybe I don't. She's been here a lot longer than me.

"Two summers ago, we took a trip to Paris for that new restaurant he opened—"

"*Le Grand Oui?*" I interrupt.

"That's the one." She nods absently, tapping the ashes off her cigarette. Grabbing the rail, I look out at the city. Hawthorne doesn't appeal to me. It's nicer than Hollow Ridge in many ways, but the vibe is just as stagnant and haunting, with no promise of a future. A place where the rich stay rich and the poor get poorer. It's such a sad reality, especially for someone who barely makes it from paycheck to paycheck. If not for moving to Savannah Cove and getting a little apartment, I'd be homeless. It isn't easy living in California. Prices are inflated, jobs lack in pay, and the housing is infuriating.

Tears stream down her face all while she keeps puffing on her cancer stick. "We went to the grand opening, and there was a banquet. I'm not sure how, since I only had one glass of wine, but I ended up in bed with him."

Her body trembles.

It's a warm day today with no wind or chill. She's not cold, not in the physical sense. When people experience trauma, it inscribes itself in your bones, attacking each layer of skin, muscle, and vein until it reaches the barest of parts. It eventually grinds on the bones, showing you just how deep it can carve until you're forever stuck in a horrific memory.

"I swear, Joey, I never would have slept with him."

My stomach churns with this information. Did he drug her? It's not like I haven't experienced his disgusting tactics. Maybe he hurt her, too.

"I believe you." When her watery eyes meet mine, they're

full of hope and gratitude. "Honestly, it's why I'm leaving," I add.

She opens her mouth in shock. "I don't mean to sound like a bitch, but I thought you two were *together*." She emphasizes the together part like it's a dirty word.

"Absolutely not," I balk. "He's foul and loathsome. I'd never..." I swallow the bile rising in my throat. "He tried. Several times. I told him to stop, or I'd report him. To who, I wasn't sure. Since he's the sole proprietor, he gets away with his repulsive behavior. Inside, though, I knew something needed to be done. Last week at that stupid catering conference for Collins & Co, I recorded him. I'd just finished the Crème Brûlée for the dessert table, and he grabbed my ass." I'm shaking from head to toe in anger, trying to keep my voice even. "He asked if he could talk to me, and I nodded all sweetly." She laughs, knowing I'm not one to be sweet. I'm bitter and haughty, that's why they call me Hotwheels.

"I followed him to the lounge room, the one connected to the bathroom in the commons area." She nods, accepting my information, and I continue with bated breath, hating what comes next. "While he searched the room for lingering staff and attendees, I turned my phone's recording on. He didn't even lock the door. His confidence astounds me to this day because he believed he'd get what he wanted from me. It was easy after that; his delusions are what made him fail. If you call him forcing himself on me *easy*. He started telling me how much he liked me working for him, and that if I was a good little chef-in-training, he promised me a future at any location I wanted. He groped me, and I told him to back off, that I wasn't interested. He proceeded to call me a slut and a tease, and that if I didn't fuck him, he'd fire me and blacklist me from working for any five-star restaurant in the future."

Her cigarette, all but forgotten to the point that the ash is long enough to break off itself, falls to the ground as she hiccups. Tears flood out, her body shaking like mine. Instead of anger, hers are shudders of disgust and sadness. "But I'm okay. I kneed him in the balls and threatened to turn him in if he so much as brushed past me again."

Robbie comes over to me and brings me into a hug. I'm not much of the hugging type, but brushing her off seems callous. She squeezes me for a moment longer while I inhale deeply, reminding myself she's not *him*. She isn't hurting me. "Instead of staying somewhere I didn't feel safe, I left before he could find a way to fire me."

"I'm so sorry, Joey." After Robbie takes a long drag, she grinds the bud using the heel of her work boots, then turns back to me with a frown.

"I'm not. He reminded me why being strong is important. Now, you need to be strong, too." Robbie pulls back, her eyes red and puffy. She probably thinks I'm crazy for not shedding a single tear. But when you have certain life experiences, you tend to grow stronger, not weaker.

"I-I—" she stutters, "I don't know how."

I nod, understanding her entirely. You don't know how strong you are until it's the only option left. She needs that to be her only option. "I don't want to scare you, Robbie, but you need to walk away. He's sexually harassing you, and I wouldn't doubt that he put something in your drink that night to take advantage of you. It won't get better, no matter how many times you tell yourself otherwise. He's a sleazebag."

She seems so small right now, like my words are hurting her more than this man ever did. "How are you so wise for such a young woman?" Her question shocks me. Age is only a number in the game of life. You can experience so much at such a young age. It can define you, it can even break you, but the choice is entirely yours. My dad doesn't even know the half of it. How could he? He lives in a blissful bubble of ignorance. A palace of his own making where the only thing that matters is *her* and money.

Either way, I'm wise because it's the path I took.

It's the only choice I decided on after France.

No pity parties or slaving away at scars, it's pure drive to never be a victim ever again.

"Experience," I reply in short, watching as awareness flickers in her gaze. I nod, not wanting to talk about it. *It's the past.* That's not a page I ever intend to turn back to.

Looking down at my arms out of habit, where my scars reside beneath the knitted fabric of my long-sleeve shirt, I sigh.

The past has the ability to destroy you if you don't leave it behind.

Scars don't define you, not if you don't allow them that right.

"Either way, he reminded me of the future I'm working for.

23

He was only a step in the long staircase of my journey. It's time to move on, and you should follow suit. You're only twenty-three, Rob. You're too young for this to be your only option."

"You're right. Thank you." Her words aren't sharp or pointed, just acceptance. And with that, I turn and leave Lucien's chop-block for a new road. Too bad my rent is due and my boyfriend doesn't like when I'm late with my half. Not that he ever seems to be on time, but of course Joey can't fuck up—it's unbecoming.

We don't share any more sadness or stories after it's said and done. I plug in my number on her cell, telling her to text if she ever needs me.

CHAPTER 3

JOEY

AS I MAKE MY WAY BACK TO MY SHARED APARTMENT, I smile. *I'm free.* There are no strings attached any longer, and I can search for a new job. My dream job. It may be another breakneck kind of hell I've been doing for the past year, barely scraping by, but it'll be for a much better company, I'm sure of it.

Wesley and I live in the lesser half of Savannah Pines. Even though it's a Podunk town, it's all we could afford outside of Hollow Ridge. At first, when I met Wes, it was a nightmare. He was *that* guy, and I avoided him at all costs. But everything changed when Dad married Marsha. I'm sure that's what drove me to him. He's everything my dad hates. Bad boy with long surfer hair. Pothead. *Careless*. He dropped out of school, got a job at the fresh age of sixteen, and worked his way up at this tiny surf shack at Savannah Cove.

While it paid next to nothing, he was happy, blissful, and trying. Something I think every human could hope for—joy and contentedness, even while unrealistic.

When Dad put a ring on that psycho bitch's finger, I rebelled. Can you blame me? She stepped in, being this perfect trophy wife, doting on him at his time in need. In reality, Marsha made Meredith Blake look charming.

I hated her and, in turn, hated my dad too. A spoiled brat? Perhaps. A daughter abandoned for fame? Sure. A broken shell of a girl, forced to grow up? Definitely. Call it daddy issues or whatever you think is befitting, but after Dad threw me wherever he could, moving me from place to place, and marrying that gold-digger, Wes became everything I needed to get back at him for moving on.

Mom had only been missing for four years. We don't even know if she's alive, safe, or scared.

Yet he moved on.

How could he?

Either way, Wes became more than just a ploy. We bonded through our fucked-up upbringings. I mean, he had it bad. He's poor, never staying in one place for too long, and always struggling to live. At least I'm loaded. *Or was.* We both went through a lot before turning eighteen, and it built this safe place for me to go to. Even while he doesn't know my entire story.

Climbing up the steps to our place, I notice a tattered package leaning against the door. *Sweet.* Maybe it's my custom apron that I've been waiting for since graduating. It has J. Moore embroidered on the left breast pocket. It was my one splurge after Dad stopped sending me checks. I really couldn't blame him since I'm his mess of a daughter. The one that refused to study law or become a politician like he wanted for me. The one who defied, partied, used his money for trips across the world, and did whatever I wanted because I could.

Josephine Moore, the mayor's damnation.

Tabloids loved to hate me, and I hated to hate me.

My fingers wrestle the key into the lock, and I unlatch it to head inside. Pushing the battered door, it makes a loud yawning noise. When the package nearly slips from my grip, I tuck it underneath my arm.

It's an absolute mess in here. The couch is covered in used blankets, Wesley's clothes are strewn about, and the goddamn dirty dishes everywhere makes me nauseous. He's a slob, so much so, that I feel like a maid rather than a girlfriend.

Shutting the door, I'm immediately met with the sound of moaning. It fills my ears obnoxiously, in a loud shrill way that could only mean one of two things.

Porn or—

"Oh, Wes! Harder, Wes!"

—my boyfriend cheating.

My ears bleed. Not physically, but the pain is just as brutal. The eardrum bursts open as I hear the sounds of her mewling like a porn star. My heart collapses in my chest, deflating like the balloon my neighbor Sarah popped of mine on my fifth birthday.

My mind flips through the past few days, months, and even the almost two years we've been together. Memories flicker in my mind as contemplation sinks in, and every situation, mood, and days spent away from Wes skitter across my mind. No matter the imagery, I can't recall a change in him. Did I love this blindly? The notion to run floods my veins like wax drying, thick, heady, unmovable. What did I do? It has to be me. *It's always me.* The constant hours, the never being around… it's my fault, right?

Instead of freaking out, I allow a calm to settle. Like when you straddle a board, waiting for the surf, and just feel the ocean beneath you and the air surrounding you, it frees me. I open our bedroom door to her on all fours while my boyfriend's dick thrusts in and out of her ass. *Bare.* It takes everything in me not to gag. We've never done *that*, let alone without a condom. I'm glad. With my luck, this isn't his first pump and dump in a cumdumpster.

He doesn't turn immediately, not until she gasps. "Wes, stop!" He turns to me then, all six feet of him staring at me in surprise.

Well, yeah, motherfucker. I'm surprised too.

His eyes are red-rimmed and bloodshot, sunken and dry. He's high again. I turn away, not wanting to see the visual of him inside her for longer than I already have. It'll be burned into my brain.

Memories don't fade.

They reside on our skin like a living brand, making sure we never forget the past.

"Josey," he gently tries, his voice heady with emotion. Hurt blooms inside my chest as I shake my head at him, going to our closet. Whenever he called me by my dad's nickname, my body ached in an intrinsic way. He did it to connect with the broken part of me—the one that misses my mom, wishes my dad wasn't heartless, and hopes life would be less of a dick.

I grab my travel bags from our closet, realizing they're not nearly big enough to carry everything. Two years of growth. Dust wafts from the movement, and I start piling everything I can fit of mine in them. I have a lot to bag up, and not all of it is physical either. Some exist deeper. Emotional damage, the wounds that never drain and heal will only get deeper, sicker, and more detrimental with time.

Years I've wasted. That's the one thing we never have. Time. It tricks us, thinking we have it, own it, and have the capability to manipulate it, but that's the biggest lie of all. It has *us.* It owns *us.* It manipulates *us.* We're just too dumb to see it.

"Hotwheels," he calls out from behind me, the pet name from a story not meant to be slices through me. I refuse to turn to him. Refuse to see his body that's tainted. Refuse to be broken by something I can't control. *Again.*

I'm not weak. I'm not malleable. I'm not a *victim.*

"Don't," I bite out, barely holding in the tears. *No.* I won't cry. Not for him. Not for them. Not for *me.* "Let me get my shit so I can leave."

"It was a mistake," he pleads, his voice small and apologetic. My hand grips a hoodie, my fisted fingers crumpling it as the pain of his betrayal presses into me.

"A mistake is falling off your surfboard and causing someone else to crash along with you. It's not sticking your dick in some random chick's ass in *our* bed. And fucking *raw*. You're so dumb, Wesley. We're done." I say these words with a fierceness I don't feel. It's all a façade. It's a front to save myself; it's my mesh guard for the cold bitter bite of love.

"Please look at me, Josey. I'm not lying," he implores, his voice softer than I've ever heard him. But it doesn't matter because he's not getting a second chance. Second chances are for people willing to change. Yet for as long as I've known him, change isn't something he's capable of. He's okay with staying as is, being content but not happy, being financially fine but not stable. He's accepting of a standstill, but I'm not.

I turn to him, seeing his chest, the one I've touched and loved and cuddled. It's all him, it's us, it's nothing.

Tears prick my eyes as they catch on eight words tattooed on his rib, the one I have a match of on my own. His inscribed with *still like the sky, free like the waves* while mine is *be free, not still.* The one that's tainted now. He has done that. And it's *not* my fault.

"It's over, Wesley. *We* are over." A clean break. Like a goddamn butter knife to the flesh.

Ever heard of sarcasm?

His eyes close, and he folds his arms over his chest. I'm

30

afraid if I stay, I'll forgive him. If I let him talk to me, he'll convince me that he's a good guy... but he's not. He's not a good guy. He's the villain of this fucked-up fairy tale. Or maybe it's me. Wouldn't be the first time.

Opening his eyes to gaze at me, tears well up. "I'm sorry," he apologizes. The sincerity is there but makes zero sense. If he's sorry, why'd he do it? If it was a mistake, why'd he risk it? If it wasn't meant to be, why'd I ever love him?

"I've forgiven you for many things over the course of our friendship and relationship, Wes. But this..." I gesture to the room behind us, a heaping mess of never-meant-to-bes. "This is not something I can move past. I'm not even sure how I'm not stabbing you right now," I whisper, my throat constricting with fresh wounds.

"It's because you fell out of love with me," he replies, matter of fact, his voice bereft. He scratches his chin as our gazes meet with confusion. "Don't you see it, Josey?" He waves his hands, gesturing to the room, but refering to our relationship. "You stopped caring what I did ages ago. It was always about being a chef and what you wanted. You forgot what we built together. This wasn't the first time, but you never noticed. At first, I wanted you to notice me, feel the pain you brought, but you abandoned me... just like your pops did to you."

"That's not what happened," I bite out, bitterness coating my tongue, threatening to spew out and be as morbid as my thoughts.

"Then tell me, what the fuck happened to us?" he implores, running both hands through his hair before pulling it at the roots.

"I died inside." With those words, my scars burn. All of them, the ones across my entire body, meaty and grubby. My answer is as close to the truth as he'll ever get from me. He could have done so many other things in this world to get answers, but this? Anything but this. In the entirety of our relationship, he never asked about them.

Not the ones on my arms.

Not the dozens on my thighs.

Definitely not the ones on my chest.

"Babe," he tries, using the single most boring word in the world, but one I allowed for the sake of his care. "Talk to me."

"It's too late for that. Don't you see? This is goodbye, Wesley. It was fun while it lasted."

"Don't leave," he begs, touching my arm. I whip it back, feeling like he's invaded my space, my life, and my traitorous heart. I smack his hand away hard and take my bags with me. To hell with all the stuff I didn't get. He can keep it. Along with his stupid surfboard he bought me. As I leave the apartment, I close another chapter in my life.

Dad isn't going to be happy.

Will he even help me this time?

Fucking Marsha. Fucking Wesley. Fucking Lucien.

They can all deep throat a cactus.

CHAPTER 4

TOBY

LET ME START BY SAYING THAT I NEVER INTENDED to fall in love with my best friend, who also happened to be married to my brother. I never wanted to break apart a family or derail my own life in the process. I never wanted to be my father. Married to the bottle, lusting after the pain, and sleeping with someone who wasn't mine to sleep with.

Whether my intention or not, it happened. It's my fault. It is what it is and isn't.

I made my bed, and now I must lie in it.

She chose him, and I lost. Now, it's time to pick myself back up and stop moping.

Many things contributed to the fall of Tobias Hayes, restaurant conglomerate business owner. *Me.* I've done it all to myself, but even with that acknowledgment, I'm bitter and have been hugging the bottle again. Some would belittle me for my lack of purpose these past few months, but I blame love. Love ruined me. Kissing me with death and lies, love promised everything by masking it with *feelings*. In the end, it gave me nothing but a heart sickness that darkened my existence.

That was over two years ago. Since then, I've been on a constant bender. Drinking. More drinking. And you guessed it, even more drinking. When Jase asked me to leave, I wanted to fight tooth and nail against it. Why did he get to choose? Listening to him belittle me while I threatened to erase myself from his life wasn't something I'd kindly accepted.

Then Lo—his wife—asked me to, and it changed my entire outlook on the ordeal. It's her. She matters. Her happiness means the world to me. It has since we were sixteen and met for the first time.

I'd destroy anything if she'd only ask.

And that's the problem.

I always push even when the door says pull.

Her asking me to vanish triggered this spiral. After two years, it's time to move forward. As much as a man like me could go.

She visited me after Jase kicked me outside of their house, practically begging me to give her a fresh start. And in return, it'd give me the same.

"It's too hard, Tobe. Being around you is difficult enough, but

being around you while Jase and I are finally on the same page... is impossible. I know. It's not fair of me to ask, it's not even okay to, but I need you to go. Whether it's for a while or to one of your other restaurants in another state, I need this. You need this," she pleads. Her eyes shine with unshed tears, and the sincerity in her voice has me nearly falling to my knees.

She needs this.

Me... gone.

"You're all I've got, Sparkle. You're everything to me," I mutter, stunned speechless by her request. She wants me to go away? No more morning runs, coffee stops, late-night phone calls, movie nights, or times with Ace and Jazzy? My stomach implodes on itself, dropping entirely with implications of what this will mean. She takes my surprise as her cue to continue.

"I'm not meant to be your everything, Tobe. You know it as much as I do. We were destined to break each other, not fix each other." Tears spring in my eyes as hers pour over. "I'll always love you, but it's not the kind of love that'll last. Not the love you deserve—definitely not the life you deserve," she finishes, her voice smaller than I've ever heard it. My best friend, the one I've spent my entire life loving, caring for, and wanting, she wants me out of Hollow Ridge, my home.

She sobs, noticing my silent tears. Her shoulders shake, almost as if this admittance hurt her more than me. All this time, she knew—she knew it'd never be more, but she selfishly clung to me—stealing all my opportunities to find and secure a forever kind of love. She did that. And actually coming to terms with this hurts a hell of a lot worse than I thought.

"Okay," I concede, realizing this would be the last gift I'd give her. I won't argue or fight it; I'll just let it happen. Because regardless of how much we both wrecked each other's lives, she deserves to be happy. As does my brother. Even if he hates me once again. Even if I did this. Even if I deserve every disgust-filled word he slings my way.

She doesn't say anything else but rises up and kisses my forehead as I've done to her on so many occasions. My eyes close on their own accord, absorbing the last morsel of love she offers. She lingers for a moment too long before pulling away.

"Goodbye, Sparkle," I whisper, my heart detaching from my chest with my last flattened words.

But it's too late because she's already gone.

I walked away. For once, I did the selfless and right thing. To my own stupidity, I thought it'd make me feel better, but it didn't. All I feel is this insatiable loneliness. One deeper than the bottomless ocean, vast and wide and never-ending.

Now, I'm stuck on repeat like she was once before. Except in this story, I don't have someone to rein me back—to fix me—to save me.

She had me.

I have no one.

Two months ago, I woke up in some random hotel, deciding to stop boozing it up. It should be simple enough, right? This isn't how my story has to end, which is why I made the choice to change. I've been in Hawthorn ever since. It's not where I intended to go, but it's far enough away from Hollow Ridge that I can breathe and so can they.

Getting out of bed, I take a quick shower and decide to start my changes. First on the agenda today, I need to do what I should have done two years ago.

Calling Daphne, the head hostess at *Su Casa*, I'm given a newfound hope.

"This is *Su Casa*. Where everything that's mine is yours," she chirps cheerfully into the phone.

"Daph," I say, "Will you get Raul on the phone? He's supposed to be there right now."

"Of course, I'll check in your office. One moment please." She puts me on hold, and I straighten my spine, gathering courage to not bail out. She asked me to leave. Now, I'm finally doing it. Took five months, but I'm ready. I can do this.

"Raul, here," my financial adviser answers.

"I need you to draft some papers for me. It's a perfect time since you're already there."

"How convenient," he says exasperated. "What for?"

"I'm signing it over to my sister in-law." He makes an unrecognizable noise at the back of his throat.

"Are you sure? She's never managed a business before. She might burn it into the ground."

I smile, knowing he's wrong. Whether a new job position or the weight the world is brought down on her, Sparkle would thrive.

"Positive. Have them delivered to her by the end of week."

"You don't want to take a day and think on it? This is a huge gamble. She hasn't been back here in two years, Toby.

She's probably already moved on."

"It's worth the risk. Get it done."

"Of course," he mumbles; his lack of faith has me smiling even wider. At least he'll be surprised when it soars, just like I know she will. She deserves to be happy. I want that for her.

By the time I get everything in order over the phone, I'm searching my email for updates across the country. I've missed many conference calls and updates on my new venues. But life goes on even if I'm not around. It's the beauty about having a manager at every location. They can handle all the stuff I'm not babysitting as long as all the numbers add up.

One email stands out as I'm scrolling.

You're invited to our seventh annual... clicking on the link for the email, I scroll, noticing it's from the Culinary Con event coordinators. Their names are signed at the bottom. They're always trying to get me to attend this event. Every year, I donate, but not once have I shown up. It's one of those events where boring businessmen and women pile together and flash their money. They buy chefs, hookers, and they drink profusely. Either way, it's a shitshow.

RSVP here, a link sits, waiting for me to make a dumb decision. *Sobriety.* I'm supposed to try that.

I hover over it, wondering if I should take the dive, but before my head decides, my phone rings.

"Yeah?" I say, picking it up. It's my business cell.

"Toby," Erik, my Hollow Hills location manager, says on a labored breath. "We have a problem." My mind runs many miles a minute, trying to figure out what could go wrong at Hollow Hill's *Mi Casa.* As a mini version of *Su Casa,* it offers the same but isn't as elegant. The hotel manages everything sans the restaurant, so there shouldn't be an issue. And with him saying otherwise, my nerves are heightened.

"What is it?" I eventually ask. I don't want to know. There's already so much on my plate. This will only worsen my mood.

"Debra'sgone," he says really fast, as if that'll lessen the blow. It doesn't. Debra's the only chef we have at the hotel. What the fuck am I supposed to do now? I have no one, and finding a stellar replacement is out of the question.

"I-Is she okay?" The first thing that comes to mind is some horrible accident. She's been with me for five years. It's not like her to miss a day, let alone be gone indefinitely.

"Oh, she's fine. She fell in love and decided that was more important than working here. Which means we either have to shut down for a few days or you're going to have to find a chef. *Tonight.*"

How the hell am I supposed to get a trained, schooled, and professional chef on short notice?

"Boss, did you hear me?"

"No, what'd you say?"

"I can call Daph. I'm sure she can find someone—"

"No!" I practically yell. "She has too much going on. I'll figure it out." She'll be dealing with Lo's first appearance soon, so risking this kind of stress when Lo will be in charge could ruin the chances of her accepting.

"But—"

"I said no," I bark. "I'll be back in two days. I know what I need to do."

"But—"

"Shut it, Erik. Calm down and trust the system."

"Oh-kay," he mutters, his voice shaky.

"The world won't end if we are closed for a few days. Whatever happens will happen. But I have it handled."

I hang up before he can come up with other what-ifs that will only cause more stress than I've already got. Opening the email I had abandoned to answer the call, I click *RSVP.*

CHAPTER 5

JOEY

"GRAY," I NEARLY CRY INTO THE PHONE AFTER she answers. "I-I need somewhere t-to go." I'm not sure why I called her. Gray and I met in France two years ago when Dad married Marsha, and she was my first and only friend while I was out there. We haven't spoken much since I came back to Hollow Ridge, and even then, it was a text here and there. The flood of tears won't stop as they leave my eyes. My blurred vision isn't safe while I drive over to the cove.

The place where I met Wes is the last place I want to be. It has many memories and most are the best of my life, but one is now the worst. It's only been a day since I caught him doing the *deed*. However, residing in my car in an abandoned parking lot, as sleep never took me, isn't ideal. Since leaving, my mind has jumped all over, and I haven't been able to concentrate since. One thing I know is that my dad won't be happy, so I can't call him crying. He'll just make me feel worse and tell me, *I told you so, Josey*.

"Come here!" she suggests as though we're still in France. There's no way my dad will help me afford a move there. Even a temporary trip is out of the question.

"Really?" I cry. She never asks questions; she's just inadvertently here for me. I don't have enough saved for more than the flight, but the thought festers.

"Of course, babe. I'm here for you. I'm staying in Hawthorn now," she explains. She's here and less than an hour away? We found each other by pure coincidence. I was in France, escaping Marsha. My dad felt bad when he dropped the ball and got married without telling me, so he sent me away for six months to *detoxify my drama* as he called it. Gray and I were at the same coffee shop every day. One day, she left the shop, and a car came straight for her. Gripping the little backpack on her shoulders, I tugged her away. Luckily, the straps didn't snap. We've been friends ever since.

"Wait, you're in California?" She said Hawthorn, but she could mean any Hawthorn.

"Yeah, Dad and I came back to visit family and check out the colleges. He wants me to go to Brookewood like him and Uncle Jase, but I'm not too sure. I have a while to decide if we're moving back or staying in France with his family. I'm leaning toward croissantland, though. This place has so many memories…" She pauses. "…not a lot of good ones. It's been months, and I'm really just not ready to see the faces of those I left behind."

What's her story? We never really dived deep into it because she cared more about mine. All I know is that we love the same bands, and she's around my age. That's it.

"Who'd you leave behind?" I ask, knowing there's an answer that I'll probably never get.

"My past," she stalls, not wanting to divulge any further. *Fair enough.* No one knows what I went through, not even her.

"How long are you here for?" I deflect for her benefit.

"For the summer, at least."

"Wow, small world," I muse, entirely shocked that she's so close.

"It is. I'm originally from Hollow Ridge," she explains.

"This is crazy!" I practically squeal, feeling the sadness abate for a moment. "I'm from Hollow Ridge, too."

She gasps. "How have we never met in this small town?" I think of the tiny rich town I grew up in, the stuck-up brats that allowed their parents to pay for everything, and how I did everything to avoid contact with others. I'm not a people person. I'm barely a person sometimes. I'm driven and focused and the last thing I had time for was friends. That's why I graduated early and went to college before everyone else. I did that. Succeeded.

"How old are you?" I murmur, wondering how I missed that information. We always talked in the same way, and our references are in the same timeframe as though we were the same age. But now that I think about it, maybe she's younger than me.

"Seventeen," she states.

"Wow." I laugh. "I'm nineteen." It's so crazy how a number defines a person, their past, their future, but doesn't explain the truths hidden behind each year.

"I'd have never guessed. So you were seventeen when we met?"

"Yup, fresh out of my second semester of college."

"College?" she repeats thoughtfully. "That young?"

"Yeah, it's probably why we never met. Back in school, I'd been a completely driven youngster. I still am, but I've graduated and moved on. I have a Bachelor's in Culinary Arts."

"Like my aunt," she mutters softly as though she didn't mean to.

"Who's your aunt?"

"Oh, you've probably never heard of her. Loren Collins."

I think of the name, wondering if I've heard it. Then it dawns on me. "Oh. My. God."

"What?" she asks on a laugh, and I can imagine her now. Her stark black hair and melted silver eyes.

"Loren Tanner! She was the top of the class in her day. She literally has a plaque in June's classroom."

"Huh?"

"June McTavish. She's the culinary professor at Brighton. She told me I was the next Loren."

"Holy crap! You must be legendary then! Before she got pregnant and married Uncle Jase, she was the chef all the businesses wanted. Like Gorden Ramsey and Bobbie Flay."

"I hope to be that awesome when I'm her age," I respond, thinking of how amazing it'd be to be wanted around the world.

"Coming, Dad!" I hear her yell in the background before answering. "Maybe you will be, but I have to jet. I'll text you my address, okay?"

"Thank you, Gray… for everything."

"You saved my life once," she teases. "I owe you a few."

But I didn't want her to owe me anything. I didn't want anyone to feel that way about me. When we hang up, I'm stuck in those feelings. Of being a burden. Do I bite the bullet and just ask Dad for money? Will he help me? Should I suck it up and go back to Wes?

It'd be great if my mom was around. She's missed so many things. She'd have been there for me through the worst part of my life, I'm sure of it. Gray texts me soon after with her address. *And by the way, even though I owe you, I'd still want to hang out. You're pretty cool, J.*

The text has me smiling all the way to her place. I have the car I paid for after my dad took my money away, my bags, what little savings I had, and my dignity. But that's it. I left my laptop, cooking utensils, and my fucking phone charger. *Dammit.*

Yet I was aware enough to grab the stupid package.

Smacking the steering wheel with my head, I pull over. I dig through my smaller duffel and find my purse and iPod. Thank fuck. *Who I now worship.* I plug it in the auxiliary and find my *Rager* playlist. Yes, I have a playlist for when I'm ready to ditch the fear of ugly jumpsuits. Which is right now. NF's "WHY" rings out. Within seconds, the familiar instrumentals and bass fill my ears. I start singing and continue my drive.

After what feels like no time at all, I pull up. The house I pull up to—correction—the *mansion* I pull up to is glorious. It's absolutely massive, tall with a Grecian feel to it in brown and red, and mixes of orange with cobblestones like a Spanish Riviera home. I didn't know Hawthorn had buildings this large. I'm surprised my parents didn't come here instead. It's less cliché than Hollow Ridge for sure.

Standing outside is a tall man. He's not looking at me, but I notice his hands resting in his pockets in a comfortable posture.

With his face downcast and shoulders that any linebacker would beg for, he gives off a strong and intimidating presence. Tall—really fucking tall—and gorgeous as can be. He has the silkiest looking sandy blond hair. As though he's paid millions of dollars to keep it shiny and wavy in that easy-going kind of way.

A trimmed beard lines his stern jaw all the way to his stony gray eyes that suddenly hit me with a curious expression as I come to a full stop. Who is he? And why does he look like he's the cover model of every *GQ* magazine ever?

When I climb out of my car and try to handle my bags, a warm hand engulfs my elbow.

"Allow me," the deep voice says.

Seriously! Who is this dude? And why is his voice French and dreamy? Warmth skates over my skin, giving me a different kind of shiver. My stomach does a weird floaty thing inside as I watch him grab my bags easily. Older men always catch my attention. It must be that I'm wired wrong. My eyes appreciate their graying temples and dad bods. But this man? There's no *dad* bod. It's just all *bod.*

"Dad! Don't go scaring her away!" Gray yells from the front entrance. My mouth hangs open as realization dawns on me. *Shit.* Gray's dad is a DILF. He turns to me with the hottest smirk I've ever experienced.

"She likes me, don't you, *ma coccinelle,*" he muses happily. *My ladybug.* Heat creeps up on my cheeks, making my stomach flip. His accent is thick and dreamy, smoothing over me like a strong shot of whiskey. God, I need to get it together. It wasn't more than a day ago that I caught Wes cheating on me. And *this*—hot dad with an amazing body—will *never* happen.

"Dad! Good God, you're going to make her faint. Stop it!" She's hollering, but it's with joy, as though this happens often, and she's always after him for it. Well, if he calls just anyone *his* ladybug, they might be catching some fists.

"I'm Francis," he finally introduces himself when we're at the landing. He smiles at me boyishly, a dimple poking through his scruffy cheek. That action alone makes me squirm, and I feel like an actual teenager—one adored. And to me, that makes this entire trip worth it.

"Joey," I reply, offering a hand. His teeth show when his grin widens. That's when I notice he can't shake my hand with all of my bags in his grasp. I have to keep myself from biting my lip to stop from smiling so much. It's unlike me to feel this swoony. *Is that even a word?*

"*Ma coccinelle,*" he teases with a larger than life grin. I cover my face because I'm not used to this kind of attention. The non-pervy kind that's just friendly and sweet. It's such a French thing. Even after six months in that country, I never got used to it. Americans always come off as sleazy when they flirt. *Like Lucien.*

"It's nice to meet you."

He sets my bags down and instead of grabbing my hand to shake, he pulls me into a hug and kisses both cheeks. I'm out of breath as he pulls away. Watching me with a flirtatious quirk to his lips, he leads me into the enormous foyer. "I've heard a lot about you. And how you saved *mon lapin* from an untimely accident."

I peer at Gray, giving her a thankful expression. She must really like me. No one likes me. I'm not really a people person, and I'm surprised she's had a good impression from someone like me.

The lost girl.

One who never belongs.

Bitter. Mean. Cruel.

"Thank you for allowing me to stay," I merely whisper, grabbing my throat in shame. Depending on others has never been my strong suit. It makes me feel weak, less, unworthy. The gratitude in my voice must show because, somehow, his smile widens even more.

"*Pas de probl*ème," he says.

"Really, Dad. *English*. Jesus," Gray complains with her signature eye roll. I've seen that a time or two. She bites her cheek as if she's amused at the fact that her dad seems to have taken a liking for me.

"My bad," he grumbles. "I've only been to the States three times in the past seventeen years. It's easy to go back to what I know." As he explains, his accent goes in and out, as if he's trying to correct himself with each word.

It's cute.

We walk together, all while my eyes devour the inside of their home. The halls are filled with art that probably costs as much as my existence. Each one has hanging lights, each piece highlighted and expressed with care. The designs of the walls are filled with the kind of damask wallpaper that reminds me of Gothic historical homes. It's beautiful and done well enough not to appear tacky. As he shows me around the ground floor, he explains every piece of art. Gray eventually becomes annoyed with his knack for details and leads me through the rest of the manor. She's too excited to show me my guest room. In reality, this *guest room* is more of its own town with its own zip code. I'm from a wealthy politician family, but this house is something else.

The room she leads me into is vast and wide. A massive poster bed rests in the center, taking up no room at all. It's themed with ivory and blood-red crimson, each accent teased with gold. The bed could fit five people at least, and it only makes me want to sprawl across it and never leave. It's beyond breathtaking in here. It's too elegant and expensive, almost making me want to avoid touching anything in fear of ruining it.

"So you think my dad is hot?" Gray questions, interrupting my incessant gawking.

I stop in my tracks, my face flaming and my stomach churning. "What?" I squeak, my voice too high. She bursts out laughing, her face amused. When she bends, gripping her stomach, my shoulders relax.

"Joking! Everyone has a thing for dear ole Dad. I swear, if he had me earlier on in life, he'd be less burly and more like a soft teddy bear."

"What do you mean? He can't be older than forty. That means he had you at least at twenty…" I trail off, wondering how she's never mentioned him. They seem extremely close. If my relationship with my father reflected theirs by even a little, I'd be at peace.

Her face eventually drops the happiness. She shakes her head lightly, changing the subject. "I just mean, he's never stressed because I'm awesome. So he looks like a young man instead of the old one he truly is."

I nod, not wanting to have her shut down on me but also wanting to know her story. We've never really done more than mundane chatting. This is… different. We're friends—

close even—just not in the way that mattered.

"Get settled in, and Delia will have dinner prepared."

"This is so cool."

"What?"

"You being royalty."

"How'd you—"

"I wondered. French bodyguards, palace-like mansion, and your dad looks all regal. Makes sense and you just confirmed it."

"Please don't treat me any differently," she implores. "I didn't even know until I went to France."

"Don't worry, you're still that lame chick who drinks chai tea and calls it an energy boost."

She scrunches her face as if to say *fair enough*, making us both laugh before she leaves me to unpack and settle in.

CHAPTER 6

JOEY

UNLIKE MY DAD AND STEP-MONSTER, GRAY'S dining room is welcoming and not stiff. The table isn't huge like you'd expect. It's quaint, enough to fit six people or so. Mine at home could fit twenty people easily. We all crowd at one end, sitting together with idle chatter. Gray's debating schools, and Francis is trying to convince her to go to Brookewood. His argument is that they have a great teacher program.

Gray wants to teach. She hasn't decided on the subject, but it's her dream to guide kids.

"What do you think, Joey?"

I'm in the middle of chewing a bite of salmon when he asks, shocking me. Swallowing down the bite, my throat feels dry. I grab my water glass, thinking over a proper response. My father would never invite me into a conversation like this, so being asked about it has me thrown off.

"It's not a woman's job to make decisions, Josephine. That's why you'll marry one of the nine families. It'll keep you in line and our family strong. Don't you want to make me proud?"

My face scrunches at the memory, and it must make Francis worry with how he reacts. Not even a second later, he's wiping his mouth to make sure I'm okay. "Is it the salmon? Too hot? Not tangy enough? I can have Delia fix it right—"

"No, no, it's perfect!" I stop his worry, not wanting him to stress over something like a warmed home-cooked meal. "I'm just *shocked* that you care about my opinion enough to ask."

His brows furrow as his lips flatten. He stares at me as if I've grown a third nipple, and it's in the middle of my forehead. "I'm not sure what men you've been around, but women's opinions are just as important to me as anyone else's. So, tell me, where do you think she should go?"

"Honestly?" I wonder aloud, and he nods encouragingly. "Wherever makes her happiest is where she should go. If I could redo my degrees all over again, I'd study in France. I'd let the best and brightest teach me and have culture on my side. It's something I regret from being at Brighton because it limited my growth."

"Brighton? Culinary arts, hmm?" he asks with a newfound interest.

"Yeah, Gray over here mentioned her aunt went there? Loren Tanner. She's my idol!" My excitement gets the better of me, thinking of the chef that made me work harder than any other lesson could. I watched videos of Loren in class. June used her as our case study for what to strive for. Her hand techniques in cutting a chicken within thirty seconds was how I learned stealth and concentration.

"Ah, yes. Lo. Maybe Gray could introduce you two," he offers, scratching his chin thoughtfully. His fingers trace his fork, the distraction in his eyes reminds me of a burdened man. Is that what he is? A man who hides behind niceties to feel less alone?

I start to say *yes*, but Gray shakes her head at us both. "I'm sure Lo is super busy with everything going on, *Dad*. You know how it's been there since *everything* happened," she enunciates slowly as though there's a hidden message that I'm not quite getting.

Francis stares at her thoughtfully, his eyes saying more than her words did. Something transpired and there must be bad blood, he's giving off too many unsubtle vibes. Whatever it is, I want to know. Curiosity always has been my worst trait. Gray almost seems scared of the topic, so again, I change it to benefit her.

"Brookewood is great, though," I add. "I've heard the best things about their programs. I'm sure if you want to go, you'll like it." I direct my words at Gray, and the gratitude from saving her again is reflective in her gaze.

We eat in silence, almost stuck in a pregnant pause of uncertainty. Subjects that are better left unsaid.

After dinner, Gray and Francis hang out by the pool, and I excuse myself. My dad deserves to know I've monumentally messed up. Especially the information pertaining to Wes. He'll either be extremely happy or severely disappointed. There's no in-between with him. He wasn't always this way. Not before Mom disappeared and not before *her.*

"Josey bear, what do you think?" he questions, holding two very normal ties up to his chest. One's dark navy and pinstriped with cornflower, and the other is argyle in shades of red. I remember Mom saying red shows absoluteness and almost a headstrong quality, while blue shows understanding and gentleness.

Tonight is Dad's biggest political speech for the next campaign. Tonight, he's discussing how we're treating humans at ICE facilities. He should represent blue. Prove he's trustworthy, show he's not like them, *convey to them he's willing to change the world for the better.*

"Blue, Daddy. I like the blue."

He smiles sweetly at me, his eyes wrinkling at the corners. "You're right, it's the perfect color. Thank you for always showing me the right direction when I get lost. You're my compass, Josephine. Don't forget that."

Tears stream my face at the memory. He used to care. He used to respect my opinion. He used to ask for it and take it into consideration. Then, one day, all hell broke loose, and I lost everything. I miss our dream team. Making decisions together, hanging out, and being best friends. Would he have saved me if he still chose me? Would my choices and life reflect differently now if not for his lack of care?

"Josephine?" he sounds out on the other end of the phone. His voice is strained, almost sad, yet nearly emotionless too. He's stuck between a lifeless marriage and a soul-sucking career choice, and I'm the red-headed stepchild.

"Daddy," I sound out, my voice still small. The wetness from my eyes leaks down my cheeks in heaps, hitting my shirt as I'm unable to control the emotions swallowing me whole.

"What's wrong?" he asks. His concern isn't like it once was, but you can tell the man who raised me is still in there; he's just lost. "Talk to me, princess."

"I-I—" I start to cry but am interrupted by Marsha's cruel voice.

"*Clay!*"

My heart dies at that moment, his voice void of any emotion when he returns.

"What do you need, Josephine?"

"Just wanted to talk, Dad. I'll let you go."

"*Is that Josey on the phone?*" I hear Marsha in the background right before she picks up the phone. "Hello." Her normal chirp—the façade—slices through my eardrums. "So nice to hear your voice. You never call anymore." I roll my eyes in response. She's so good at faking it. So fucking good that I almost believe her.

"Yeah, hey," I mutter, not feeling it. I swipe away my stray tears and straighten my spine, unsure of why she wanted to speak to me. We don't get along. We can't stand one another.

"I'd like you over for dinner tomorrow night. We need to discuss your *future*." She says future like it's taboo and I don't have a career plan already. Must be another of her wedding scheme bullshit ideas.

"Sure thing, what time?" I play it off like it's the simplest thing rather than the single most painful thing I'll be forcing myself to do.

"Six. Your father is on a tight schedule." *Of course, he is.*

"See you then," I respond, not leaving room for more pointless words to be shared.

"And Josey, don't upset your dad. He has enough going on as it is."

I close my eyes, forcing the tears down, and nod, realizing she can't see me. "See you tomorrow, Marsha." I hang up before she hurts me even more. I didn't even get the chance to talk to my own dad. She controls everything, especially us.

Tomorrow will either fix everything or further ruin what I've tried to build.

Either way, I'll survive. I always do. Even when the person I love the most hurts me each step of the way.

CHAPTER 7

JOEY

"THEY WANT ME TO GO TO DINNER TONIGHT," I tell Gray the next day when she's emerged from showering after her swim in the pool, all while we sit eating popcorn. Best post-breakup day: popcorn, chick flicks, and shit talking. That's why we're here in the media room. *Yeah, they have a fucking media room.* The TV's as big as one at a real movie theater. They even have an area dedicated to snacks and drinks and shit. It's like I'm on cloud nine while being dragged down by memories. At least there are carbs.

"What do you want?" she asks tentatively. I stare at her, contemplating my answer. *What do I want?* My mom back. My dad back. Wes? *No.* He was a waste of my time. No one cheats unless they're missing something or an absolute asshole. *Or both.* The fact that I didn't realize what we were missing just shows we were lacking somewhere.

"Honestly, I need his help. Not just financially, but he's the best decision maker I know. It's the only reason I agreed. While it's a shitty thing to say, I feel cornered. Between my job gone and Wesley and I not being together… I'm fucked." She nods as she places more popcorn in her mouth. She's understanding in ways most chicks aren't at her age. As if her life experiences—like mine—have taught her things she shouldn't know yet.

"What about Wes, any reparations there?" she questions quietly, almost like it was out of habit and not because she believes there should be. I shake my head before answering, and she almost smiles.

"We were only meant to last what time we did. It's like he was what needed to happen to get me to a new position in life. It's an asshole-y thing to say, but it's true. It hurts. Even thinking about it right now makes me sick, but it also provides clarity. It should hurt *worse.* I should be absolutely *devastated.* But I'm not. And that's more telling than what I witnessed." I rub at my eyes, wishing I could bleach them of that memory.

"Understandable. Even if relationships make zero sense to me, I've witnessed cheating and what it does to those around the ones involved. I'd jump ship or run far away. It's just not for me," she admits, drinking her Dr. Pepper to wash down the words.

"You okay?" I'd avoid asking her this altogether, but I can tell she needs to get something off her chest. It's not always about me, even if she deflects to make it so.

"Just remembering the past few years of my life."

"What happened?" She bites her lip almost too harshly. I watch her, seeing the way the life drains from her face. She's sad; that much is obvious. Being burdened by life at such a young age isn't something I'd wish upon a bad person, let alone someone as kind as Gray.

"I had a best friend," she whispers, and her tone relays death.

"Who was she?"

"He," she clarifies. "He was my entire world. We grew up together and were born two weeks apart." I nod at her to continue and watch as she swallows another sip of her drink. "His dad and my mom…" A single tear floats down her face, resignation forming in the desolation of her expression.

I drop the bag of popcorn. My heart in my throat. Is this why she smiled when I said there's no coming back?

"They had an affair. Our parents. His dad and my mom." She wipes at her face, her cheeks blotching with sadness. I wish to drench myself in her pain and take it off her shoulders, though handling the burdens of others isn't something I'm unused to. If anything, my entire life is piles and piles of others' garbage.

"It destroyed us all. What they didn't realize is how detrimental it was to *him* and me. Our friendship suffered. The one person I loved and confided in, the one who kept me up, protected me… he was taken from me with the knowledge of their betrayal." Tears freely stream down her face now as her eyes mirror storm clouds full of rain, waiting to plunder the world beneath as it bleeds of its burdens. With a shaky nod, she finishes. "I knew, and it broke him." Her body shakes with sobs that I feel in my throat as if they were my own. I scoot closer, wanting to give her comfort but not knowing how. I'm not a touchy person; it's just not me. Not since *then*. It's like she knows and brings me the rest of the way into her embrace as she lets out all the hardships forced upon her. "He hated me. So much. He still does."

"He doesn't hate you," I attempt even though I don't know the whole story. But if he can't forgive her for being a kid with a secret she shouldn't have had to keep, then he's not right for her.

"He does," she admonishes. "After this mess, he abandoned me—our friendship." She hiccups, and I pull back, seeing how upset she truly is. "We had a plan. Finish school together, go to college together, get married someday."

My face scrunches with realization. "You *loved* loved him?"

"Unfortunately." She nods, giving me a derisive snort. "He uses it against me now. In school, he ruined my life. Until I left for France, at least."

I nod, surprisingly understanding of how this goes. Guy is a dick, guy likes girl who takes it, and then he changes. That's what she's going to live through. Hopefully, she gives him a run for his money. Hopefully, she hits him back with a strong exterior rather than being a punching bag. It's apparent in how well she's handling all of this that she's resilient.

"Maybe he'll grow out of it," I emphasize the grow part, hoping he doesn't turn out to be a complete loser. "Sometimes guys can't express the pain they experience so they gravitate to being assholes rather than speaking about their struggles."

"Maybe," she concedes as she wipes at her face furiously. "But I won't be around to watch. It's what I've been trying to tell Dad. I don't want to come back to school here. Not unless I know he won't be there. He doesn't deserve me. Not with how he is now. I want to live and be free of the horror my mother has put our families through."

"I understand." And I do. My mother's disappearance ruined our family's reputation by stealing my father's kindness and bringing me a horror film monster for a stepmother.

She sniffles a bit before we try to go back to our movie, but our mood has soured it. The cutesy love story of J-Lo and Ralph Fiennes seems unrealistic and so far from reality. Love isn't this easy or kind. There's weight to every choice, repercussions for every action, and consequences no one plans for.

By the time I'm supposed to head to dinner, I'm dreading it. I don't even shower before getting ready.

"You've got this," I whisper into the mirror even though I'm not feeling a single word of it.

"You really do," Francis's voice hums from behind me; his words like a Band-Aid, healing me and promising protection. "Don't stress about your parents. I'm sure they're going to bend over backward for you. *I would.*" Is he… *flirting* with me? From my position in front of the mirror, I watch him as if he stood in front of me. His eyes roam my body unhurriedly, drinking me in. The admiration caresses me with hope, offering something no one in my position should take. Reaping the benefits of his home is one thing while taking advantage of his body is another.

I blush. Turning to him leaning against the doorjamb, I watch as he smiles. "The only bending backward that they'll do involves them laughing. They're not cool like you."

His chuckle makes flutters rush my body, my palms perspiring along with it. I wipe them on the boyfriend jeans I'm wearing and pray he doesn't think I'm being a dick, rather than my dry as gin humor.

"You'd be amazed at the affect you have on people," he says softly, almost too low for me to hear him as he looks at the floor. *He's a charming sonofabitch.* "Drive safe. If you need a ride or just someone to talk to, I'm only a phone call away."

I eye him skeptically, wondering if he's serious or if my jaded heart expects a string or twenty tied.

"I don't—" I start, but before I can finish, he places his hand outward, gesturing to my pocket.

"Phone?"

Handing it to him, I watch as he types quickly before giving it back. "If, by chance, you need anything, and I mean *anything*, don't hesitate to call." When our focuses collide, he's smirking, displaying his signature dimple. I'm melting like that green bitch in *The Wizard of Oz*. Trying not to laugh at myself for how odd my mind is, I offer a tentative smile.

"Thank you," I barely muster, feeling many things, though none of them acceptable. Especially when his daughter is my friend and three rooms down. As I walk away, I check my phone before pocketing it.

Mon Roméo.

My Romeo.

That's what he put in my phone.

I've been called stupid on many occasions, but this won't be one of those times.

CHAPTER 8

THE DAY BEFORE

JOEY

AS SOON AS I ARRIVE AT MY DAD'S, I'M A BALL OF sick and nervous energy. This can't go well. Especially when Marsha's here. My fingers stumble over the gate code, reminding me that the worst he can say is no.

But where does that leave me?

Homeless.

Jobless.

Worthless.

Swallowing the bile slowly rising from anxiety, I wait as the gates open. My car glides in as I allow it to coast. Parked only ten feet from the entrance, I debate whether I can survive this or not. Can I? Will I accomplish anything at this point?

Why didn't I save more money? Usually, I'm one to plan so far ahead that my plans have plans. This time, though, I didn't think it through. My loyalty to Wes was double his to me, if not triple. He betrayed me, my trust, and made me believe a backup plan wasn't necessary.

Guess when it comes to love, I'm flawed.

"Josephine," Marsha calls out as I make my way to the front door. She opens it before I get the chance, but that's just like her, wanting the upper hand on everything. "You're late."

"I'm on time," I argue.

"If you're not early, you're late," she reprimands, a conniving smile on her face. It makes her face appear uglier. If not for her polarizing attitude and degrading humor, she'd be beautiful. Marsha has that politician wife look. Her hair is always pinned up. She's twenty-seven, blonde, and tenacious as hell. It's not a far reach that she went for my father, and he fell for it. When you're lonely and suffering unspeakable loss, it's easy to fall into the venomous trap of a black widow.

"Come, come." She ushers me inside like a dog, or a doormat, or in this case both. I stare at the walls. It's a routine, especially since I only visit every once in a while. The pictures have changed again. Almost every single one of Mom and me is gone. There's only one left of Dad and me. *Graduation.* It's sad, seeing how these pictures are plastered all over like a memorial.

Here lies Josephine. She's not dead… just non-existent.

Dad sits at the dinner table with his newspaper in hand and his mood unreadable. Our relationship is as stagnant as this silent air. If I didn't remind myself to breathe, the darkness would take me, and it's not looking too unwelcoming right now. He grips the paper when he hears Marsha's heels hit the tile floor, and I try to not smile. In his world of politics where he has to pretend to be happy and in love, he can lie. But here, where no one is around but her and me, he hides behind nice words. His facial expressions, though, give away more than he'll ever admit.

"Hey, Daddy," I call out in a small voice like I'm a little girl all over again and not a woman who's suffering every day. The newspaper falls to the table, and his eyes meet mine. Amber, the exact shade of mine, stares at me. Understanding flickers. Care. For this moment, this tiny morsel of breaths collectively stolen, he shows his love. In his expression, you can see he misses me, that he's sorry, and he wishes things were different. It's not enough, though. The simple glances of love and support don't rectify his actions.

And those speak volumes.

He abandoned me.

Killed my hope.

Didn't notice when someone stole my innocence.

Lost time is forever gone but memories trickle through the crack of my mind on a continuous loop.

"Hey, Josey-pie," he greets, his voice warm and happy as he stands to hug me. *It's been so long.* His arms are a welcome reprieve. He holds me together at this moment, collecting my pain and borrowing the weight so it's not unbearable. Then as soon as it's there, it's gone.

"Your father and I would like to speak with you," Marsha interrupts our tiny moment, the little span of time we'll never get back. Remember time is the biggest liar of all.

Don't be fooled.

"Sit," she suggests, waving me to the table. Dad pulls out a chair, and as I lower myself, he tucks me in. My stomach feels all sorts of uncomfortable with the simple fact that Marsha's leading this family dinner. Whatever comes out of her mouth is usually bad. It holds no merit, but he allows it. Every single time.

Wherever Clayton Moore disappeared to, I'd like to file a missing person's report.

"Your dad and I were discussing your absence..." she drones on, and I don't listen, using this time to think of all the restaurants in Hollow Ridge and Hawthorne and wondering if any needs a head chef. Since we've met, I've learned to block out her talks and gibberish about being a *family*. She's not kind, she's fake, and we have enough plastic in the Hollow Ridge Bay that we don't need her polluting it further.

"Josephine Ellis Moore." My dad breaks me from my silence, reprimanding me for my lack of respect.

"Sorry, Dad. I have a lot on my mind." It's a lame excuse, but truthful, nonetheless.

"She asked why you're not working tonight," he reiterates.

"Ah, you see... I quit." Taking in a haggard breath, I blink the disappointment away. For a moment, the thought of lying occurred to me, but then I realized Marsha and her goons probably stalk me enough to know I'm falsifying that information. Neither seems surprised, and they both exude an almost vague understanding along with their disappointment.

"Again?" Marsha goads, placing her hand on her hip with judgment in her expression.

"This guy—"

"Enough!" my dad interrupts. Whenever Marsha and I spat, he gets aggravated, usually shutting us down with his booming voice. "Let's eat, then discuss. I'm famished."

And at that, we're no longer speaking.

Just like normal.

Voiceless meals with miserable human beings.

Cheers.

Dinner goes on without a single word passed among us three. I'd say it's peaceful, but we all know that's a lie. It's awkward and stifling, almost like being locked into a room without windows. I'm not a fan.

"Marsha and I were discussing your future," Dad finally breaks the cloak of invisibility I tried clinging to. He takes a swig of his wine, then pats his mouth like he's regal and important. He is, being a mayor and all, but he's not to me.

Not anymore. "We want you to move back home. My next campaign—"

"You're fucking joking," I spit, my voice louder than I've ever allowed it to rise. Never at my dad. Never swear. Never show weakness. Never bend. "You cut me out of your life for *her*, and now you suddenly want me to pretend I'm okay with that?"

"Lower your voice, Josephine. We don't raise our voices or curse in this household."

"Again, until she showed up," I let out, frustration seeping from my pores.

"I need to show a solidified family front and not a daughter shacked up with some surfer urchin who doesn't know the difference between a salad fork and a dinner fork."

A snort escapes me. I can't help it. It's an accurate depiction even though that isn't the issue. The real one is the fact that he still believes he has any control over me. He lost that when he practically disowned me for my choices.

"If you're not home, you set a bad precedent, showing others that they don't have to respect me and my image if my own daughter can't," he continues, as if I didn't laugh at his previous comment.

"I'm not moving back here," I bite out, folding my arms across my chest.

"I think you are," he challenges with wrinkles lining his forehead. "I know you're struggling. Why else, out of the blue, would you call me? Money talks, honey. It's screaming that something went wrong." He brings his hands together and sets them on the table, something he wouldn't ever do while eating. "You're easy to read. Did you get fired? Is that why you called? You can't afford rent with that lowlife? You're just going to ask for money and run home to him, supporting his pot smoking and alcohol habits...?"

My tongue hurts as my teeth pinch the life out of it, holding back every bitter thing I want to say. As much as he's callous toward me, threatening with words and belittling me, I can't react. What choice do I have? But I can't hold it in, not when his snide smirk comes through, all triumphant and golden, like he's the *man*. He must forget that being *the man* isn't the same as being *a man*.

"For your information," I snap, "I left him. Caught him fucking a tramp on our bed. So, no, Dad. I'm not going *home*. I've been at my friend Gray's house for the past two days, and that's where I'll stay." He goes to say something, but I can tell where his confidence falters and his face falls with sadness, and I don't allow him. "I came to you because you're my dad. I needed someone to talk to, to help me, support me, and maybe even tell me it's not my fault. I didn't sign up for this. None of this." By the end, the betraying tears leave my eyes, and my voice is hoarse with emotion. It's not like I cry often. Or ever. But my dad and his words, all of it hurts me. This distance he's put between us, the way he allows his wife to talk to me, and the way he now speaks to me as if I'm not his daughter.

It's a mess.

I hate it.

I hate *him*.

Scooting my chair back, I leave without another word. His money is useless to me when he's such a despicable man. I'm not even remotely okay with the way he behaves. And as he calls after me, chasing me out the door, I don't stop.

Like the stand-up guy he is, he doesn't follow me past the front door, saving whatever useless pride he has left when he lets me leave.

Goodbye, Dad. Don't worry. I didn't need you then, and I don't need you now.

CHAPTER 4

JOEY

AFTER THE TRAIN WRECK OF A DINNER—IF YOU could call it that—I go back to Gray's. She's out with some girl from high school who begged to see her. Honestly, I need her here to talk, listen, or even just vent to so I'm not alone. Being alone is miserable. It's one of my most troubling traits since Mom disappeared. Being abandoned is the other. Clinging onto things that matter seems to be my default setting.

I fell asleep right after taking a long bath in the Jacuzzi tub. Not sure how I didn't spend every spare moment in that thing. It's like a mini hot tub for my own pleasure. As I sit here, staring at the package I took *that* night, I bite my lip. Contemplation runs thick through me. It's not my apron. Took me reading who it was from to tell me that it's something bigger.

Much bigger.

Instead of dwelling, I open the box, wondering if hell froze over.

Inside sits a little four-by-six note. *You've been cordially invited...* Flipping it over, I read the back, shock slicing at me like a paper cut.

Dear Ms. Moore,

We were eager to see your application for Culinary Con. It's not surprising to see your long list of accomplishments in your short life, but we're proud to represent you on this new venture.

It brings us great pleasure to select you for the Raffle Chef Contest. Your donation was greatly appreciated, and we hope you find your dream career. All restaurants involved are hugely renowned for their service and etiquette. They'd be lucky to have a dedicated chef such as yourself.

The event will be held the twenty-seventh day of May. We know it's a last-minute addition, but we couldn't resist the recommendation letter we received in your honor.

Please accept this outfit, we were informed by Mayor Moore of your size. See you there.

Sincerely,
Culinary Con Founder, Ted Gehrig

Application? May 27th? That's today! My eyes nearly bug out. Anger. Horror. Excitement. It's infused in each intake of breath. How could he? How can I not accept? What if I'm given the chance to get into a top-five restaurant? It's not like I could jump into this career otherwise because I'm considered inexperienced.

But Dad.

He did this.

With him, there are always strings attached. It's not like he did this out of the kindness of his heart, because he has his own agenda. He always does. I remove the packing paper to see what rests inside. My eyes connect with black material, and I inwardly groan. It better not be a dress. Dad knows exactly how I feel about the lack of style dresses have.

Pulling it out, I notice the material is stiff. It's going to make my skin itch, I'm sure of it. That, or it'll crawl. Especially knowing my dad is basically selling me to the highest bidder—his own personal hooker for hire. I've heard of Culinary Con. It's only for the highest-ranking chefs and restaurant moguls. You're put into a drawing raffle, and the more tickets you buy, the largest chance you have of winning a chef. That means I'll go to some dick who's loaded, I'm sure. It's fate, isn't it? Probably someone my dad greased palms with. Because why the hell not?

I'm tempted not to show up, so my dad's *generous* donation will go toward nothing. He deserves it. It'd show him right. But I don't have a choice. I'm jobless. And homeless, as soon as Francis and Gray get sick of me.

I hold the dress up against my body in the mirror. It's going to be a tight fit, showing off every little detail of my body.

Yay.

Rolling my eyes, I decide to take a shower. After two hours of blow-drying my hair and making it presentable, I start to wonder why the hell I'm putting myself through this. Another hour passes by the time I'm done with my face and wearing my outfit. My skin is already irritated with the restraining feeling of the expensive material. If jeans and a crop top were acceptable, I'd change out of this in a heartbeat.

Deciding to pack them in my bag as a *just in case*, I face myself in the mirror. I don't look like me. I look like *her*. And her. And her. And her. All the women who live for this shit, the ones who have to work so hard to be pretty on the outside because their insides are dead. That's exactly what I appear to be trying to do right now.

Knock. Knock. The door sounds out from beside me. For once, I closed it, knowing I'd be nearly naked the entire time I got ready. Opening to see who is on the other side, I spot Francis.

"Hey," he says awkwardly.

We've got to stop meeting like this. It looks bad. Very, very bad. Not that I mind the company or the view, but it makes me look shady. Not to mention that if Gray walked in on the way he flirts, she'd probably kick me to the curb.

"Hi," I reply lamely, not knowing what to say.

"How did dinner go?"

I cringe.

He stares at me as a million things go through my mind. It was *bad,* and that's understating the disaster it truly turned out being.

"That well?" he jokes, but he doesn't know the half of it. I bite my lip, holding back all the words I want to say but can't. Then I realize how weird it must feel not to invite him in. We stand weirdly at the door, and I open it wider, waving him in.

"If a train wreck with a bazillion passengers is considered good..." A laugh escapes me at the euphemism, knowing it's overdramatic. He chuckles at me, shaking his head. Tonight, he's wearing distressed jeans, a button-up that's rolled at the sleeves, and his hair is brushed back. I stare for far too long before he winks, throwing me back out of my headspace.

"Could be worse."

"Really?" I ask, exasperated.

"Well, you could have your wife try to run you off the road, try to take your inheritance, and make your daughter believe you're a drug-abusing dead man for fifteen years," he explains simply as though this isn't something bigger than it is. The amusement in his tone should make me laugh, but I'm completely speechless. "What? Cat caught your tongue, *ma coccinelles?*"

"You drop, like, the biggest bomb on my lap, dude. What do you think?" I mock. Is it true? *There's no way—*

"Yeah, Gray's mom was a peach," he confirms.

—*it's true.*

"Wow," is all I get out. I'm seriously at a loss here. How the hell does one cope with that level of crazy? No wonder Gray keeps her distance when it comes to topics of the heart. That'd be rough.

"Yeah, but it's all over now. I'm happier than I've ever been." As he says the words, I see the possibilities of everything he and Gray have been through. It makes me want to hug the sadness out of them, fix them somehow, and help... but how do you help a man and a kid who have everything?

"That's good," I finally respond.

"Anyway," he starts, staring at me with interest. "Where are you headed in that?" He says *that* like he can't say anything more without being too forward. I appreciate it. I'm so close to just asking him if he's interested and seeing if it leads to anywhere. *It couldn't. I wouldn't. But God, does it sound nice.*

"An event my father pimped me out to," I groan. Hanging my head in shame for just thinking it's something I'd do, I hope he doesn't see me as weak. We may barely know one another, but for some reason, him seeing me as *frail* makes me sadder than it should.

A few seconds pass, the silence feeling like sensory overload rather than the opposite. He tips my chin up; his soft fingertips—nothing like how a working man's hands would feel—caress my skin, feathery soft, warm, and with care. I can't hold back the tiniest grin, loving how each move feels calculated and kind. Full of promise and suggestion. Two things I'm not allowed to want. I shouldn't even consider it with what happened with Wes only three days ago.

"Don't go," he whispers, so close—too close if we consider Gray.

"I-I," I stumble over excuses and reasons, not knowing which way is up or down. His warring gray eyes, stubbled cheeks, and rosy lips mere inches from mine. "I have to." It's a weak attempt at words, but it gives me some ground.

"You can always stay here... *with me*," he suggests. His breath is warm on my lips, yet I'm shivering and unable to think of words. Gray's dad is too much. And if I allow myself to stay, things will only get bad—better for me—bad for Gray.

I won't do that to her.

I can't.

Begrudgingly, I pull back. The need to seal my lips to his, to take his mouth with everything I have, and have him make me feel good, burns my skin. It's prickled with unused energy and unsatisfied desire. "I'll see you when I get back, Francis." It's all I can offer. It's all we can ever be. I look back at him before leaving the door, and his gaze sets my skin ablaze. His desire swims in his irises like nothing I've ever experienced. I bite my lip to avoid running to him, but it seems to only propel him to me. In the next moment, he's face-to-face with me, cupping my jaw tenderly.

His lips descend on mine in a hot second, brushing mine with soft fervor and passion, making my heart rebel against my chest. We kiss for only seconds, moments flurrying like embers to the sky, and then we break apart. My gaze lands on him, seeing the ardor seeping from his expression, letting me know everything I need to know.

I have to leave.

"I'm sorry," he placates, his voice grittier, his accent stronger than ever. "I didn't want to live the rest of my life not knowing." Words are stuck in my throat, my need to get out of here increasing, so I grab my overnight bag and force my legs to move outside the room and out the front door.

CHAPTER 10

TOBY

I ARRIVE IN VEGAS THREE HOURS AFTER CLICKING RSVP. Dale called me immediately, excited for me to come. He said since it was such a late addition, he wouldn't be able to have a reserved seat for me.

The party is in five hours, and I have my best black and white three-piece Dior suit ready for the occasion. The plan consists of doing my normal ten-thousand-dollar donation and then some for raffles.

That's how this works.

Shake some hands. Grease some palms. Get recognition.

You raffle for a top-of-the-pyramid kind of chef. They're

well-known, experienced, and know their shit. It's exactly what I need for tonight. Before taking the trip, I called Francis. He told me to stay sober or I'd lose my balls. He's trying to warn me because Ellie basically got him wasted and married him. *Ellie.* My mind travels to the Antichrist herself. She fucked up a lot before her untimely demise.

The best thing that came of her death was Gray being reunited with Francis. That was the worst-kept secret. It made zero sense as to why he stayed away. I get he had a kid he wanted to protect, a fortune, and even his family name, but Gray grew up thinking her dad died drunk. Seeing her face when we brought up Francis over the years made me sad. Nate and I were in the loop. We knew and couldn't say anything. What kind of people does that make us?

Gray forgave Francis.

Hell, she flew across the world to learn about their family and what it means to be a Satoray. She grew to love him, and he updates me often about their adventures. Like now, they're in Hawthorn for the summer, and part of the next semester, while Gray decides her future and Frankie goes wild.

After all the drama of Ellie, I didn't think I'd survive. I was able to be with Lo. Truly be with her. Then she got into that accident, and I thought even then that maybe she'd pick me. But what I didn't realize—or refused to—was that she and Jase had more than us.

They were real.

We weren't.

And in the end, I was the one who suffered.

Pulling up to the hotel in my Z51 Corvette, I practically cry when I hand the keys over to the valet. He's eighteen, maybe. His eyes light up like mine used to when I got a new video game.

"Scratch it, you die."

He chuckles as if I'm joking. I'm not. There are only twenty-five of the limited edition charcoal dust color to be ever made. That's as limited as it gets for Corvettes. "Bro, I'd—"

"Not your bro, *dude*. I'm serious. I'll hunt you down if she's even surface-dented. Buffable or not, this car is worth more than your entire existence," I say harshly. The kid visibly swallows as his excitement drains from his face entirely. *Good.* No joyrides for him.

"Got it," he mutters, his hands shaking when he reaches the door to drive off. I smile at him and wave, not caring that he might have pissed himself. Better not get that shit on my seats. A bellhop waves me over, taking my bags and suit and carrying them to the front. Handing him a hundred, I shoo him away. As soon as I'm checked in, I'm practically running for the room. When I notice the minibar, the one I specifically asked to be empty, I choke down the dryness swelling my tongue.

Is this what life of an addict will always be like?

Craving a single drop like I'm stranded without sustenance, and when it's placed in front of you, in all its taunting glory, you have to abstain from indulging? That's what I'm experiencing as I stare at the little bottles of Jack,

Jameson, Jimmy Beam, and Crown. It's like they knew whiskey was my weakness and wanted to test me or force me to spend a shit-ton more money. Rehab. I did the twelve steps, though I skipped huge details on a few. Catherine Bobbie—goes by Bobbie—Nate's and my sponsor, she saved me. Brought me from the cusp of drowning and dragged me out, drying each oversaturated inch.

Closing my eyes with what little restraint I have, I change into my gym shorts and racer tank. Instead of sitting in a room that would more than likely push me over the edge, I head to the gym at the top floor, the one only suites have access to.

Scanning my room card, I'm allowed entry. It's empty. *Not surprisingly.* There are several events this weekend, and most people dread working out while on vacation. For one, it's business. Two, it's the only thing that keeps me from dousing myself in woodsy goodness. And three, it's productive and healthy. It's what I do to keep my mind off *her* and how happy she must be right now.

Two years.

Bet she's radiant.

Why did my happiness have to reflect solely on hers? When will I find the part of myself that deserves happiness and run with it?

Will there ever be a day when I can smile and know that I'm worthy of love?

Heading for the treadmill, I decide to sweat all the cravings away. It'll take some time, but it'll happen. That, I'm sure of.

I stretch, wondering if the burn will be less with this much preparation. There are two ways to work out. The right way, which is painful if you do it right, and the wrong way, which hurts no matter how long you go. The only difference is that the wrong way can cause irreparable damage.

After warming up, I start at a slow jog. Ten minutes in, my calves are feeling stretched and heated, so I pick up the pace to a run. Wanting the exertion, I need the blinding sweat to seep through and remind me why being sober is important.

Forty minutes in, my body feels the burn. It feels the exhaustion and lack of stamina. During these past two years, I've let myself go. Not just with binge-eating, booze, and everything else bad, but with this.

The one thing I made sure both Lo and I did was keep up our health, but then I let it go to trash. I couldn't help it. She put me in the worst darkness I've ever been in. Where stars didn't exist. No moon. No light. Just blackness. Nothingness as it consumed me along the way.

She wrecked me. And like the fool I am, I let her.

My heart pounds, my head following soon after. I check my watch and realize I've been busting ass for two hours. How am I still going? No water. No breaks or breathers. Sometimes, the mind consumes, and it's not always in the best interest of the person, either.

When I make it back to my room, a sticky note resides on my door. When I flip it open, I notice a short message. *Be ready in forty, registration is two hours in advance.* My stomach flips.

How am I supposed to un-exhaust myself, all while looking dashing doing it?

Ice bath?

Ice. Bath.

Closing the plug to the tub, I find the wine cooler besides the fridge and head to the ice machine near the gym. I fill it up and go back and forth between my room and the machine until half the tub is full. Turning the water on the coldest setting, I let it run. As soon as it's ready, I remove my shirt, shoes, and socks, and lower myself into the bitter cold. My nipples are hard before the water touches me, and my balls are drawn up in preparation, knowing the drill.

I settle inside, my entire body shivering from the initial cold. You'd think I'd be used to it; I've been taking ice baths since high school. Since *he* started beating the shit out of me. My mind travels to dear ole Dad, and I shiver for an entirely different reason.

"You'd think being half of me, you'd be less worthless than that prick you call brother," he hisses, spittle leaving his lips with each word as he shouts inches from my face. People wonder how parents get so angry, why they're upset, or even vicious.

Mine, tonight, has everything to do with the bowl I dropped in the sink.

Not even six inches above the bottom of it, as I washed it, it slipped, crashing into the stainless steel sink. It shattered. Never before has a bowl smashed without force, yet it did. Immediately, he howls. "What the fuck have you done now, boy?"

My body stiffens, readying for attack, knowing he's going to lay it on me, hurt me until I can't breathe...

Breathe.

How was one supposed to with a punctured lung?

My dad beat me that night with his fist wrapped around a pillowcase. He forgot one thing, though—ribs break easily. Not *that* easily, but easily enough that a grown man only needs to punch once in the right spot. Mom rushed me to the hospital as Dad claimed it was a varsity accident. And so, my beatings began.

As did my ice baths.

I shake my head, noticing the moisture leaking from my eyes. The memories never fade, even if the man is buried six feet under.

My skin hurts from the blistering cold, and I empty the tub, stepping out. It takes too much time to get my body back up to temp, so I jump into the shower, cleaning off the remaining grime. By the time I'm suited up and ready to walk out the door, a knock sounds out.

Jacob, one of the co-hosts of Culinary Con, stands at my door, looking smug as fuck. "Hayes," he mutters as though we haven't spoken in ages, which is not wrong. We haven't been in the same room for at least five years.

"Jake, my man," I greet, pulling him into a side hug. He slaps my back, then smiles, his face one of happiness.

"Toby, man. It's been too long. And you're looking younger than ever," he muses, staring at me in awe. "There's no way you're in your late thirties." I give him a wry smile in return, not realizing how old I'm getting day after day.

"Thirty-seven in October," I remind him, wondering how time has flown by so quickly.

"Damn, son. We're getting old."

"Speak for yourself, old man. I'm young as hell." But I'm sure the amusement doesn't reach my face since he changes the subject.

"Ready for this?"

"What? Giving you money for something I see no return on?" A chuckle leaves him, his face alight with humor. "Wouldn't change it for the world," I lie.

We make it down to the conference room's foyer. There, in the front, is a table set up with three women. They're wearing shiny sequined dresses that only make them look old and trying too hard to appear young. They stare at me with wonder and it has me smirking. *I've still got it.* Even when my life's a fucked-up mess, I've still got it.

"Ladies," I coo, acting all grandiose when I feel anything but.

They all giggle in unison as if they've practiced this time and time again to get it right. "Sir," the far right says. "Name?"

"Tobias Hayes," I pronounce, and her eyes bulge out.

"*The* Tobias? Our golden sponsor every year?"

"That's the one," Jake booms from beside me, clapping my shoulder again. By the end of tonight, it's going to be sore from his bear paws. "He's been more than generous for years. I'm honestly proud to call him friend."

Friend, my ass.

Moneybags is more like it.

"Here's your ID badge and envelope of chefs," the middle one explains. The one on the left stares at me in admiration, like she wants to flirt but won't. I notice the ring on her finger and decide to tease her.

"And your name, gorgeous?"

"P-Penny," she stutters.

"Ah, Penny. Such a pretty name. What is it that you have for me?" The other ladies glower as I give all my attention to the respectful woman at the end.

"Raffles," she says breathily. "For the chef contest."

"I see," I muse, touching her hand and the ring on her finger. She doesn't pull away, but she should. I've been known to ruin marriages. "How much?"

"Fifty dollars a ticket," she explains, her face red and flamed from the skin-to-skin attention. "The money goes toward the foundation. It's basically a donation."

"Have a piece of paper to charge my account? I'll write down a number, and you put me in for that much, okay?" Her eyes widen as if she's not used to this kind of situation. She hands me a piece of paper, and I write down a one and five zeroes. Her mouth hangs open, and she types into the spreadsheet on the computer. "Jake here has my information. Feel free to charge my account."

"This is huge, sir," Penny finally replies. "You're such a philanthropist."

I chuckle. *What's ten thousand to a man like me?*

She hands me a receipt, and I pocket it without looking at it. By the time I'm seated at a table, I'm beyond ready to drink I can't see straight. These events are boring and so are the people involved. A waitress hands me a bottle of sparkling water, which tastes like ass, and not the good kind. Ten minutes pass by before Jake stops to see how I've settled. I take a big drink, hoping he decides not to stay.

"I can't believe you bought a hundred thousand dollars' worth of tickets," is the first thing he says to me. And that drink I just took comes spewing out with a fit of coughs.

"What?"

"That's what you wrote down. Penny showed me."

"Fuck," I curse, pulling the receipt out of my pocket. Sure as the day I was born, it says one hundred thousand. I'm not sure how I'll explain this to Raul. And fuckity fuck. If I don't get a chef with this amount of money, I'll be pissed.

"What's wrong?" he asks, his eyebrow raised in amusement.

"I thought I wrote ten thousand," I mutter, clearing my throat. "Raul is going to kill me."

He laughs. "Too late now, Toby. At least you'll be a shoo-in to win."

"Fuck off," I growl. He continues his chuckling all while heading to the podium and grabbing the mic.

"Tonight, is a special night. Usually, we have only three chefs, but this year, we have four. One is especially important. She's a prodigy, and I've heard nothing but praise about her.

And she's a spitfire."

I try not to roll my eyes in exasperation at his poor etiquette and wait for the stage to fill with the four contestants. They're getting paid good money to simply exist. By being selected, you get a five-year contract with the company that wins and a salary that's way more than fair for the first three years. After the money I've spent on this stupid event, I better get the best one.

He starts inviting them up to the stage, talking about their work and qualifications. When he gets to the last one—the auburn-haired spitfire, as he called her—I try not to grunt. What is she, fifteen? She stares directly at me as if hearing my thoughts. Her eyes connect with mine on a different level. They're wise and angry. A kind of anger I understand and feel. The event proceeds, and her gaze stays locked on me.

It's unnerving and uncomfortable.

"Our Golden Sponsor, Tobias Hayes!" Jake's voice booms, and I'm unsure of what has happened since this chick has siphoned my every thought since arriving on stage. My attention is stuck on the girl who's angrier than anyone ought to be, and it's only gotten worse. The thundering disappointment flashing in her eyes has me confused.

"Toby," Jake announces again like I'm an unintelligible imp.

My gaze meets his.

And I know.

She's mine now.

CHAPTER 11

JOEY

THE DRIVE TO VEGAS FEELS LONGER THAN IT TRULY is. By the time I arrive, I've only got thirty minutes before the raffle. Luckily, I decided to get my dress on before leaving. Francis and his lips were way too distracting. *And wrong, Joey. Don't forget wrong.*

Putting on my way-too-tall pumps before giving the valet my keys, I head inside to sign in with the registrar.

A man named Jake takes me to the back of a stage, telling me I'll be called out when they're ready.

"Where can I put my bag?" I ask before he runs off. He's too energetic, moving from place to place too fast. He gives me a curious look, wondering why I'm not checked into the hotel, I'm sure.

"I'll take it," he offers.

"No, no," I argue too quickly. My entire life is in that bag. If he takes it and loses it—which I'm sure he will—I'll be screwed.

"Miss," he starts. Someone from beside us calls his name, and he's shaking his head. "Here, get a room." He hands me a card, and I wonder what the hell I'm supposed to do in the meantime. I have less than thirty minutes at this point, and if I'm late, it'll make me look tacky.

Don't dwell, I remind myself before rushing toward the lobby. It's not easy in trashy heels, that's for sure. I'd be much more comfortable in my Vans.

"I need a room," I rush out as soon as I get to the man standing behind the counter.

"ID?" he questions like I'm a fucking child. I'm not old enough to rent a room, but he doesn't need to know that.

"My dad asked me to do it while he holds his event," I lie, watching him stare at me in disbelief.

"I can't—"

"She's with me," a man says briskly from behind me. I turn to him with a grateful expression. He looks familiar, but I'm not entirely sure from where. The service clerk doesn't appear to want to deal with the man standing behind me. Instead, he takes the card Jake gave me and types in some info.

"There's only the honeymoon suite left," he mutters absently, clicking more keys.

"That'll just have to do," I urge. It's not my money anyway. He nods, his fingers tapping away.

"Here you are," he confirms, handing me a receipt to sign. Scribbling some unintelligible name, I get the room card and find a bellhop.

"Please take this to my room." He nods at me with a smile and takes my bag. Checking my cell, I notice it's been fifteen minutes. I have only six to get back to the stage. Stopping at the nearest wall, I use it as leverage to take off my heels, then book it to the event center.

By the time I make it back, putting my death traps back on my feet, they're calling us out on the stage. My face must be sweaty since I've run in this stuffy building back and forth on a time constraint. *Oh, well. It's not a beauty contest.*

"Zachariah Billings," Jake reads the name of the winner for the first chef. "Raise your hand so this fine young woman can meet you." He raises his hand, a man in a stiff suit and an even stiffer looking expression waits for the first chef to make her way over.

The other two beside me get their business owners while I stand awkwardly. As I'm debating how much I hate the life choices I've made to get to this point, I find a man staring at me.

His hair is sloppy and purposely so. His suit—perfectly committed to his body as sure as he's not committed to any woman in his life—fits him effortlessly. The look in his eyes as he watches me makes me nervous. It's how Francis looks at me, but this man differs. His expression is one of a man who'll eat me alive and spit me out. Francis's was more of a *take my time* kind of hunger. As I'm busy wondering what this guy's story is, a name is called.

"Our Golden Sponsor, Tobias Hayes!"

No one stands to greet me, making me hopeful they didn't show up, and I won't be stuck with some dick who doesn't know the difference between a spoon and a ladle.

"Toby," Jake repeats from beside me. *Fuck.* That means the dude is here, and Jake knows him. So much for not getting paired. Holding in the groan of disappointment, the man who was analyzing every breath I took stands and saunters toward me. *No fucking way.*

He's not only too young to be a stuffy businessman, but he's too hot to be into something so mundane. Right?

As Toby makes his way over to me, each step is another nail in my coffin. If I thought Francis was hard to handle, this man—with his sexy come-hither eyes—is impossible. A smirk tilts at his lips, and for some reason, that makes me want to smack it off his face.

Smugness isn't attractive.

He better not be a douchebag.

Jake hands my new warden an envelope. One I'm sure that lists my good and bad traits, my name, age, and everything else my father decided was pertinent to know. Like how much men controlling me isn't something I allow.

The man doesn't say a word as he leads me back to his table. Awkward silence fills the small expanse between us, reminding me how uneasy this entire shindig makes me feel. Sitting down in the chair, since he still hasn't said a word, he eyes me skeptically.

"Toby," he practically growls to me as he sits, offering his hand. I stare at it, knowing how disrespectful I'm being by not offering mine to him in return. He opens the folder and begins reading to himself. Stiff air swims around us, more potent than the booze we both desperately need.

"*Nineteen,*" he mocks as if all I've accomplished in my short lifespan is a disappointment. He's shaking his head, reading on. "Josephine?"

"Joey," I correct, my eyes narrowing with each second that clicks by.

"A pleasure, I'm sure," he mutters with disappointment.

God, if I knew it was going to be this awful, I'd have avoided this altogether. He probably spent tens of thousands to win me, yet he treats me like leftovers. It's appalling and unacceptable. A waitress passes by, and I stop her. "Champagne, please." She nods politely, bringing me a flute back moments later.

"You're not old enough to drink," Toby reprimands, not giving me a second glance.

"Maybe you're just too old." It's a lame comeback, but my blood is boiling, and it's the best I have. I should have stayed in Francis's arms, his lips against mine, his body...

"Everyone!" Jake hollers over the mic, interrupting my

pleasant daydream. "We're going to do an icebreaker. Get ready to be put into groups." Toby and I are at a lonely table with no seatmates to pair with. So as we wait for instructions, Jake meets us at our table with a woman on his arm and another couple.

"Let's play a game," he says in his best *Jigsaw* voice.

"Never have I ever," the woman next to him jumps in and suggests. I try to contain the snort rising but fail miserably. Of fucking course these old shits want to play an inappropriate teenage game. This may be the only time they can get their socks off.

"Okay, shots every time someone has done something, yes?" Jake questions, making sure the same rules as always still applies.

Everyone nods, but Toby's face falls. "Problem, old man?" I taunt, raising a challenging eyebrow at him.

"No, *Sous*. But I'm sure you'll regret this." *Sous?* I'm no one's sous. With a grunt and the need to flip him off, I pay attention to anyone but him.

Jake waves a waitress over and tells her to bring us six shots of whiskey and to keep them coming.

"I'll start!" the blonde next to me offers. "Never have I ever gotten wasted." I chuckle because even I have, and I'm only nineteen. Everyone around the table drinks. When I glance back at Toby, he watches me as he slowly takes back a shot too. His eyes melt me more than the whiskey down my throat does. Chills skate up my bare thighs, and it's as if he knows because his eyes wander over them, taking in every inch of me like a contract, making sure every detail is up to par.

I've nearly forgotten how bare my arms are when his eyes home in on the scars. Like he knows exactly what they are and their meaning, he quirks a brow.

Does my pain make me less annoying, old man?

As if realizing he's staring, he shakes his head and doesn't look at me again. The questions keep going around, and by the time it's to Toby, I'm beyond tipsy. If there's a *right before wasted* word, that's where I'm at.

"Never have I ever broken the law," Toby mutters. It makes me wonder if he even knows the rules of the game. You're supposed to suggest something you *haven't* done, and I'm sure he's broken several just with his looks alone.

I raise another shot to my lips with a wink, unable to stop giggling. It's not like me. Alcohol swims through my veins like a fish does through a channel to the ocean. I'm hot and sweaty and slowly feeling too friendly. *I'm not a friendly person.*

Toby watches me with tempting eyes, ones that promise a good night but a regretful morning. He's a drug I'd easily partake in. But unlike Oxy and Percs, I'd be addicted with one dose rather than seven days' worth, unable to return. And I've never been one to turn away any kind of vice, especially if it feels good.

"Your turn," Blondie squeals, poking my thigh. My eyes meet his hazel ones, seeing the little green tracing the outer edge of the irises. I bite my lip, knowing what I want to know, begging it'll give me courage to do something stupid. Something I'd have done with Francis if not for circumstance.

But I can't do this with Francis. I can't. *I can't.* I won't.

My inhibitions are being tested, and like the Chicago Bears every football season, I'm failing. And fast.

"Never have I ever…" I pause, gathering courage. "Fucked in public." It's too bold, stupid even, but as the fire in Toby's eyes turn from embers into a full-fledged bonfire, I know it hit where it was meant to. He takes the shot glass, licking the edge slowly while keeping my eyes locked with his, and tips it back. Immediately, I find myself watching his throat bob with the swallow, wanting to bite the skin there and feel the roughness of his stubble on my lips, between my thighs, and everywhere else that's sensitive.

With the way he licks every trace of whiskey from his plump lips, tasting every drop, savoring even, I'm wondering how this business will work when I'm insanely attracted to him. He's not like Lucien. There's no forced come-ons and disgusting groping.

He's a power trip I want to ride until it's all drained away.

This will be fun.

But we all know it's the booze talking.

CHAPTER 12

JOEY

I DRANK TOO MUCH LAST NIGHT. NOT SURE HOW since I'm not even twenty-one yet. Guess money buys anything.

Not *my* money, of course.

Theirs.

The rich dicks. Dirty liars. Uptight whiners.

My parents. Or rather, my father and his disgusting wife.

They forced my hand in coming here, and then, I end up in bed with some random asshole who thinks it's remotely okay to say sexual jokes and get his rocks off. If it wasn't for his fantastic witty comebacks, I probably would have kneed him in the jewels before leaving. *That face doesn't hurt, either.* The sharp jaw lined with dark stubble and the way his eyes hunt me, calculating in the most disparaging way.

It wasn't my intention to do anything other than follow my father's underhanded demands and get a new job, using whatever he offered. I can't even remember if I got the job.

I need that job.

Any job really.

The worst part is not many snippets of lingering memories flitter through. I drank way too much. It's been a long time since I've had that much booze. Between studies and work, it wasn't possible. Yet free booze makes me easy. Fuck. Who was that guy anyway?

"Going to ride my cock, Sous?" It's a challenge, a bet without winnings.

Are the stakes worth the fun?

"Fuck you, old man."

"Isn't that the plan?" he bites my shoulder, gliding his teeth down slowly. "Fucking you until you coat my cock with your hatred..."

I shiver, thinking of how foggy that memory is. What did I do?

The moment leading up to this morning isn't pretty, but it's my life. Sometimes, that's all you can do. Use what you have and not complain. Is Francis going to think differently of me for ending up with someone else? Do I care? *Yes.* I'm not sure why since we mean nothing to each other, and he probably just wants to sleep with me... but I care. It's not even the situation of nowhere to stay that has me worried, it's that he won't like me anymore for it.

Then there's Gray. She deserves more than my misguided feelings.

My head throbs as I walk to the lobby. "Excuse me," I nearly groan with the words. Even my own voice has my head hurting. Closing my eyes, I try to remember anything.

"Miss?" a woman's voice prickles my senses. Her voice is soft as though she knows I'm hungover. *Why am I at this desk?* My eyes fling open as nausea forces its way up my body. I search for a trash can and can't find one nearby. The plant by the desk becomes my victim as my stomach sloshes, and I heave until my body breaks out in a sweat.

"Oh, God!" I hear the same voice exclaim. "Sweetie, are you okay?" she asks, worry laced in her tone. I look at her, feeling disgusting and stupid. The embarrassment of vomiting in public makes me want to cry. She probably thinks I'm a tramp or a hoodlum. It's not like I'm wearing the expensive dress and pumps from last night, I don't even know where they went. And my bag. Fuck, my bag. "Who can I call for you?" Her voice should soothe me and make me feel safe and less gross, but it doesn't. It reminds me of Marsha and her need to involve herself in everything.

"I-I'm so sorry," I start. Then *his* voice is sounding out from beside her.

"Can you get her a washcloth?" he demands even if he

sounds nice. It wasn't a question toward the nice lady. I stare at him. His perfect hair with his un-hungover face. How is he fine? How isn't he puking? He must be a fucking alien. There's not a single droplet of sweat on his perfect brows, and I feel like I've run a mile on an empty stomach.

Empty stomach. No wonder I'm a mess. I can't recall eating a single thing since breakfast yesterday. And since I didn't eat anything when I went to Dad's… How am I alive?

"What do you want?" I hiss, hating that he's seeing me fragile. I'm anything but fragile. He smirks at me, and again, I'm caught with the desire to slap his stupidly handsome face. No one has the right to look like he does after the night that we had—even if I can't recall the events.

"Such an angry troll," he taunts. "One would think you'd be grateful to the man who found *your* bag that you so rudely accused me of stealing." He tsks at me like an adult would do to a child.

"Fucking Christ," I mutter, peeved beyond ever before. There's the need to kiss the stupid smugness off his face and hit it repeatedly. He's not the only one wondering which I'll do. "I'm not that short. It's not my fault you're a giant! And troll… really?"

"Your hair *is* red."

"So is two percent of the world, and that's not counting the people who dye their hair."

He laughs at me as the lady comes back with a warm rag. I wipe my face, feeling nothing less than disgusting. "Can I have my bag?" I grumble, handing the rag back to the lady. You'd think she'd show disgust, but the look in her eyes proves she's a mom, and a good one.

"Is this man bothering you, Miss?" she requests, eyeing Toby with unspoken disappointment.

"Oh look, babe," he jests. "This hostess thinks I'm bothering you." *Babe?* And I thought this couldn't possibly get worse. Pet names can be cute, but starting with Gumby, going to troll, and ending with babe? Hard fucking pass.

"No, ma'am," I return to the lady, spotting her name tag. *Cheryl.* "Thank you, Cheryl. For being kind." Reaching into Toby's back pocket, hoping there's a wallet there and not a random grope from me, I feel it. Opening it, I take two twenties out of the top, noticing he has way too much cash on him. She shakes her head when I try to hand them to her, but I insist. "Please, my dad didn't raise a woman of freebies."

Understanding flickers in her eyes, and she takes the cash. Toby doesn't say a thing as I stuff the wallet back in his pocket. "Thanks, old man. Till next time," I mock, returning his smug grin as I yank my bag from his hands. Giving him a two-finger salute, I pass by him without a second glance.

Let's hope I can make it to Francis's house before retching again. The hotel doors open before I have the chance to reach them, the bellhop keeping the entrance clear so I can tote my bag along. As I make my way to the valet, I hear *him* call after me.

"Hey!"

He doesn't use my name, and it's only now sprung on me

that he hasn't said my name once this morning. What's his name? Fuck. I've never had a one-night stand. Is that what last night was?

"I need to get back home," I respond, not turning toward him. His hand clamps on my elbow, stopping me in my spot outside the main building doors.

"I'm sorry for being a dick," he says, almost sounding earnest. If not for his constant joking behavior, I'd believe him. But I've met men like him. Ones who tend to be from my father's dinners, but similar all the same. He rubs a thumb across his chin, his eyes imploring and apologetic. Fakeness can be hidden in the hottest men and most beautiful women. My trust isn't asked for, it's earned.

"I don't have time for this," I reply sharply, the prickliness evident in each word. And it's the truth. *I don't.* Francis and Gray are probably worried. *Shit.* Where's my cell phone? Putting a finger up to silence the rebuttal I know is coming from him, I place my bag on the concrete and search inside. When I spot it, I mentally chastise myself for being so dumb. I'd be put back a lot if I lost it. Especially without a job. Trying to unlock it fails and the screen stays black.

"Goddammit," I curse, hating myself even more. I've been careless. Really fucking careless.

"Need any help?" he offers, forcing my gaze up to his. I bet he loves this, me practically on my knees at his feet, his benevolent face peering down at me with all the power. He probably gets off on it. As if answering my question, he smiles. "Guess not."

I flip him off, raising myself to find my claim card. Turning away from him without a goodbye, I find the valet and hand him the ticket.

"Leaving so soon?" he asks with a cheerful smile.

"What does it look like she's doing? Standing there like an idiot?" my one-night fuck deadpans.

I turn toward him, grumbling under my breath, "Don't be such a shithead. He's only doing his job."

"He's obviously flirting with you," he argues, and when I turn to the valet, he's blushing.

"I'll be back," the valet mutters uncomfortably.

"*See,*" he grouses.

I try my best to ignore him but can't. People who are dicks just for the sake of being a dick irk me more than people who litter the streets. My eyes meet his, and his are full of amusement while I hope mine are filled with malice.

"You need a reality check—" I go to say his name but don't recall it.

"Toby," he offers, "but you can call me *boss.*" I eye him, my mind not connecting the dots.

"—Toby. People work to live. That's what he's trying to accomplish. Plus, you're not *my* man, let alone a man who has any right to tell me whom I talk to." He's smiling so big it's aggravating me further and flustering me at the same time. "Even if you were my man, I'd tell you to fuck right off with any attitude that acclimates *ownership.*"

"Calm down, Joey," he pacifies, putting his hands up in

surrender. I can't help but roll my eyes and make a noise of exasperation while doing it. He's incorrigible.

"So, you know my name…" I question. "What else do you remember?"

"That you suck a mean—"

"Here's your car, Miss," the valet interrupts, saving me from being even more embarrassed. Heat flames my skin as I grab my keys, staring at my cherry red Toyota Avalon, the last nice thing I own.

"See you Monday," Toby says as I walk to the driver side of my car.

"Why do you keep insinuating we'll see each other again?" I can't help but complain.

"Because I own you now. You signed the contract. For the next five years, we'll definitely get to know each other."

I balk as the contents left in my stomach curdle at the thought. In all my nineteen years, I haven't been speechless from anything. Not even when Mom disappeared or when a man took my innocence away. But now, knowing I slept with my manager, the man who I've signed my life over to, and the same man I should have never crossed a line with, I'm out of words.

No explanations.

Not a single excuse.

Stunned stupid.

Guess I'm my father's daughter after all.

Proud now, Daddy?

CHAPTER 13

PRESENT

TOBY

THE WAY SHE FIGHTS ME AT EVERY MOVE SHOULD be a turn-off. The fact that she's now an employee should also be taken into consideration, yet I don't care. With any other woman, her attitude would probably disgust and annoy me. But her? The red-haired insult maven, I find myself getting off on it. She's treacherous with her tongue, and there's a battle in every word and a backhanded comment in every sentence. It's enticing in the worst way, *Lo really messed with my head*. Her softness is nothing like Joey's steeling gaze. Her spunk isn't comparable to Joey's fire. But one thing is certain, I find myself thinking of Joey the entire drive back to Hawthorn.

My mind travels over the night before. I was sober, alcohol free, and trying to change. With that one provoking old man joke, I knew I'd show her up. I'm anything but a lightweight. But thirteen shots of Jameson on an empty stomach? I'm lucky to be walking this morning. It's easy to understand why Joey was hurling her guts up. She really doesn't remember last night?

"Follow me," I husk, unable to control the hunger coursing through me. She's half my age, so this shouldn't happen. Jameson disagrees as he urges me on, telling me to take and take and take.

She nods up at me. Her eyes are glassy, but she seems as sober as I am. As in, not sober at all. Should we do this? Drink and screw around? Will she regret it tomorrow? My mind can't catch a thought for long except her bare legs and how sexy her pumps make her look.

We make it to a family bathroom, flinging the door open. She comes after me, her lips connecting with mine furiously. I can feel anger and bitterness with each nip. Pulling back as much as she'll allow, I try to think coherently.

"We shouldn't," I mumble, my chest heaving while my dick tries breaking through my slacks.

"Too scared, old man?"

I groan as she pulls me onto her mouth, claiming it as hers *for the night.*

I stiffen in my pants at the way she looked at me, the way her lips felt warm and savage against me—demanding even. How I wish I could remember more. If we went further. *We had to.* We were both naked. *In bed.* Practically cuddling.

The joke about her being good at sucking dick was just to

jab at her, but I can see it was too far. She pushes my buttons, ones I didn't even realize I had. It's like her entire purpose is to whip me back just as badly and not let me get away with anything. The challenge to beat her at our tongue duels is the most fun I've had in months. Monday can't come soon enough.

Screw fucking random chicks. Verbal battles with Joey is a better aphrodisiac. Maybe even better than booze.

Don't get ahead of yourself, Toby.

My head spins at the reason why I'm here. Drinking. Calling my friend sponsor, I hope he doesn't be a dick.

"Tobes, my man," he answers on the first ring.

"Hey," I let out. The guilt of last night weighs heavily on me. My body shakes as the urge to make a pit stop overwhelms me. I pull off to the side of the road.

"What happened?" he questions. There isn't an ounce of accusation or confrontation, just understanding.

"One sec," I respond, right before opening my door to puke. My lungs constrict as I retch out the fluids my body doesn't have. The pills and water I drank before running after Joey wasn't enough, and as my body convulses with each gasp, I keep heaving even as the contents of my stomach no longer exist.

He always knows when I drink. Like with Nate, he's a fucking psychic. "Last night," I mutter softly into the phone after picking it up, not wanting to be weak anymore. The burn in my lungs from holding my breath becomes too much. "I fucked up, Francis."

Yeah, my ex-best friend's ex-best friend's ex-husband is

the one who keeps my head on straight.

"How much did you drink, T?"

Again, the utmost concern is all that I hear. He's too good to me. "I'm not sure. I can't even remember everything. Whether it be from a full blackout or from selective avoidance, I fucked up."

I can imagine him nodding, mulling over how to respond. That's just how he is. "How far are you?"

"Barstow." I only made it this far before giving in to call.

"You waited that long to call me?"

I cringe, hearing the disappointment in his voice. He's right, I could have crashed. Alcohol runs through my veins more than blood. If you sliced me open, that's the only scent that would fill your nostrils. That and self-loathing.

"Yeah. Didn't realize I made it this far, to be honest."

"Then you shouldn't be driving," he chastises.

"You're probably right. I have a fuck-ton on my mind. Like a new chef, giving Lo the main *Su Casa* location, and realizing how fucking dumb I am for drinking."

"Well, you're beating yourself up enough for the both of us. Tell me more about Lo and your restaurant."

Of course, that's what he wants to hear about. Since I barely utter her name, he tries lobotomizing it from my brain whenever it's mentioned. "Nothing," I divert. "My new chef is feisty, though."

"New chef? Why did you need a new one?"

Man. I completely forgot it's been days since we've really

talked. "Debra walked out, I guess. I had a limited time to get a replacement and decided to show up at Culinary Con."

"Isn't that some big ordeal that lasts all week?"

"Not for me, it doesn't. I got what I came for, gave more than I should, and now I'm trying to convince her to show up to work."

"Good luck with that," he mocks. "If you say she's feisty, then she must be a helluva catch."

"Yeah, if you crave being drowned by a fucking siren. She's smoking hot, but that mouth… it's going to get her into trouble."

"I guess it's a good thing you dig that kind of thing."

"Not before now," I argue.

"That's not true. Lo used to be a contender for witticism. She didn't bow down until all that shit went down." I nod my head at his response, not realizing he can't see me.

"I guess."

"That's awkward," he starts, a teasing lilt to his words. "Tell me, how do you feel?"

"Like I died and came back to life just to experience the agony all over again."

"Nothing new, then? How about you come to dinner Sunday? We can catch up, and you can meet Gray and her friend."

"Teenagers? No thanks."

"Believe me, she's not *just* a teen. She's something else."

"Is that admiration in your tone, Francis?"

"It's a lot more than that."

"Color me intrigued."

"Oh, and Toby…"

"Yeah?"

"*Sors-toi la tête du cul.*"

"Huh? What's with the French, dude? You never spoke French in high school."

"That was before I spent eighteen years in France where my family only spoke French." He scoffs, then continues, "It means, get your head out of your ass before you ruin someone else's life along with yours."

"Thanks… glad to have you as a friend."

"Believe me, I'm being kind. You're really dumb sometimes."

"Tell me something I don't know."

"See you Sunday, man. Bring some wine."

CHAPTER 14

JOEY

"I WAS WORRIED ABOUT YOU," FRANCIS COMMENTS immediately when I come down from my room after a shower and change. I wish he wasn't here, standing in the foyer like a caring person who has no reason to show me an ounce of kindness. Wish he didn't see me this way. Ragged. Hungover. *Disgusting.*

Vegas has that regretful film once you leave, lingering, permeating, slipping through every moral of yours until none are left. Yet all of us who shame the city of endless nights always return one way or another. Hypocrites, the lot of us.

"I'm sorry," I respond lamely. What do I say? *I'm sorry*

I didn't stay here and be with you, but I found another hottie and enjoyed him? Did I, though… enjoy him?

Yes. My body doesn't hurt in the wrong ways like it did in Paris. *After that morning…*

This feels like I let loose, explored a man, and got too drunk. Am I selectively regretting or forgetting something important? Can't believe I was so reckless while in the presence of men. Not all good men, I'm sure.

"Did you have fun?" He doesn't grill me or ask with malice. Like he cares, he sits on the sofa in the front room. With a wine glass in hand and soft features, he waits for my response. He's so sophisticated. Too mature for me. Too much my friend's dad…

"I don't remember," I reply honestly. I don't know why I find myself being open, but I am. He nods, his face curious as he pats the seat next to him. I make my way over, wanting to know how he makes me feel so comfortable.

"I remember those days. The forgetting. Getting high and drinking until I got alcohol poisoning with munchies on the side. It's not fun. Don't do that." He chuckles, fingering the edge of his glass, almost stuck in the past. "It didn't last long, though; the reminder of what my life became kind of drowned that out."

This is the most we've spoken that hasn't been flirtatious and *hot*. He's giving me an opening, and I'll be damned if I don't take it.

"Was it your release?" It's a simple question. Simple for folks who don't struggle. Ones who live blissfully where nothing seems to go on. But for people like him and me—the

ones who hide their battles in smiles and charity events—
it's a gun, waiting for the bullet to be chambered, giving an
ultimate destruction.

"Until I met her."

"Who?" I question. Not out of jealousy or worry, but plain
curiosity.

"Gray." It's a simple one-word answer, but as I look into
his raging storm eyes, I know it's anything but. When I sit next
to him, my leg bumps his accidentally. As I try to move from
my mistake, he grips my bare thigh. Warmth spreads through
me, starting from where our skin connects and causing a flush
all across my body.

"What do you mean *met?*" I attempt to direct his attention to
anywhere but my thigh and the goose bumps he left in his path.

"We just met," he whispers, emotion sticking to every word
like glue, molding to each letter, marking their memory like tree
roots to the ground. Chills break out over my skin as confusion
settles in. The ebb and flow of his pain, wrapped in the air,
whizzing erratically like my heart, flows over me, absorbing
me, telling me there's so much more than I could imagine.

Breathe, Joey.

Letting out the stale air in my lungs, I ask him so many
questions with my eyes, hoping he sees them and answers each
one. Because while I may be brave on a good day, exhaustion
overwhelms me and keeps me from spouting off each one.

"Francis," I mutter, not knowing how to force him to
go on. *How do you?* It's *his* story, his pain, his history. It's not

something that should matter to me. We've just met, after all. But I care, even if just for the sake of him and his daughter.

"I mentioned my ex..." When I nod, he accepts this as a cue to go on. "She was the love of my life. Or so my seventeen-year-old self thought. Putting a smile on her face brought me the most joy I had ever experienced. Honestly, I was just a love-struck idiot."

I'm entranced, and he hasn't said anything I haven't heard from anyone who lost a first love. Regret. Hurt. Cynicism. His face doesn't give a ton away either, just knowledge and acceptance. He burned his burdens, eradicating them from his soul, and rose from the ashes in return.

"She knew everything about me. My family, our royal bloodline, the inheritance..." he veers off. I flinch, thinking of how Dad always warned me not to date beneath me—that in doing so, they'd only love me for what I was financially worth.

"I'm so sorry," I finally say, my heart breaking with the realization that he was used. It feels like shit. I'd know.

"Me too," he mutters. Taking a much larger than necessary gulp of his wine, he squeezes his eyes closed. It takes several seconds before he opens them, his eyes—ones with too much experience—sinking deep into me, telling me more than words ever could.

"What did she do to you?" I request. It's so loaded. I know it from the little detail he told me the other day. The one about his near-death.

"That's the question, isn't it?" He laughs, but there's no humor on his face. It's a pitiful sound, one full of so much disdain. It's surprising a man this kind could carry such a weight. "When we were in high school, I was dumbfounded when she asked me out. *She* asked *me*. Eleanor Graves, the most popular girl in school. The one with dark raven hair that was never curly. It was slick straight, like she flat-ironed it for days just to keep it so stiff. And her face, almost angelic with sharp cheekbones and a tiny nose. Some would say she was flawless... *they'd be wrong.*" He shakes his head sadly. Nostalgia doesn't lace his tone, derisiveness does. "Not for the fact that she was a psychopath, but because she had a tiny scar underneath her eyebrow. It was always covered with make-up, but after you spent time with her and she skipped her cover-up, it was there. I always thought it was adorable, it reminded me of when a cat scratches you and you remember it years later fondly. She hated it, though. Whenever I mentioned how endearing I found it, she'd freak out and call me stupid." He lets out a long exhale. His eyes are wide and filled with the need to talk faster, explain more. They run rampant and expose everything he holds within himself.

"It's okay to breathe," I offer, hoping to calm the wildness seeping through his skin, inking the floor with all the indecision and regret.

He closes his eyes, as if he's already forgotten that it's a necessary action to survive, calming himself with each passing second.

"She was cruel, but I loved her. She was hateful, but I forgave her. She was crazy and in love with my best friend, but

I kissed the ground she stomped upon, covering and forgiving each hellish thing she did. But it wasn't love. That's where I got it all wrong."

He finally releases my thigh, the imprint of his fingers on me has him scrunching his face in disapproval. As soon as he's opened up, the conversation is over. He's shut down the topic completely, every flutter of emotion he had is gone.

"I've had too much to drink," he chastises himself. "Ironic, really… since I just told my best friend to stop drinking himself to death."

"You still talk to him? The one who slept with your ex?" I accuse, shocked that he could forgive him. Whether that's some kind of superpower or stupidity he wields, the jury's out on that. Whether his best friend was a part of his ex's love or not, he had to have given her ammunition for that, right?

"Fuck no," he curses, his voice lower and raspier than I've ever heard. I grip my chest from the hatred that spills out with those two syllables, realizing I made a major mistake in judging him. "That's an entirely different story that we're not ready to have."

He polishes off his wine and stands, offering his hand to me. "Let's eat and save such dark topics for another time, hmm?"

I stare at him in mouth-open-wide shock. How can he just brush over all of that? My heart is still racing from his admission, and he just ignores it like it didn't change his life.

Why does alcohol make people weird?

And why do I want to beg him for more answers?

CHAPTER 15

TOBY

"DO I REALLY HAVE TO COME OVER?" I ASK FRANCIS the following Sunday. He called me, telling me how excited he is to introduce me to *"Ma coccinelle."* Whoever the fuck that is. This weird French shift with him has thrown me off.

Nate, Francis, and I kept in touch after Ellie tried murdering Francis, but it seems his acclimation to France made him more French than American in the sense of language and accent. It's like he's an entirely new person, one I don't really know anymore.

After my happenstance with Jameson, I called Bobbie, my actual sponsor. The most worrisome part of that call was her telling me she hadn't heard from Nate in a long time. He was on a bender, and he called her when he nearly caved. When she checked in on him, he seemed okay. After that, nothing. No correspondence at all. It worries me. Since leaving Hollow Ridge, I've been a bad friend and accountability partner.

It doesn't help that I've been drinking up until several months ago, and the guilt made me stay away. Nate has his own shit to deal with. He's temperamental and in the worst situation. How could I bother him with my addictions when he's riddled with his own?

"We haven't seen each other since Eleanor's funeral, Toby. Yes, we need to see each other and talk. Especially about you drinking last night when you swore off alcohol." His tone is chastising as much as it's full of concern. It's not news that whiskey is my weakness when no one expected a thing.

Being accustomed to alcohol on every front isn't hard to hide when you matter so little. No one pays attention to the single uncle, son, brother… they care too much about their own lives to bother. So it's not a surprise really, not with my childhood and fatherhood. If anything, that made it fateful. "Between you and Nathan, I'm not even sure how to keep you both sober."

"You've spoken with Nate?"

"Yes, he called, strung out of his mind. He's hurting." The realization dawns on me; he's suffering and I've been a shitty friend. If Lo knew I kept in contact with her brother just to avoid being a good friend, would she hate me even more? "Might as well start with you, and then I'll go save him, too."

"Save me? You told me to bring wine," I chide, unable to jab right back at him. He chuckles on the other side of the phone, light-hearted, unburdened, happy. Something I haven't felt in a long time.

"For me, idiot. You hate wine," he argues.

"It's booze. And reminds me of *her*. Of course, I hate wine." The apathy in my tone is laced with condescension and negligence. Not apathetic at all, if we're being honest.

"It was meant to end this way. You leaving, you discovering other venues, me getting my daughter..." he trails off. "Fate, Tobias. Definitely, fate."

I shake my head, knowing he can't see me. If this is fate, as he claims, then why does my chest still ache as if the pain is physical and not emotional? I've never been one for destiny or *God's plan.* I'm all about the details. There's no proof this was set in stone ages ago. It's easy to refute a life that you absolutely abhor, and I've yet to accept my future. Whatever it may be.

My mind wanders to Joey. The woman from last night, the one who smacked me in the face with her words as much as this whiskey hangover, is something else. She's the only reason I'd love to believe in this exhaustive universe of *fate.*

"I'll see you tonight," I grunt, hanging up soon after. My mind continues to replay what I can remember from our night together.

"Bend over," I hiss, my voice not even slightly slurred while my vision spots a little. She turns, her hips shaking in the little black dress she sports. The heels do everything for her figure, making the globes

of her ass sit higher. And fuck, this woman has an exquisite ass.

"You're a bossy dick," she grumbles, sashaying to make a point of how much control she has here.

"Yet your cunt is soaking for me," I challenge, wanting to ram my cock deep in her and feel her squeeze me until she screams my name.

"Definitely not your doing," she snarks, turning toward me with a smirk.

I stalk over to her, and the sound of my palm smacking her left cheek echoes in the bathroom. "Bet you'll cream as soon as I touch you."

"Is that a challenge, old man?" she taunts, wetting her bottom lip.

"Bet your goddamn ass, Sous."

My mind tries to remember more, her moans, the way she felt around my cock as I sank into her. It's crazy to crave the memories when every other time I've blocked every single one out. I couldn't give a shit who was on the receiving end of my dick, as long as I had a good time. Until Joey.

I get ready for the night, jeans—which I usually never allow myself to wear—an untucked button-up, my Richard Mille watch, which is my most prized possession, and my loafers. After grabbing Francis's favorite Château wine, my mind settles on the fact that I'll have to be sober for whatever conversation we have.

Château is nothing I'd enjoy, that's for sure. It costs way too much and only tastes good to wine drinkers. To whiskey connoisseurs like myself, it tastes like a flower arrangement crushed into a fucking vat of dirty water. *Hard pass.* I'd definitely drink, but I have to get the hotel restaurant up and going with Joey. Being hammered on the job isn't exactly acceptable behavior.

The drive to his mansion isn't long as he lives only fifteen minutes away from me. I remember when he bought this place, it was before Gray even knew he still existed. He asked me my opinion, and I told him how lush and unnecessary all the space seemed to be. Of course, he argued, then bought it anyway.

As I pull up to his huge drive, I smile at how the sun sets, orange and purple hues mix vibrantly in the west. His house faces east, a perfect view to see the beauty the world has to offer. He's leaning on the column right outside his door. The smug bastard stands with kindness and a tinge of a tipsy lopsided grin. It's nice seeing him at peace now when a huge part of his life had been missing. It's so vastly different than I expected.

"Tobias," he announces like we didn't just speak on the phone. I wave the wine at him, seeing his eyes light up. Whether I'm an alcoholic or not, Francis fancies his liquor as well. Even if he appears sophisticated with a bottle while I probably mirror a drunkard.

"Frankie," I return, using his old name. A chuckle breaks free.

"Haven't heard that in ages."

"I'm sure. It's not posh enough," I joke, knowing how he converted into the royal behavior. He used to piss all over it in college and high school, but that changed quickly when it was the only option he had.

"Oh, fuck off. Let's eat, yeah?"

With a slight punch to my shoulder, he leads me inside, and I see how much this place has changed. It's completely different than the empty place he asked me to check out. It isn't familiar in the sense it doesn't remind me of him—or rather who he used to be—or even Gray. It seems stiff and impersonal.

In the kitchen, there's Gratin Dauphinois and Coq-au-vin, an entire French feast that's clearly been thought out. If not for my time in France for the expansion of the French restaurant I plan to open in Hawthorn, this meal wouldn't have crossed my mind. French cuisine isn't my specialty.

Someone familiar stands at the stove, reaching for the oven below. My eyes trail the body, not realizing it may come off as pervy. Shaking my head to remove my eyes from the person standing there, I get a smack to the back of my head.

"If you don't stop staring at my daughter, I might have to castrate you," Francis hisses, his tone both amused and angered.

"Fuck, my bad. I wasn't trying to look at her like that." Which I didn't. It wasn't her ass I was paying attention to.

"Tobes?" I hear Gray practically squeal after she sets a tray down. "Oh my God!" Her excitement throws me off. I figured she'd hate me along with everyone else. She jumps into my arms, and I barely catch her in time.

"Hey, pretty girl." She squeezes me, her arms around my neck. I return the love. Like Ace and Jazzy, I spent a lot of time with Gray. Taking care of all three kids as if they were my own became second nature. When everything imploded, she had the shortest stick pulled. She didn't deserve everyone's avoidance. They treated her too much like she, too, was fucked like her mom.

"No fucking way." I hear *her* voice. *Her* as in the hot as fuck, off-limits, gorgeous spitfire—my newest sous.

Gray pulls back with a raised eyebrow. My mouth is stuck open at the fact that she's standing here. In *Francis's* house.

"*Ma coccinelle,*" Francis calls out sweetly with a soft grit. The way he says it, how it rolls off his tongue, and how she blushes in return has my haunches rising. No fucking way. No. No. Nope. This isn't happening. *Not again.*

"How?" I accuse, not sure what I'm trying to ask. She heaves in a breath, one that causes her shoulders to stiffen, and offers me a glare that makes her face seem almost inhuman.

"Are you seeing Gray?" she sputters, almost *jealous?* Or maybe, it's worry. I don't know, but I like the former better.

"He better fucking not be," Francis barks from behind me.

I roll my eyes with a groan, unable to contain the annoyance. I'd never touch Gray. Ever.

"Absolutely not," Gray hisses. She punches Joey in the arm light-heartedly. "He's basically my uncle!"

"I want to hear *him* say it," Joey demands of me. I laugh. Unable to keep it in, I fucking lose it.

"You jealous, Sous?" I taunt.

"Sous… really? Don't have anything original?" she mocks, placing her hands on her hips.

"You aren't denying it." I smirk, loving how she narrows

her eyes hotly.

"So, dinner," she deflects with a clap, "should be done in ten." She ignores me by going and checking on all the food. I turn to Francis, pointing with my thumb toward his study. He nods pensively, leading me the way. Unable to resist, I turn and glance at Joey, seeing her staring at me with many emotions. Fear. Trepidation. Anger. After winking, I follow Frankie down the thick expanse of the hallway.

"Why is she here?" It comes out as an accusation, because from where I'm standing, there's something going on between them. With the short time I've spent with Joey, I know that blush only comes from attention she's been given.

"Not that it's a matter to you, but she's staying till she gets back on her feet."

"Why?" I ask again, my voice strained with aggravation.

"Because she caught her boyfriend fucking some chick, and her dad is a piece of shit," he answers. How does *he* know this much info?

"And you know this—"

"She's Gray's friend, and Gray let me know so I wouldn't kick Joey out on the streets." As if he knew I was about to ask, he hurries and continues. "I'd never do that, but she was definitely worried. We're still new to each other. Also," he pauses giving me a pointed look. "How do you know her?"

I swallow, not knowing how to answer that loaded question. Nodding to gather the courage to admit how I fucked up two days ago, I let out a sharp exhale. "Uhm," I start and stop in the same breath. "Last night…" I don't know how to explain any of this. The quizzical expression he gives isn't one of amusement. It's one of hostility.

"Did you fuck her?" he prods. I can't tell if he's pissed or worried for her. Both? Neither? Why do I care?

"What does it matter?" He shuts his mouth, almost saying something but changing his mind the last second.

"She's young," he offers instead.

"Yeah, but she's an adult," I argue.

He nods disappointedly. "That, she is."

"You guys done debating over me?" Joey pokes her head into the study. "As much as most women enjoy being talked about by two men, I'm neither impressed nor endeared. Dinner is ready, so let's eat."

"Bossy little thing," I mumble.

"What's that, old man? Let's go," Francis demands, his tone throws me off more than her living here. Why is he acting this way? And why does it seem like he's hiding something?

CHAPTER 16

JOEY

FRANCIS'S ATTITUDE DURING DINNER POLARIZES me, putting me in an awkward state of wanting to leave but also not knowing where to go. This is my temporary home after all. There's nothing I can say or do to keep me here, and if I'm unwanted, it won't take me any time at all to pack up my shit and hit the road.

He can't blame me for whatever happened between them in the office, right? They seemed heated, and that's the last thing I need. Two men vying for my attention when my focus is simply to survive.

Men make zero sense to me. Especially since Wes, by

no means, *was* a man. He may be twenty-two, but he may as well have been fifteen. He didn't fight for me, argue about my well-being, or really care for me. At least, only for as much as I could help him. Every time Toby brought up me living here, Francis's face masked into indifference. I'm not sure why, but it made me feel like a leech. I'm a guest, this much is true, but feeling absolutely isolated for a reason I couldn't control hurts me.

Whatever silent battle they're having, I don't want any part of the war they are waging.

"So, Tobes, what's it been like since I left?" Gray breaks the mold of pregnant aggression. Toby grabs his glass, bringing it to his lips all while staring at Gray—not in annoyance or appreciation, but in more of a silence contemplation kind of way—as she waits for his response.

"Yeah, *Tobes*," I mock dryly, watching as my best friend turns her head to me, eyeing me as if I've grown a dick on my nose. The man in question sets his drink down, his jaw clenching a little while he directs all his animosity to me instead of Francis. These two are a goddamn handful, and I barely know either of them.

"Well," he starts and then lets out a heavy exhale. "I'm here because *Mi Casa* in Hollow Ridge needs a chef." It's not explanatory to either at the table. But to me? *The* chef in question. It's a big fucking deal. That's who he is? Tobias Hayes, owner of all twenty *Su Casa* locations and their sister restaurants? *Wow.* He's much bigger than I gave him credit for. I'm absolutely shocked and hope it doesn't appear that way on my face.

"What are you supposed to do?" she asks, making me slowly scoop potatoes in my mouth to seem busy and not nosy as hell. My fork clinks as his next words escape those stupid heart-shaped pillow lips.

"Just ask little *Sous* over here. She's the new chef."

All heads turn to me, but it's Francis's expression that takes my breath away. His nostrils are flared, the vein in his forehead seems larger and more pronounced as though it's as pissed off with me as the man himself. If diamonds could be cut with teeth, the grinding of his molars would turn them to dust. I hadn't had the chance to inform him of my new job… not that it's his business or that I knew Toby was his so-called *best friend*. This is so stupid.

The silence envelops us like a bubble of stale club air. It's unappealing, unpleasant, and definitely unnecessary, but here we are. I'm not sure what to say, so I swallow and bite the inside of my cheek. After several long and awkward minutes, I cross my arms, feeling the utmost uncomfortable sensation of eyes on me. It's not something that appeals to anyone of my solitude-loving caliber, but it doesn't seem to matter.

Folding my arms to give myself some semblance of peace, I hear someone—*Gray*—clear their throat.

"You didn't tell me Uncle Tobes hired you," she muses, but behind the soft words is hurt and betrayal. Is that information so vital to both her dad and herself? Why does it matter? I don't even remember taking the job. If anything, it was a *fuck you* to the rich go-getters and schmoozers like my parents. It wasn't intentional for me to get selected like a whore for the taking to become some chef. Now that I know it's for *Mi Casa*, I'm absolutely thrilled. Having that on my resume will change my life, no doubt.

"Honestly, I don't recall that night much. Didn't seem pertinent enough information," I nearly spit, hating the way it sounds escaping my lips. Toby's glare makes the hair on my nape rise, and the fact that I can feel him and his emotions is more telling than the fact that him being upset has me giddy.

"It should. This is your livelihood. I'd think it matters," Toby chastises, shaking his head at me. My heart races with the disappointing tone. Well, shit luck. He doesn't own me, my personality, or how I react to anything.

I take the napkin off my lap, wiping my mouth before standing up. No words are shared between us. Gray looks confused, Francis is silently raging, and Toby won't look at me. These people, for as much as they call themselves family, they don't act like it. If anything, they seem as if they're almost strangers. Besides me, there's something deeper going on here. It's more than what I've walked into. It has something to do with what Francis won't tell me, what Gray refuses to accept, and whatever has Toby stiffening whenever Lo and Jase are brought up.

Whatever they shared before I came into this home stifles the room with a bubble of discomfort. One I have no intention of sticking around to experience along with them. I have enough baggage myself; there's no reason to carry more or continue this charade.

It's clear that I'm not welcome.

Whatever.

Even though I don't feel like being polite, like the lady Mom and Dad raised me to be, I tuck in my chair, bow my head a little, then practically rush from the room. If they think I'll stay here and be some punching bag for all of their insecurities, they're mistaken. My father and Wes did that enough for a lifetime. Continuing that kind of frustration and pain isn't in the cards for me.

I don't stop for a coat because it's not cold enough here for it. Either way, I'm leaving. Opening the door, I try not to let the built-up pressure in me tumble over. It's not my style. Level-headedness is something I pride myself in. But as Toby's words sink in, my heart hammers in tandem of my rising anger. It presses against my temples, letting me know this won't be easing up anytime soon.

After shutting the door, my feet tap easily on the stoned pathway. Francis's guards don't pay attention to me. Like the first day I arrived, they stand, arms together, almost like British guards. Seeing yet unmoving.

That must be one helluva job, to act like there isn't a care. When in reality, the safety of everyone pertinent to the cause has to be watched without being shown they're being watched.

I roll my eyes as even more frustration settles inside me.

I'm so angry that when my toe stubs on a rock, I yell.

"Fuck you!" It slips from my lips, and I continue my warpath to my car. All of the vehicles are aligned in the massive driveway, all with plenty of room separating them, but mine stands out the most. Unlike all of theirs, it's the cheapest. Francis drives a Land Rover that makes my Avalon look like a tin can in comparison. Toby—or I think it's his—drives a Stingray. It not only shows his maturity level, but it also pushes me to believe he's loaded.

When you're a kid raised by wealthy adults who have more money than they know what to do with, you notice other people with the same predicament. Me? I'm homeless, loveless, and penniless. It didn't dawn on me that my dad would abandon me and make me live in debt. At first, when I'd pissed him off, it felt like he cared again, but it soon was proven that he didn't. It wasn't even him cutting me off that hurt, it was *her*. Marsha. Who he let control him.

It never bothered me that he wouldn't pay for schooling. Between scholarships and me willing to work, I wanted to make something of myself, and he underestimated it. At first, I thought it was tough love, and when I showed him how well I was doing, he didn't care. But no, it wasn't tough love; it was a woman who told him I used him.

It's true, I was dramatic and made mistakes. Hell, I even dated Wesley to garner his attention, but she made me out to be reckless and childish, and told him to not help me anymore.

Without siblings, the sole pedestal was on me. All the marks against me were too heavy, and when he brought that gavel down, it made me realize his standards were always going to be too high. It's why I let myself go. Allowed myself to love Wesley, to go to school, work two jobs, and be independent. What I didn't realize in all of that was that he wasn't going to be there for me in the emotional times.

Like Mom's birthday.

Whenever that day comes, I don't celebrate, I mope. How do you celebrate the life of someone who could be dead or alive? She's *missing*. It has been six years. I should be over it. I'm not. Dad moved on too fast, too quick for me to realize it, and now he has a woman who's soulless, stealing his heart and money with a flick of her wrist.

Why her?

Why not some stay-at-home mom and not a hot model who spreads her legs easily? She's barely older than me. He definitely fucked my mind with that tidbit.

I hate him.

Everything he's changed into.

He disgusts me.

My hand connects with the door of my car and when the handle pops from me pulling, I nearly fall to my knees with tears. Life was never meant to be fair. It has always been burdensome and mopey, like a teen that doesn't get their way. But does it eventually settle? Like when they finally surpass the hormonal age and grow up, would life do that?

I smack the window as saddened anger rides me like

a trainer to a horse. It hits me again and again like a crop, whipping me until I'm near tears and wanting to just give into the darkness. I let out an unladylike growl and bow my head.

Going back inside, I look for my purse. Toby makes a beeline for me. It doesn't take a genius to know he's up for a confrontation. Turning back to where I came from, once again forgetting my goddamn keys, I run.

CHAPTER 17

TOBY

"WHERE ARE YOU GOING?" I PRACTICALLY SPIT, watching her short legs move faster to get away from me. It's funny, seeing her try to speed up when she's so short.

"Anywhere. Just not here," she hisses, not giving me her eyes—those goddamn telling eyes.

"Scared to admit you feel something?" It's a dumb question. Why should I expect her to feel anything when we've only just met? Fuck, we have an insane amount of chemistry, even if it's only filled with hatred and lust. It's something. Saying otherwise would be a mistake, and we both know it. Even if it's like pulling out her teeth to get that information from her. Before dinner and even during, I could feel her. For some reason, I know she somehow felt me too.

"The only thing I feel, Tobias, is a headache. One you're bound to be behind."

Joey's steps falter, and she finally stops, letting out an annoyed breath when she tries to open her car door, but apparently doesn't have the key to open it. She didn't think this through; anger and something else drove her out here. If she was prepared, she'd be rushing out of this courtyard and probably across town.

She's a runner.

Like me.

When I've made it to her, I come too close. It isn't like me to care, but it also isn't like me to invade personal spaces.

"Is that so?" I finally respond, boxing her in against her car. Her chest rises sharply, her cheeks slightly flushed.

"Yes," she bites, her cheeks sharp from locking her jaw.

"I hear orgasms are a great cure for those." It's a whisper, said right below her ear. I'm not sure when I leaned so close, but my lips brush her with each word. She inhales sharply, the sound warming me. Temptation spreads through me, knowing she's affecting me as much as I am her.

It takes everything in me not to push her against the hood and show her just how well orgasms reduce pain. Placing my palm on her jaw, I grip her chin. She worries her lip between her teeth, bringing my gaze to the way she's avoiding looking at me.

"Is that what you want, Joey? To come and feel some of

that ache leave?" Wiping my thumb across her bottom lip, she moistens it with her tongue, taunting me.

"What if it is?" she practically growls. Her eyes dark with lust, sharp with anticipation, but underneath the surface, I can see her hatred. The abhorrence living beneath the surface of that dainty exterior.

"Spread your fucking thighs," I command, not willing to test the theory of her resistance. She's giving in, and I should accept it—take and feast upon my goddamn winnings. That's what we both need, isn't it? Release. To see where this connection is going, how far it will rise to the occasion, and maybe it'll be so fucking good that neither of us will be able to let go.

Or maybe *that's* exactly what we need.

To let go.

Instead of debating my head, I tap her thighs. "Open." Her eyes narrow a little with argument; she wants to fight and, in a way, I want her to. Being pliant isn't attractive, but being destructive is as hot as a fucking ice bath.

Her legs split with her gaze intent on mine, telling me to go fuck myself.

Now why would I do that when she's right here to give and give and give?

"Turn around," I all but hiss.

"No," she refuses, shaking her head, but she bites that goddamn lip telling me a different story. I press into her, her softness cushioning my hardness. Every inch of our shared warmth blazes. We fit perfectly. I grip her throat, making sure not to press too hard but wanting to feel her pulse beat beneath my touch. Maybe she doesn't like being manhandled, but she looks fucking spectacular beneath my grip.

"Turn the fuck around."

She smiles coyly as if she doesn't realize how bratty she's being. "Gonna make me, old man? Or are you too weak? Old age and everything..." she taunts, just like she did in Vegas. Coercing me to show her that I could hold my liquor. She likes the game between us. The one where she pushes, and I'm forced to press right back.

I release her neck, watching as she momentarily pouts. Pulling her away from the car by her arms, I twist and shove her against it. Luckily, it's not super lit out here, or I'm sure Frankie's cameras would catch us. Or his guards. If they're smart, they'll look the fuck away.

Pressing her chest against the glass of the car, she moans. Goddamn. She likes being handled, pushed, and I fucking love demanding.

"You seem to like pressing my buttons, Sous. Bet you don't expect how much you like being controlled, huh?" She grunts but grinds against my dick. "You want my cock deep inside you, don't you? Stretching that tight little pussy as you scream for *more*."

"Fuck you," she hisses, but she doesn't stop rubbing against me. Her body wants me, even if her mind is dead set on denying it.

"Oh, I will. I'm going to thrust inside that slippery cunt

of yours and you're going to beg for more."

"You talk too much," she grumbles as I undo the button and zipper of my jeans. Hooking my fingers into the little loops on her shorts, I slide them down her thighs. As soon as my eyes catch the tiny scrap of material between her cheeks, a guttural noise escapes my lips. She's getting restless, and I'm loving the way she doesn't stop fidgeting. She's got it bad.

My hand rests on her backside, rubbing up and down, wanting to press my palm against it harshly. Needing to leave a mark she'll feel tomorrow, serving as a reminder that she loves my ownership.

I slip my fingers between her folds, feeling her drenched. "Fuck, you're so wet, Sous." It comes out hoarse and needy. She's fucking soaked for me. I rub her clit, watching in awe as she grinds into my fingers for more friction. Trailing my fingers to her hole, I dip inside and she's panting.

"Fuck me already," she groans.

A smile takes over my face at her words. Pulling my stiff cock out, I rub it up and down her folds like it's a paintbrush, wanting to test every goddamn color on the palette. Her tiny gasp escapes as I inch in slowly. Halfway through, my body can't contain the adrenaline rushing through my veins. Desperation clings to me as I thrust into her, my hips pushing her body flat against the door of her car.

"Shit." Her voice is raspy with lust, and the sound alone

has me wanting to drill into her. My hips move on their own accord, chasing the pleasure shooting through my balls, wanting to rise and escape into her. "Toby, faster." It's a breathy demand. I love the way my name sounds leaving her lips, kissing the air with promise and urgency.

I reach for her clit and start flicking it roughly, making it a point that it hurts as much as it feels good. She bows into me, her body only held by me and the car. A goddamn mess of curse words and moans escape us both as we chase our releases. Picking up my pace, I grunt as my cock goes in and out of her, slipping and disappearing between her cheeks. Pleasure zings through me, but I need her to come before I do.

"Come for me, Sous. Coat my cock with it."

"Such a dirty fucking mouth," she groans as I harshly rub in circles across her bundle of nerves. She cries out, the cadence of the sounds surrounding me like a fucking wet dream. That's all it takes to tip me over the edge. Thrusting a few more times, I throw my head back and groan out into the night air, feeling my heat coat her walls.

Fuck. Fuck. Fuck.

No condom.

Staring as it leaks from her, it hits me. It'd be a goddamn shame not to watch us sin when the entire world could bear witness.

CHAPTER 18

JOEY

AFTER THE ENCHANTING HIGH WANES, MY HEART spasms, softening me and hardening me continuously. What did we just do, and why do I want to keep going until I'm a messy puddle at this asshole's feet? What is he doing to me?

As distressing as this is, he eviscerates me with his eyes, confusing my heart further. He's gazing at me long and hard as if he sees the gears inside my head moving, trying to understand the emotions I'm sure are slathered all over my face.

Instead of asking, he interrupts my invasive thoughts by turning me around and pushing into my chest. His palm flattens against the rapid thrumming. As if the organ itself seeks his touch out, it further palpitates, oscillating against my ribs in a steady staccato. When I don't breathe, he lowers as if tying his shoes, his face level with my hips.

"Put your thighs around my shoulders," he demands, smacking my bare thigh, then deftly grips it. This is definitely not where I imagined this going, but the voracity of his gaze isn't one to riot against. If anything, it's enabling the way my legs begin to spread.

"Toby, I don't think—" Nerves take hold, warning me. We're in public. This shouldn't be happening. Not when his release hotly leaks from me, tracing my thighs and possessing every inch they coat.

He stops my words by kissing the sensitive flesh he just spanked and raising my legs around him, where his mouth presses against my *very* drenched center. His breath tickles and thrills all in the same motion. Tendrils of desires wrap around me, holding me hostage as he coerces my submission. It's daunting to know we're in the middle of the driveway where anyone could see us or catch us, but fuck if that doesn't drive me toward him more.

My chest rises rapidly as he nuzzles my slick flesh, groaning in a husky way that has me squeezing his head. Running my fingers into the russet hair that's messy in the most purposeful way, I battle with bringing him closer and pushing him away, slaving against my last ounce of control.

"I'm going to lick your pussy, Sous. I want to feel how you taste on my tongue now that you're *mine*."

Shit.

His mouth.

His? Did he just say his?

Stopping my train of thought with his scruffy cheeks, I can barely process anything. Not just from him touching my most intimate place while it's still wet from *us*, but he always uses his tongue as a battle sword, fighting me with each word. I never know if it'll be a caress or a plundering, but it's always hot.

Raising his head, he trails his nose up my pussy, dragging it between the seam of me where I'm bound to be coated in our shared release. I groan as his tongue joins the war, waging my emotions and life for pure pleasure.

He'll win.

He always does.

I never stood a goddamn chance.

"Scream all you want, Sous. The whole world should hear me claiming you as mine," he grits, swiping my clit with his tongue. It's slow and savage with as much power as leisure. It's torturous bliss, and he's well aware.

His hooded eyes meet mine as he's buried between my thighs. The hazel hues—bluer like a nearly black sky—glint with mischief and promise as he licks from my ass to my center, not letting me lose concentration.

It's intense, being eaten out while a stare such as Toby's penetrates me as surely as his tongue does. It's seductive and maddening, feeling every sensation from both his ambitious gaze and wicked mouth. He's wrecking me with each stroke, killing me with every jab, and stealing me piece by piece with every pleased grunt.

My eyes close when a finger enters me. It's an automatic response as I attempt to absorb each tendril filling my body. He surprises me with his teeth, biting down, forcing my gaze open once again.

"Watch me, Josephine," he growls after pulling back an inch. "Watch me take you. No one will ever have you after this. No one will make your cunt clench like me. No one will ever be *me*."

And fuck, with another lick across my throbbing clit, I'm moaning his name as he laps up our shared release as if he's been blessed to do so.

My chest bows with each pant, my body spent in the best way. He rests my jelly-like legs on the ground, gripping my hips to keep me from falling.

Before I can say a single word, his palm cups the back of my neck, pulling my lips to his. He takes my mouth with an intensity that feels as powerful as the erection pressing into my stomach. *How is he already hard again?*

His tongue teases my lips, wandering, exploring, *claiming*. It's such a passionate exchange, and that fuzziness overwhelms me. My stomach feels warm and electric, like a live wire, waiting to be touched by something living and visceral.

He bites at me when I close my eyes once again.

"Don't hide those icy eyes, Sous. They're meant to watch."

I nod as he drags his teeth across my bottom lip, wanting

him to bite harder, wishing I didn't want him so much. He feels essential. If I don't have him, my body will wither; that's how he makes me feel. How is that possible? How is any of this happening right now?

Toby pulls back, looking at me with heat, his eyes glint conspiratorially. It's endearing, and I hate that too. That we've never been more than this moment, but it seems we should be.

Dragging my eyes from the glistening of his jaw and throat, all the way down to his stiff dick, I practically heat right back up, wanting him to take me again.

Bruise me.

Claim me.

Take, take, take.

What is happening to me?

"If you keep looking at me like that, I'm going to get better acquainted with that pussy."

I blush, feeling it hit my cheeks. My body warms at the smile that tilts his lips, and I want this moment to stay. To wrap it up with safety-tape and keep it tucked away where reality won't tarnish it.

"What if I want you to explore more?" I question. It comes out a lot huskier than intended, but the way his eyes narrow, darkening his irises, I'm pleased with the outcome. My hands flatten against my car, needing something to ground me since the cobblestone beneath my feet seems just as unstable as the emotions warring inside me.

"Fuck. Joey. You're killing me here."

I can't help but grin because he hasn't called me Joey yet. It sounds desperate coming from him, and it's something I shouldn't get addicted to.

"We should go then, old man. Especially if someone your age can't handle it," I taunt, biting my lip at the glare he returns. Instead of arguing, he flips me against the car, spreading my thighs once more.

"Can't handle it?" he mocks, smacking my ass. "It's you who should be worried, Sous."

Then he's thrusting into me in one go, pistoning against my ass as if it's meant to slap. He growls when I push into him, forcing him deeper. He slides a palm up my spine, making sure to leave chills in its wake, and trails it to my hair. His fingers delve into the frizzy mess, fisting it while he uses it as his own rein. I cry out as he angles his hips to hit me *there*—that bumpy spot inside me that Wes never found—making me shake. Sparks break out over my skin, hardening my nipples with the chill.

"So fucking tight. Did you know that? You're squeezing me like a fucking vise, Josephine."

With my name on his tongue, I'm gripping him tighter, flexing as an orgasm takes over. He tugs my loose curls harder and deepens his thrusts.

"Shit. Shit. Shit," he grunts, and then I feel him release inside me again, heat swimming through me, soothing me from the inside out.

Sweat lines my spine, forehead, and arms, coating me with

lust and satisfaction. When he pulls out again, I'm shaking from head to toe. Not ever experiencing this kind of sex with Wes and never this intense of a workout either. Even though I surf often and run just the same, it's like Toby worked muscles I didn't know my body had.

"We should probably leave before someone comes out," he mentions, and resituates my shorts, patting my ass gently. "But next time you test my stamina—" he traces a finger to the crease of my ass. "—I'll show you just how many ways I can stick my cock inside you and *still* keep going."

His words send shivers of promise through me, and I've never wanted to test a theory more. Especially when I wiggle back into his groin and feel him already half stiff.

"Guess I should lay on the old man jokes thicker next time." The tease no sooner leaves my lips before he's smacking my ass and making me yelp at the sting of pain. And if the little slut in me doesn't jump in glee at the sensation...

"Move that ass, Sous."

"Yes, *boss*," I mock, batting my eyelashes.

"Cheeky girl," he muses, kissing my nose affectionately.

At that moment, I was no longer the homeless, penniless, and loveless girl who just lost everything.

I was *his*. Tobias Hayes's.

And not even I realized what that meant at the time.

... a number ... £90 ...
... so ... I ...
... called at night John ...
... and ... me he had ...
... — ... I asked ...
... to you which ...
... last did ... Have you ...
... the German soldier who had ...
... asked the Irish prisoner ...
... near. On the way ...
... German's head but ...
... the fact ... On ...
... the good ...

PART II

INTOXICATED

You never realize your life is destroyed until
there are only scraps of what hope looked like.
It's like an invisible tornado.
Chaos and destruction remain, even while you
can't see the curator of the damage.
Yet unlike an invisible storm, you know even with the
shambles, there's a required clean-up.
There's no simple fix in starting over. Not without a hefty cost.
Not without giving up the possibility of recovery.
Not without accepting you've *really* and *truly* fucked up.
And that's what's truly intoxicating about pain.
You can realize it, mend it, and even overcome it. But if you're like
me, you *love* it, live for it, and thrive off its nasty bite, hoping in the
end, you suffer *endlessly*.
Forever damaged.
Forever lost.
Forever empty.

- JOEY

CHAPTER 19

THREE YEARS LATER

TOBY

IT'S BEEN THREE YEARS.

Long, hard, life-altering years.

I'm married.

I hate her.

She hates me, too.

Maybe this is my penance, my dues for being a piece of shit and trying to steal my brother's wife. I deserve her hate and give it back tenfold. Now, it's our routine. I'm not sure what life would be without our constant bickering.

Peaceful, maybe. *Lonely.* Lifeless, definitely.

She deserves more, but making her suffer with me has

become a game, and she hasn't walked away either. Maybe she lives for it, too.

Hollow Ridge.

I'm back here.

My home.

Or rather, it was, until I screwed everything up.

We all make choices. Some that burn us, some that light the way, and others that have no reaction in either direction. My choices—mine and Lo's—ruined my life. Yeah, being a willing participant is what brought me to this moment. I wouldn't even change it for the world. That is, unless if I could change from ever meeting her.

She gave me a great life. Up until the end, that is.

We wouldn't have worked out. No matter how much I wanted it, no matter how hard I worked for it, and no matter how many memories we shared.

Her and Jase were fated.

It was stupid of me to think I could come between that. Be what she needed, what I wanted, and still make her as happy as him.

It wasn't meant to be for us as much as I tried.

We were circumstance, and they were destiny.

No matter how much I repeat that, acknowledge it, and realize it, the pain doesn't falter. My pursuit for the connection I felt with Lo hasn't come. Maybe it won't—maybe it wasn't meant to be in the first place.

I try and try and try for love. I did. I do. Yet I can't find it.

I can't find her; I can't find the other half of my soul.

Until I did.

She sets my soul aflame and burns me, leaving me with scars on every inch of my skin. With her, the pain doesn't ease. It cuts and digs, burying itself inside every crevasse my body offers. My new love—turned hate—absolutely devitalized me.

My run, like every day since coming back, is tremulous and exhaustive. My heart pounds in sync with the soles of my shoes smacking the gravel road. It's like the patter needs to be in unison or I'll collapse. I'm doing too much, I know I am, yet I can't stop. It's like my newest binge. Instead of booze or drugs, it's exhaustion. A high I can only get from nearly crumbling. Though that doesn't stop me from voraciously swallowing every drop of Jameson we own.

Today, I don't stop at the coffee shop. I can't. It's burdensome on my heart, and no matter how much I'd love the extra energy, it's too painful. Every time while passing it, her eyes haunt me, the child's face haunts me, and then the hatred for my wife grows more cancerous.

That shop holds horrors and memories like a personal scrapbook of my past on constant display. I can't count how many times we experienced a smile, a laugh, or a small touch in that little place. There's no way to explain how it retains all the good and bad and in between. The only thing I can offer is that it was once my home away from home, but no resurfaced trigger is worth the brown liquid gold.

As I run past it, my stomach feels empty of food and

everything altogether. It's not like me to eat anymore. If I didn't keep up my protein, exercise, and water intake, I'd be scrawny. It's unhealthy what I do to myself, dragging my body through as much as it can take, and even sometimes going past what it should be capable of.

My life's a mess.

My heart's non-existent.

My soul was lost long ago.

Worst of all, I no longer have any fucks to give.

My legs ache as my body pushes me toward Hollow Hills on the coast of the town. It's where I'm staying. It's not home, but after selling the house we bought for our future, it seems along with a failing marriage, we may as well have a place that isn't a home.

As soon as I'm in the lobby, I'm using my special penthouse suite badge to get to where I'm staying. It's a long sixty-floor journey, but it takes a lot less time than you'd think. When the elevator stops, I'm met with a hallway leading to hell. With a few paces toward the double doors, I'm face-to-face with her and immediately notice her glacial stare.

My worst enemy.

The biggest liar of all.

My goddamn wife.

"Where were you?" she accuses, ice lacing her tone like it does the windows when snow falls. Crossing her arms, I watch the hand that brands her as mine grip herself tightly as if it's the only motion keeping her from raging out.

Our daily routine consists of not getting five feet before she's grilling me and I'm spitting treacherous words in return. Round and round we go, killing each other with every lie we've spun. *Does it hurt, Joey? Knowing you're this fucking dangerous to me... because I didn't know or I'd have never fucked you three years ago.*

She started this war, not me. The only difference between her and I? I've decided to win.

She played dirty, only realizing too late that I play the dirtiest.

"Running," I bite back, glaring at her. Her hands hold her hips like I've done many times. Her rich auburn hair is straight and as silky, long enough to pull but not as long as *hers*. Even though I hate my wife, she's stunning. She's fucking sexy even while she disgusts me with every fiber of my being. And God, the things I've done to her even while hating her... yet here we both stay.

I stare at her, mesmerized, while also lifting my nose in the air as if she's lesser than me. With her petite but generous curves, tiny nose, and whiskey amber eyes, I'm enthralled. She's a fiery siren waiting to hunt me down and steal my soul after she drags me beneath the black sea.

Too bad there's nothing left for her to take.

Once upon of a time, she could have been everything to me. She was.

Fool me once... *never again.*

She can fight all she wants for this dead, binding relationship we have, but she'll never own another piece of my heart.

When we met, I thought she was the perfect distraction. Now I know better; she's the catalyst of everything I once held dear. And we'll destroy each other eventually.

With my answer hanging in the air, she's giving me the most disdainful look. She wanted this. Wanted me. Used me. Destroyed me.

"Is that all you were doing?" she nearly hisses. The venom spewing from her lips is enough to have my haunches up. She doesn't get to accuse me. She doesn't get to question my whereabouts. She doesn't get *anything* from me.

"Whether that's all I was doing or not, it's none of your damn business. You lost that privilege when you fucked up this relationship," I all but yell.

She closes her eyes almost in pain, but she doesn't know my pain. She doesn't feel what I've felt since that day changed our lives.

"I care," she says, her tone bereft of all the anger she threw at me moments ago.

"Bullshit!" I call her out, knowing her true intentions, knowing she was never here for us.

She lets out a ragged breath, huffing like a child unable to get what she wants. "You're still my husband, Tobias."

"And you're my biggest mistake, Joey," I spit.

"I love you," she barely whispers.

"I fucking hate you." My words deliver the last blow as they usually do. It's my only response before walking into the master bathroom, undressing and heading into the shower, hoping to clean all the dirt, regret, and grit away.

Maybe I'd call Bry and get some much-needed frustration worked out. I need to unwind, and my wife isn't the one to do the job anymore. It only entangles us further, damaging what's left of my soul.

CHAPTER 20

PAST

TOBY

I STARE AT YOU WITH TEMPTATION. WHY IS IT something so beautiful and fierce came into my life when I needed it the most? That's what you are, a cirrus of glowing fireflies with the capability of harm but instead chooses light.

You giggle. Your eyes alight with a glimmer of something I haven't felt in years. It's a reminder to be young at heart, even if life ages us. I love the way your smile is a little crooked, your teeth overbite the bottom ones, hiding them nearly entirely, but what gets me the most is the way your face lights up with the same rays as the sun, giving so much and asking for nothing in return.

"Do you want kids?" she asks me, throwing me out of the revelry of her. Her eyes are serious, but there's also softness. As though she doesn't want to push me even while wanting a response. We've been married a year and slowly getting to know each other. It's weird. The hate we had for those short months before changed, morphing into something incredulous—something I couldn't imagine experiencing with anyone else.

"I do," I answer, unable to keep my grin at bay. Seeing little babies with my attributes has always been a craving of mine. When I was younger and Lo had Ace, my heart swelled so much. The love unfettered and unruly in its wake. I can only imagine what it'd feel like if the kid was my own.

Finally glancing at her, she has an unreadable expression, one that reminds me of grief. Not the kind like Lo experienced, where it overtook her entire mind, but a gentler, more subtle kind that has a meaning I'm not privy to. She licks her lips, distracting me from her change of mood at her own question. Did she want me to *not* want them? I'm nearing forty. That age in many people's eyes is almost too old for children. To me, the craving won't ebb until I've had my own. My desire to bring life into the world has never wavered.

"Oh." It's such a simple response as if it took her every ounce of energy to release that one syllable, and I want to know why. But again, she licks her lips, hiding whatever it is that's bothering her.

"I've always wanted a child to hold, teach, and watch grow. Not that I'm saying I'd be a great father or anything," I admit, shrugging shyly. Reaching behind my head, I rub my neck.

"You always do that when you're embarrassed," she muses with a flushed smile. Her cheeks are rosy like her hair, tinged with redness that shows how angelic she really is.

"I do, don't I?" I don't mention *she* told me that on many occasions, or that it's something I've tried quitting for the simple fact that it reminds me of my past. I just enjoy the way her eyes zero in on me biting my inner lip.

She closes the short distance to me and presses a yellow-painted nail to my mouth, brushing the pad of her soft fingers across my sensitive flesh.

"Smile, old man. I want to feel it under my fingertips."

Even with the desire not to give in to her for the old man comment, my lips break into a grin, making her eyes sparkle with joy. I'm finally getting used to her nickname for me. Albeit, it's still sad. She's nearly half my age, so the term is appropriate, but it's still depressing nonetheless. Someone this young shouldn't be with a man my age. It stunts her growth and life experiences. I'm already an adult and know what I want and need. She's at the age where one day, she wants *this,* and the next, she wants someone like her loser ex-tool of a boyfriend. It's how everyone is. Not me, I've always been driven to love— even if the love was unrequited most times, I still sought it.

She brings my thoughts back to her crinkled nose. The splashes of freckles dusting her cheeks and nose are more and more appealing with each glance. She's enjoying this, teasing me. Her soft touch has me aching in other ways, ones I've kept at bay for weeks, unwilling to tarnish this new modesty we've grown with each other.

"Kiss me, old man. Show me how those lips feel." I close my eyes at her words, knowing her kisses drive me to madness as keenly as her touch. Bowing my head, eyes still shut, I wait for her move. One thing I've learned about Joey is that she likes controlling the situation.

Her lips touch mine, tentative at first, then stronger, almost greedy with their pressure. She tastes like nature and lemons—like sweetness and joy—like mine, mine, mine. The tip of her tongue traces the crease of my lips, and a groan leaves me as I allow her everything she wants. Unlike the women from years ago, before I met Joey, she isn't trying to be frenzied or sensual. She's towing me into her radiant depths of twilight—not light nor dark—but effervescent, securing me and marking me as hers, hers, hers.

Her teeth nip my lips as a tiny moan leaves her throat, forcing my eyes open. I see her, those amber glazed domes reflecting brightly, soaked with delight and warmth. Our kisses split me in half. The half stuck on our bond, and the other thrust into fear of fully accepting it.

We know so little, feel so much, and battle between the challenges each day brings. Neither of us went to that fundraiser out to find whatever this is, but we did. We found each other. Whether it means something or not, she brings contentment and fear and exhilaration.

"Do you want kids, Sous?" Her face falls before she can

catch it. One thing she told me that has stuck was how her dad taught her to school her features at all times. It's where the newspaper got stuck on her title as the ice queen. She's the youngest person I know who hides her emotions better than someone who feels nothing. Right now, as she gives me the fakest grin, I'm realizing she's hiding something.

"Yes," she finally answers. Her eyes gloss, reminding me so much of pain. Pain I know. Pain makes sense. Pain has many faces, and this one is the most common.

"Do you?" I prod a little, seeing that simple grimace barely contained.

"Toby," she rushes out, her voice so small and scared. The way she utters my name makes a tightness form in my chest. It's one of years of acceptance and tribulations. But she's only twenty. How many trials of experiences could bring this kind of knowledge?

"Talk to me," I offer, hoping it comes off soft and supportive and not demanding. She may be my wife, and we might even be learning what we feel for each other, but I care. Fuck, I care. Seeing her cry for the first time clicked with me. Seeing her agonize over what we did in Vegas… I witnessed and fell before I knew I tripped.

"I-I can't h-have kids." Her words are as choppy as the rise and fall of her chest.

Four words.

More damning than a gavel hammering down, more agonizing than letting a murderer free, more heartbreaking than any loss I've felt, yet I can't cry with her. Because what I see in her distraught expression as sorrow leaks free from her eyes is need. Need for me to be okay. Need for me to be strong. Need for me to pick her anyway.

"C'mere, Sous," I coax as she lets her grief free. Her peachy lips warble a little, the freckle—my favorite one—beneath her bottom lip trembles, but she finally comes into my open arms.

"You're not mad?" she whispers, her voice smaller than I've ever heard it. No. How could I be? She shakes in my arms. My little warrior, who always fights tougher than any person I know, cries silently. If Joey could be described simply, it'd be impossible. She's calculated and calm, unruly and incredibly sexy, captivating and consuming. She fights for everyone who needs a voice and doesn't back down when pushed too far. In the year we've known each other, she's only cried twice. This being the second.

The first... a time I wish I could take back. A time when I hurt her without knowing she cared.

"Hey," I say gently, pulling away to tilt her chin up to me. My eyes catch hers, seeing the redness blotching her soft features. I kiss her, unable to see the torment in her eyes a moment later. She whimpers in a way that squeezes my vital organs, begging to fix it—soothe her—something. Anything. "How can I be mad at you?"

"You just said you wanted kids. That's something even my twenty-year-old body can't offer," she explains, sniffling.

"How do you know?" I try, not meaning she didn't know

for sure, but what if fate decided differently?

Her eyes shut, the motion telling me she doesn't want to answer. I can tell because her lips are tight and her body is stiff. I shouldn't have pushed. It's her body. It's her choice. Almost as if she's made a decision, she nods a couple of times, then stares at me. The way she bites her lips and pulls herself away from me strikes me with worry-filled tension.

"When I was seventeen, my dad shipped me off to Paris." She inhales deeply as though a reminder to breathe is necessary. "He didn't want to put up with the harsh reality that his new wife was only eight years older than me, and I couldn't handle it."

I nod, waiting for the punchline. She paces a bit, gnawing on her finger and avoiding eye contact with me.

"It was beautiful there. Not as they make it out to be in the movies, but it had an ethereal beauty. Something you feel deep inside. Inspirational almost, thoughtless expression within your reach, you only had to grasp it." As she describes it, I know melancholy is attached, and she's just avoiding narrowing it down to words. I can see it in her struggle and the way she switches from biting her bottom lip to grinding her teeth. The tenseness of her jaw is present with her rapid breathing. I step toward her, wanting to offer comfort, but then immediately see the shift in her. The jolt as she nearly jumps out of her skin when I reach for her has me halting immediately.

"Please," she implores. "Let me get this out."

I nod, needing her to know I'll keep my distance. "Talk, I'll be here when you're ready."

"Paris was everything I dreamed it would be. The art, the streetlamps... the food." Her eyes lighten a tinge at the mention of food but fades just as quickly. "With its beauty came the dark. Like any other place on this planet, it had its downfalls." She takes in a sharp breath, her eyes glossing again. God, what I'd do to hold her, reassure her, breathe safety into her disarmed bones.

"I'd just had a croissant from this little shop. It was golden, flakey, and delicious." She chuckles lightly, and I watch as it fades to a sad, unimpressed smile. "No one makes croissants like the French..." Her eyes well with tears. They topple over, and my heart fucking breaks at the moment she stares at me with hopelessness. She cries as I watch from afar, unwilling to allow me to barge into her space. Space is something imperative at this moment, my gut pushing a pin into the problem, screaming, "Someone hurt her!" It knows—*I* know— and it fucking hurts feeling this helpless.

"It was early—five in the morning. I remember everything about that day so clearly. The coffee I'd been sipping with the croissant, taking it with me when I left. Hazelnut. Bitter but sweet at the same time. The day—dark but promising, little spurs of pink drifting over the horizon, waiting for the sun's kiss, stuck on its lover, waiting more patiently like no man could be. The beige beret I wore, the wool cardigan, the plaid red, black, and white scarf. The black Vans, pleated black skirt, and leggings." She huffs and sobs at recalling the memory.

Fuck. I just want to ebb away this burden she carries. I want to kill the fucker who hurt her and make it all go away.

"To get to the flat my dad paid for me to stay in, I had to travel across several dank alleys, two of which I knew weren't exactly safe." She knots her hands together, her eyes shutting, but she doesn't pause for long. "It didn't have many rays of light, shielded by shadows. I knew, like my soul, it'd brighten with time. It took me only a few breaths to realize that day would be bad. Almost like an acrid odor or taste, I could sense it. I trailed the alleyway, holding my coffee to keep the breeze from chilling me." Her eyes stare at the ground, focusing too hard, hating whatever came next. "I smelled him before I registered his grip on my wrist."

I close my eyes, my stomach concaving with what she's about to say. I already know. It makes me sick, bile rising, promising to release with so many words. It hits me, the scars, the ones I've loved and cherished, the ones I've touched and kissed, they're from pain. They're a mirror of what she feels because that man took from her.

"He smelled like an ashtray. Stale. Piss-poor. A grungy, disgusting and vile man. The harsh scent infiltrated my nose as his grubby hand wrapped around me, forcing me to the brick building on the east side of the alley. The meek scream that left me did no good because his palm covered it easily." She cringes, her body scrunching in displeasure. "His fist connected with my face as I struggled, and I remember thinking, *I wish I was bigger, taller... a man* because he was too strong. Even as a homeless man, he was stronger than *me*." Her cries sear my soul to the bone, digging into me more than the knife I took to the gut in college.

"He raped me in the dark confines of that street. Ruining my childhood and taking my innocence along with it." Her voice croaks at the admission. She bends over and heaves, and I feel the nausea overwhelming me too, unable to imagine what it must have felt like for her.

"A month later, I woke up sick. Vomiting, heaving, shaking as blood leaked from me. It took everything in me to go to the hospital because leaving the flat was near impossible. I didn't feel safe, didn't know up from down, left from right, life felt unlivable."

No. Please don't say it.

"I was pregnant." *Fuck. Fuck! FUCK.* "I'd been losing the child. A child he forced into me. As cruel and sick as that man was and what he did, I thought it was fated in all sense. How fucking tragic, right?" I don't answer because I can't. I just let her talk it out. "The doctor informed me I had chlamydia. So, on top of the rape and pregnancy, I had an STD." She combs her fingers through her hair, pulling harshly, making my skin chill. "The disease caused my fallopian tubes to be blocked, decreasing blood flow to the baby. It killed it. *He* killed it." She lets out a shaky breath, tragedy hardening her features. "It made me unable to have babies by permanently damaging my tubes."

Standing here speechless, I wait for the words to form as she tells me the most horrific story known to man. How do I help? Fix this? Ease her guilt? Do any-fucking-thing? How?

"Joey—"

"I'm going to take a shower," she interrupts me, her face red, blotchy, and barren of any emotion. She walks past me, not even offering a glance, keeping her distance. Why am I such a piece of shit? I let her walk away.

Because I'm a coward.

CHAPTER 21

PAST

JOEY

GOD. WHY DID I ADMIT ALL OF THAT? SEEING
the pity on his face made me squirm more than the recount.
Not my dad, Gray, or even Wes knew about Paris and what
that man did to me in the alley. No one knew the status of
my health or that he ruined my body for the future. They
couldn't possibly know the extent of my pain, losing a
child I didn't even know I was carrying. Everything hurt.
Admitting it, getting it off my chest, it didn't ease the reality;
it only made someone else aware of what I had to live with.

Lying in that hospital bed alone.

Crying as they listed all the traumas.

Bleeding for days after losing my baby.

It killed me. Most of all, it made me hateful.

When I found Gray three weeks later, it wasn't merely coincidence. It was fate.

"You can come home in a month or so, Josey. I don't think right now is the time." Of course, Dad would think me a burden. How could he know a man raped me in the streets almost two months ago, stole my purse and money, gave and took from me, and now I'm living off what's in the flat. My stomach churns thinking of the cigarette smell and odious perfidy that man exuded.

"Please, Daddy, I can't stay here," I meekly beg, praying he tells me it's okay. This hurts. I want to die. My body wants to give up.

"Josephine Ellis Moore, is paradise not enough for you? I'm spending all this money for you to take a holiday while Marsha gets settled in—"

"It's not that... I miss you, is all," I lay it on thick. Not untrue, though. I missed Dad—just wish he loved me as he once did.

"Baby girl, only a few more months."

"Daddy," I cry, finally letting the ache from my soul burden him for a moment as it does me daily.

"What is—"

"Clay!" Marsha yells, stealing his attention. He sounds muffled on the other end, like he's covered the phone so I wouldn't be able to hear their conversation. "I've gotta go Josey-pie. Talk soon."

He hangs up before I can respond.

Tears leave my eyes, dripping, dripping, dripping, until nothing's left. I pull out my leather-bound journal, the last thing I can remember Mom ever giving me. I've always had a wild streak and wanted exploration, to be free... She gave me this journal for my travels. She believed I'd explore the world one day.

I wonder if this is what she imagined.

My body hides within itself as I replay that fateful night over again. If not for being in my bra, my phone would have been taken too. Did Dad not notice the lack of charges on the cards? Or did the vile man use them?

How could he not feel my pain? Was my voice too soft, too unbroken, too insincere? If not for Dad being the mayor of Hollow Ridge, I'd have told someone. Maybe. Possibly. Probably not. The shame that constantly stabs me isn't alleviating anytime soon. I get off the tile floor, heading to the master bathroom of the flat. Dad didn't spare any expense. It's stocked full of groceries, even now, over two months after my arrival. It has two bedrooms—one made into an office for my studies. The kitchen grand and beautiful, expertly decorated for my chef skills. Everything super detailed and elegant.

As I run the bath, I pray for answers. I'm not a religious person. How can I be after what that man forced into me and then stole soon after? If the world was created by a man full of wisdom, hope, and faith, why did I carry none?

The water level begins to rise, and I go for the cupboard. Searching. For what, I don't know. Pills? Anything to erase the imagery invading all my senses. Inside, there's nothing. Not a single depressant. I can't even buy alcohol, not that I'd want to leave my place anyway.

I grab the scissors from my drawer, knowing this is my only means of escape.

Bleed.

Cut.

Relief.

The scars are hideous. They dance across my skin, pretending to care, but the pink and white raised skin does nothing for the memories plaguing my mind. Maybe this time, if I dig a little deeper, the memories will bleed out of me.

I go to the clawfoot tub, not even undressing as I sink in. The water is scalding, not cool, not even hot—it's fucking feels acidic as it burns my flesh. The steam comes off in flurries of heat, the clouds whirring around as my lungs breathe for me. After minutes of pain, it all ends, and though my flesh is pink, my need for more hasn't abated.

Feel.

That's what I want.

Pain.

That's what I need.

Nothing.

That's what I get.

Gripping the metal shears in my palms, I rotate them, creating a peaceful routine. Back and forth. Flip. Flip. Flip again. When pain grips me from the scalding heat, I change my mind. There's something I need to do.

My skin is pink as I get out the tub, thinking of what changed. Maybe it's the coffee shop where it happened. Maybe that's where it all will end. Go away. Fix me. Stripping myself of the soaked clothes, an ache flushes my skin. The abraded feeling of my long shirt, jeans, and socks, reminds me of why this all needs to be over. If hurting myself is the only sustenance life can offer, then what's the point in living?

After drying myself, I leave the flat. My feet touch each cobblestone as I venture as far from home as I've done in weeks. The sky is gray and dreary like me, matching my soul, my heart, what's left of me. There's no rain; the air isn't even chilled. It's almost stagnant, without motion, seamless and still.

I make my trek to the shop, but it doesn't take long. No, it's not far, and that's the worst part. If I'd only managed a few hundred more paces, I'd have been safe that morning. Only a thousand at most, yet that very thousand cost me everything.

Spotting the little place that used to alleviate my sweet tooth before fate soured it, tears spring. They don't fall, though. There's not enough life there. No energy exists behind my eyelids right now. There's a crosswalk nearby, a ton of little shops, and even a park, too. Yet none of these things saved me. I'd lost. I'd lost. I'd lost.

A teenage girl walks toward the light and crosses to the opposite street. She's ten feet or so away from me. She's so absorbed in a book cradled in her palms, she must not realize where she is. If she keeps her path, she'll surely get hit. Her pace doesn't slow as she's headed straight for the crossing. I rush her, not wanting her to feel pain like me, even if her pain is different. It's pain. And pain knows pain knows pain.

I tug on the straps of the little backpack wrapped around her arms, hauling her against me right as a car honks at her, speeding through the light. She's so goddamn lucky. What if I wasn't a good person? What if the man who hurt me came back for her? She's small. Dainty, even. She could have died. My eyes finally release tears. Not for me, no. For her. This innocent girl. A passerby. Someone who matters.

My eyes shed tears remembering the moment she peered into my eyes, her soulful gray—nearly melted solder—eyes, ones that gave me hope. They reminded me that I'm a fighter. We spent a ton of time together that day, just talking. She told me she'd been studying abroad, I soaked up the info. She sounded American—like me—and she saved my life. One little moment suspended in time gave me a reason to persevere. It threw fate the middle finger. It mooned its ass to the fucker who stole from me. It killed my doubt, filling me with hatred, making me brim with newfound purpose.

The child aspect, though… no matter how it changed me for the better, it didn't erase the knowledge that no babies on this earth could biologically be mine. Ever. And seeing Toby, watching that hope die, it reminded me all over again of that hopelessness I felt before meeting Gray. He wanted something so mundane and beautiful, something with poetry and prose, something I could never give. He deserves more than that. He deserves a family with kids, a wife who can give them to him, a woman who can offer more than brokenness.

Whether he sees it or not, I can see his barely abated memories. The ones he has nightmares about. The one with a woman named Sparkle. The ones that keep him from falling for me like I've inevitably fallen for him.

His boyish charm—annoying as hell at first—caught me off guard in the end, making me spiral into a coma for Tobias Hayes. It warmed me, defrosting the icy exterior, weaving hot new trickles of sweetness around me like a blanket.

I'm falling for him even more.

For real.

And he's offering me so much in return—everything but his heart.

That kiss we shared before all my past troubles came about seared me like the two-thousand-dollar steaks at *Le Grand Oui.* Something so soul-burning about the bereft way he allowed me to own it, take it, and not force it from me. It filled me with delicious spurs of hope. Something I haven't felt since before Paris. It's more than a crush, more than what I felt for Wes, but less than love. An almost love. An almost hope. An almost future.

I shower, warring with what to do next. My heart tells me to go to our bed and let him hold me. My soul says to bask under the stars and let them guide the way. Yet my body, the most present part of me, begs me to have him eradicate that man from my mind. Replace the moments stolen with ones given and asked for. It wants the patience Toby will give. When we were together at the beginning, it started with our bodies, so why not restart the same?

This time without hatred.

This time *with* every string attached.

My choice.

His choice.

Our bodies coming as one.

CHAPTER 22

TOBY

MY FEET HAVEN'T MOVED.

They're still planted on the carpeted ground of the living room.

The water ran for a half hour, and I listened in silence, beating myself up for pushing. It doesn't help that all I can do is feel horrible that she got her choices taken away from her. Isn't that exactly what I did? Take advantage of her in the sense of us both being wasted, having a fucking drive-thru wedding, and then not knowing for weeks?

Guilt wraps around me like barbed wire, slicing me up on the inside while simultaneously marring my heart. It's times like these, when I'm at my rawest, that Lo forces her way in.

"I'm sorry, Sparkle. I didn't mean it." If she can't hear the sincerity intended, I'll hate myself.

"You can be sorry all you want, Tobe, but sorry doesn't mean a damn thing if some change isn't in your future," she scolds me, her eyes narrowing to slits. We eat popcorn, watching Dirty Dancing *for the fifty-billionth time this month, while she waits for Jase to pay her some attention.*

He's only been in college a year, and he has already abandoned their relationship.

Sports.

Parties.

Excuses.

She acts like it doesn't bother her, but then she sees the pictures of him uploaded by Ellie and Francis. Like tonight. I showed her a new one Ellie uploaded. Jase had his arm wrapped around her waist, her eyes were glassy and so were his. They'd been drinking. Frankie invited Ellie to the party, but Jase didn't mention it to Lo. I'd pointed out that maybe she needs to break it off. Wait until his partying streak ends, but she took it badly.

What did you think would happen? *I close my eyes, pull her closer to my chest, and kiss her temple. "I'm learning, Sparkle. If it happens again, it doesn't mean I'm not sorry. It just means I'm trying."*

She nods and ignores me for the rest of the movie.

I think of Joey—her eyes glimmering with hurt, her face sunken with horror, and her lips tight and stiff with the inability to speak. Her hurting feels different than Lo's hurt. It feels like my heart's being excavated from my torso and used for a tool to beat at the wall senselessly.

When did that moment change? Probably when the woman I'd loved for as long as I can remember became a memory abandoned to time. Loving Lo was a choice, something I decided time after time after time. I held onto it, kidnapping the feeling, praying it'd be returned. With Joey, it's not a choice. The moment I woke up next to her, her attitude after—the sarcastic asshole personality that rivaled my own—forced me to feel. It touched a part of my soul that closed off years ago.

Both her persistence and stand-offish behavior weaseled its way into me, consuming me somehow, borrowing my heart—not telling me it was for keeps.

Her pain has become mine. Her happiness, mine. Her lust, mine. Her love… that's mine, too.

As I stew in my own hatred, I realize we're pretty screwed on the hotel front. *Mi Casa* will be without a cook again. Joey has done an amazing job as the chef, but I don't want to stick around Hollow Ridge, not if I don't have to. I want us to fall into whatever this is, in our own time, away from here. Hawthorn, maybe. Anywhere but this tainted town with people I've been lucky not to run into.

I head into my office, turn on the computer, and write up an email for Raul. Joey isn't going to be happy that this choice will be made without her, but she can have a job anywhere. I'll take her to wherever her heart desires, help her in every way to give us a chance.

After clicking send, I go over my calendar, noticing the memos from Raul about *Su Casa* and how well Lo has taken over. He's probably shitting bricks at how wrong he was about her management skills. They don't call her the *Prodigy of the West* for no reason. At first, I worried she wouldn't take the job, wouldn't risk being this close to me even if we never communicated directly. It never crossed my mind she'd fail. She only proved me right.

Several knocks rapping on the door make my eyes shoot up. Not expecting to see her so soon after her shower, I'm happily shocked by her small smile. She's wearing a silky robe, one she hardly wears, but I love seeing it on her. It's this pink color with daffodils all over—her favorite flower.

Her arms are held tightly over her chest in a vest of protection. She bites the inside of her cheek, making the subtlest dimple pop inward. It takes everything in me to stay seated and not brush the stray auburn hairs from her face. When she's like this, soaked from bathing or a pool, her hair is even more tantalizing. It's darker, but still has that red glint when the light hits it. She's breathtaking in every sense of the word.

"Hey," I offer gently. The whisper of my words has her cheeks flushing. Whether embarrassment or charm, it's a beautiful tint to her soft peach complexion. She bites her lip, nerves coming off her in waves, but I don't know why.

She's everything most women aren't. Vivacious. Absolute. Bold. Her finger goes to her teeth, sinking in lightly. "I'm going to call it a night." The shyness in her tone has me smiling. I can't help it; it's young and free. Warranted.

"Why, Mrs. Hayes… are you asking me to join you?" I tease, loving the way she takes a huge inhale, her chest rising as a flush creeps up her chest and throat, making me want to touch her and see how low it goes. She hides her face as I stare openly at her, showing how much I really do find her beautiful.

"Y-Yes," she stutters a bit, then she straightens her spine, almost like she hates seeming fragile. She's not. She's the strongest woman I've ever met. And that's saying a lot. "If you're ready for bed, that is." The way she changes her voice to sound less forward has me rising from my desk and stalking toward her. The way she backs up a step just to stop and hold her ground has heat gathering in my chest and groin.

"T-Toby," she stumbles over her words again. My dick twitches at it. The way she's so small in comparison to me. Like a tiny doll that I'll keep forever if she'll let me. Her hands slide up my arms, caressing, telling me without saying a word, but I want to hear it.

"Yes?" I prod gently, wanting her to be open about what she wants. I crave it. Need it. Savor it.

"I want you," she breathes softly. Almost missing the promise in her words, I suck in air, not knowing if she's ready for it. *For me. For us. For this.* Especially after our conversation tonight. She waits for my response, not looking at me but gripping my arms at this point and trying to convey it with the pressure.

Tilting her chin up, needing to see her facial expressions, I lick my suddenly dry lips. "Josephine," I request gruffly, unsure of how much restraint I truly have. "I need you to be specific. Tell me what you want, spell it out for me. I don't want to cross a line."

Her eyes flutter slowly, sweetly, the lashes meeting her cheeks. "I want *you*," she enunciates, her expression alight with fear and desire, swirling together to make a toddy mixture that swims through me. What does she want? Me to hold her? Kiss her? Love her? Fuck her?

Maybe she just needs me to be here for her. Maybe she needs a sweet and platonic touch. Her expression can show so much but tell so little. She pulls on the waist of my slacks with her right forefinger, her touch separated by my tucked-in shirt. Even then, it takes a lot not to groan. We haven't touched in months. It was my attempt of trying not to push, knowing she wanted more than fucking.

"I need you to give me something better to remember on this night, old man."

"If I push too hard, tell me, okay?" I request, hoping she sees that tenderness is what I'll offer.

"You won't, but yes, okay." She nods as she says this, almost as if she needs me to both see and hear she's sure.

I grip her face, wanting to feel her pale rose lips against my mouth. Swiping my thumb across her chin to put this moment in memory, I watch her smile. Her teeth nip at me as she playfully shakes her hips.

Instead of swatting her ass like I want, I kiss her. Her lips are stiff for only a breath, her surprise leaks away with my control. We battle, her tongue fighting mine, her teeth hitting mine, and our flavors intermingling. She's sweet like I remember, perfect like I can never forget, and all mine for now.

She moans as my tongue brushes the ridges of the roof of her mouth. I guide her backward toward our bedroom, the one I've yet to taste, touch, or experience her in other than sleeping. After she nearly stumbles, our lips not leaving one another, I lift her, waiting for her to clutch me in that delicious way I crave.

Joey doesn't disappoint, digging her heels into the dimples on my lower back. As we make our way to the room, she rips at my shirt, uncaring that it's Tom Ford and expensive as shit. She pulls it from me right as I lower her on our bed. Her expression heated, she touches her puffy lips with a grin.

She leans back, and her robe comes undone, revealing her lack of attire. She's bare. One hundred and ten percent naked. It's almost as if she's untouched and innocent and not like the vixen who battled me for months with her tongue, body, and words.

"Fuck," I grunt as she pulls the robe off, leaving it underneath her like a display, making her my very own meal platter to feast upon.

"What's it going to be, old man?" Our eyes connect as she bites her bottom lip, the way her teeth glide over the flesh has me coming undone. I've waited for this moment, and now that it's here, my nerves overwhelm every inch of me.

What if I hurt her?

CHAPTER 23

JOEY

THE WAY HE'S EATING ME UP WITH HIS EXPRESSION alone has my legs quaking with need. Desire pools in my belly and lower, wanting—no—needing his touch. He's been so sweet and gentle, and that's not what I want. Though the memories are few and far too many, I remember the way he handled me in Vegas and at Francis's house. I'm not a gentle doll who desires sweet touches; I'm more of a fuck doll who likes being hammered into, and he knows it.

"Fuck." His single word has me nervous with excitement. It's that kind of thrill that skates up your skin, buzzing along the way.

"That's exactly what I want," I respond, trying to hide the heat flaming my skin. His eyes are connecting with mine, and there's a question there, possibly more, but I don't want questions or reassurances. Him inside me is my only desire right now. Stroking deep like I know he can and gutting me from the inside out with his cock—that's what we need.

I waggle my finger at him, desperate for him to touch me, to go faster, get rougher, and take, take, take.

He smirks, his lips tilting at the sides. That fucking smirk always gets us both into trouble. It breaks down my barriers and fucks me the same way I know he can.

He slowly shrugs off the rest of his shirt. The one destroyed by my impatience and costs a small fortune—not that I care. It stopped my hands from roaming, so it needed to go. It gives me the opportunity to stare at him. Really stare at him. He's usually super stand-offish when it comes to his body. There are scars everywhere, I've seen glimpses. You can tell he tried hiding them with tattoos, covering up his past, something I know nothing about. When he reaches for his pants, my impatience rises. He's purposely going slow to torture me.

I sit up, and my hands go to his slacks. His eyes devour me as I unbutton and unzip them. Dragging them down with his boxer briefs, my eyes connect with his cock. It's huge. Way bigger than I remember. It doesn't help that I gulp loudly, and he chuckles, only making me more nervous. Without asking, I touch his velvety length, loving the feel beneath my fingertips.

"Josephine," he hisses, his face one of pain.

"I'm sorry," I croak, knowing it's not from me doing something wrong, but more than likely the three months he's gone without sex or intimate human touch. I grip him, not knowing how he likes it but hoping the knowledge I have is enough. A guttural groan escapes his thick throat as he glares down at me. It's not an angry one, but heated, like fucking coals that have basked in the flames for hours.

Toby's knees connect with the mattress, forcing me to lie back. He kisses my left shoulder, trailing to my collarbone, all while I stroke him softly, teasingly, wanting more but unable to push him to the brink. His lips, feather-soft and hot, make their way to my throat. He licks, swirls over the veins, and sucks with purpose. Marking me. Claiming me.

I moan as his left hand grips my hips, rubbing his thumb in circles, taunting me. "Please," I whimper as that same hand grips my breast, kneading it reverently. He flicks my nipple, making me hiss in approval.

"Please what?" he torments, moving his mouth over the pebbled flesh and flicking his tongue over the tightened bud.

"Fuck me," I plead, widening my legs.

"Shh, Sous," he hushes, bringing our lips together. A moan tries slipping out as his fingers spread me, dancing flagrantly over my clit. I buck into him, wanting him to fill me. It's been so long; a slow, torturous burn that exceeds anything I've ever had to wait for.

When he pulls back, his eyes are vibrant green, edgy, full of worship and lust. He's holding back, but this time in his eyes, it's not because of anyone other than us. The way he gazes at me is with remembrance and hope. A future.

"I love you," he whispers, the bereft moment without air as I'm trying to gain back my mind hits me. "Breathe, Josephine." And I do. Dissolving into a pile of ashes beneath his strong body, I flutter away, soothing the air between us.

Letting out a strangled noise that doesn't match the heady sentiments rushing through me has him halting.

"I love you, too." It's merely uttered, barely there, not hesitant but cherished with the emotions displayed between us both. He cants off the bed, using his arms as anchors and hovering over me with ease. His tattoos blare at me, each one telling stories of love and pain and a life that brings me the man he is today. He's going to make love to me. Something I've never experienced before.

"You act like you've never done this before," I utter as he worships me with his eyes. His expression morphs into a shy boyish grin.

"I haven't."

"What do you—"

"Let me show you," he promises, interrupting me, before kissing my mouth. It's chaste and soft, sensual and sweet. His arms flex as he lowers himself, tracing his lips over every sensitive piece of flesh visible. I shake with barely abated desire, needing more, wanting everything he'll offer.

His mouth hovers over my center, his breath hot and decadent as he waits for my go-ahead. "Please," I nearly hiss. He's much more controlled than me right now. Keeping my hands to myself and stopping him from going slow is killing me.

When he lowers, a sigh escapes me as the press of his tongue swipes languidly down my slit. Contentedness and desperation mingling in one breath. My fingers brush his scalp, unable to hold still.

He spreads me with his fingers, his mouth taking control of every spasm raging inside me, seeking exit, yearning for release. He touches me in a way of remembrance, as if it's our last day, soft like snow, fragile as ice, savoring me like a last sip of wine. His grunts only further my devotion to keeping his head between my thighs, and the way I'm tugging his hair only makes him go slower.

The bed shifts as he rises, but before I can complain, he's lifting me. My heart races, thinking he's going to impale me, but when he only rests me on top of his abs, confusion takes over.

"I need you to take a memory from me, too, Josephine." Our gazes connect, and there's pain there, not residual but effervescent, cresting through his chest into mine; it's subduing me with its strength. "Purify my sins, Sous. Ease them like only you can and replace them with yourself," he pleads, gripping my thighs. There's an unspoken vow.

He lifts me, forcing me upward. When my thighs are nearly around his head, he places a gentle kiss on me. "Erase every memory, Sous. Every touch and taste before you, make them dissolve. Love me until it's only you and me." With a shaky nod, he's placing me on his mouth. The first swipe of his tongue has me grinding down on him, hissing as his teeth bite into my flesh. He holds my thighs with brutal rashness, bruising me and pressing his fingers into my soft flesh as if touch'll fix this. *Fix him.*

Whenever this moment went from my ease to his, it doesn't matter; the only thing that matters right now is the current flushing through my system, eradicating every bad memory experienced without him.

We'll slay our demons together.

Our love will set the world on fire.

Darkness binds us, branding us at this moment, and as he becomes reckless beneath me, pushing, biting, flicking his tongue masterfully as if re-memorizing a nightmare as a daydream, I'm gripping the headboard of our bed to carry the impact.

As the stars in the sky expand and swallow the dark, Toby beckons me in the same way. His body interlaces with mine, taking every ounce of fight by embedding us together, taking, taking, taking.

"Toby," I moan, and he clamps down on my clit as I let go. I'm riding his face as the sky explodes around me, detonating my vision of rudimentary intimacy, switching it for sublime euphoria.

My high settles, and he's moving me down him, his face red and slickened with my release.

We are neither here nor there but exist in a time lapse. We are stolen kisses. Unspoken truths. Midnight wishes. Everything and nothing, as our eyes communicate and our souls merge, sealing our fates as one.

We are soulmates; we are purloining constellations, revering the sky.

"You breathe life back into me, Sous." A tear slips past me, not understanding what memory I replaced, but the hope on his face, swallowing the fear he reflected often, makes every wordless action crush my chest with the affection I've long thought were lost to me.

Breathe, Joey.

"It's my turn to do the same for you," he promises before flipping me over and taking my mouth and body for the first time since we've reconnected. Cherishing, caressing, loving every scarred inch of us both, replacing every heinous memory with pure ones.

CHAPTER 24

JOEY

MEMORIES OF SWEETNESS BLUR MY VISION, reminding me how far we got before snapping. Our love a bone under too much pressure, fracturing until useless.

Toby has every right to hate me. Even *I* hate me.

After the door practically yells at me as he slams it, the shower starts running.

What are we doing? Why am I still here? And the more pressing question is, why is he?

We're married, yes. I love him, yes. If that's all there is, what's the point?

I want to be the couple they write songs about.

Where there are books and movies based upon the passion they share.

Never-ending. Constant. Inspirational.

Is that too much to ask?

It's been over a year since everything went to hell.

It took him time to gather himself, but now we're back here. Hollow Ridge. The place we both openly loathe. Where *she* is. He acts as if I shouldn't care, but even when we were happy, he loved and adored her, all while lying in my arms.

The bandages our love wrapped around him were temporary gauze, faulty enough where her love always leaked through, wreaking its infection throughout us both.

You don't know true pain until you're making love with the man of your dreams, and his mind is stuck on the one woman he's always loved most. He calls me the ice queen, the bitter bitch, the frigid north, but does he not realize he's made me this way?

He did this.

To me.

To himself.

To us.

We *were* happy.

In love, if I'm truthful to myself.

Our days were spent together. At *Mi Casa*, watching movies at night, exploring each other's bodies. Everything was perfect. Even after I told him about my inability to have children, we were good. Then we collided, a frisson of explosive anger and resentment. A destruction of hate and loathing waiting for the right time to fulminate.

My curiosity came with a cost.

At the time, it didn't occur to me that the cost would be too much.

No one ever does.

The splashing of water droplets drowns out my despondence. I didn't lie to him when I told him I loved him. Tears trail my cheeks as the emotions kept at bay finally frees. There are ten minutes tops to get it all out before he's back.

This is our routine.

He runs.

I charge.

He disappears.

I drown.

My chest that once barricaded a heart now houses a veinless appendage surrounded by ice-covered shrapnel. Frigid as ice, lifeless as the dead, voiceless as silence.

It's as lonely as I am.

Can he not feel that?

He used to care. Once, his heart made mine fonder, helped it grow, changed me... but I've ruined it.

Only, he's not the only one bitter about it.

Standing in the same place he left me, I swallow back the emotion. I have seven minutes left. Checking the watch on my wrist, I watch as time fades a little more. *Six.* Instead of waiting for him, my mind sets on its target. The wine closet.

He did so well. It took me a year to know his truths and see the lies he hid behind. Now, it's apparent more than ever. He's broken again, and I've taken so much.

' I'm the bad. He's the good. We're the tainted.

The nickel under my hand sends icy tendrils through me. It's not the cold from the metal; it's the awareness of what I've accepted. The failure of love, the one I can't seem to let go.

Turning the handle, I peer inside. Wine isn't my alcoholic beverage of choice, but it gets the job done and puts a dent in his wallet, so maybe then he'll notice me. Bringing anything stronger into our house only leads to dangerous situations. Regardless of our shared hatred, handing him ammunition won't be happening any time soon.

Picking the bottle closest to me, I take it to the kitchen.

Another reminder of what I've lost. The counters are bare, as are the cupboards, walls, and everything in between. When passion is lost, is there a cure? Or is it the one thing that never grows back, like a lost limb? Cancerous to the body once detached and unable to be lively once more.

I don't even frown when thinking of that loss. What does it compare to the rest? It's nothing. Just like me.

Four.

The clock blatantly makes me aware of how little time I have to soak into this pain. Then I'll hide it like he does his love. Opposites. Opposing forces that battle constantly. Hatred and the lack of disposition fill my nerves every day.

The cork sounds out, popping like a knuckle as I strain

to consume my emotions. *Let it breathe*, Dad would always say. Too bad for us both, I've never cared to be formal. Near the stove, hanging upside down, my wine glasses stare at me. Again, it hits me that not caring is a symptom of despondence, but it changes nothing. Lifting the bottle to my mouth, I drink.

It doesn't burn, it slides, it soothes, it fabricates fairy tales. It whispers happy fictitious dreams, making it easier for me to accept the reality that has become my life. They say there are some hard to swallow pills in life, but they didn't tell you that you'd soon choke on those words, nearly dying to swallow back the hand you're dealt.

Two.

The resounding clock in my mind ticks, promising dread and telling me life isn't going to be any easier once our door to the bathroom opens. Not that he has a heart to care anymore. It's like it shriveled inside him like a dying plant. The essence fading away with each day it lacks water and sun to sustain it.

I watched him die like a wilting daffodil, the yellow turning to brown, the petals flitting to the ground, the stem slowly deteriorating as life around it prospers. It's beautiful. It's ugly. It's our reality.

The door to the bathroom swings open, smacking against the door stopper I bought for us when the last few walls received holes from his anger. His temperament doesn't scare me; it's never been directed at me, even if his hatred has. Sometimes, I'd rather him beat me black and blue than give me this nothingness. At least with bruises, there's something.

Color. An existence of manifestation and not resolve.

It's painful to watch him hate on me, love on work, and pretend I'm the one solidified by ice. He made us this way. The warmth and light I offered left the first time he called me a mistake. Now, it's depleted, and like a dying organ, that'll never change.

"I'm going out," he barks, his voice no less cruel, his actions no less depressing. "Don't stay up." His bare chest glistens with the shower, trailing down his sculpted body, marking every inch and making my mouth drier than the wine already has.

Even after all these years, he's delectable. His body is as chiseled as the ice sculptures from our reception. Each dip is sharp and prominent, and the happy trail that leads lower, to a place I haven't been deserving enough to touch in ages, makes me clench my jaw. He's too sexy for his own good. Too much everything.

"I'm going out, too," I lie easily. My words convey it, though, when they tremble with the sadness I've barely hidden. So much for a full ten minutes to cry and become frozen again. It's not like a goddamn switch as much as I'd like it to be.

He smirks cruelly, his lips tilting harshly, promising nothing but asshole remarks that'll tear me up even more. Hatred is something Toby used well, a crutch, a weapon, the most damning tool in his arsenal.

"I'm sure you will, Joey. Tell Francis I said hi." It's bitter and tasteless, making my wine just as lancinating. Fuck him. Fuck *him*. "And when he's fucking you, try *not* to remind him that his cock will never be *mine*."

"Oh, honey. I will," I coo, gripping the bottle as if it'll stop me from falling to the ground in a heap of sobs. Benign pain can be subdued, but this malignant torment can't. This is what he's subjected me to. A lesser woman. One who lies, swallowing the pain back as one does water.

Maybe in spite of him, I'll go see Francis.

His eyes narrow at my response, showing very little. What was once jealousy is resignation. He doesn't have a heated stare; it's empty, just like his fucking heart. There's no way for me to beat it alive, but it sure as hell doesn't hurt any less knowing he'll be spending his night between the legs of some whore.

And he calls *me* Satan.

"Don't want to make your side bitch wait too long, Tobias. She might find another dick to fill her," I grumble, bringing the wine to my lips, drinking in front of the man with an addiction problem. We both have vices. His is alcohol; mine is his torturous love. They're both hurtful and detrimental for our health, but neither of us have the willpower to win.

I fell in love with the lies, marrying the pain.

He's divorced to the truth, addicted to acrimony.

We cheated love, lusting after aspiration.

There's no savior for our damnation, no hope for our salvation, and no justice for our actions.

"You're right," he huffs, pausing feet in front of me. "My dick definitely needs a companion tonight. Such a shame your pussy doesn't do it for me anymore." He turns and strolls out of the kitchen, leaving me with the largest fist inside my chest, beating against my heart, hoping to make it live once more.

As soon as he enters our bedroom to get dressed, I hiccup, feeling the tears springing free. Crying is so hideous. Especially on me.

My body shakes as the pent-up turmoil overflows through my eyes. I sob and sob, and he doesn't come out to check on me. It's not like he's unused to my fits. After a heady fight, destructive words that dig deep, and jabs that are meant to destroy, I break down. Usually, I try to wait for him to leave, but this goddamn wine broke the little barrier I gained.

My walls fall as I admit how fucked-up we are. We stay. Why the hell do we stay? He could leave. I could leave. Or maybe we can't?

Dad set our marriage in stone. We could have walked away. Sex doesn't mean everything. And while we have some of the most passionate fuck fests, even while screwed up, it's not enough to sustain a marriage. I fell hard and fast for this man, and what did he do? Belittle me, push me away, and make me want to die.

Great marriage material, sure.

When he comes out of the room, he takes one look at me, his eyes on mine for an entire five seconds before he turns. He can pretend, but the wrinkle in his brow and grimace on his face show how much he cares, even if he doesn't realize it. He hides behind his asshole persona because the Toby I hurt is the one who refuses to come out.

"I love you," I barely whisper. He stops at the door, halting entirely. His fingers dig into the frame, whitening his knuckles as he restrains himself. Instead of turning and coming to me, kissing me, loving me... he opens the door and practically runs away.

Where did we go wrong, Tobias?

Did I fail us?

There's no more fixing to be done, is there?

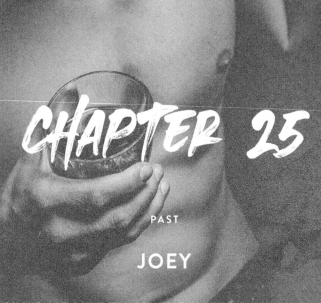

CHAPTER 25

PAST

JOEY

"WHY IS HE LIKE THIS?" THE WORDS TUMBLE OUT of me. The breath I held in hopes to give me courage finally escapes. It's loud and exhausted, much like me.

"He's been hurt so much," Frankie mutters. He grips his wine glass. Emotions clouds his normally forgiving eyes; it's bitterness and degradation at its finest. "He fell in love."

"With Loren," I add. Jealousy gives me nothing but depression, but her name brings it by the ton. "He says her name sometimes when he's tossing and turning and has had too much to drink."

"We were young once." He tips the liquid back, taking

a large gulp. Francis isn't one to overindulge. Unlike my husband, he drinks for the palette chaser, not for the aphrodisiac qualities. "He met Lo at random, but the change in him was immediate."

I nod, unknowing where this is going.

"He wasn't my best friend back then," he explains. "Jase was." Bitterness seeps from those two words like licking baking soda. "He changed almost overnight, Toby did."

He readjusts, forcing me to do the same. This air between us is stiff as it is every time we talk about anything serious. Francis has a way of storytelling that makes you uncomfortable. Unlike people who love telling stories and flourish on parts that aren't pretty, Frankie gives it to you straight, no sugar, no chaser, just the bitter truth.

"Even I could see the change in him. Lo brought out a side that was carefree, much like you do."

Our eyes meet.

Storm and amber.

Two very damaged people.

In this, we're one. Twins of a long-lost hope where love exists and doesn't hurt.

"What made her special?" The distasteful way my words leave me has us both cringing. While I'm mature in many ways, this is one thing where my inner bitch just can't shut up.

"She was his light. His dad, Brant, beat the shit out of him."

My eyes widen at this information, at a loss for words. "What?"

Francis's eyes widen as if he's given too much that wasn't his to offer. "He didn't tell you?" I shake my head, sadness creeping in.

That's what I am now. Sad. A fucking mess of desolation and the need to not be alive.

"Brant wasn't a good man, though Millie wasn't much better. Brant would beat on her, then she'd dope up on Xanny and booze. After Toby would get home, it would happen all over."

Disgust fills me. It silences all responses while bile rises. How could a parent hurt their child? Their wife? How could they willingly cause pain?

"Millie wouldn't leave him. In turn, Jase got beat too."

"They both did? Is that why they weren't close?" I ask, needing to know how two brothers could hate each other so much.

"No." He rubs a palm down his face, the wine nearly emptied. At this moment, staring at the remnants of liquid in his glass, I'm suddenly feeling the urge to consume some of my own medicine.

This dose of reality isn't welcome. It's heavy and drowning. Pain does that to people.

"While I discovered they were both being abused, neither knew the other was. It actually caused a rift later on when Jase fell in love with Lo."

"Fuck," I let out.

"It was bad. Toby loved her. Endlessly. Obsessively, even." Cringing at that, he rubs a reassuring hand on my shoulder. "He didn't love her like he loves you," he explains. "With you, it's real. It's something tangible and revolutionary. It's nothing

I've witnessed from him before. With her, she saved a broken kid inside him and brought him strength. In turn, he held onto that and ended up destroying her marriage and his family."

I go to say something, and he stops me. "He wasn't the only one at fault, no, but he could have walked away and didn't."

At this moment, understanding dawns on me. Even without knowing it all right now, it's apparent why my husband is the way he is. Abandonment.

His mom did that.

His father did that.

His brother did that.

Lo did that.

How the fuck does one expect a man to be strong and resilient if he can't trust himself to love and let go? And with him not believing me and Francis, it makes sense.

"He had an affair with Lo," Frankie says a moment later. "Emotional at first—hugs, kisses, love in a profound and comforting kind of way. Then, when Jase admitted to his affair with my ex, she full-blown used Toby."

Fuck.

Fuck.

What the fuck?

"Why?"

He shrugs. "I thought it was revenge, but then, after they slept together, she begged him to leave and give her a chance to be happy and reconcile with Jase. So I don't think that was it. I think her comfort in Toby clouded her idealisms of right and wrong. In the end, that never mattered. She broke Toby, and as a result, he and Jase haven't spoken since."

Warm anguish runs down my cheeks, pain as primitive as dying flowers consumes me. Toby's reaction to Francis hugging me, holding me at that moment, must have triggered his regression.

My body aches as reality sinks in.

I have to love him enough to fix this. Whether painful or not, no matter what he does, I won't fucking abandon him. No matter how bad it gets.

"I'm surprised you've stayed," Francis sounds out as I'm lost in my own head. When our gazes clash, his are full of confusion. "He hurts you so much. Fucks around, terrorizes you."

"I choose to sleep with him even after he's with others," I argue, seeing exactly what he means. I'm degrading myself, allowing his behavior to carry on. But if I were in his shoes, would I be any less unforgivable? "He doesn't want me to want him, but I can't stop."

"Why? What does this do for either of you?"

"Love isn't always pretty, Francis."

"Isn't always ugly, either."

"I'm not giving up on him," I promise. "He didn't give up on me at my lowest. When I cut and he came home to find me covered in blood and tears and sorrow, he stayed. He fixed me. He *loved* me." My body trembles with the tears and sobs wracking my frame. "I love him," I whisper through my sorrow.

"Love isn't always enough, Ladybug."

"It is for me."

"He'll continue to hurt you," he tries, running a hand through his hair. Gloss covers his eyes, the storms wage in them, they're turbulent and fierce. "I don't want to see you hurt."

"Then don't watch," I argue. "I'm staying, I'm fighting, and when he's finally ready, he can earn me back."

He nods, but the unhappiness is there. Toby is his friend, but so am I, and I can already see which side he's choosing. Knowing someone else is giving up on the man I love most burdens me with sadness.

"It's my choice, Frankie."

Our eyes collide once more, and this time, when he explains the entire story of Loren, Jason, and Toby, I'm a mess of sobs.

I come to grips with a lot of new information.

Lo has a baby.

That baby could be my husband's.

And Toby has no fucking clue.

Ideas filter through my fog, warring with right and wrong, consuming me.

By the time I'm driving home, I know what I need to do, even if I have to ask the devil himself.

"Daddy," I say when he answers. "I need a favor and I'm willing to renegotiate the terms of our arrangement if you follow through."

"Consider it handled, Josey."

Let's hope my husband can avoid me now. I'm bringing his family back together.

CHAPTER 26

TOBY

HER TEARS GUT ME.

Limb from limb, as if my chest was filleted open and each important organ tore from my body, she slaughters my existence with those whiskey eyes.

Fuck.

I hate seeing her like that.

Yes, I hate her.

Yes, she fucked me over.

Yes, our marriage is a disaster.

But seeing those tears? It obliterates my soul and then some. She's not who she was. I'm not who I was. Our marriage is as fake as the strength I pretend to have.

I'm jaded. She can't expect anything less, but fuck, if her breaking down doesn't tear me up inside. My heart was never a good decision maker. If I had the strength and passion a husband should possess, I'd rush back in there and fuck our love back into her and myself.

I'd fix this gap between us.

I'd forgive her and her mistakes.

But Francis.

That's who she'll run to. It's who she always runs to.

Just as Lo did with me.

How can I be in the same place now that I was five years ago with Lo? She chose him. Just as Lo chose Jase. How did I fuck up the same way all over again?

It's not right, but I'm human.

At least, that's what I tell myself.

I hit the elevator button five times before it beeps. We're in the tower of Hollow Hills. We've been here for nearly two years. We should have a home, not an entire floor we've taken residence of.

That's the thing. Two years ago, everything stopped.

Now, we're in a rerun of *Supernatural*, the Groundhog Day episode where Dean dies in every goddamn way until Sam loses his mind.

I've lost my mind.

As the elevator opens and I'm standing in there, my heart aches. It hurts worse than when Lo didn't choose me. It terrorizes me with promise, reminding me that I don't deserve happiness.

And fuck if that doesn't hurt more.

"Toby?" Bry's voice sounds out after she answers my call. Not realizing I dialed her, I attempt to shake the fog. Desperation claws its way up my throat, voicing the words my heart doesn't feel.

"Are you available?" I mutter, hating myself more and more.

"For you, sugar? Any time. Give me a half hour to clean up. Then we'll meet at our usual place."

"See you then," I reply, hoping the hatred inside me doesn't seep out and taint her too.

I shouldn't have called her.

Hell, I shouldn't be walking toward our meetup.

Yes, walking.

Our meetup is twenty floors below, room four-fourteen. It's the room I have booked forever. Or at least since we started hanging out. Is it cheating when your entire wedding is a sham? When she agrees to letting me go? When separation is a single world between two entities who don't know the meaning?

It's not like any of it was real. Not for me, and certainly not for her.

But fuck if it doesn't hurt when I leave her behind, and she's a wreck.

How did we go so wrong?

I know how, but it doesn't make the brutality of it any less painful. We did so well; I thought I finally found a slice of happiness without Lo. A place of peace between heaven and hell. Unlike purgatory, it was welcome. It was serene. It was *mine.* As the elevator lowers to the fortieth floor, my stomach knots.

She started this. She fucked Francis and ruined us. She chose him; she *didn't* pick me.

After everything I went through with Lo, I knew I couldn't stomach going through it all over again. I refused. But that's the problem with marriages. You can't just walk the fuck away. I mean, you can. My brother did it to Lo, so why couldn't I?

The metal box stops, the light on the front of it letting me know I've arrived. Seeing it illuminated has me regretting this before it starts. The doors open, sliding to my doom. That's what Bry, Serena, and Tamara are. My end.

They bring me momentary peace. It's not even pleasurable. Not love. Not lust. It just… is. They distract me. Now, as I'm walking toward our room with my head down, I can't stomach the thought of touching her like I miss touching my wife. I'm not drunk enough for this shit. I'm fully sober, riding on the high of hatred, but it doesn't feel the same. Alcohol soothes the pain, bringing a buzz and promises momentary bereavement.

It's a lie.

My life is a lie.

Joey is a goddamn lie.

Pulling out my wallet, I smack it against the door's scanner. You'd think I'd have a secret badge for this entire hotel. It's not like my brother doesn't own it. But no, I have a regular generated fucking key that only solidifies how fucking twisted I've become.

I chose this.

To defy her.

To ruin me.

To hate myself.

Think she hates me more than I hate myself? Fat chance. Pretty sure the bottom of the cesspool of disgust has nothing on the absolute abhorrence I have for myself. But that's life, right? You reap what you sow, and goddamn, I sowed an entire fucking village of clothing. Fucking my brother's wife, loving her, wanting her comfort even now… I've really screwed up everything and all I have to blame is myslef.

The light blinks after I tap it again, the lock sliding out of place. Opening the heavy door, I shuffle inside. Before even caring for waiting on Bry, I stop at the mini fridge. They know to stock it with the good stuff. The good stuff being *whiskey*. There's nothing quite like the burn of despoliation by booze. As I raise the bottle of Jameson, a little ease slips into me. The glass is cold and heavy in my palm. Its promises are false, but I open it anyway. Its warmth is faulty, but I swallow it back. Its aphrodisiac qualities are temporary, but I keep going.

It no longer burns.

If it did, I numbed it out. How could I not? It's supposed to suppress pain, not conjure it.

She said thirty minutes, which means I have at least twenty to drink and get my dick prepared. Taking the entire bottle with me to the bedroom, I lie back and open my phone, hoping for some type of memory.

When Joey and I were together, there was no faking. Getting hard was expected and impossible to ignore. But with these women I use? It's nearly unbearable. It makes me drink more, makes me hate myself with each breath, and the loathsome reality that I've become my father settles in me each time.

I open my Google drive, seeing all the images of Joey and me from our short happiness together. When she smiles, it's radiant, glowing as brightly as her fiery hair. I start with the selfie she took of us when we flew to Paris, deciding to pave our own path together. We're standing in front of the coffee shop that meant the world to her. Even with the tainted memories, she wanted me to fix them, change them, and make them better. So I did. Wherever she felt trapped, I remade memories with her. And in turn, she did the same for me.

Seeing myself in this picture causes my heart to pang. Happiness lines my eyes, my smile is full and bright, and the way I'm looking at her as if she hung the goddamn moon only makes the disgust for myself rise.

"What have we done, Sous?"

She can't answer me. She's twenty floors up, probably drinking, or maybe… just maybe, she's fucking the man I thought was my best friend. Why would he do that to me? He hated Jase for what happened with Ellie, so why would he do the same to me?

Our friendship ended that godforsaken day. He tried reaching out, maybe to apologize, possibly to gloat, but either way, I didn't give him the chance to explain.

"Where do you want to go?" I ask her, seeing love swirl in her warm eyes. Unlike I thought when quitting for her at Mi Casa, she took it well.

"Paris," she hums. It's such a beautiful sound leaving her throat. The contentedness in her voice has me aching in places I didn't realize could ache.

It's the soulful kind, the one that lets you know it's real love and it's fucking pure.

"I'll book us flights," I offer immediately. "We'll travel, and I'll work from a laptop."

She smiles innocently, but after the two weeks of pure unadulterated fucking we've done, I know she's anything but innocent. Taking the kid gloves off changed us both, making us inseparable and desperate for each other's touch.

Climbing off the bed, she prowls toward me in the swivel chair. She's wearing a pale pink nightie that rests high above her knees, barely covering her pussy. She's watching me like an animal does its prey. That's what I've become—her meal for the taking—and fuck, she's incredible when she takes charge.

It's not often as her tastes are more for me pounding her while holding her down, but sometimes, she switches roles, and I'm weak beneath her fingertips.

She saunters over, biting her lip in the most sensual way. Taunting. She's fucking taunting me. After she comes over to me, she places both thighs over mine, and I hold her down as she straddles me. The chair whines with our shared weight. It's old. A vintage piece she bought from the little shop in town.

It's hideous. Floral patterns that not even my grandmother would want. And it's pink and beige. It matches nothing in our home, but we keep it.

Seeing the sparkle in her eyes is worth every moment of staring at the ugly thing.

She wiggles above me as I contemplate how long to make the trip to France for. My dick hardens instantly as she keeps her pace. I peer into her gaze, and she smirks. My little Sous. The best part of my existence.

"You don't play fair, Sous," I mutter, thumbing her lower lip. The need to bite and taste it is strong, but if we want to get the ball rolling, I need to set dates, dive into details, and get everything in place.

"Guess you should try to calm your dick, old man. It's giving me ideas," she teases, biting my thumb. She widens her mouth, and I press into it. She sucks on my thumb, and my cock throbs with the idea of having her mouth wrapped around it instead.

No, behave.

I mentally smack myself and pull my thumb out. She pouts, her little lip outward and adorable as she flares her nose at me.

Rotating us, I open the laptop and start looking at flights. "How about we leave tomorrow?" Weekdays aren't as busy, and while we'll be flying in a private jet, it's still better to be there when it's least eventful.

"That soon?" She perks up, and her ass grinds onto my stiffness again. Letting out a ragged sigh, I give her my full attention, gripping her hips.

"You're a fucking menace, Sous. My cock isn't a fan of your wiggling."

213

"Liar, he loves it when I—" She presses down, the wetness from her bare pussy rubbing on my boxers more apparent. *"—rub all over him."*

"Fuck," I hiss. She leans forward, taking my mouth, and I let her. She consumes and tangles our tongues. She takes and gives and fucking moans in the best way.

My body vibrates with untapped lust, barely tampered by the need to get details in order. She knows what game she's playing, and I love that we can do this back and forth.

"Paris," I grouse. *"Three weeks."*

"Cock," she deflects. *"Inside me."*

Those words are the only push I need before sliding my dick out and impaling her while on the swivel chair.

I keep drinking from the memories, feeling the warmth settle in my gut. Booze doesn't affect me like others. It's not so much a relaxant when I can't sleep anymore. Being blackout drunk is the only way I can survive these days. I'll binge, drink and maybe fuck someone, then I'll hate myself so much that I attempt to asphyxiate on my own vomit.

Usually, I wake up days later, numb and depleted. You'd think I'd become numb, fix myself, go back to AA—to my sponsor, Bobbie—something. *Anything.*

I don't.

This pain is what I deserve. It's my fault.

Seeing the folder labeled *private*, I open it using my pin, and my breathing catches. Joey and I used to do this thing where we'd take images in super public areas and send them to each other. It all started in Paris when I went searching for a new winery for my French expansion back home. She was at the hotel and sent me an image of her in a kimono that rested open, split in the center, showing me a lot of side boob and her bare pussy.

She asked for an image in return. So I excused myself from the Frenchman explaining the grapes and plantation. Surrounded by grapes in a remote area, I took a picture of myself gripping my cock while grapevines surrounded me. It was our new game. One I could fully commit to. It got hotter and hotter. Her at our restaurant, me at the corporate building in Hollow Ridge, and more and more and more.

Nothing stopped us, and the thought of being caught was thrilling. She drove me mad. Following that first true initial time after she told me her story, it was hands-on all the time. We'd sneak quick fucks in the industrial fridges, in the pantry that housed all the stuff for cooking, and across my desk as she soaked all the papers with her pleasure.

We burned, and eventually, that wasn't enough.

It crashed.

It dissolved.

We were ruin.

My dick stands rock hard thinking of her and seeing all these pictures of our sexcapades. The one video I stop on is one of her squirting. Who needed porn when your wife willingly reenacted every dirty fantasy you could ever wish for?

She's spread wide as my fingers pump into her. Her hips

bow off the bed, and her soft mewls of satisfaction ring out, making my cock ache from the memory.

She holds her tits, pinching the little barbell in her left tit while rubbing her right with slow and sure movements. I block the camera's view as I lean forward and take her cunt with my tongue. Her flavor is unlike anything I've ever had.

Even now, I won't go down on anyone, kiss them, or give them more. It's too intimate. It's something reserved for someone I love, not some woman who probably fucks every guy she wants.

The throbbing in my shaft becomes painful as an almost tangible fog settles over my eyes and I watch myself move away from my wife and rub her little clit until she's screaming my name. She's lost in her ecstasy, not even able to open her eyes as she comes and leaks all over the bed.

Fuck.

She's so fucking beautiful.

Even now when she's not mine. She's still the most beautiful woman I've ever had the horror of loving. No one is her. No one compares. No one ever will. I shut down the app and slurp back my friend Jameson, knowing he'll help keep my mind off the pain and focus on that video.

"Tell me something, Sous."

"Like what?" She lays on the opposite of our loveseat with her feet nestled on my lap as I rub the tenderness from them. She's been working non-stop since starting at Mi Casa. *Her work ethic is unparalleled.*

"Tell me something you're afraid to say, even to yourself."

She closes her eyes a moment, running a hand through her tangled hair. Then her gaze locks with mine.

"I'm terrified of losing myself. I'm one to hide from myself and protect my heart. People always leave, Toby. Always."

Something about her words hit me square in the chest, unraveling what little guard I had knitted over my heart, the only protection I had left for this woman who somehow changed everything for me. That little safety net was all I had left not to be open with her.

"What about you, Mr. Secretive?"

"I like you," I admit. *"A whole fucking lot."*

A smile changes her serious expression to one I'm growing to love. I swallow the feelings clogging my throat and tell her what I've been holding back all along.

"Giving you my heart fucking scares me." A sigh escapes her. She clutches her hands, and I know it's so she won't reach out. She's like me, a rowing boat in the Riviera wanting a destination, but gazing up at the stars, she looks for a guide, just to be greeted with a bleak, lightless sky.

"What if we trade?"

"Trade?" I ask, feeling my pulse pick up. The way she bites her lip is indicative of the gears in her head moving. They're always turning and trying to decipher the exact words and how she wants them to play out. It reminds me so much of myself that it keeps me feeling connected to her.

"Yours for mine. A one-for-one deal. I steal your heart, and you steal mine."

The pinch I feel beneath my ribs aches in an entirely new way.
Is that what she wants, love?

As I sit in my self-loathing, I hear the lock turn and the door opening, but I don't care. I cradle my most loyal friend and realize I've already downed half a bottle.

Tonight will be one of *those* nights. Where there are so many regrets to memories unknown. And truly, it's what I've always deserved.

"Toby?" Bry's soft voice calls out to me.

"One sec!" I holler back, hoping I can stay hard for her. It's sad when you can't even force your dick to rise to the occasion when choosing to cheat. If it's not for pleasure, then what's the point? But luckily, looking over Joey's and my personal porn, my dick is awake and ready.

She saunters into the room, noting my bottled friend, but ignoring it. Joey wouldn't ignore it. She'd grab it, then chuck it at the wall or pour it down the drain, all while screaming at me to stop hurting myself.

Because even though the hatred runs thick between us, her love still powers through. Just like before we were married, she killed me with hatred and soothed it with a bite of lust and a whole lotta love.

I hate her so damn much.

It runs deep.

Intrinsic and depraved.

But fuck, her body could fulfill every fantasy of mine, drive me through the wall with pleasure, and it'd sate me. It'd do something none of these women ever could. It'd bring me peace. She doesn't deserve it, though, not while she shares her body with Francis.

Is that what she's doing right now? Riding his cock while she wears *my* ring? My anger builds, and as Bry drops her trench coat and reveals a lacy number, I pretend it's her that has me hard as a rock. I imagine Joey is fucking my best friend, letting him into her tight little ass like I used to. And then I'm grabbing Bry, throwing her on the bed, and sheathing myself before sinking in. She's wrong. Not the same tightness. Not the same heat. Not the same. Not the same. Not the fucking same.

I growl as I think of my wife's perfect pink pussy, how she screams for me and milks my cock. I think of her perfect *real* tits and not the fake bubbles I'm gripping as I thrust. It's Joey's whimpers and lip biting I'm fantasizing about and not the woman making loud noises that don't turn me on.

And as she's getting louder, the only thing that's pushing me forward is the thought of my wife with another man, and I have to make her feel this pain. She needs to feel what I feel. She needs to fucking hurt, and I want to be the bearer of every ounce of pain. She will feel it all and then I'll hate myself more, pretending it's what I want. Sadness manifests inside me, but you know what's stronger? What absolutely overwhelms me until there's nothing but *it*?

Hatred.

It immobilizes me, taunts me to push, and threatens to take ownership.

So, I let it.

Faking an orgasm, I still in Bry, pretending it's because I'm spent. Before pulling out of her, I grab my cell and take a picture of me holding one of Bry's tits, my eyes are closed in faux pleasure. Before thinking twice, I send the image to Joey, hating myself more. In that hate, I find peace. Because neither of us should like who we've become, and until one of us wins this stupid fucking game, we're going to despise every shaky breath.

Pulling out, I make sure to hold onto the condom, knowing I'd never fuck someone bare again, especially not this person who means nothing to me. She smiles at me with a look of sedation and yearning glistening in her eyes. I need to cut this shit off. She's going to grow attached, and I can't have that.

Regardless of how much I'm turning into my father, I will, under no circumstances, become Jase.

Throwing the condom away, I put my softened dick away, zipping up. I should stay. She likes when I stay a little longer and get her off. Pretend she matters. But I don't give a single fuck how she feels. No matter what, she knows what she's signed up for. There are *no* strings; I refuse to have a single attachment. Whether that makes me a piece of shit or not, I don't care.

Grabbing my bottle of Jameson, I walk away. As if she knows, she doesn't follow or call after me.

Maybe she'll grow jaded too and realize love is overrated and a fucking joke. It's not meant to have and to hold. To cherish or fucking keep. It's meant to tear you to shreds and swallow you before throwing you right back up.

Love is weakness.

It's my retribution.

It's my burden.

It's my death sentence.

The entire way back up to Joey's and my suite, I think of how much I hate her and what she's done to me. I thought Lo was bad, but fucking Joey? She's like a decomposing stab wound that will never heal. The knife dug in, leaving a forever stain on the tissue and muscles, forcing them to keep the memory of the action. Replaying it with each remembrance of the word.

I'm so fucked, and I did this to myself.

Why am I such a lost cause?

When will I learn?

Was I ever worthy of love?

The bottle gets lighter and lighter as the elevator dings on the sixtieth floor, letting me know the entire floor that's mine and mine alone is waiting. Maybe Joey is in there. Did she invite that cocksucker back here to pleasure her?

He can't please her like I can. He doesn't know how to flick her clit the right way or how to squeeze her nipple too hard, just the way she begs for. And fuck, there's no way his cock fills her like mine does.

Does she let him come in her? Taint what's not hers to offer him?

Fuck. I hate her.

Hate him.

Hate me.

Hate every-fucking-thing.

I drink and drink until the bottle is as barren as my chest. Funny how that works. Items representing ourselves. Alcohol is mine. Not just my vice, but my descriptor. Hurts like a bitch, takes and soothes momentarily.

Lie.

Lie.

Lies.

Fuck.

Getting to my door, I hit the black pad with my wallet and watch as the light flickers. When I twist the handle, my vision blurs, revealing my worst nightmare. My stomach squeezes at the sight in front of me.

She wouldn't fucking dare.

CHAPTER 27

JOEY

AS I WALLOW IN SELF-PITY AND ATTEMPT TO DROWN my sorrows, my phone chirps. Reaching above me on the counter to get it, I tighten my fingers around it, realizing it isn't the man I'm desperate to hear from. My eyes land on Francis's text. *Ma coccinelle, are you okay?* It's been a few days since we last spoke, but he keeps me grounded. Not in a way Toby used to, but in a way that shows he cares. Or at least, I hope he does.

Yeah, just dandy. How's Gray?

I can imagine his disapproving glare and the forehead wrinkling as he shakes it.

Deflection doesn't work on me, sweetheart. He's good, I'll give him that. Toby thinks I find comfort in Francis. *I do.* It's just not sexual. It hasn't been intimate in any way since that kiss we shared. Once Toby and I were together, Francis became strictly a friend. Hell, he's my best friend's dad. I wouldn't break that trust for anything. Not even if he was good in the sack.

You're ignoring what matters, Frankie. How's my best friend?

When everything between Toby and I imploded, Gray was going through something herself, and she hasn't quite recovered. If I didn't witness it myself, I wouldn't believe a single guy could wreak as much havoc as Ace did on any given day.

Why do men hurt the ones they love? I ask myself this daily. Regardless of how much Toby tells me he hates me, it's a lie. It shows in the way he always comes home. Even if he spends nights with other women, he always comes home. It's a silent promise, like no matter what, he will always come back to me. How he used to constantly fuck me after he'd fuck other women is telling too. Coming home after being inside them, then being inside me. Dirty. Depraved. Diabolical.

He purposely doesn't shower. It's his punishment to me, making me smell them on our sheets, on him, and everything in between. If he knew I'd never fucked Francis, would he hate himself more? Not that he could feel a single fucking thing. He drinks so much it's a miracle he could see at all, let alone think enough to hate himself. How he works every day, fully functioning while polishing off bottles in his office, is beyond my understanding.

Alcohol is his medication, his loaded gun, and he continues to fill the chamber with bullets, pulling the trigger on his personal roulette game. He hurts himself more than I ever could. But we stay. We fucking stay, and it makes no sense.

It may never.

But he keeps going back to other women, and I just lie here with my battery-operated boyfriend and find peace knowing I never crossed the lines in which he has.

"Divorce me if you think I've betrayed you," I hiss, pushing at his chest with tears welling in my eyes. It hurts. It fucking hurts knowing he believes I'd choose Frankie over him. I couldn't do that. Ever. Toby saved me. He mended my most broken parts, soothed the scars, and eased the pain. He did that.

I'd never ruin us for something as simple as sex.

Deep-seated resentment takes residence in my bones, infiltrating my love and rotting it with each harsh word he snaps at me.

"Fuck. I can't even look at you," he bites, turning away from me. I reach out for his arm, but he yanks it away as if I've hurt him by touching his skin. Tears spill free, painting my cheeks with warpaint I didn't realize I needed. How could they not? He won't look at me. Toby is a man all about connection. With mind, soul, and eyes. He made sure to let me know that eyes are the windows to the soul every time he made love to me.

"I didn't—"

"Stop talking!" he barks sharply, turning all that loathing onto me. His hand raises to grip my face but drops deftly before the skin connects. "This is how this will work."

I stare at him, dumbfounded. What does he mean? The way he straightens his spine with resolve, narrowing his eyes with concentration, and clenches his jaw austerely has me on edge. He's almost too calm, masking his emotions like he's a marionette and no person pulls his strings any longer.

"From now on, you're not my wife, Joey. On paper, sure. But in the real world, where it matters, where marriages are of love and bullshit? That's not us anymore." His contentious mask drops for a twinkling moment as pain pigments his features with agony. Worrying his lip, he lets out a Herculean exhale. "You fuck who you want, Joey. And so will I."

"Nonono," I whimper. "That's not—"

"Shut the fuck up," he growls so deadly that I hiccup, feeling my chest deflate as it loses every ounce of love it ever attained. "We're done. We won't become Lo and Jase. They both cheated. Us... this won't be that. No. There won't be any love or feelings involved."

"Then why stay?" I cry, my chest aching beyond repair. I grip it, wondering if it still beats, still thrums even as his words slice deeper than my razors ever could. Wes couldn't have ever hurt me this bad. My dad abandoning me never ached his much. Mom disappearing doesn't compare. This inherent torment, swirling with sorrow inside my soul, is not attainable even as my body carries it like a thousand-pound dumbbell.

This is savagery in living form. Corrosion. Destruction. Pure decrement.

I fall into a heap of sobs and instead of comforting me like he always did, he turns his back on me. "I'm going out. Don't fucking expect me to come home." As the door slams, I break.

Absolutely.

Entirely.

Forever.

He didn't hear my side of the story, I tried. I fucking tried.

For nearly six months, I kept trying. That's when he made it noticeable that he'd been fucking other people. He's paraded his hickeys, lipstick stains, and the way he smelled like them. Sex. Perfume. Booze. Then he'd come home and fuck me with their scent wrapped around him as sure as their legs were.

And I let him.

I let him.

I let him.

He was a train wreck I couldn't stay or look away from. Still, I'm here.

Hate is my darkest lover, cosseting me with twine, branding me its slave.

I know why I stay, but why the fuck does he?

She needs you. Come by? Francis's texts ping as I cry from the memories of my darkest days coming to light. Looking down at my bare arms full of inch to two inches of raised healed flesh, I feel. Pain is a blossoming flower, rooting in the veins, sprouting itself through the skin and flourishing in the tears of pure agony. Beautiful. Ugly. Damning. I bring the wine bottle back to my lips, kissing the glass as its comfort is all that ties me here.

When? Toby isn't home. I have time.

It's true. I could drive over, be there for her, and maybe get a night's sleep where Toby isn't here to hurt me with his disheveled appearance. As words blur together with my tears and wine, it's apparent that driving isn't in my future.

Have you been drinking?

I bite my lip. He knows me well. Whenever my husband is gone, I drown myself in *his* vice, knowing full well that it'll destroy whatever is left of us both.

Maybe a little. I barely type it before bubbles are coming and going from his typing and stopping.

I'll come to you.

He cares. Maybe he wants more? It wouldn't surprise me. Men can be fickle and one-dimensional. Even someone as charming and kind as Francis Satoray.

Okay. It's all I offer. If he wants love, I have none to offer him. If he wants sex, I'm taken. If he wants to be my friend, I'm all for it.

So many minutes pass before he's arriving. By then, I'm nearly polishing off the bottle. You see, while I waited, my phone beeped. When my notification said *Tobias,* I got excited and opened it right away. Maybe he was apologizing, telling me he loved me, that he hates this separation as much as I do.

But no.

Nothing could prepare me for the image that hit my inbox.

Like all the memories of me doing this exact thing with him, in every country and state we visited, he's continuing our game. Tainting it. Just like everything else he touches. That fucking bastard!

He's on top of a brunette woman with a butterfly tattoo, her eyes are closed in rapture and so are his. They must have snapped this as he orgasmed inside her. They're both sweaty and entirely naked. It fucking guts me to see him like this.

I stare at it as I down the very expensive and nasty wine. It no longer possesses a flavor, though. I'm too far gone. And by the time Frankie shows up, using a spare room card that I've given him, he sees me. He's too late. I'm already a mess on the floor.

CHAPTER 28

FRANCIS

NEVER KNEW I'D SEE A DAY WHEN I HATED TOBY as much as I currently hate his brother, but alas, here we are. Someone always has to be a villain in another person's story, so that's probably why Toby made me his. In reality, if we take a step back and truly look at this particular picture from an outsider's glance like I can, it's easy to spot that Toby is his own villain.

Respect. A foreign word to many, especially in this day and age. People believe they deserve something that isn't theirs. They take with no regard to the ones they hurt, and they don't cart guilt around for their misdoings. It's a word that holds a vow for my friends and family. One that pushes me forward to only ever be honest and kind. Once upon a time, that wasn't me. Not that the world lived with that version for long, but we all make mistakes.

The only thing that separates me from this sad woman on the floor in a heap is that one word. It doesn't come from a deep admiration for my best friend, nor does it derive from a pedestal I see Toby on. It simply has been ingrained in me to treat the street sweepers the same way they treat royalty.

In my eyes, we're all the same. Only our circumstances are different.

My eyes strain to see in the mostly darkened room, the only light coming from the kitchen night lamp. Joey lays barely coherent, mumbling about how she deserves to die and it'd be easy. "Please, just do it," she slurs. "Take away my misery."

Her eyes are droopy as she's holds the bottle like it's her only weapon, shielding her like her husband should be doing. Pain this gruesome shouldn't be worn every day, tattered and decrepit, bleeding the spirit dry with pinpricks of antipathy.

This is the problem with Toby; he doesn't realize he fucked up and continues to do so. He has such a beautiful life, woman, and future, but he allows alcohol to rule over him. He lets fear and his past and insecurities own every semblance of reality.

Did he not realize when he believed I was fucking his wife that he already sucked the bottle like a goddamn tit? He slurped and savored and regaled, not seeing his life falling apart around him.

But no, *I'm* the bad guy.

"Josephine," I coo softly. She tries opening her wet, red-rimmed eyes, but she scrunches her face in displeasure instead. "I'm so sorry, Ladybug." She cries more, and I can't help but want to fix her. I've kept my distance. She chose Toby, and I respect that, but I'll continue to stay by her side. Because she deserves to be loved and cherished. She deserves to be fucking worshiped.

But not by me.

I'm not that guy.

I'm not Jase or Toby. I'm me. The person who knows his limits and worth.

Crouching down, I wipe her eyes and wish to ease her struggles. How can someone claim to love her yet continue to hurt her at every turn? If she was mine, I'd literally kneel at her feet. She'd be my queen, and no one would ever come between us. Petty differences, stubbornness, and every other emotion wouldn't stop me from fixing it. Does Toby not see how he's depleting her? How with every push, she falls apart even more? Does he not understand she lost, too?

It's not one-sided. A marriage never is. Where she swallows it all, he acts like a child. As if he's the only one who lost and surrendered.

She gave up more, sacrificed everything, and yet still, he walks away?

He's not the same person who kept my secret for fifteen years, protecting me, my daughter, my legacy. No, he's less than that man now. A shell that somehow still exists. At least Nate tries to battle his addiction. Even now, as none of us can reach him, he's trying. He broke when Lo tried killing herself. He literally relapsed from the guilt, but he's pushing through. That's the difference between my two best friends. One wants to make a difference while the other wants pity.

Until he mans the fuck up, I'll be here like a goddamn father figure for him, scolding him, taking care of his wife, and hoping that he finally pulls his stupid ass out of the clouds and loves her. Does he not see Lo in Joey? The dejection, the ruining, the barely-there woman who was once a goddess? The one who fought back, battling, conquering as if fighting was her only sustenance? Does he not realize the patterns are nearly mirrored, desperate, seeking help, and he's just too goddamn stupid and stubborn to save her?

What made him save Loren? What made her special?

Because as I cradle my daughter's best friend in my arms, holding her to me to keep her warm and watched over, I'm not sure what the fuck changed to make Loren more suitable for his love than the woman he vowed to cherish.

He's despicable.

His behavior is unacceptable.

She's a tree infested with beetles that harvest each livable root, consuming and devouring until it eventually dies due to its gluttonous actions.

"The fuck are you doing here?" Toby's loud bark slices through me, rattling my cage like an aggressor. The way it hits me isn't with fear but more with worry. His words are slurred and heavy. He's fucking tanked, and the way he staggers toward us with a bottle clutched in his hand has anger rising inside me.

Since I left America for France, I've kept my temper in check. It's what's necessary for someone in my political position. Being stupid and aggressive isn't acceptable, and as I watch him trip over his own two feet, I want nothing more than to punch him in his face. Screw my image, he needs to fucking learn.

He's past his normal drunk. Toby can hold his liquor. When a normal person gets to the point of no return, bordering on alcohol poisoning, that's when Toby is at his calmest. When a normal person would be dead, that's when Toby is incoherent. Like now. He can't focus, but his rage is barely tamed. Haunted eyes stare back at me, desolate of morality, readily corrupt and damning to vanquish.

I don't let Joey go. Even as she whimpers in her sleepy daze, I hold her and wait out the storm that is Tobias Hayes.

"You're n-not fucking welcome, F-Frankie." His words are getting choppier. Messy like his disheveled hair and attire. Who was it this time? Bry? I bet it was her. She's the only one who willingly drives here at a moment's notice.

"Neither are you," I bark. The harshness lacing my tone comes off deadly. It's venomous, leaking disgust and hatred. What has he done to himself? To his wife? With his red-rimmed glossy eyes and his strained face, he's hopeless.

Looking at him with his sadness seeping from his pores like the whiskey, I feel bad. But right now, he doesn't need me. She does. She's the one hurting. He hurts her. He always fucking hurts her.

"S-She okay?" He stumbles, looking at her as if seeing her for the first time. For the first time in a year, I see worry behind that loathing. Actual tangible care. It's slim and muddied by booze, but maybe that's when he's most honest.

"Would you be?"

His eyes fly to mine, challenging but riddled with loathing, and he shakes his head. "No. She d-deserves better."

"You're goddamn right, she does. You fucking twat."

With a pinched expression, he comes closer, but I halt him with my palm. "Take a fucking shower. You smell like a washed-up drunkard who fondled one too many whores."

He scoffs at me as if me telling him what to do is blasphemous. Maybe it is, but he's not getting a single step closer. I'll knock him out easily. I refuse to let him taint her even more. She's already broken. So goddamn broken.

Right now, she's his rag doll that got taken from orphanage to orphanage. Hit way too many times, spit on, kicked, and buried in the dirt. Lifeless, but hanging on to hope.

What hope is there?

Toby doesn't look like he's ready to change, but seeing the way his eyes are glazed over with emotion makes me wonder if he's not a lost cause after all. Maybe he only needs a push in the right direction.

"Shower. Now. Or I won't let you see her."

He nods, staggering into their bedroom. Good. Because

beating him was in the cards if he didn't listen. He may be my best friend—even if he's an absolute dickwad—but unlike him, I don't give up on people. Right now, though, Joey concerns me most. She uses pain to drive her to live. She cuts to satiate the numbness. She bleeds to cleanse herself of loss. Toby does this to himself, and Joey doesn't know how to stop. She's young, unused to the brokenness of the man in the other room.

Now if I can somehow mend these two or sever them completely for their better interests... Now that's the biggest and truest challenge, isn't it?

I need to fix them.

Somehow.

Any way physically possible, it'll happen.

Especially since they don't seem to know how to do it themselves. But I won't be Toby. I'll keep my love platonic, even if I could love Joey better. There's no corruption in my future, and I refuse to wreck another marriage. I already did that once. Even if I had to walk away to make sure I didn't ruin myself, too.

I wonder if she still thinks of me. I do, especially when I'm on the isle where we met.

Some romances aren't meant to be written about.

"I'm going to fix this, *ma coccinelle*. I promise," I murmur against Joey's forehead. Leaving a kiss as she's finally lost the pained expression. Maybe she's dreaming of a happier life. A safer one. I'll do anything to prevent these two from killing themselves, if it's the last thing I'll ever accomplish. They matter too much to me to not intercede.

When Toby sobers up, he's going to either fight me or he's going to listen. No matter how much I repeat the notion in my head of him being settled, it's more than likely he's going to choose the former. Good thing I'm not the dainty kid I was in high school, so he'll have a good partner to spar with.

And maybe when this is all said and done, the isle will call me home, and I'll finally find peace.

CHAPTER 29

PRESENT

GRAY

A LITTLE BIRDIE MENTIONED YOU WERE IN TOWN.
The first text comes through, making my heart run rampant.

I'm coming for you, Storm.

My hands are clammy as they grip the bottle of kombucha I've forced myself to drink. Its little chia seeds having me internally gagging. Eating has never been easy for me because I'm picky and textures set me in a spiral of heaves.

Something about the texts have me trembling. Deep and strong feelings of abandonment rise inside my chest. They beat and puncture the walls of my flesh, pressing forward, begging for access, and unless I battle them, he'll win. That's what he does, isn't it? Win.

You can ignore me all you want, Gray. I will come for you, then after I've broken you, you'll come for me too.

I shiver, swallowing back another gulp. The glass feels heavy in my palm while my phone feels like a brick in comparison. Dad said he'd be right back. That was hours ago.

It's Joey.

Something's wrong.

We haven't been hanging out as much as we should. Doesn't help that Ace breathes down my neck whenever I'm most vulnerable. It's why leaving the house is a feat in itself.

He can't rule me anymore. Not after what he did, not with how he ruined my life. I refuse.

When my phone beeps and vibrates in my palm, I peer at the screen, wondering what he wants now. He never gives up. He's tenacious, even more than he was in high school. Ace Collins scares the living shit out of me.

He's my bully, the pain to my ache, and the grim reaper to my murder.

If I allow it, he'll end my life.

I miss you, mon beau. At the text from Range—Ranger Godefroy—my not-so-temporary Paris fling, heat surfaces on my skin, blanketing it in warmth. That's what Range does, he soothes my aches and promises endless care and a name my father would approve of. I roll my eyes at that. He might be royalty to my French grandparents and my father, but he's just Range to me. The kindest man I know.

Miss you too, Range. Visit me this summer?

Wouldn't miss it for the world, ma petit. Special occasion?

Just needing you here. Especially since you haven't seen my home.

I'll book my flights then. He sends and then another message pops through. *But, mon beau, I will follow through with that promise.* My body flames at that. Where it warms from his sweetness and adoration, it melts with his promise.

I don't know what you're talking about. I lie, wanting to distract myself from the asshole who fucks my head up with every jab he throws my way.

When I get there, your pussy is mine. Tu comprends, ma petit?

Yes, sir. I joke, but inside, my body squirms with possibilities. Since the day we've met, he's wanted me. It's why I never pushed for more. If I gave him what he asked for—my body—maybe he wouldn't stick around.

That's what Ace did.

Used me.

Chewed me up.

Spit me back out.

I've selected the first week of June. See you then, Gray. Don't miss me too much.

But I will. So I respond with a winky face and then head to my kitchen, needing to wash the strong kombucha flavor from my tongue. Opening the huge stainless steel fridge that could feed the entire town of Hollow Ridge, I scan for something not so bitter.

"Guess I know why you're avoiding me."

I screech, banging my elbow on the shelf, knocking it down along with every condiment I've ever seen. My eyes connect with the mess. The ketchup bottle's cap broke, spraying red everywhere, and the mustard did the same. It's the pickles that made the biggest mess.

Broken, in a pile of green saltiness, they brine the floor with their potent smell. My gaze focuses on everything but the voice that spoke. Was he watching me? How did he get past the guards again, let alone barge in here?

"I'm fed up with your silence, Storm. You will kneel for me, and you'll fucking beg for more." His hand grips my wrist, and I'm faced with the hate of my life. Love lost itself in the mix, creating a monster that ate at my sanity, driving me crazy as he devoured my soul.

"Ace," I whisper, not knowing how to react to the icicle touch on my skin. He's cold, subhuman, like an insensate vampire who preys on me until I'm weak. I'm not weak anymore. The fragile teen he fucked with and pushed over the edge is dead.

Just like the love we once shared.

"Who is he?" he barks, clutching the fridge door as if to keep himself away. He moves, closing it, forcing me to walk backward, all while his boots crush pickles, spreading their juices all over the floor. Delia isn't going to be happy about cleaning this mess.

"Who is who?" I play dumb. There's no way he knows about Range. No way. He's my best-kept secret. Even Dad thinks he's just my friend, though mémé was the one who pushed me into his arms.

"Don't act like a daft doll, Gray. That's beneath you," he hisses. We walk back until my spine connects with the opposing counter, and tingles of heat zip through me. We're not teenagers anymore. We can almost legally drink, but with him hovering, pushing into me, I feel like that high schooler he ridiculed until I escaped. The one he did unspeakable things to and stole something that wasn't his.

"A friend," I offer. It's not a lie. *It's not the truth either.*

"A friend," he mocks. "Do you fuck this friend, Storm?" His chest brushes mine, thick and threaded with muscles. Ace has grown since our last encounter, the one that separated us entirely. Making him the villain and me the loser in our story.

He towers over me, making my five-foot-five form seem smaller than it is. His palm presses against my pounding chest, and the feral look in his eyes has me unable to breathe. What does he want? Why did one action ruin everything?

"Has he touched what's mine, Storm?" The deadly way the question comes out has the hair on the back of my neck rising.

"Not yours, Ace," I grit, barely able to grapple the strength to bite back. A cruel smirk curves at his lips, the way it says more than the very few words he said to me in the past five years.

"That's where you're wrong, Gray. You've been mine since birth," he enunciates, acting as if I've forgotten our origins and how we were born exactly two weeks apart. "You have five years." He taps his wrist, signaling time. "The clock is ticking." Then he's moving away from me, stealing my breath all over again.

My heart doesn't know whether to pound or slow as it erratically tries escaping my chest, going in every which direction. His form daunting as it still closes me in. The ringing of my phone has him tilting his head toward it.

"Looks like Daddy is calling. You should probably answer." He lifts my phone, unlocking it with the code I never changed. "So predictable." His fingers glide over my texts, invading every ounce of privacy I thought I had. Instead of getting mad or feeling betrayed, a smile breaks free.

While Ace believes he's winning and has the upper hand, it's me who'll win. Because unlike he realizes, I'm moving on, pushing past our memories. I'm *living.* It doesn't occur to me how angry he is until he's tossing my cell onto the ground and breaking it with his boot in the next breath.

My gasp lodges in my throat after he stares at me with dead eyes, intent on ruining everything.

"Can't wait to meet him," he growls, pushing forward to grab my throat. His fingers grip me in a way I've dreamed about, handling me in a way that both frightens me and makes my body ache with neediness. For a slight second, his eyes, that have been blacker as of late, seem to soften into the vacant sea ones I grew up loving. One second, he's rubbing circles into my throat, and the next, he's biting my lip, scraping his teeth against it.

A whimper escapes me; he steals it, swallowing it as his mouth devours mine. And when I don't think I can no longer sustain the emotions bursting through me at such a short and simple touch, he's gone. Fluttering my eyelashes, I have to wonder if I've imagined it all.

I haven't.

The pickles and other liquids are still spilled and scattered, but he's gone.

I touch my lips, feeling the swelling and wetness. Dragging my fingers across them again, I notice the blood. He marked me.

On the floor, surrounded by a mess, my phone is amidst the chaos. It's cracked, the colors on the screen are wrong, but the light is still on. Picking it up, I notice a slew of messages.

Won't be home, mon lapin. *Please make sure you eat. And no, cotton candy isn't a food group.* Tears slip down my face as my life feels like a mess. Ace rattles me with every confrontation, and that's what it is. A battle. Something to win or lose, and while he's always got the upper hand, this time felt different.

Is she okay? I respond even though it's been ten minutes.

She will be. I'll make sure of it.

It makes my heart both swell and crash. There was a time Joey and my dad shared looks that scared me. Not that having a stepmom almost my age was scary, but it just didn't occur to me it could be my best friend. But as time went on, they proved a kinship that made me jealous. They got along in a way Dad and I have never been able to connect. It was as endearing as it was infuriating.

Dad takes care of Joey and Uncle Toby. Their marriage is in shambles, and I feel as if I'm watching Lo and Jase all over again. The difference being Joey's will to fight. It's admirable if not stupid. Holding her as her world implodes isn't easy, but it's worth it to know she's still here.

After the last time I caught her hurting herself, it terrified me for what her future held.

She thinks I don't know.

She thinks I don't see.

She thinks I don't understand.

I do.

Just keep breathing, Joey.

Just keep breathing.

CHAPTER 30

JOEY

PAIN.

Pain.

More pain.

My eyes pinch as a drilling digs into my skull. *Fucking Christ.* This is why I don't like drinking. Even in the quiet of the room, I can hear whispering. The light noises filtering into my ears sound obnoxiously loud. My head throbs, agony needling into my temples over and over, reminding me that wine *is* the worst drink to get drunk on. It always makes me feel like death and fate fucked me at the same time. Since no one could win, I got the brunt of the pain.

My body feels gross. Like when you go to pass out in bed without showering and are still in the day before's clothing, make-up, and sweat. It's an unpleasant sheet that seems to stick to every crevasse of me right now.

Begrudgingly trying to roll over, I nearly fall on my ass. Noticing that I'm not on my bed, but rather the chaise lounge in our spare room. It's big enough to fit me and Toby... *don't think of him.* We spent nights upon nights christening our rooms with our ravenous fucking, this particular piece was Dr. Orgasm Gifter. Sometimes, it was sweet love. Most times, though? With his demanding nature and my need to be controlled in the bedroom, rough fucking was what ended up happening. Toby always gave me so much power by letting me choose to be bound and pushed.

Now, he doesn't touch me. Not to hug, kiss, or be intimate in any way. It's insane how we went from breaking all my walls down and learning so much about each other, to him being unable to look at me. I knew telling him my secret would burst in my face, but I just didn't realize it'd be the thing to ruin us.

He says it's not.

But we all know it's the *exact* reason.

My body aches as I shuffle around the room, noticing I'm still in my sun dress. Heading to the walk-in closet that has a standing mirror, I nearly break down. My face is full of mascara. It's smeared and dried in streaks down my face. It's ugly and grotesque, and I hate it.

Francis. He came here.

Shit.

Walking over to the closed door in the room, I lean my ear against it, hoping to hear better. The voices are less muffled. It sounds like... *Toby?* My heart races. He came home? Rarely does he show up this soon after leaving. He hates being in the same place we fell further in love.

Why did I have to meet Loren?

Why did I push?

How can he not see I wanted to help?

Everything spiraled from that moment.

More so now than before, he hates me. He's going to ruin me when he finds out the information I discovered. It wasn't my intention to hurt him. I wanted to build a bridge, get him to love me more, but he ended up hating me in the end. More than he already did.

"You can't keep doing this to her," Francis's voice strains, talking to what I'm guessing is my husband. They lost their friendship last year. Frankie didn't stop trying, but Toby flinched every time at the mention of his name.

"She did this to us. *You* did this to us," Toby's low and lethal tone makes a shiver run up my spine.

"I told you, we didn't fool around. She isn't like that, and I sure as hell am not you or your goddamn brother." The hiss of Frankie's words has me uncomfortable. He's furious, even if his tone sounds lighter than Toby's. The way his French accent thickens with hatred shows how much he's ready to explode.

"She deserves better than you."

"Fuck you. *Leave.*"

"I'm not leaving you alone with her. If she saw what you looked like when you showed up last night, the empty bottle, and your clothes… You're a mess. She doesn't need to see the fact that you let someone use you last night."

Tears prick behind my eyelids, and a whimper escapes me as the words tumble in my mind. Nausea builds up, pinching my insides with a cruel fist. I'm rushing to the bathroom to heave when I hear the door open.

"Ladybug?" Francis's soothing tone rings out. I don't look up to see him when he enters the bathroom. His hands collect my hair, holding it back as my body shakes and tries emptying, but there's nothing there. It can't purge itself of disgust and heartbreak. If it could, I'd have left, nothing would have hurt me, and Toby wouldn't matter. But it doesn't work that way, and Toby is the only person who can single-handedly destroy me.

He rubs soothing circles into my back as my body launches several more times. When I finish, I wipe my mouth with the back of my hand and rise from the floor. Frankie's eyes are laced with concern, his forehead worrisome. It's amazing that a man this attractive and kind wasn't here to be *with* me but rather to take care of me.

"You okay, sweetheart?"

Placing my hands under the running water, I scrub them until they redden. Even then, I rub them more and more until they hurt. Once they're clean, I try for my face, but the sobs break loose, and I'm a mess. He doesn't look away or show pity. The only thing he offers is comfort. He's too nice, and I hate it. Being around someone as cruel as my husband, you get used to not having much kindness directed toward you, so when it's offered, it's as polarizing as happiness.

I'm reduced to the sorrow that haunts me and the love that conquers me.

He wraps me into his arms and holds me. Bet Toby ran off somewhere. He could never stick around for the tough shit. Unlike he claims, he's just like the men he hates most. Disloyal. Weak. Childish.

"It's going to be okay. You are strong and resilient." He pulls away enough to lay a kiss on my forehead, and when we pull apart, the venom-filled gaze of my husband interrupts.

"How fucking charming," he bites out. His expression is nearly expressionless. The only thing that gives him away is his eyes. They're always liquid hate when he's angry. They shine in a dark light, letting me know he's anything but happy.

"Ignore him," Frankie says, not looking back at the man he once called a friend. "He's in a pissy mood because he fell asleep before he got to shower last night." It's then that I look behind him, but he looks like his normal fucked-up self. Clean, fresh pressed pants, and button-up. Nothing new.

"Worried you'll see the woman I fucked left on me, Joey?" It's a taunt, but it's so much more with the expression he's wearing. He wants me to know I'm unworthy of him, but that's not true. It's *him* who's unworthy of me.

He doesn't get to be with other women and act like the jealous husband.

Not anymore.

"No, I'm worried the man I fucked last night stuck around," I jab, narrowing my eyes. Today feels different. The battleground between us has opened up a pit, and instead of standing on the sidelines, hoping my guns outmaneuver his, I'm jumping in, hashing it out with my own two hands. He won't win.

If he wants me back, he can fucking earn me.

Toby takes two steps forward, but as Frankie stiffens and moves me out of his reach, I smile, making sure Toby sees he hasn't won.

"Don't worry, honey," I mock. "I made sure he wore protection."

Toby's nostrils flare and his jaw clenches, and for the first time in a year, I haven't seen him look more attractive. There's something arousing about a man who wants to kill the person who has touched what is his. Almost as sexy as a man who takes what is his and never lets go.

Too bad Toby can't be the latter. We'd never be in this mess if he'd just listened and took what he wanted.

He turns and leaves, but not before he gives one last scathing glare. That's more emotion than he's offered me in ages. It's almost adrenaline-inducing; something I want more of now I know which buttons to push.

"That was really fucking stupid," Francis hisses after the bedroom door slams, more than likely splintering. That door has taken a beating over the last year. I'm lucky it is still attached to its hinges.

"He had it coming," I complain, rubbing my temples. The discomfort, nausea, and disappointment laced with the adrenalin release has me in so much agony.

"You should drink some water, eat some food, and rest, Ladybug."

"You're probably right, but I have to work tonight. And whether or not I got wasted last night, I don't have a choice."

"Going to tell me why you drank your life away? That's not like you," he chastises lightly, trying to not sound as disappointed as he must feel.

"I went and saw Loren."

Francis's face sobers, almost like he knew this would eventually happen. In retrospect, it's his fault since he's the one who mentioned her and told me the entire story. Good lord, the story Toby, Lo, and her husband Jase had, it's pretty insane.

"You shouldn't have done that," he remarks, pinching the bridge of his nose. His shoulders sag a bit, and I'm almost regretful that I betrayed his confidence this way. He asked me to promise him I wouldn't reach out if he told me their story.

I lied.

I broke it.

I regret nothing.

Well, not nothing. I regret hurting him.

"I had to. After everything we experienced, I needed to know what made her special. Why did he stick around, love her, care for her, yet abandon me?! What makes her so fucking special!" I hiss, tears pooling once again. I despised how weak love has made me. Hated the fact that Wesley could not have ever hurt me this badly while Toby did so on the daily.

"She's off-limits, Josephine," he growls, showing me just how pissed he is with his eyes. The way he grimaces and bows his head is almost worse than betraying myself by doing it.

"She has a baby, Francis."

"Yes, and it's none of your fucking business."

He's right. Except for the most important part. It's half of my husband. And after the expression on his face, I know he's not unaware of that tidbit.

"It is. Biologically, yes, that child is Toby's."

He scrunches his face and turns. Pacing back and forth, he fists his palms with heated anger. After several back and forth strides, he raises and connects a fist with the wall, making a loud fucking sound. All of ten seconds pass before Toby bounds back in here. Fury and worry strain across his face, reminding me of the husband I've lost. He's still there. Hidden, but there.

"What the fuck?!" His words come out as an accusation, looking over me and then glaring at Francis. "Did you—"

"No!" I hurry and reassure him. "Just got some bad news."

He looks over me as if he doesn't believe me. Of course, he doesn't. Why would he? I constantly lie to him. He grips Francis by the arm. "Nothing makes you this angry. Not unless it involves Gray."

When Francis refuses to look at Toby, I make sure to peer

elsewhere. My lying skills, in spite of Toby, are great. My capabilities when it's something like this? Below average.

He sidesteps his best friend, and for the first time in nearly a year, he touches my chin. "Tell me, *Sous*," he practically spits with the calmest tone known to man, using a pet name that makes my thighs clench automatically. "What is it that he's furious about? We both know it isn't your best friend, or you'd be more upset."

I attempt to shake from his grip and piercing eyes, but he holds me steady. He even leans in closer. Too close. Way too fucking close. I can smell him. That intoxicating scent that brought me peace and salvation once upon a time. It's so spicy and male and Toby. It's him, and I couldn't imagine a more potent scent.

"H-He," I try, looking at Francis behind him.

"Don't look at him," Toby criticizes, gripping my chin harder. My lips part with the sensation of him touching me. "What did I tell you? Your eyes belong here." In his eyes, a familiar heat simmers. It's something I thought died long ago, withering away just like our love, but here it is, festering in those hazel eyes that have scolded me more times than my own father's.

"L-Loren," I stutter, knowing as soon as her name leaves my lips, it'd be the end of this skin-to-skin connection that feels like home when it should be anything but. No matter how much he has hurt me, he's still my comfort. My love for him runs scarily deep. No matter how riddled with diseases and decay, it's filled to the brim for this man, and I can't seem to let go.

His hand falls from me, his eyes almost appearing haunted.

"So you went there with malcontent?" he grits, his jaw once again hard. "Did you *hurt* her?"

I stare aghast at the accusation. *Hurt her?* Was he fucking joking? She hurt *me*. Not with just the information of biology, but with her power over *my* husband. How could he think I'd incite pain on that woman and her child?

"You bastard," I growl. "You goddamn bastard." My hands fist and fly to his chest. I know it's wrong. I know no one should ever raise a hand to anyone. I know it'll cause damage that isn't physical, but I can't stop the pain flowing through me toward his chest. "I hate you! So much! Fuck you!" The words are hysteric, just like me and the tears drowning me. The pain is vital and real. The ache ripping open into a cavern of self-loathing and disgust.

"Joey," Francis tries, but my vision is too blurry. The tears won't stop, and the hurt won't ease, and the hatred won't go away.

Toby grips my fists and holds them as if they're as precious as they are despicable. If he knew just how much damage these hands have caused me in the last year, would he care? He doesn't even know I started cutting again. That my mental health sank because of his lack of care. His tactless cheating and unredeemable behavior left me on the verge of suicide, but he doesn't see me.

The ice queen. The frigid. The *invisible*.

CHAPTER 31

LIFE HANDS YOU CARDS.

Pick a card, any card! It doesn't warn you they are placed for our ruin, and it's up to us to make sure we win and they do not.

"Peaches," Jase says, smacking my mind back to focus. I'm cooking street tacos. Whether Ace will admit it or not, he lives for coming home during his breaks to eat my food. He's jaded, my baby boy. Since Jase and I fell apart six years ago, he has been this hollow version of himself. It's only when we're alone and watching movies that my little man comes out. It's been a long time since I've seen him smile and even longer since I've witnessed him laugh.

The only time he truly breaks free is when no one is watching and he's outside with Jazzy and Lev. Jazz is a teen now, it hasn't been as worrisome as I'd have imagined. She's soft-spoken, kind, and needy.

It only hurts wondering if all the pain Jase and I caused will ruin her for when she's older. Codependency has its downfalls. One of them being falling in love. When Jase is gone for more than a few hours at nights, she gets skittish.

She has a lot of friends, and when they fight, the world tends to be ending in her eyes.

It scares me for her future.

Maybe I'm a glutton for anxious thoughts, but all I want for my babies is happiness.

"You okay there?" Jase muses, carrying a dirty Lev. He's smudged from head to toe in ink.

"I'm about to ask you the same," I say on a laugh. Lev hides behind his dad, and I know he's been caught doing something he shouldn't be. "What did you get yourself into, mister?" Lev refuses to look at me, and Jason just chuckles.

"As you can tell, he's been sneaking into the office and playing with my signature stamp." He kisses our boy on his nose, and my heart melts. It's like Lev reset something in Jase. Even while his temples gray a little, showing his age, he's taking being a new-again dad with ease, and I'm somehow more in love with him.

These past few years, I struggled. The overwhelming feeling of not being enough killed me. That's why he stopped running Collins & Co, stepping down so I could become a full-time chef. It took him time to adjust, but it was well worth it.

Counseling saved us.

Love fixed us.

Our pain brought us closer.

When Jase places loud kisses on Lev's cheeks, he giggles and stops hiding. "There's my little prince."

"Mama," he coos, and my heart feels like it's being squeezed in all the right ways.

"That's right, baby," I say, kissing his little nose. Diving into his sides with my fingers, I make him break out into a fit of laughter.

When I look past Jase, I see my other baby boy, who claims he's not a baby anymore. "Hey, baby boy." He rolls his eyes, and I melt. He never does that anymore. It's like the world—my damage—hid the mundane emotions in a barrier of hatred.

Jase turns to greet Ace, but his expressionless mask is back in place, and I'm still unsure how to fix any of that. It hurts to see them against each other. "Will you wash up Lev?" I ask him, wanting a moment with Jase to tell him what happened today.

Or rather, what has been unfolding for a while without really realizing it. After Toby signed *Su Casa* over to me three years ago, my life changed for the better. Jase had finally transferred the reins to Jeremiah, and it was my turn to work. Somehow, the business fell into my lap.

I wanted to reach out to tell him thank you and ask him why, after all this time, did he believe in me.

The worst part, I wanted to tell him about Lev.

His son.

Tears prick my eyes as Ace grabs his little brother. His mask doesn't drop until he's nearing the corner, then he's like the rest of us, wrapped around Lev's little finger. The power that little boy has over us all is freeing in every way.

Jason grabs my hips and kisses me, taking my mind away for a breath. He consumes me, leaving me breathless as his lips own mine once again. It's like this every time—my body gets hot, and my heart beats a little too quickly.

I'm madly in love with him.

My heart beats to watch his do the same.

"Fuck, I missed you today."

"I missed you, too," I whisper against his lips. He gives me one more before smacking my ass. When I yelp, a mischievous smile comes over him, and I'm stuck in my mind, wondering how I could be in this place.

Happy.

In love.

Alive.

"I met someone today," I mention when he starts setting the table. Since we went to counseling and struggled through our issues, we made it our mission to have dinners together—all of us—always talking. No phones or technology are allowed.

The moments around this table are just us.

Our family.

"Yeah? Is that why you were gone?" he asks with a smile.

"How—"

"Came home to surprise you with a little one-on-one time," he teases with a smirk. God, I've missed that smirk. We rarely have time to fool around with Lev so still young and disastrous. He gets into *everything*. When we do, it's usually a fast fucking against the shelves in the pantry or him eating me out while I'm on the dryer, pretending to do laundry. As always, though, my favorite times are when Lev is at Millie's, and Jase spends every waking moment inside me.

It's like we're teens again, unable to stop pushing boundaries, not wanting to spare a moment.

"Don't pout, Peaches. I have it on good authority that Lev, Jazzy, and Ace have a date with their grandparents tomorrow." My face heats, and he saunters over to me, taking my mouth again, sending shivers up and down my spine. "And tomorrow, when they're gone, I'm going to fuck you so hard, you'll be feeling me for days."

A moan shakes free, and it almost makes me forget why I needed Ace to take Lev. Shaking my lustful fog that Jase has no issue putting me in, I press a hand to his chest to force some distance. He's the best distraction, but a distraction nonetheless.

"For the past few weeks, I've been talking with a local chef. Her and her husband are looking to expand into Hollow Ridge, and she asked me for my opinion." His eyebrows shoot up, almost as if he's as surprised as me.

"Why you?"

"She had the same teacher as me in culinary school," I say,

wondering out loud. "Which maybe piqued my interest a little."

He laughs lightly. "That or you were happy someone cares about food as much as you do."

Smacking his arm softly, I watch him grab a finger full of guac and pop it in his mouth. "You're incorrigible."

"Yet you love me," he teases.

"You're distracting me, Jase," I complain, shooing him away from the food.

"Okay, Peaches. Talk," he mocks, leaning against the kitchen table. His legs are widened, lazy, and fogging my brain a little too much. Closing my eyes for resolve, I finally open them to a smirking Jase with that tongue-in-cheek look I adore so much. "So, what happened?" He gestures for me to keep going.

"She showed up as I was ordering and told me she had to use the bathroom. After a half hour, I got nervous and went inside, and she wasn't there. She made a huge deal about this meetup and then basically stood me up."

"That's odd," he muses, scratching his head. "Did she seem on drugs? Maybe one of Nate's—"

"No, no, nothing like that. She was young, seemed really nice, but something made her not come back to the table."

"Maybe she was too nervous to meet her idol?"

"Perhaps," I accept with a shrug. "But when I went on Facebook to ask her what was up, her profile was deactivated."

"Well, if there's a red flag, that would be it," Jase sounds out, and when I go to respond, Lev comes running into the kitchen in his little dinosaur jammies and wet brown hair.

During these moments, he looks so much like Toby that it physically hurts.

Would he forgive me if it came out about Lev?

Would he hate me more?

Would he want to take him away from me?

My heart shatters with that. No, that'll never happen. Not ever.

"Mama!" Lev yells and bounds into my arms. "Ace-y said I could have ice cream after dinner if I was good in the tub."

"Were you good, little prince?" Jason asks from beside me. Lev looks at his dad with a toothy grin and nods.

"He only soaked the entire ground," Ace admits. "I'd say, he's a charming little prince." I smile at my son, seeing the light and dark battle inside his ocean eyes, wondering when they became so dreary and dejected. He's not the little boy who drank hot cocoa and cuddled with me when I was sad.

He's tragic and beautiful, and I wish I could fix the past and make his heart glow again. He'll find the person who does that, and when he does, I'll be here. I'll always be here.

"Tacos?" Jazzy asks, slipping under Ace's arm. She's grown so much in the past five years. She's sassy and spunky, but also quiet and reserved.

It's like she's in the middle of the battle of her life, and all for something I can't offer her, so all I can do is try to understand and guide her. But we're not close. Not like her and Ace, and definitely not like her and her father.

Our dynamic is hard, but I'll never stop trying.

When we're all seated at the table with the tortillas I made from scratch sitting in the center, and the garnishes and extras sitting in a circle around it, we all dig in. It isn't until we're all into our second and third tacos that Jazzy speaks up.

"Bobbie called today," she admits. The immediate feeling that overtakes me is dread. But she wouldn't call Jazzy to tell us Nate is dead. She wouldn't… right? Heat and cold fight for power over my skin. Heat from worry, cold from that numbness that always tries to burst free of the confines I've locked it in.

"Yeah, she said Nate is doing better, but it's Toby she's worried about." My eyes burn with awareness. Bobbie and I connected three years ago. When Toby gave me the restaurant, she reached out, telling me that he fell into his vices. He'd been going to Alcoholics Anonymous for months, and the only step he couldn't quite accept was making amends. Step eight. She reached out because Nate and Toby stayed close, being accountable together, trying to overcome.

Is Toby drinking again?

Did his spiral happen because I ruined him?

Choices.

We all have them.

Why does guilt make me believe I forced some of his?

"Why's that, baby?" I ask, not hinting to anything, but the way Jase grips his glass tells me I'm not being as subtle as I want to be. Regret for what happened with Toby eats me alive constantly. How could it not? I gave birth to his child.

While Jase and I decided not to have a test done, I took

one when Lev was two and started looking more like Toby than Jase. When Jason found the papers, we fought a lot. We ended up going back to therapy because, at that moment, I broke his trust.

Now, Jase accepts that Toby is biologically Lev's father, but he is his dad. Always will be.

"Uncle Frankie says he doesn't go home sometimes and disappears randomly. Bobbie only confirmed the same. She has tried getting in contact, but he ignores her. While she doesn't believe she has a duty to keep pushing, she cares about him."

I nod, wondering when my daughter got close to Francis, Bobbie, and Nate, all while I feel out of the loop.

"How's Nate?" I ask, deflecting the attention from the taboo subject of my ex-best friend.

"He's thirty-seven days clean," she answers after she swallows some Pepsi. I stare at my daughter who mirrors me in every way but our hair. She's blonde like her father, but as she ages, she's looking less and less like me and growing into a beautiful young woman. It makes me choke up to think that in only five years, she'll be leaving for college, too.

"That's good," I try, tears blurring my vision.

When will the pain become easier to bear?

Will I ever overcome the havoc I brought upon the ones I love?

Can I fix my soul and spread the tide, in hopes I won't be eternally damned?

My face flames, feeling someone watching me, and when

I look up, it's Jase.

Inhale.

Exhale.

Breathe.

He moves his lips with my mantra, and a few salty droplets leave my eyes.

"*I love you*," he mouths, and I fall in love again and again, wondering how two lost souls could break so much, yet always find each other again.

CHAPTER 32

TOBY

AS SHE BRUSHES HER TEETH, I PACE THE FLOOR outside the bathroom. Not sure how I did, but I convinced Frankie to leave without any more arguments or fighting. Told him—promised—I wouldn't hurt her. Not that I'd ever raise my hand to her for anything other than what she wanted. She liked being manhandled a little in the bedroom, but I'd never physically hurt her otherwise.

Why did she see Lo? Why do I hate my best friend? Why does my blood boil with the need to fuck my wife and remind her that no one will ever be me and can't satisfy her like I do?

My body is hot as hell, my skin inflamed, and the hangover

hammering into my head doesn't help matters. I'm so pissed I can barely function.

After my girl sobbed, holding onto me in a way I haven't felt in a long time, I couldn't hold back. It's like her icy exterior defrosted and started to melt for me. She showed me more passion and pain in those five minutes than she's offered since our separation.

She's so fucking beautiful.

I hate it.

I despise how radiant she is even while being a mess. It's insanity, knowing she'll always own this important part of me.

She does. She owns me, every fucking inch.

Even last night when Jameson helped me fuck Bry, it was Joey I was fucking in my mind. She has the power. All of it. She could destroy me, and sometimes, that's all I want.

Her anger brought me some type of satisfaction. The depraved kind that shouldn't thrive on such emotions. I can't help the way it got me hard, knowing she was unreasonably jealous that I cared enough about Lo. I can't stop that either. It was built into me at a young age. It's something that lives in me and never died even when our friendship did.

I hear the water shut off, and a moment later, my wife walks through the door. Her eyes are sunken and red, but for the most part, they're not teary. She's such a goddamn mess, and I haven't seen her look more beautiful. I can't help the part of me that drives me forward. There's no resisting the urge to touch her face, cup it, and rub circles. I'm losing. I'm fucking losing this battle with my heart. But she doesn't look happy or proud. She's back to being that woman with all the walls, the hardened ice queen who feels nothing. Her scars may be visible, but that thick scar tissue around her heart is as numb as she is.

If she didn't remind me so much of Lo, I'd probably care. But I can't be that guy again. *A second choice.* I can't leave either. Not just because of her father's threats, but because losing her feels like a death wish. She's vital to me. Not a moment goes by when she isn't fighting her way into my mind. I love her. I hate her. I wish we were in a better place.

She deserves better.

I deserve better.

This is so fucked up.

Seeing her with Frankie broke something in me last night. It couldn't have just been him with her and the chance of them fucking, even if he denies every second of it. It was the fact that my wife was *feeling*. She was *broken* and instead of *me* holding her, fixing her, and being the man she needs, it was *him*.

He held her.

He eased her hurt.

He fixed what I couldn't.

I stood by like a fucking onlooker the entire time and that hurt. No one gets to touch her like that. No one gets what is mine or loves what isn't theirs to love.

She's mine, goddammit.

"Why are you glaring at me?" she mumbles, her voice

wobbly with emotion as I tentatively go to hold her face between my palms. And fuck if that doesn't ignite something deep inside me. She's something else. The power she wields over me is unreal.

"I'm not," I say, bringing some of my own walls back up. When she shuts down, I have to do the same. If I care when she doesn't, she hurts me. Since she never feels, I'm always suffering in the pain of being alone. She abandons me every time she escapes into her mind.

She hurts me more than Lo ever could, and if she knew that she held that much power, maybe she'd destroy me entirely.

"Are too. You have that big-ass wrinkled forehead and narrowed eyes. It's how you look at me when you leave and fuck random women."

The word *fuck* and *random women* shouldn't be used in the same sentence, coming out of her mouth, no less.

I drop my hand from her face, knowing that if I continue this physical connection between us, I'll cave. Why I hold on so unapologetically, I'm not sure.

I'm just waiting for her to leave me, too.

That's what they all do.

Toss me away.

Choose better paths. Find something easier. Leave.

"Why did you meet up with Loren?" I ask, stopping her questioning eyes. Her face scrunches like she's even worse off than moments ago. I want to hug her and reassure her, but that would only create a false sense of comfort. Lies. I've cheated on her. She cheated on me. We're a hot-ass mess.

"You've always been so obsessed," she admits, her voice small and uncertain. I did that. I took a strong and fierce woman and turned her into one who doesn't feel that anymore. How could I ruin such a beautiful part of her?

"I loved her," I whisper. The only admission she'll get.

"*Love*," she corrects. "You *love* her and always will. I'm not sure why I tried to compare. There's nothing like a man's first love, the one who got away, the one they'll always pine after." The words are bitter and empty as though she has every feeling toward them but refuses to allow them to filter through. I don't blame her. For the past year, I've used every word of hers against her.

"I needed to know what made her special. It helps that I work for you, that I'm a chef who went to the same school and had the same professor. It was easy asking for help. Seeing if she had any advice for me to finally leave."

My breath comes out ragged, the sharp intake of air as her words hit something vital inside me, warning me I've finally lost. She gave up. The battle is no more. The pang of hurt that slices me shouldn't cut so deep, but it keeps going until it breaks through the bone protecting the lifeless heart that beats inside.

She wants to leave.

She plans to leave.

She's going to leave.

The words play on repeat in my head, smashing my

thoughts of everything away. She's not going to fight anymore. What did I expect? For her to live with our choices and keep the agreement to fuck who we want? Obviously, she wants more. Maybe her new fuck buddy showers her with love and orgasms. Maybe his dick is bigger than mine. Maybe he's what she's leaving me for.

Rage blinds me as I cup her face again. My eyes slice into her, needing to get deep, needing to hit it where it matters, no matter the pain. Her chest rises with a quick breath. She worries her lip, and I watch in amazement as her eyes fly to mine. They're so telling. They give me what I need when I can't stand her numbness. They melt for me, giving me life when there's nothing to offer.

"No one will ever be me, Josephine."

The words are harsher than intended, but as I said, pain will come whether I'm opposed to it or not.

"Heard that one before, Tobias." She raises her eyebrows. "And guess what? I'm not fucking impressed with what I get from you."

Walking us both backward to the chaise lounge, I push her down gently, guiding her body to where mine covers it. "It seems you've forgotten how good I am to you when it's beneficial for me."

She smacks my palm away. "That's the key ingredient, isn't it? *Beneficial for you.* I'm done with this shit. Get off me."

It hurts to hear those words. But with her past and what's she experienced, I don't push. I rise up on my feet and watch as tears gloss her eyes.

Fuck.

I can't believe I pushed her to tears. Did I break her trust again? Did I lose all the progress I finally gained?

"I'm sorry." I mean it. It's sincere. Her trust is something I'd never betray. Her heart, I've obviously lost that battle. But her body? Never. That's hers. It's her choice.

"Don't be… I just…" she sniffles. "You were with someone else last night. Having you that close, I hate it."

I swallow back the dryness. She's right. I'm a prick. "No one is you either, Gumby."

Her eyes connect with mine with a ferocity that hurts to see. "Don't fucking call me that. You lost that right when you stepped out on me."

"Stepped out on you?!" I holler, unable to refrain from raising my voice. "You *fucked* Francis first. You cheated *first*. I just followed in your footsteps."

"Fuck you," she hisses. "I'm done with this. You're like a fucking tornado, Tobias. You spin me around and around, leaving a chaotic mess of me, and then when you're done, you apologize. It's bullshit. You are bullshit."

She heads toward our room, and a few minutes later, I follow. I can't let her leave like this. Not while she's upset and angry. I've walked away so many times. I've hurt her, and now I need to see what makes her stay.

It's not my money.

It's apparently not my dick.

It has to be something like her dad threatening her too. She's no Lo.

She doesn't stay for love. No one in their right mind would.

"Go away," she growls as I close the door behind us. My eyes roam her lithe body. The wide set of her hips, her long legs, and when she turns, her bare breasts overwhelm me. She's fucking gorgeous. It's why I keep my distance when she changes or showers. I need to be strong because seeing her without clothing is too fucking maddening. Not just to my dick, but to my soul. She shreds through me.

She shouldn't be allowed to be naked. Not when passions are heavy, especially when they're the angry kind as it brings me little control.

She holds all the power. She always has. It's why I'm not jumping her right now, reclaiming what's mine and fucking her into submission. But, God, I want to.

"Fuck," I breathe, loving that the freckles I've fallen in love with still go beyond her cheeks and nose. Her body is a masterpiece. She's so beautiful and so goddamn mine. Even if we've both forgotten that fact.

"Don't come any closer." She sighs, and it's in those words that I hear the weakness. Either I need to test this limit and touch her, or she needs to smack me.

My feet move before I can process what's happening, and she doesn't stop me. I halt several steps away and wait for her to tell me to leave her. We have that trust. She knows she can tell me no. It's something I love about us.

When my feet touch hers, she bites her lip. It's an expression I've missed. Our hatred is turmoil, how it burns and ignites by contact. We're the gasoline, and the fire is our passion.

We're a disaster together, but apart, we're non-existent. I need her. She needs me.

"Tell me to stop, Joey. Tell me to fucking stop." The heat of my words has her licking her lips. There's something in her expression. It boils beneath the surface, and I want to touch and taste it. See if it burns as much as it looks like it will.

She doesn't say anything, but she tilts her head to give me access. I bend and kiss her throat. Fuck. The taste of her is so fresh and lively. She's a goddamn treat after the staved dryness I've experienced. I don't kiss women. Joey being my only exception.

Just as going down on them isn't allowed, kissing isn't either. My relations with them were strictly meant to hurt Joey. It had no value in connection. It did nothing but make me loathe myself further.

She can't hate me any more than I hate myself. Of that, I'm now certain.

I could die and be at ease, but then she'd have to live with my ruin.

No one deserves that burden. Even if she asked for it.

"This means nothing," she whimpers. "Hate can feel just as good as love."

And with those words, she's walking into our bathroom and leaving me with the hardest erection I've had in ages.

Fuck. That resilience. It's what drew me to her. It hasn't ebbed even an ounce. She's just a good fucking liar.

So am I.

CHAPTER 33

PAST

JOEY

"I CAN'T BELIEVE YOU." I HEAR WESLEY BEFORE I see him. Why did the front doorman let him through? Didn't Francis tell them he wasn't allowed here?

He wasn't allowed to breathe in the same vicinity because no one wanted an STD. Especially when one walks straight through the front door.

"I'm sorry, you've mistaken me for someone who cares about what the hell you're talking about," I bite out, gripping the *Hollow Ridge Post* and reading all the new shit about my dad and Marsha. They're campaigning for senate. Mayor of Hollow Ridge wasn't enough, so they had to keep rising higher.

Guess the power-hungry whore finally convinced Dad.

"This, Josey!" he yells, and I don't spare him a glance. My eyes are stuck on an image where I'm photoshopped in. Literally. No one could say this is me with them. For one, I don't go home, and two, it's been weeks since we spoke, and this outfit is the one Marsha wore at dinner that horrible night six weeks ago.

Those fuckers.

They knew I wouldn't campaign with them and make them seem perfect. Why lie for them when they do it much better than me?

"Stop ignoring me, Joey. Fuck," Wesley complains. I almost forget he's here. Folding the newspaper, feeling much older than my nineteen years, I see him standing there right beside me. His hair is disheveled, his eyes red, which for once aren't because he's high, and his clothes are in a state of disarray. Seems like our split did way more for me than it did for this loser.

Rolling my eyes at his disheveled appearance, I set the newspaper down on the coffee nook and stand. "Why are you here?" It comes out more scathing than intended, but he doesn't deserve anything less. He starts for me, holding some document in his hands, and I'm already bored.

He doesn't get to waltz into my new home, one where happiness thrives and cheaters don't exist.

Wasted time, that's all I got from this idiot.

"This," he hisses, nearly crumpling the paper in his hands. "What the fuck is it?!" It's an accusation, but one which makes zero sense.

How the hell would I know?

Am I a magician who conjures answers out of my ass? VOILA! Answers.

No, dipshit. That's not how any of this works.

"You ask me as if I'm aware of what you're going on about. I'm not. So, leave."

"That's just great, Joey. Just fucking superb." He sets the paper down. "Don't act like you don't know that you sent your marriage certificate to my apartment." *Not yours, fuckface.* It was in my name.

Wait. Did he say *marriage certificate?* Out of all the words he said, those are definitely the strangest. He couldn't have. I'm not married. Not... *married.*

"Did you say marriage certificate?" I balk. The information trickles through my veins like spiderwebs weaving. There's no—

"That's what this says right here."

—way.

My eyes widen, and I feel them trying to pop out of my head as I grip the paper he discarded. The paper, unlike most, is fancy and thick. The watermark of Las Vegas all over it and the holographic emblem on top confirms how *not fake* this document is.

What the actual fuck?

"When did you get married? The week we broke up? Or were you so enamored with this Tobias Hayes that you didn't wait even a day?"

I start to interrupt him because there's no way I would have married anyone, especially Toby.

"No, let me tell you since the paper shows. This was filed three days after we broke up. *Three days, Joey.* God, I knew you were in your head while we were together, but it seems this Toby loser was probably seeing you for ages, and I was none the wiser."

"Oh, fuck off. I didn't cheat on you. This must be some joke from Dad. I didn't get married."

He scoffs, folding his arms across his chest. It's then I notice how gaunt he's gotten since we broke up. What, did he finally realize how big of a douche he was?

Only took him two years.

Too bad it was a little too late for us both. I'm happy here with Gray and Francis. They're kind and supportive, and they push me to strive for more. Hell, even working at *Mi Casa* is nice. There are no strings—other than a five-year obligatory contract—that keep me here. I like it.

Working for someone like Toby was nothing I was prepared for. Unlike his outside demeanor, he's an amazing manager. His books are perfection, his employees are absolutely wonderful, and he doesn't belittle me unless it's in private.

Which is a daily occurrence, but almost like some creepy thing I expect.

"Well, thought you should know about this," he mutters unhappily. "Figured you already knew and celebrated." He looks around the McMansion and grinds his teeth. "Must be a rich sugar daddy with nice digs—"

"Do you talk to all women this way, or is Ladybug just special?" Francis scolds, joining the commotion between me and Wes. His eyes are dark and hardened. The usual soft exterior of the man who's saved me from being homeless is nowhere to be found. He looks two seconds away from ripping Wes apart. If not with his handsomely striking looks, it'd be with the power behind his words.

"You must be Toby, Josey's husband."

My mouth falls agape at the words Wes purposely unloads. Francis's eyes shoot to mine. Intrigue and betrayal glittering in the pretty gray storms residing there.

I shake my head, hoping he can read the *he's insane* look. It has to be a joke. Has to be.

"Ah, no. I'm Francis. Her, as you blatantly slurred, sugar daddy." He adds a thick French accent and directs a saucy look my way. It warms me. Since moving in here, Francis and I decided to stay friends and save Gray the hurt of seeing her best friend and Dad doing more than just talking. I mean, it'd be hot and sensual, no doubt, but Gray means a great deal to me. Him, too.

Wes's face is comical, his jaw open and wide. "You really are a whore—" he starts, but Francis stops him.

"It's time for you to leave. We don't appreciate name-calling in this household, especially not from the likes of a beach bum."

I smile gratefully at Francis, loving that he said something before I could make an ass of myself and charge Wes.

"Goodbye, Wesley. Again. Next time, just don't."

"Josey—"

"No. This conversation and any remnants of our friendship are over. Leave."

He walks out, and I watch as the two guards make sure he's escorted off the premises. Francis doesn't let anything slip.

"What did he mean when he said *husband?*" His eyebrow hitches up, and it's almost like he bites the inside of his cheek.

"Honestly, I don't know. He gave me this document and said it showed up at his place. It looks legit enough, but I don't recall ever getting married." Handing him the piece of paper, I watch as Francis's eyes widen. Awareness and apprehension lick his features, coating them with disbelief and annoyance. It's the same expression he had at that dinner with Toby. The one where he fucked me and ran off.

I thought it'd be different. That we'd hit it off. He called me *his,* and since then, I can't tell you how many times my BOB brought me pleasure with him in mind. That night blew my expectations. *More.* That's what I want.

"You married Toby," he whispers, his voice solemn. The subversiveness hurts to hear. It almost slices through me like my favorite knife does through vegetables.

"It must be a joke. My dad has been on my case, wanting me to help with his campaign by getting married, so he probably did this. Made me have a leg to stand on. Maybe it's his attempt to force my hand."

"I promise you this, Ladybug. This is real. It's as legitimate as it gets. You're married. To my best friend, no less." His face pales. "Why wouldn't he tell me?" The hurt isn't something he can mask. It's right there on his forehead and in the long frown he probably doesn't realize he's wearing. It's in the way his eyes seem lost and perturbed, but mostly, it's in the way he holds himself like it's ruining everything.

"He couldn't have... could he? Why wouldn't he say something?"

"Maybe it was a game. Either way, you two need to discuss this, and I definitely need a fucking drink."

I stare at him with a deep sadness. Disappointing people you care about sucks, especially when they never swear and can't resist the urge. He lets the document fall to the floor before heading to his wet bar. Fuck. I really messed up this time and don't even know what to do.

"Y-YOU'RE WHAT?" GRAY ASKS AN HOUR LATER after she gets home, her face pale, a perfect match to her father's. Almost like she's as shocked as I am.

"Married. Toby and I apparently got married that night in Vegas."

"Jesus Christ, Joey. This is insane. You married my uncle."

"I'm just as shocked as you are," I grab the bottle of Goose I stole from Francis's bar, bringing it to my lips. "I really fucked myself over. Who would willingly marry a man like that?" But even with my scathing words, I don't feel them. Toby is a dick for sure, but there's something underlying there. A hurt man.

Secrets. Maybe even some heartbreak. Either way, if he loves as well as his body fucks, he's got to be a good-ass guy.

"He's not so bad," she muses. "When I was younger, I used to tell Ace that I was going to marry him." The words tumble out, but Ace... that name. Ace must be that childhood love of hers.

"Is that so?" I ignore the nagging inside me that seeks more information. She'll tell me her story when she's ready and I'll be here for her.

"Yeah." She giggles and takes the bottle from my hand, taking a swig and choking on the fumes. "Uncle Toby always took care of me. I was in love."

My heart feels warm at her words, and it has nothing to do with the alcohol.

"I guess it made sense, especially since my mom hated me and my father was dead. Toby and Jase were stand-in father figures to me. I loved them. So much." A tear slips free. "Lost them both so easily though."

I take the bottle from her and chug for a second. There's not enough booze in the world to mask this girl's hurt. Hell, if not for the booze and my hardened interior, I'd be her. A sad mess of tears and resentment. But that's what happens when you harden yourself to pain.

Not even the good stuff slips through.

"Reconnect, Gray."

"Can't. I don't want to be a burden. I don't look like my mother, but I'm a reminder of all the havoc she wreaked on everyone."

283

"Try. Especially before you run back off to France."

"H-How'd you know?"

"You had pamphlets on the table in the dining room. Figured you had your mind set on starting afresh."

She nods solemnly. "I don't want to see Ace again."

"Then don't. See Jase and his wife. Go reconnect. What if this is your last chance?"

"You're right. I'm scared."

"Fear is for the fish. Be you and fierce. Don't let anyone stop you. Not even some tool with a silly name like Ace."

She chuckles and nods at me.

We drink until the bottle is empty, which doesn't take long since it wasn't full to start with. I'm riding a buzz, and Gray is passed out. Who said drunk texting was for the birds?

Got some news today, I send to my boss. Fuck. He is my boss now. Isn't he? We have this mutual nothingness. Like we don't talk, fuck, or anything in between. We exist, but right now, with a fifth of vodka swimming through me, I want him. It comes and goes. That's what my vibrator is for, to satisfy the ache Toby left me with.

Is this about work?

No.

Then why are you texting me, Sous? My body warms at the name, and I can even hear his deep timbre saying it. Fuck. Fuck. Fuck. I'm so far gone for this asshole, and he has no idea.

It pertains to you, dick. Shit. Maybe calling your boss a dick isn't the brightest idea. I never said I was the brightest light bulb in the package, though.

Call me dick again, Sous. I'll definitely show you how true that statement is. My body warms and fucking boils moments later as I remember him taking me against my car and telling me I'm his. But he didn't keep me. Maybe I'm only his for when he's ready and willing. Wouldn't be a surprise. Men like Toby, with possessive streaks, only want to be controlling when it's in their best interest.

We're married, Toby. Did you know that? It's all I could offer. A Band-Aid. Telling him I want his dick inside me isn't an option. He's my boss, and this job has been phenomenal. Not just an experience, but for my mood. Everyone loves my cooking. The restaurant's ratings have skyrocketed because of me. If that's not an ego boost, then I'm not sure what is.

Instead of a text message, my phone lights up. Toby is calling, and I really want to be a teenager and chuck the phone across the room. As tempting as that is, Gray is sleeping next to me, so I have to be quiet.

I tiptoe out of the room before I answer. "H-Hello," I mutter, my words a little slurred.

"So, you *are* drunk. I honestly had a heart attack."

"Oh, I'm serious as shit," I mumble. A giggle escapes me, and I have to slap my hand over my mouth.

"Who have you been drinking with, Sous?" It comes out dark and threatening. I can't help but clench my thighs. What the fuck is wrong with me? When did men being demanding dicks turn me on?

"Gray," I say, stifling another laugh.

"She's fucking seventeen. If Francis—"

"He's drinking too," I interrupt.

"With you?" he accuses, sounding all burly and jealous. God, it's so hot. He's so fucking hot. "While I know I'm hot, Sous, I'm your boss, and you probably shouldn't be saying that."

"I said that out loud?" I'm mortified at the slip up. I've been good for so long that I've forgotten what it's like to be reckless.

"Yes. Why is Frankie drinking?"

"He saw our wedding certificate. Seems he's not happy about the outcome."

"Fuck."

"Fuck," I repeat, unable to stop laughing at the way he groans. "Wes." I enunciate the 's' because I'm tripping over the word. "He brought the certificate over. When did we tie the knot, hubbykins?"

"Don't ever fucking call me that again," he grumps on the other end. "Remember Vegas?" His voice is gravelly and wetness pools between my thighs.

"Can't say I do, old man."

A grumble on the other end of the phone has me smiling wide. "Me either. Which means, that's probably when we fucked up."

"Please don't say that word anymore, Toby. It's doing weird things to my body."

"Joey," he complains huskily, and I can imagine his hand between his thighs stroking up and down. A moan slips out, and I can't even stop it. "Fuck. Fuck. Fuck," he grouses, and I'm so hot and bothered, hating and loving vodka with each passing second.

"Come over," I taunt. "Unless you're—"

"Don't finish that fucking sentence."

"Why, old man, can't handle my sass?"

"I can handle you well, Sous. Or do I need to remind you of that?"

"Hmm," I tease. "It's been too long."

"I'll be there in thirty minutes. Don't you fucking move." My phone beeps when he disconnects the call.

I take a picture of myself in one of the guest rooms, only wearing my short shorts and camisole without a bra, and send it to Toby. I'm leaning against the bed, my legs wide.

With the caption: *Like this, old man?*

I bet he's growling.

I love it when he growls.

CHAPTER 34

PAST

JOEY

"YOU NEED TO COME HOME."

"That is *not* my home," I return, hating that I sound as upset as I do. My father grumbles something under his breath, making me clutch my phone tighter.

"If you don't, I'll be disappointed." Like I fucking care at this point, but seeing him with an emotion other than the ones his wife forces onto him is too enticing to ignore.

"Fine. I'll be there in fifteen."

I press my code in the front gate, and as it opens, I almost wish I could destroy it and his perfect storybook house. He thinks that being in this big castle makes him any less sad. He's a very lonely man. His wife doesn't love him, he doesn't love himself, and he's slowly losing my love too.

His heart that used to be full of kindness is now hollow and desolate.

"Miss Moore, so nice to see you," Gareth mutters, I groan, but otherwise ignore him. We don't like each other. He always told on me to Dad when I snuck out.

I enter my old house with a bitterness in my gait, making sure to smack my heels loudly so he's aware I've arrived. He hates noise and unnecessary drama. I'd just gotten the news yesterday that Toby and I are married. While he took it well, I'm not sure why. As I round the dining room, I see him seated with Marsha. When my eyes hit the opposite side of the table where I normally sit, my heart sinks.

Toby.

In the flesh.

"Toby?" I question, watching as his annoyed gaze and posture meet my surprised ones.

"Joey," he addresses me, not giving anything away.

"Sit down, Josephine. We have much to discuss." The scathing glare my dad sends my way makes Marsha smile and never in my life have I wanted to smack a look off someone's face as much as I do now.

I sit next to Toby, putting a hand on his thigh for comfort. It isn't until he stiffens that I realize I've overstepped my boundaries.

"Have you watched the news recently, Josephine?"

"Does a bear shit in the woods?"

Toby coughs into his champagne, and I smile in kind. Fuck these rich dicks. They're horrible to me and expect me to bend over to their every command.

"Josephine," Dad chastises. "Not now."

"Oh, I'm sorry, *Father*. Where are my manners? Does a bear defecate in the forest? Is that better?"

Toby tries really hard and fails to cough over a chuckle, and for some reason, I find that endearing.

"In the Hollow Ridge news yesterday, a story ran."

"When does it not?" The snide remark slips out before I can contain it.

"Would you stop interrupting me?" he hisses. "You're being petulant."

"My bad, should've sent me to somewhere other than Paris then. They speak their minds, the total opposite of those brain-dead guppies such as your wife."

"Enough!" he yells, using a voice I haven't heard since I was really little. Toby switches places and squeezes *my* thigh. "You *will* listen to me, Josephine."

"Okay, *Father*," I mutter unenthusiastically.

"News broke out that you eloped with Mr. Hayes over here."

Now it's my turn to choke. Dad never lets me drink champagne, yet here as I choke on it, I'm very aware that this occasion is a rare one.

He wants something.

I stare at him agape, wondering where this is going.

"You are to stay married to Tobias."

"Are you—" Toby grips my leg tighter, stopping my words.

"We've already controlled the situation. Made it out as a story of a man and a woman desperate for each other but scared of their family's approval, so they made a rash decision."

I'm trying to keep calm, but Toby's hand keeps rising. It's making me flush in every area of my body. It's been over a month since we slept together, and my body misses his and the way it plays me like a fiddle. His fingers trail upward, and I have to adjust in my seat before I moan.

"Okay," I say, and Toby's hand rises. It's like he's calling me a good girl with every slide of his fingers.

"Just like that?" he grouches across from me.

"Why not? We don't have to be in love to fuck each other."

My father's face looks like a ripened tomato. Red, swelling, with that vein on his forehead popping outward.

"You're being unladylike," my father chastises all while Marsha grins as if I'm making her night. My theory was right about Toby because his fingers halt at that comment.

"I'm sorry, you're right. I'm sure we're going to fall in love at any moment." I only say the words to test Toby and see if he'll finally reach where I want him. Widening my legs a little, I'm pleased to feel his fingers edge my panties. His face gives nothing away, but the massive bulge in his slacks tell me everything I need to know.

He wants me.

He'll do anything to have me.

As Dad discusses why we have to be together for his image, he also explains that with me cooperating, I'll be receiving my entire inheritance as soon as we sign a contract to be married until his election ends.

Easy enough.

"Bring the documents. I'll sign them right now."

I say the words with a chipper demeanor, but in reality, none of it matters, except for the orgasm I'm bound to have right in front of my father and his stupid wife. Just as I imagine, his fingers move my panties to the side, and between my legs is a wet pussy that's craving some major Toby attention.

"Josey?"

"Yes," I mutter, clearing my throat and hoping the flush I feel from Toby's fingers isn't visible.

"I'm proud of you."

They are my dad's words, but they're as fake as his Botox injections. Yet I smile at him and practically moan as Toby fingers me knuckle-deep.

I squeeze his thigh as I ride the high of him finger-fucking me while my dad sits a mere five feet away. I'm practically humming with the feeling of an impending orgasm, but right as I'm about to detonate, Toby pulls his fingers away just as the wait staff drops off our plates on the table. He makes a show of touching his lamb with the finger that was inside me, then he licks it slow and sensually, his eyes not leaving mine.

"This lamb is absolutely divine," Toby muses. "Perfect, even."

"Tease," I grumble under my breath, knowing only he could hear. With his cocksure smile and smirk thereafter, I'm sure this night will end with his cock inside me.

CHAPTER 35

TOBY

SHE'S FUCKING STUNNING. SPENDING AS MUCH time away from her as possible was the deal. Being around her breaks my barriers, but fuck, I want her. Day in and day out, she's all I think about. I haven't even been with a single person since we were together against her car. The taste of her cunt is all I imagine; it's all I dream about and savor. It's all I want and all I need.

"So, that was awkward," she mutters as I'm escorting her outside.

"The fact that we're married and can't remember? Or the fact that we just signed contracts because you deserve every penny of your inheritance?"

"What? That's why you did it?"

"Yes," I say easily, but it's a lie. She doesn't need to know any other details. Because this is enough for me.

"What's in it for you?" she questions, folding her arms in a *don't fuck with me* manner. It's charming to say the least.

"A warm cunt I can sink into every night, morning, midday. Actually, it's for whenever I'm starving and desperate. You know, it's just what I want. You. Beneath me. My cock filling you."

She lets out a puff of air, and it's adorable. Unable to help myself, I lean forward and take her mouth. She tastes like champagne and dinner. And something sweeter that must be all her.

"You have a large ego, Toby."

"I have an even larger cock, Joey. Or have you forgotten?"

"You may need to remind me," she challenges, and my dick stiffens entirely in my slacks. Pushing her against the hood of my car, I listen to her moan. It's such a velvety sound, soaking me in hot liquid heat.

"You don't know what you're asking for, Sous."

"I'm asking you to prove your words are true."

"Not sure your daddy will like me sinking my cock in his little princess. Especially when I'm filling her with my seed, making her scream my name, and feeling her clench me like she'll die if she doesn't have me."

"Toby," she moans. It's more of a whimper, something we

both can get behind.

"Yes, Sous?"

"Fuck me before I break your dick."

"So demanding."

Unzipping my pants but keeping the button closed, I slide my dick out and hover it over her opening. Moving her panties to the side, much like I did at dinner, I tease her center but never touch her where she wants me to. She writhes and makes the sexiest little whimpers. "I always knew you enjoyed public outings, Sous. Just didn't know you wanted my dick inside you each time."

"Toby, I swear to fuck if you don't—"

She moans as I sink inside her. Her body arches into me as my cock fills her up. She's a mess of wetness and moans, reduced to the sensation of me filling her and hitting her exactly where she wants and needs.

"More," she demands, her face flushed. I raise her up, angling us both to hit her G-spot, and as I'm rutting into her, I slide my palm between her thighs and pinch her clit. "Fuck!" she practically screams, the swollen bud beneath my fingers only makes my dick swell.

I start rubbing in harsh circles, just like she likes, and it doesn't take long before she's coming around my dick, squeezing me so fucking tight that I see stars.

"So beautiful when you fall apart, Sous."

When she smirks beneath me, I lose all sense of control and start hammering inside her. Sweat drips from my forehead as we fuck in broad daylight underneath the Californian sun. It's sweltering, but the sun has nothing on the heat she brings me with her sassy mouth.

After a few more pumps, I'm releasing, coating her walls with every ounce I have, and she's moaning beneath me. Looking at her lying across my hood, I want her to be pregnant with my child. As I pull out, my cum slips from her, and it takes all of my self-control not to scoop it up and shove it in her, then fuck her ten more times, just to be certain she's filled to the brim with my seed.

Shaking my head, I'm thrown out of my mind. How could I want that when she's a practical stranger who's so young and doesn't know what she wants to do with her life?

What the fuck is wrong with me?

"You're thinking too hard, boss," she muses and readjusts herself. "Don't worry, I'm on the pill."

I open my mouth to speak and am at a loss for words. "That's not the problem," I mutter.

"Either way, you're okay to fuck me bare. I kind of like it."

"Let me show you then," I challenge.

"Again?"

"Are you challenging my stamina again, Sous?"

"That's not the sound of your cock filling me, Tobias. I'm starting to think it's all talk." She no sooner gets the words out before I'm filling her to the brim with my steel length again. She moans loudly, and I have to slap a hand over her mouth. Her legs rise, and I wrap them around my waist as I sink all the way in. She makes a choked noise when I pull out and slam inside her, and fuck if I'm not on the brink of coming already.

"Right there, ohmigod." Her muffled moan surrounds my hand. Her teeth dig into me as I rut into her. I've never felt so complete than I do at this moment. Not only is she my wife now, but her moans bring me solace, her fight brings me happiness, and her cunt brings me pleasure like never before.

I pull out and slam into her time and time again until my balls tingle, and I'm emptying into her. She's breathing heavily, and as she stands, my seed seeps from her, streaking her thighs. It's an image I never want to forget. One that'll be prime jerking material for the rest of my life.

"Guess you should come live with me, wife."

"Wife. I can get used to that," she muses, touching her chin. I grip the same flesh.

"I can get used to watching my cum spill down your thighs."

She smiles with red tinting her cheeks, and before I let her leave me again, I reach between her thighs, swiping my seed that's dripped out, and with the most purposeful hand ever, I force it into her cunt over and over again as she whimpers. Then when she's practically falling, I rub her clit until she coats my fingers all over again.

"Next time you want to challenge me, Sous, I'll take your ass, just as I promised last time."

"Promises, promises, Tobias. You keep saying you're going to own me, but I think you're mistaken."

I growl and pull her mouth to mine, biting, nibbling,

making sure she has bruises, whether visible or not.

"This is the start of us, little chef. Just you wait."

"I'll believe you when my ass is a little less virginal."

Twenty minutes later, she's following me into my hotel room, and I'm fucking her in every position. I make sure to finger her ass, preparing her for the next time when my cock takes its place.

CHAPTER 36

PAST

TOBY

"YOU'RE HAPPY," FRANKIE MUSES, SITTING NEXT TO me. We're driving to Hollow Ridge to see Gene. He promised me Mom's ring. And while the story behind it isn't the prettiest, it matters to me. It's all I have of my family. Or will be, once it's mine.

"I love her so much," I respond, gripping the steering wheel. Love makes us mad, yes? Well, Joey's love makes me sane. Absolutely sure and secure. It breathes life back into me.

"Does she know why you guys are leaving all of a sudden for Cancun?"

"No, but she'll be freaking the hell out when you, Gray,

Nate, Bobbie, Gene, and her dad show up."

He smiles, his face full of happiness. I thought for sure he'd be jealous of our happiness. It's not like I could hide my own jealousy when Jase and Lo got married. But he seems at ease. Like this information makes him as happy as finding love himself would.

"Nate doing okay?" Francis's jaw clenches.

"He's not horrible. You know how he gets," he mutters. It's not disappointment lacing his tone, it's worry. I feel the same, though their friendship is longer and more intertwined than Nate's and my own.

"Do you think I shouldn't have invited him?" Not having him there would feel wrong. He's meant to witness this. Something happy. No more guilt.

He wears that like a full body tattoo. No amount of scrubbing can clean his conscience, not in his mind.

"With Bobbie there, I think it'll be okay. She grounds him."

Understanding fills me. Bobbie is his as Joey is to me, his hope. He may not see it—the drugs and depression may cloud him so much that he can't see it—but she's going to save him. When he's ready, maybe she'll even allow their love to be real between them and not full of lies.

"I'm excited to marry her. For real this time," I mention as we drop the heavy subject.

AFTER WE MEET WITH GENE, I'M HOLDING THE RING

in my hand. The one that's my mom's. It's beautiful and perfect for Joey. I drop Francis off on the way home, and while Joey is still at *Mi Casa*, I pack it in my bag, hoping it doesn't get lost.

Days later, when we're at the cabana in Cancun, my body hums with acknowledgment. She doesn't even know it, but today is the day.

She's perfect in her short burnt orange sundress that makes her pale skin beam and her eyes seem even brighter somehow. Her hair is down in waves, tangled with the wind, and blowing toward me, begging me to pull it as I thrust into her deeply.

While Clay—her father—wanted this wedding for show, to make it seem like this big-ass notion for his campaign, it had nothing to do with him and everything to do with Joey.

My one stipulation was Marsha couldn't come. It's obvious she's an absolute waste of air, especially while in the presence of my wife, but I truly wanted her dad to be here.

She may say he doesn't matter anymore, but I know that's a lie. She loves him endlessly, even while he's forgotten what it means to be a father.

She grabs my hand as she hops in the sand, her eyes alight with joy and promise. "Sex on the beach?" she asks, and I raise an eyebrow.

"Pretty sure that's illegal in every country, Sous."

Playfully, she smacks my chest, a giggle escaping her. "No, you perv, a drink." When I smirk, she rolls her eyes. "But that other thing," she whispers, leaning in conspiratorially. "Wait for tonight and I'll sit on your lap while no one can see what's going on beneath my dress."

I bring her in for a fierce kiss, the ache in my dick present as she leads me to the bar that's surrounded by water. The first day we came out here, I about died. Unlike my Sous, swimming with the sharks doesn't appeal to me, and this bar is entirely in the water. It's not deep, but every chair is barely above the surface. So when you're sitting, your legs are with the fish. Literally.

We take a seat at the bar, and I fall more for her as her eyes take in the ocean. She's breathtaking like this. Carefree. Happy. No sorrows to consume her.

That's why it's perfect that we're getting married soon, at sunset, when everything will be in place. She told me she wanted something special for the two of us eventually. Getting married didn't have to be a show, but she wanted to experience it with me. For real.

Where booze and bad decisions didn't guide it.

She orders her drink while I sip a virgin mojito. I don't have an entire hold over my addiction, which is why I've been attending weekly AA meetings. My sponsor takes care of me, and I own up to everything.

It's that one step.

The making amends.

I've nearly skipped it.

While it doesn't make me any less dedicated to going further with my recovery, it does staunch my ability to let Joey fully in. That's why we're here.

I'm ready.

She's mine.

I'm hers.

We're perfect for each other.

After we talk about her ideas for a French version of *Su Casa*, I'm wondering if France is in our future. What if I could fix her memories like I promised? Take them away by expanding the restaurant she wants to be a part of so much, while extinguishing her demons?

Noting that idea down for *someday soon*, I lead her away toward our suite.

Later that day, when we're supposed to be going to dinner, I tell her to dress for a fancier place. Though not many exist on this resort, no matter how distinguished it is.

She does.

Fuck does she.

My wife steps out of our ensuite with her hair cascading down her back. Red fire flaming lips greet me with a smile. Amber golden hues watch me with anticipation all while I barely hold my dick down in my pants. *Down, boy. Later.*

"Absolutely breathtaking, Sous," I whisper. My voice a mix of huskiness and admiration. She's perfection. When we first met, you couldn't catch her in a dress, but somewhere along the way, that changed. She became in love; maybe it was our constant need to fuck in the open, or maybe she's growing into the beautiful woman I've seen since day one. Either way, she's radiant when she's comfortable and happy with her body.

I love it.

I love her.

Her cheeks redden, matching the color of her lips.

"Thank you," she murmurs, her voice small, meek, and so unlike my wife that it has me smiling.

"Ready?" I offer my hand, and her small one attaches itself to mine a moment later. Heat overwhelms me, flooding my system with her fire and presence, and I'm in love with this very moment.

In a country far from home, a place that has only brought us closer, I'm in love. The scents, the colors, everything intertwined is welcome and beautiful.

Leading her out the door and down the elevator, she follows, not asking a single question. The vibrant coral and tangerine sky bleeds across the horizon. Enveloping and sublime, it's perfect for tonight.

"An outside fancy restaurant?" she muses, her eyes full of wonder. As we walk, I stop us. "Shoes off."

"Bossy, old man?"

"You don't complain when I'm sinking inside you."

Her face lights up, and that red tint comes back, making me well aware of where her mind just went. She reaches down, but instead of letting her take them off, I kneel.

She peers down at me with so much heat I'm sure the sun's rays are weak in comparison. Her eyes twinkle, and when I kiss her ankles, the tiny moan that escapes her has my dick jumping.

Fuck.

How are we supposed to get married when she's filling me up with these kinds of emotions?

I continue kissing her exposed flesh before undoing the straps of her heels. She uses my shoulders to keep from falling as I kiss the pads of her feet. Then as I repeat this with the other foot, I swear I hear her moan again. She's killing me.

I slip off my own shoes and lead us down the beach. Our hands are entwined, our hearts following suit, and as the sun paints the sky with more vibrant colors, we finally make it to our destination. Stopping where I'm at, Joey's eyes scan the area.

Amusement flickers at the edge of my lips. Tamping it down is near impossible, but somehow, I do. She turns back to me, her face one of confusion. "Where's dinner?"

A chuckle escapes me. Only she would be worried about food when we're on an abandoned beach and a bunch of people are standing in the distance.

Gripping both of her hands, I kiss them, making sure each finger gets enough attention from my lips. She's smiling, but what else is present is the love I constantly feel. The pull of seduction and amorous sensations are something I'm very used to now, but it still amazes me that someone as perfect as Joey could love me. All the bad parts included.

She dived in with me, she loved me, and she hasn't stopped seizing to amaze me.

"Josephine Ellis Moore," I recite, my voice thick with everything currently rushing through me. Her eyes glisten, like her body is aware of what I'm about to say before I actually follow through with it.

"Toby," she says, her voice airy and tight with affection. It's beautiful to see every emotion she has to offer, ones most would be ashamed of. The kind that people hide behind and pretend don't exist. Joey lets them flow through her freely. Allowing them to bleed to the surface without causation.

The thud as my knees connect with the wheat-colored sand almost yawns in the air with how silent everything else feels. The crashing waves on the shore are neither loud nor quiet. The sun has neared its apex and right now couldn't be a more perfect time.

"We've been through a lot in the year we've been together. Probably more than the average couple since I'm a dick by nature," I muse. A sharp intake of air followed by a small choking laugh escapes her. "But fuck, Sous, I love you. If the world told me you didn't pick every star in that sky and hang them yourself, I wouldn't believe it."

Tears fall, the little droplets wetting the sand by my knees. She's a beautiful sight. I savor every drop, knowing it's an honor to be given that kind of emotion and experience this level of love and adoration.

I'm a lucky fucking bastard.

"You're my sunshine, Sous. My goddamn little chef who cooks me food that shouldn't be real. You're perfect. Scars, sadness, and all, you're perfection."

She starts bending to my level, taking my mouth with

hers, but I need to get this all out. She deserves this.

"I've never felt more in love in my entire life. Not a single human compares, or even comes close. You're my happiness. When you hurt, I hurt. When the days are endless and barren of love, I experience that with you. And fuck, when those eyes leak with emotions, like they do now, I feel pure, like I found *the one* and deserve to have this happiness with you. I love you so much, Sous. Will you marry me... again?"

At the little added touch of that last word, her mouth breaks into a smile, and she's nodding while her eyes fill to the brim with more tears. I'm up in a flash, lifting her, bringing her body to mine, right where it fits, and then I'm taking her mouth and consuming her emotions and sharing my own.

I twirl us around, because fuck, I've never felt this hyped or happy, and then our mouths are fused together again. When she reaches for the button of my dress shirt, I swat her away gently.

"I should've asked, will you marry me... right now," I whisper into her ear, and she stops moving. We break apart and wonder is written all over her face.

"Right now?"

"Yes, beautiful. Right fucking now."

"But I don't—"

"You look perfect, and there isn't a better moment than right now while our families are standing a hundred feet away, waiting."

"What did you do?" she muses as a myriad of feelings wash

over her.

"I decided we should have a real wedding where you're the queen and the whole fucking world bears witness."

She grabs my face, and we resume kissing. It's consuming. Effortless. Blissful. If this is the start of the rest of our lives, I'll never wish for another thing again.

She's all I need.

"Let's get married then, old man. Wouldn't want you to die of old age first," she teases, smirking at me. I set her down entirely and smack her ass.

Squeals escape, and then I'm leading her to our forever.

The place she'll truly be mine.

Josephine Ellis Hayes, my wife. My lifeline. My sobriety chip.

CHAPTER 37

JOEY

I BOTTLE THE RESENTMENT AND HATRED AS ONE would a black widow and praying mantis in a jar, wondering which would strike first and who would conquer all.

One time, Wes caught one of each in two separate jars. It annoyed me that he captured two beautiful creatures just to hold them hostage and watch them waste away.

He set the glasses side by side, mirrors, almost doorways, to see how calculated each species was.

The intrigue in his eyes terrified me, let me know something inside him may be darker than I bargained for, yet I did nothing but watch.

His fingers caressed the one housing the bright green mantis. He leaned in close, his eyes narrowing on the stillness, I'm sure.

When the insect didn't move, only keeping a stock-still position, I wondered if maybe fear kept it frozen in place, but like Wes knew something I didn't, he smiled.

The way his lips tilted at the edges conspiratorially made my insides squeeze uncomfortably. As a predator or person with a lack of empathy would, he gave me chills, but for some reason, it didn't force my eyes away.

Like the impact when music hits really loud, the bass bumping throughout your body, I could only prepare for the cacophony of bulldozing emotions.

After deciding whatever he needed, he stared at the widow. Its red stomach patch faced away from us as it protected itself by hiding in the lid, but Wes saw. Tapping the lid several times, we watched as the spider plopped to the bottom.

He bit the inside of his cheek wordlessly, causing an insane curiosity to bite at my mind.

It made zero sense.

This was barbaric, but I didn't do a single thing to stop this from escalating.

He unscrewed the lids, lifting both cylinders at the same time. Nothing could prepare me for what I witnessed next.

Anxiety gnawed at my stomach, creating an untamable distress to bubble through my chest. It burned and ached, acting as an early warning system as the two foes faced off.

Neither moved.

They both stood motionless, almost calculating, watching, observing the opponent.

It never occurred to me which would win, but staring at the black widow, knowing its bite was as deadly as it was vicious, my mind had made itself up.

It struck first. The widow went straight for the jugular, and that was its first mistake—taking the easy shot, the uncalculated risk of striking first.

The mantis, as if knowing all along, gripped the spider with its pincers, holding it like it was sushi, his arms the chopsticks of death.

It squeezed and squeezed, making sure to eat its legs while it writhed in its hold. Nausea built inside me, suffocating my every breath, but the mantis didn't stop to recognize how uncomfortable I was.

How could it know?

This was a dog-eat-dog world. In this case, a mantis-eat-widow one, he did what he had to do to survive. He won, eating his winnings like a gloating king after battle.

And I learned something valuable that day: always watch your six, don't trust words, and never take the first shot. I'd never lay victim to a man ever again.

Mondays were created by a traitorous cunt who thought a new start of the week was a good idea.

The clock reads two in the afternoon—my allotted break was over two hours ago. Toby would kill me if I didn't take one. Stopping at my locker in the employee portion of the restaurant, I grab my spare joint tucked into my bag. It's one I keep close by. Smoking isn't something I partake in often, especially not after Wes and his dickish behavior. It tends to remind me of him, and that's not something I like to relive.

Heading toward the back, I leave a rolling pin between the door to make sure I don't get locked out. It's not a risk I'll ever make again.

It's been days since we both got drunk. Dad hasn't stopped calling, Gray hasn't stopped texting, and I'm stuck in a play-by-play work life and sleep life. Toby is always home. He sleeps next to me every night, but it's weird. We don't talk. We don't touch. We just don't.

Come over, Joey. Or we're breaking up. I laugh at her message. *Only if you have hot Cheetos and cheese.*

I thought you stopped getting high. I chuckle, loving that she's so attuned to me.

Never truly stopped. But seriously, I'd die for both. As I'm sending the text, I stop at my locker and get my little copper cigarette holder. It has a white front with a red rose stamped on. It was my grandmother's. It's also where I keep my blunts.

What're you doing? Gray's message pops up on my phone. Swiping up to see her others, I notice she messaged me five times, simply to say hi.

About to take a hit on the back-truck entrance.

You're smoking right now? Is her automatic response. It's insane—for how much we talk, we don't really talk. We've grown closer over the years, but her staying in France ninety percent of the time takes our friendship to a text-and-call-only kind. She's doing better now, Ace is far away, and she's seeing this new royal dude. He treats her right, so that's all that matters to me.

Started again, seems to be the only thing that helps my depression. Shivers overtake my frame. It doesn't help that it's a little overcast and moody, bringing a chill that only furthers the one already sweeping over me.

I didn't know that. She messages back. *Bring some over tonight. Need to let loose.*

It just dawned on me that she's in the States and not France.

You're home? I check the calendar, noting it's spring break. Wow, time has flown right on by.

How the hell else would we hang out, weirdo? Just flew in to see Dad for spring break. I smile at that. Francis loves his little girl. How they've bonded over the years is amazing. I'm proud of him for taking care of her. He never stops trying to make her life the best it can be.

I'll be there at seven-ish. It's not a late night for once. I'm actually going to be slowing down here. Last night only pushed me further. I'm going to find a new job away from Hollow Ridge, and I'm going to thrive there and eventually divorce Toby. Something makes me cling on. Maybe it's the thought of giving up, or maybe it's the inability to live without him. Either way, we only hurt each other, and it's exhausting.

We deserve more.

I light up, and for the first time all day, I breathe. Fuck. It feels good to let loose. Even if my way to do so isn't conventional.

Toby wanted me the other night, so after my shower, I went to our room. But he wasn't there. Good thing, I was nearly combustible seeing the lust swirl in his eyes, wanting to give in. But he fucked some chick, and I have more self-respect than that. *This time.*

It's not even the fact that he cheats that makes me hate him; it's that he has this idea that I'm worse than he is. He's the only man who has touched me since Wesley. The only one.

Yeah, Francis and I shared a single kiss, but we never got intimate. The fact that Toby can't see that makes me mad. It pains me that he thinks I'm intentionally hurting him too. Who lives like that?

And why does the desperate girl inside me want to fix him? I want that so much it's sickening. I'm allowing myself to stay in this horrible relationship all while walking away *is* an option.

The fact that I'm still here says how weak I've become. I love him so damn much, even as he finds his pleasure in others, I still want to be the one he comes home to.

I want to be the only one.

Will I break before that happens again?

Why won't I walk away?

After my phone chirps several times, I set my bud down to see what the rush is. *I need you to come home right now. I know you still have four hours, but it's important.*

Toby.

Of course, something is wrong.

Please.

I already called Sanje, he's covering.

Sanje is our other chef. When Toby and I left Hawthorn and Hollow Ridge behind, we traveled the world together. We grew Hayes Corp and the Casa Conglomerate. We went French cuisine and Italian, all the way to Thai and Korean. We didn't stop the expansion until we had to come back once again to truly change the Hollow Hills' *Mi Casa*. We hired Sanje and his protege Dominique. They've been the best decision we've ever made, and when I'm not feeling like working, which tends to be every other day, Sanje takes over. Once I'm gone, he can have full rein. I'm done being here and crumpling beneath all the weight.

I read over the texts two more times, wondering what he could possibly need. The desperation in the texts makes me feel so many things I've avoided. He needs me. It's probably nothing important, but either way, the feeling is still there. After taking another huge inhale before putting out the blunt, I tuck it into my little box.

I'm heading up the elevator in the next ten minutes. Working where you live has its benefits, like being less than five minutes away.

Using my penthouse card, I go the extra ten floors no one but the owners have access to. The metal makes noises as it goes up, and not even the shitty music can dull my nerves. I'm always on edge when it comes to this man.

Scanning inside our home, I don't see him. It's odd, but I don't worry too much. When he's not in our room, an unsettling feeling arouses. But it's when I go to our office that my heart stops entirely.

Inside the room is my father, and besides him... my mother.

"Mom?" The soft voice that trickles out of me has me unnerved.

"Fix this, Tobias. Now."

It's all my father says before looking at me with an inexplicable emotion. Then he's leaving, all while my mom, who's been missing for nine years, stands in front of me.

CHAPTER 38

TOBY

THIS SHOULD FREAK ME OUT. THAT MY WIFE looks as if she's about to pass out, but I remain calm. One of us has to. Before she came in, her father and I had a chat. More like he threatened me once more.

The truth of the matter is, he hid Lianna from Joey all these years.

Like me, she's an addict.

The difference between us, her addiction is meth while mine is whiskey.

She abandoned my wife, tore her to shreds. All for a craving.

I may be a loser that drinks his sorry existence away, but leaving Joey isn't something I can do. Whether our hatred outshines our love, it keeps me grounded.

At first, it didn't. I'd disappear for days at a time. I even lied about it being because of other women, but I'd binge-drink and end up in the hospital.

Gene always came. Though my mother keeps me at a distance, my stepfather is there for me. He's forgiven me for what Lo and I did. He loves me still.

Mom sticks to her favorite son, just like she always has.

The only thing we've ever had in common was the bottle. *Isn't that right, Ma?* You hug it and I grapple it. You married yourself to the way it made you feel. I divorced myself of feelings so I could drink.

Why did you pass your addiction onto me?

Why did you let me get wasted as a child?

Why did you fucking suck?

My resentment rises as I watch my wife silently fall apart while her doped up mother hasn't moved from her spot. She hugs herself and sways a bit, making my blood boil. How could Clay bring her here, expect me to fix this, and then walk the fuck away when he knows her mother's a soft spot for Joey? It's been nearly a decade since Lianna disappeared. Clay's action only prove that his political gain is more important than his daughter's emotional state.

Does he not know she's been through enough?

That she slices her wrists as if she's her own art piece?

Did he not see the change when she came back from France? How she didn't leave the house; how no fucking person could reach her because she lived in a hell situated in her own mind? My hands shake, my body following suit, as I try to tamper down the rage. Clay has carried so much weight over me, a pull to hurt his child—my wife. He's a despicable human and the fact that he so callously disregards the woman I'm in love with only turns my hatred into a tangible and combustible thing.

"You're a-alive?" Joey's voice breaks. The little girl who was abandoned and forced into the arms of a psychotic bitch like Marsha comes through. She's so young right now as she barely keeps herself from not running to the woman in front of her.

"Joey," I say, breaking her panic-filled fog. Her gaze meets mine. Eyes that I've loved for years, amber and frozen in time, stilled and ever-feeling, look at me for help and comfort, something I haven't offered her in a long time. Something that has to change.

We are always fighting each other, pushing, colliding in a crash that takes us deeper in the thrall of hatred. The softness I'd once freely given rises in me, wanting to give and give, making sure that look on her face never comes back.

I hate her.

I love her.

I want to destroy her

Then when there's nothing left, I want to fix everything.

Instead of being a dick, I get up and close the distance

between us. She's so fragile at this moment, wrapping her arms around my middle, holding me like I'll protect her.

Oh, I will.

Even as I hate her.

She doesn't cry, but her entire body shakes with shock. Like the first time I saw Francis after his accident. He was bruised from head to toe, in casts, and connected to machines. But he was alive. He made it.

"Baby girl," her mother slurs. It reminds me of being wasted beyond my own comprehension. Unable to see straight or speak clearly but attempting to anyway.

"I think it's best if she rests," I offer, seeing her mom having a hard time standing. She's high as a fucking kite, sailing the clouds, bouncing from here to there and nowhere at the same time. It's disgusting, and I hate it. Doesn't matter that Nate is an addict and I love him like a brother, this woman means nothing to me, and being this way in front of my wife as she trembles from head to toe in my arms has me on edge.

"Let me take her," I tell Joey. She nods against my chest, not letting me go. It's endearing and so fucking sad. I pull her off me gently, tilting her head up. "Meet me in the bedroom, Sous." Her eyes lose her foreign expression and lighten a little. She nods, and I kiss her forehead, needing her to feel my support in some way. She shivers and steps away, heading to our room.

"Mrs. Moore," I sound out.

"It's just Lia. Clay divorced me years ago when he could."

"Why would you come back?" I demand, realizing how callous I sound. "Why now when his re-election is months away?"

"He doesn't deserve to be in the senate," she hisses, her eyes unable to focus on mine. "He and that whore of his don't deserve happiness."

"And you decided that ruining my wife's life is acceptable? She was destroyed because of you. You took a beautiful teenager, ready to face the world with her parents, to a woman who's jaded by all things maternal."

"T-That's wasn't my intention. My little Josephine wasn't meant to be hurt. Clay kept me away."

"From what I can tell, it was with very good reason. Look at you. You're a goddamn mess. And now that he's using me, I have no choice but to fix it."

"What do you mean?"

"Yes, Toby, what do you mean?" Joey's head peeks around the door. She looks both somber and angry at the same time. Who knew those two emotions could live side by side and hurt me worse?

"Your dad owns me, Sous." It's the first real shred of honesty I've offered her in so long. It isn't a surprise when this bit of information knocks her a step or two backward. She seems more hurt from this than she was the other night.

"We can talk later," she drawls, using that voice I hate hearing from her. It's the one halfway between disappointment and disregard.

"But you"—she points at her mom—"need a shower, some

sleep, and a change of clothes."

"I'll do it," I offer. Joey nods slowly, cold calculation in her stare. She's hurting. I can see it and feel it as if they were my own emotions. She leaves the room, and I turn back to Lianna, wondering how she could give up something as precious as a child.

It's one thing, no matter how addicted I get, that makes zero sense to me. Like I did before, giving up on alcohol is easy when it comes to the ones I love. Hurting myself and Joey are the only reasons I go back. It's a bitter tool I've used because no matter what, in my mind, I deserve every fucking mess up and repercussion.

"Our guest room is this way," I mutter bitterly, leaving the office and hoping she follows. There's no time to babysit when the world around me falls apart. When I make it to the room far west of our home, I open the door and tell her it's where she'll be staying until I fix everything or ruin Clay in the process, hoping it'll be both in one blow. He needs to be knocked down every peg, and if I have to be the one to drop-kick him myself, then so be it.

CHAPTER 34

JOEY

AS I SIT IN OUR ROOM, I CURL INTO A BALL,
remembering the worst days of my life.

A baby.

I finally got pregnant.

Would we be fixed if my body could handle carrying
a child?

Why couldn't I be stronger?

My heart sinks as I think of how much I wanted my mom
back then.

Did she ever experience this loss?

Did she ever weep for the world to ease up?

Did she beg to be deserving of a child?

I did.

Every single day and night, I begged. Hell, after a week, I tried getting Toby on board for trying again, and he refused. I pleaded with him to put another baby in me. To love me entirely and give me hope.

He wouldn't.

He said no.

Not yet.

No.

No.

No.

That word repeats in my mind.

Remember when I said my rape ruined our relationship? It's true. After getting diagnosed with chlamydia, losing my tubal function, and losing a baby, it's true.

Toby, my loving husband, he broke.

He wasn't there for me. Silence was what he offered. Yeah, he comforted me, loved me, was perfect, but he didn't live his pain with me. He didn't suffer the same, and I hated him for it.

How could he be silent when I raged at the world?

How could he act unaffected when I died inside?

How could he pretend to be so strong when he couldn't even admit he lost something too?

It's where my resentment unfurled. It's where it thrived. It's where we lost each other.

"I'll be in the office today, don't worry I've got S covering for

you this week."

"Okay," I respond, not caring. *Nothing mattered anymore. My job could suffer along with me, maybe then I wouldn't be so alone.*

He leaves and my phone chimes.

Dad told me. Come over. Let me cry with you and feed you chocolate and popcorn. *For the first time in two weeks, I smile. It's small and barely there, but it's a smile. Standing up, I head to the shower.*

Thirty minutes later, I'm arriving at Mansion de la Frenchman. It's what I've called it since living here.

Francis wasn't amused, but Gray sure as hell was.

Before I make it to the front door, I hear angered voices.

"You think you can walk away, Storm? Think that just because you flew across the fucking world, that I wouldn't still own every single breath you take? Did you forget what your whore of a mother did? What you hid from me?"

His tone is aggressive and single-handedly scary. I've never seen someone so young contain so much malice.

"Ace—" Gray whispers, probably trying to soothe him. He doesn't stop himself from pushing her into the wall of the house. His palm glides up her throat, gripping and possessive. It reminds me so much of Toby that I almost wish I had popcorn.

"You're my fucking damaged toy, Gray. Next time you decide to leave Hollow Ridge, I'll fucking follow you." He bites her lip before releasing her, then walks toward the back of the house. Interesting. There isn't anything out there but fields for miles, and right as Gray goes to chase him, someone taps my shoulder.

"Ladybug?" Francis calls out. I turn and see his big and looming figure. The worry on his face already has the tears rushing out.

"I didn't mean to show up unannounced."

"Shh," he coos and pulls me into his arms. I hug him. Just letting him hold me. After my tears abate a little, he kisses my forehead and then both of my cheeks. It's so soothing and kind, and when he drags me inside to talk to me and love me in the most mundane way, I feel at peace.

That's the day my marriage ended.

Somehow, in the short trip to Gray's home, Toby thought I'd fucked his best friend. How wrong was he?

The door opening surprises me. Though he said we'd talk in our room, I didn't believe him. He's a runner—he runs from his problems, commitments, and wrongdoings all the time.

"How are you feeling?" Toby's voice sounds out. It's skeptical, the way his words slow as if he's second-guessing them.

"Do you ever think of our baby?" I deflect, asking him what has been burning into my skin day after day for the past two years. The thing that's as real as it is painful. It's an ache that doesn't ebb; one you don't heal from, but rather, you learn to live with. It's the scars on my arms, the visual imagery of sorrow without the memories. Because we didn't get those did we? Will we ever? Will I be a mom? Will I be deserving? Is there anything I can do to be given such a gift? Am I not worthy? Tears flood me, but it's not a sob where the body shakes, it's acceptance as salty droplets trail my cheeks, heating my skin while numbing me to everything else.

"Every day," he answers, and that's when I realize he's gotten closer. His voice is louder than I expected. It's full of implications—no sadness—almost like he has a filter, not allowing the emotions to bleed through because he's scared of them.

I'm scared of them.

Imagine losing something vital to you, then deciding that holding it in was the only way to breakthrough it, then to finally let it out and experience it entirely, all at once. With that and his words on my mind, my body starts to shake. The tears come faster, the pain pinches harder, the deadness inside rots with everything I've allowed myself to hold.

"Why didn't we get to have a child, Toby?" Another question. Another answer I don't want. It's there, though; these necessary questions that I've never allowed myself to truly ask. "Am I not meant to be a mother, too?"

My chest aches. If someone like Lianna Moore could have me, then why can't I be a mother? What makes everyone else special and not me? Is it my body? Is it not strong enough? Am I too weak to carry something so special?

I think back to Paris. To that alleyway where my life changed entirely. The memory pounds into me, trickling in like a soft drizzle, and as the reality of losing a child flows through me, it turns into a tropical storm, winding me, stealing my breath, and before I know it, I can't stop the sobs.

"Josephine," Toby calls out, his hand on my cheek. He cups it, the warmth from him making me feel too hot, on fire, unwelcome and brutal. "I'm not sure why our baby was taken. Life doesn't always make sense. No matter what we did, it can't change the outcome."

"How can you be so calm?" I hiss, pushing his hand away. "How can you think logically and be okay? How is this okay and not a fucking disaster?" My chest heaves as the emotion rips through me, it slices from my chest, searching for the person who hurts me most.

It comes for him.

And I don't stop it.

"Why is she good enough?" I cry, but as confusion takes over his face, I move from the fetal position and sit up.

He doesn't know I know.

But DNA doesn't lie.

"Your mom?" he finally asks.

Immediately, my head is shaking while my heart is trying to calm. "Lo."

"What are you talking about?" he asks.

If I dye my hair, will I be good enough?

Will I look more like her?

Will you love me then?

"When I stopped you in the coffee shop. That little boy... Leviathan." I pause to breathe, inhaling deeply before letting it out. "He's your son." Toby's features tighten, his eyes pinched and his lips pursed. It's an emotion that makes me believe he knew but wouldn't accept it.

Why would he?

She hid this for five years.

Five years of time lost.

"Why do you think he's mine? Jase and I are nearly identical."

"You're nothing alike," I bite out.

"You're wrong. Besides our looks, we're the same. Incurable. Miserable. A goddamn fucking mess." He leans toward me, taking my face, rubbing circles over the tears as if smearing them will change the fact that sorrow doesn't leave when they dry. "I've fucked up, Sous." *Sous.* It's the worst and best name he's given me. It reminds me of the good times, the bad ones, and everything in between. It hurts. It heals. It digs deep.

"Don't ignore this," I plea. "DNA doesn't lie, Tobias." He shakes his head, almost like understanding bleeds into him and his features, but as if a decision is made, he doesn't push it. He grips my face harder and kisses me.

His lips demolish mine in a collision neither of us prepared for. It's timeless, the actions non-existent and coalescing at the same time. It's simultaneous and untethered. It's soft and hard. It's a claiming and a promise. It's everything I've wanted and nothing he has offered.

My body thrums with life, it hums and soothes, it feels like everything he's taken and given as they fight silently to win my sensations over. It's overwhelming as my heart and mind have it out, and I can't help but cry.

His tongue traces my bottom lip—a plea—something that isn't what he usually offers. My husband takes, he doesn't ask, and it's always been something I've needed, but this tiny moment of tenderness, the keening of his will, the offering, it's his kneeling to me.

I open for him, parting my lips with a soft moan. His tongue twists with mine as my body heats. Something in the slow, sensual dance brings me too many feelings, and my body starts feeling jittery again.

He pulls back, placing his forehead against mine. "I hate what I've done," he whispers. His eyes are closed when I peer at them, as if the connection will break if he opens them and gives me his pain. That's what I want. His pain. His presence. His everything. "You'd have been a perfect mother. So perfect it hurts that I haven't given that to you. I hate myself, Josephine. I hate every breath I take, every moment I'm here and hurting you. I hate every choice I've made since seeing you with Francis. I hate every fucking thing in this world, even you, but fuck, that's *not* true. You're my one lie. The thing I promise to hate and ruin, but love runs deep, it fucking breaks me with its power. Because no matter the pain, Sous, I can't stop. My heart beats for you, it hurts for you, it feels... *only* for you." His face is haunted and strained, and he's never been more handsome.

Pain looks me in the eye.

Hate wrings from him.

Sorrow promises me to be better.

"What do we do now?" I ask, feeling too much. My walls are all but non-existent. They're no longer standing, but demolishing, torn down by every single thing we've been holding back, and it's so telling.

"We start over."

CHAPTER 40

TOBY

"I TOLD YOU THE NEXT TIME YOU SMART-MOUTHED me, your ass would be mine."

She grins as if she knows something I don't. "Maybe I've been pushing because you're too slow. Is it your age, old man?"

I growl and push her on the bed. She's freshly showered, her skin dripping, and all I want is to taste and fuck every inch of her. Prowling on top of her, I start at her throat, making sure to suck long enough to leave marks.

"Toby!" she complains. "I work tomorrow!"

"Good, then the entire staff can know I'm the only man fucking you and you're mine."

"You're such a goddamn caveman," she grumbles, but I see the satisfaction in her eyes. She wants me to mark her and make sure the world knows I'm hers too.

I suck and lick her throat and breasts, making sure to bite her piercing just the way she likes. As she writhes beneath me, a mess of moans and groans, I lick her navel, dipping in and swirling my tongue over that piercing. She whimpers above me, and I just know she's going to be wet as fuck when I finally spread her open. I take my time to leave hickeys and bite marks on her hips to make sure she knows it's *me* that can't get enough of *her*. She won't admit it, but I think she secretly likes when I take her body and make it my own puppet.

When I reach the apex of her thighs, she wiggles, desperate for attention.

"Needy, Sous?"

"No, you don't do it for me," she taunts. Those words hit the monster where it hurts, and I'm latching onto her clit in the next breath, biting, chewing, and making loud grunting noises that can't seem to be tamped down.

"Fuck, Toby," she moans. "Right there. Fuck." They're low and husky moans and have my cock weeping for attention.

I lick from her clit to her asshole, diving into her as her essence coats my tongue. The flavor is nothing I'll ever tire of. It's sweet and tangy and all mine.

"You're fucking delicious. I'll never stop loving this cunt."

She groans when I latch onto her again. She's moving her hips up and down all while pushing my head deeper into her.

She fucks my face like I'm about to fuck her pussy, and it's unnerving me.

Before she explodes, I stop.

"Really?!" she yells, her face red and agitated.

"If I make you come before stretching you, you won't enjoy it as much your first time. Trust me."

She flops back down with a groan.

I lick her nub as a tease, and she literally barks at me like a goddamn dog. I can't help but laugh at how greedy she is with her orgasms.

Getting up, I open my dresser, wanting to get the lube as quickly as possible. Then I come back to my wife, seeing her sprawled wide, rubbing her clit.

"Naughty girl," I chastise, slapping her cunt. She screams and then grinds against my palm. "Greedy." I smack again, and she's screeching.

Kneeling, I squirt lube onto my fingers, making sure to put a ton on her rosy little hole. She shivers, and I can't tell if it's in anticipation or from the lube's temperature.

Placing my tongue over her swollen clit, I flick several times while entering her with a finger. She doesn't squeeze me like I worried. Most people would death grip, but me and my girl have been practicing.

After pumping into her for several minutes, I continue to work her pussy and asshole in tandem, watching her thrive. Adding a second finger, she bows upward, whimpering.

"Good?" I ask, knowing she trusts me to keep her safe.

"More," she demands. So, I add another, scissoring them inside to stretch her.

I pull my fingers out when she's thrusting down onto them. She's ready, and fuck, so am I.

I stand and offer her my hands. "W-What are you doing?" she asks with worry.

"You're going to ride my cock, Sous. It'll hurt less, and I'll get to look at your tits bounce while you fuck me."

She worries her lip a moment before nodding. I lie back, feeling just as nervous. I've never done this with anyone. Porn is my only direction. That and the smutty books I stole from Lo once upon a time.

She kneels in front of my cock, bending to swipe her sinful tongue across the slit. After she's done torturing me, she takes my entire length down her throat, and I nearly pass out for the sensations zipping up my spine.

"Shit," I grumble, feeling my balls tingle. They want to release, but they're going to have to be patient.

"Can't take me, old man?"

"Get the fuck on my cock before I lose control," I ground out, watching as she smirks.

"What if I want you to lose control?"

"Not your first time, beautiful, now slide that pretty ass over my cock and take it whole." Her face reddens, and I take joy in making her flush. She hovers over my length, and I squirt a ton of lube over him, coating him. She starts lowering, and her face contorts with pain. I grip her clit and start rubbing sensual circles over it, teasing her. When she's fully seated, I'm practically on edge. She's so fucking tight, so ramming into her isn't an option.

After a few moments, she's moaning and rotating above me. My cock pulses with the need to release, throbbing in a way I've never felt before. When she starts rising and falling, I'm losing control and grunting with how good it feels.

My balls tighten, and I hold out, wanting her to come first and truly experience this with me.

"Toby, fuck," she moans. "I need harder." The last three words are a whimper, but it's the only push I need. Grabbing her hips, I slam into her from the bottom, pushing my hips forward as she screams above me.

"Be a good little *sous* and rub that clit for me," I instruct, watching sweat bead on her forehead. She reaches between us and starts rubbing. "That's right, flick that bean just like I would with my tongue." As her movements turn furious, I fuck into her like my dick will fall off otherwise.

We're both groaning and moving fast and passionately. It's when she lets out a string of curses, squeezing me harder than ever before that I lose my edge and release inside her. Fuck. Fuck. Fuck.

"Your ass is divine, Josephine," I praise as she lifts off me. Pulling her into my side, I tuck her under my arm.

"Remind me to test your age more often," she teases. I bite her ear and start kissing her throat. Before getting too into it as my dick already starts stiffening, I roll off the bed, carrying her with me to the bathroom.

"Let me take care of you, beautiful."

"I'd like that," she whispers against my heart, kissing it several times over.

This is happiness.

This is what we were meant to be.

This is everything I couldn't have ever dreamed.

She's my perfect match.

My woman.

Mine.

Mine.

Mine.

CHAPTER 41

JOEY

I STARE AT THE POSITIVE ON THE STICK, SMILING SO big. This isn't happening, is it? I'm pregnant. Actually pregnant. My heart soars, and my stomach flutters. Tears run down my face as emotions clog me up. This is what I've always wanted.

Especially since that doctor in France told me it wasn't a possibility.

I'm. Pregnant.

Me.

Toby.

Us.

I call my OB and make an appointment for a full workup.

I need to know. I absolutely need to see where this goes. Toby is going to be thrilled.

Most men shy away from baby talk or wanting them, but when I finally opened up about not being able to conceive, he was so supportive. He did research, and we made sure that we were both on the same adoption page. Because it's as much as we could really do.

As I gape at the stick over and over, my heart hammers with pride and overwhelming joy. A baby. We're going to have a baby. The feeling of absolute glee doesn't push me to go tell Toby, it's the love.

Running to our office, I forgo knocking. He's on the phone, but as soon as he sees me, his face lights up.

"Raul, I have to go."

My grin widens. He's so accommodating, always considering our time. The way his eyes shine with love brings me elation. We're so good together.

Not just in bed, though we excel at that too.

"Hey, beautiful." My heart melts right there into a puddle of love and gooeyness.

"Hey, there," I whisper, unable to keep the happiness at bay. Pulling the test out from behind my back, I show him. His expression is confused for all of five seconds before his brows lift.

"I'm going to be a dad?" he muses loudly. "A dad?"

I jump up and down, squealing. "You are!" My heart flutters like my stomach, and I can't keep the elation from consuming me.

"We're having a baby!" The tears come again, sparking a fit of giggles. I've never been happier. He's rounding the desk and lifting me up.

"We're having a baby," he says seductively, his voice going from light to hot in a second's notice. He takes my mouth greedily, swallowing my moans, and carries me to our room. At some point, I drop the stick and become entirely absorbed with his mouth.

"Fuck, you're so beautiful," he husks. Setting me on the bed, he spreads my legs. Pushing my dress up, he grips my panties, sliding them down my thighs. "You're always so wet for me, Sous."

"Stop talking and take me," I demand, wanting him inside me right now.

"As you wish, wife."

That never gets old.

Him calling me his wife.

It's so captivating and sexy, especially when he's about to use me. He kneels between my thighs and licks across my slit. He's groaning as he starts feasting on me. It's so hot, having me bow upward into his mouth as he greedily bites and slurps.

"Toby," I moan, and he slips a finger inside me, pressing upward, hitting my favorite spot.

"Come for me, Sous. Soak my fingers."

And I explode as he bites my clit, grinding his teeth over the swollen flesh. Fuck me.

We're always fire together, an inferno where we both bask

in the endless heat of it all.

WE'RE SITTING IN THE WAITING ROOM, HOPING TO

get images of our little Gumby today. Eight weeks ago, when I got my blood tests, it was confirmed. We're having a baby. I sit and absently rub my stomach as Toby watches with rapt attention. His face is glowing more than mine. He's high on this feeling, and to be honest, so am I. We sit together, hand in hand, and wait to be called in. I'm barely showing, my bump is like one you get from bloating after eating one-too-many tacos. But God, does it feel like perfection.

I never thought this would be us, but I couldn't be happier. Seeing the elation on my husband's face as he rubs my stomach every night, talking to it and kissing it, makes me cry.

Stupid hormones.

He's never seemed happier, and when we make love, it's fiercer, more passionate, driving us both wild. But what I can't get over? The way he looks at me as if I'm his queen.

"Mrs. Hayes?" the nurse calls out, making my heart race. This is it. The moment we've been waiting for. We head to a scale, and I'm being weighed. Then she's settling us into a room and taking my vitals.

"All seems good," she says with a grin. "The doctor will be right in."

"I can't believe this is happening, Sous," Toby chimes, his eyes full of endearing emotions.

"I know," I cry, the sentiment hitting me fiercely. He kisses me then, holding my jaw and face, making sure I feel every ounce of love he's offering.

"You're so fucking stunning, Joey. So goddamn perfect and breathtaking. Thank you for making me the happiest man." He kisses me again, harder, longer, and as I'm about to straddle his lap, the doctor comes in and clears her throat.

"Hello," she chirps, her cheeks a little rosy.

"I'm so sorry," I apologize with heat flaming every inch of me.

"It's quite alright," she muses. She's a small thing with black hair pulled back in a ponytail, scrubs, and a stethoscope around her neck. She's dainty and cute. "Let's get started, shall we?"

She pats the table for me to lie back on, grabs the gel and a little white monitor. Rubbing the probe on my stomach, you can hear the whooshing of the insides of my body. She moves it around and again and again. I'm looking at the little black screen, not knowing what to look for. From what I've read in books and have watched in movies, this isn't how I recall any of the descriptions.

After several seconds, she turns off the machine, wipes my stomach, and before the words leave her lips, I already know what's wrong.

"The baby is no longer viable." The words hit me like a train, and my stomach hurts with realization. No. This can't be happening. This was our little miracle. Our little baby. The Gumby we were going to love endlessly.

Tears prick my eyes, and I can't breathe.

I can't breathe.

I can't breathe.

Panic sets in, making me nauseous. The realization of me not being strong enough for our baby overwhelms me, and I'm a mess. As I cry, the doctor talks to Toby, and as he comes over and tries to soothe me, I scream. The pain hurts. It's deep and visceral. It's damning and unfair. It hurts and hurts and hurts some more. It stabs at me like a knife, making sure I feel every goddamn puncture, going deeper and deeper. It's not fair, this life. It took my little Gumby; I wasn't strong enough. I couldn't home it. Take care of it. I'm not a good mom. I killed my baby.

My stomach sinks, and I'm shaking all over. Before I can make it off the table, I puke. Anxiety and hatred lace my every breath.

I cry myself into exhaustion until I eventually pass out. When I wake up, I'm naked and in the bath as my husband rubs soothing touches across my body. He holds me lovingly. He warms me. But how is he not angry?

I killed our baby. I ruined our chance. All because I hated my father and had to go to France. I'm such a selfish lech. I've ruined everything, and now, we're paying the price for it.

I cry more as he washes my sins away, trying to baptize me into a new light, a clearer one. The anger rides me, tells me it's all fake. We don't get to have any happiness. I've ruined it for us, ruined our lives, killed our baby.

He doesn't stop consoling me, even after he's washed me and dried me. He carries me bridal style to our room and kisses my forehead with so much care it hurts. It's fucking misery seeing him so calm.

Break for me.

Break with me.

Break, goddammit.

CHAPTER 42

TOBY

HOW TO BE STRONG 101: *DON'T BE.*

Like with Lo, I stay here. But internally, I'm screaming.

How did she do this? Make it through the devastation of knowing something died before it had the chance to breathe? How does anyone ease that kind of pain? How do I make my wife know I love her so much?

By staying? Done.

By holding her? Done.

By not leaving her side? Done.

I've watched her break apart, and I've loved her through it. I've hugged her and told her how beautiful she is. I cried in the silence of the night when she finally passed out from exhaustion, but is it enough?

She broke in my arms.

I broke in the emptiness of my living room.

She hurts so much. How can my hurt compare? Yes, I lost a child I didn't get to meet. I didn't get to hear its heartbeat, or see whether it'd be a boy or a girl.

But her? My strong fucking wife? She lost a part of herself. She had to experience the aftermath in her body while I stay idly by, not knowing what she needed. Her words didn't exist, but her pain screamed constantly. The way she shut down tore me up inside. It literally wrenched my heart out and pulverized it while I tried not to push her. She deserves to be happy and have a baby and be a mom. She'd be the best mom.

Tears stream down my face. It hurts to know I can't fix a single goddamn thing about our situation. I cry for what feels like hours, wishing I could do it in front of her. But my pain shouldn't rise above hers. I'll grieve in silence when she's least vulnerable, and when she needs me, I'll be there.

Dialing my mom's number, I yearn for her voice. Her guidance. Her love.

"Tobias?" she says, her voice filled with sleep and exhaustion.

"Ma," I whisper, and I crack. Just hearing her soft voice and breathing, I entirely shatter.

"What's wrong, baby boy?"

346

It's like I'm ten years old again, and I've fucked up my ankle by trying to catch up with Jase and all his friends, breaking my bones in the process.

"I-I," I stumble over the words. The hot feeling of guilt builds inside me, spilling from my eyes and taking my heart again. What's left of it? There's nothing fucking left. "I lost a baby a couple of days ago." With those words, I slam the gavel down. I ax the words as if they're wood I need to chop. It's hurtful and effervescent, so fucking raw. Admitting my loss makes it so much more real.

"Oh, baby. I'm so sorry."

I can hear it, the way she sniffles. Ma and I are alike in that sense. She holds in the pain, sucking it all up from the person who's hurting and absorbing it so they don't suffer alone.

"It hurts so much," I cry. My voice doesn't even sound like it belongs to me. It's so small and little—so sad. I'm so strong. Joey always told me that, and so did Lo, but right now, I can't be. I wanted that baby so fucking much.

Fate had other plans.

Destiny too.

My heart hammers in my chest, reminding me I'm alive, but what about the soul? Is that still intact? Does it and can it exist when death knocks on its door, stealing from it, making sure nothing but pain is left in its wake?

"I had a miscarriage after you were born," Mom explains after I sit and cry. "You were twelve years old."

Right as she says my age, I'm thrown back to a memory so

brutal, my body trembles.

I was twelve when I drank my first bottle of whiskey.

It wasn't just a sip like most kids do their first time, not simply a taste, or curiosity. No, it was the entire fucking bottle.

Unlike most, it did occur to me what it'd bring.

Dad always drank his life away. Repercussions weren't unbeknownst to me.

All the information needed, I possessed.

Going into that cabinet wasn't with lack of purpose. Every step, breath, and swallow of that woodsy liquid was intentional.

Me nearly dying in the end didn't matter. Only the purpose behind the action did. Escape. Freedom. Peace.

My hands trace the wood, my eyes scan the bottles, and my body hums with intention.

My dad finally snapped tonight, using me as his biggest punching bag. Then I had the unbearable sight of him forcing my mom onto her knees as he sodomized her. She cried—tears streaming from her eyes, the black from her mascara made crude marks over her sharp cheekbones.

I cried with her.

He finally let me leave, which is how I found myself perusing his cabinet. He only let me leave after forcing me to watch them. Something inside him is broken. It doesn't make sense to me, but I can't fix him. After I walked away, I went straight to the hutch in his office.

Grabbing some bottle that's green and tan and red, I shake it and bring it to my lips. Without thinking twice or smelling it, I chug. The first gulp makes me choke; I cough out the liquid. But that doesn't stop my pursuit. I take another sip, then another drink, eventually I'm sucking it down like my life depends on it until I'm feeling light-headed.

Ten minutes later, I'm sitting here, a bottle nestled between my palms, drinking it away like it's the purest form of grace.

I think of that night and wonder if it's the same one Mom is referring to. "I'm sorry you experienced that, Ma."

"Sometimes, it's best to think it is meant to be. No matter how emptying those words sound, God wouldn't take your baby unless it was—"

"Stop, Ma. Just stop."

"Toby, I'm just trying to say—"

"I don't want to hear it. Please. I just... I have to go."

I hang up. Not even a minute later, I'm rifling through my whiskey cabinet and see my favorite bottle of Jameson. My stomach clenches in anticipation of its burn.

If I'd known all those years ago that an amber liquid would drown me, take away all of my power, and watch me fall to my knees for it, would I have still drank it? Allow myself to become consumed by it? After knowing what it has done, how I allowed it to own me, and how it breaks me with every fucking drop, think I'd have walked away from it?

They have warning labels, so humans—as faulty as they are—will second-guess a choice. Alcohol isn't like that. There are whiskey commercials that make people look sophisticated and happy, sexy and sensual, and people talk about the reprieve it offers. What about warning us that it'll rip you apart eventually? A sign that it'll take and take and take until the only thing left is worthlessness?

What about the self-loathing?

The anger.

Bitterness.

Resentment.

The lost time?

The cold glass of the bottle touches my lips, whispering sweet nothings, promising to hide away my pain. That succulent titter, offering nothing more than regret, but lying all the same.

I open wide, guzzling another mouthful. Once, this burned. It ached as it sloshed down my esophagus. Now, it's a tantalizing zing, a high like no other, and as it weasels its way into my stomach, comfort confides in me, begging me for more, more, more.

I was almost three years sober.

Three goddamn years.

Who knew it'd take one loss to break me?

Joey saved me.

Now, it's Jameson's turn.

BREATHE

...lly a number got £70
...er. so I re...
...nith called at night sch...
...ay and ...old me he ha...
... I ask...
...mber ... to you whe...
...arlet did. Have you
...f the German soldier who ha...
... and asked the Irish pri...
... none. On the wa...
... German's head but ...
...ad of the fact. On ...
... what the goes of b...
... head shot
...ead,

PART III
DETOXIFY

Spirals. We all have them. From afar,
we can see the telltale signs
and try to catch them for other people.
What about for the ones who are experiencing it first-hand?
We try to put the bottle down.
We try to clean our palette of addiction.
We try to be better.
What if the sole person who had
endless hope for you becomes hopeless?
You spiral.
I'm spiraling.
I'm spinning.
I'm dying.
Is it too late?

- TOBY

CHAPTER 43

TOBY

MY JAW CLENCHES WITH THE EXTENT OF PRESSURE I'm putting on it, my eyes strain to unfeel everything up until this moment. *Love hurts.* If I've learned anything from Loren, it's that it can be the utmost exciting part of life while the most detrimental in the same breath.

It's exhaustive.

A cheat.

Rebellious in nature.

You can have many loves. They don't even have to be romantic. But the kind embedded in the soul that are on a deeper level than friendship, that bow inside until they seep through the pores, that's the love we fight for. It's the love we want and search for. On the same token, it's the one we take for granted, abuse, and wish to live without because it can calm as much as destruct. It can ensure pain and ease it. Kiss the heart and sink its teeth in. It wholeheartedly owns all the power and that is its right. It's not a privilege, nothing earned or borrowed, because love bends for no one, it doesn't malleate to what is needed, it is a reckless substance no one can control. Love chooses its own path, and like the saps we are, we follow willingly.

Her mom slept for hours. When she came to, I had a concierge doctor on hand. She'd be going through rehab in my goddamn house, I'll make sure of it. Joey hasn't left our room, and I don't blame her. Imagine the turmoil she must be experiencing knowing her mom is fine and only left because shooting up was more important than being a mother.

How fucked in the head is she?

To leave someone as beautiful, loving, and strong as my wife.

She missed out on seeing the most spectacular woman grow and thrive. Joey did it without her, Clay, and even without me. She blossomed with freedom and ease, she crushed all expectations, and is fighting for a top chef title.

My wife.

The amazing woman.

The one who hates me.

The one I'm starting to realize I *don't* hate.

The one who ruined me for good reason.

I don't deserve her, but I'll be damned if I don't try.

It may have taken me seeing her a mess last night, breaking in front of me, but thinking of our unborn baby, the pain, the suffering, and I'm willing to break the mold and be better. Would she say yes? Does her hatred run too deep?

Try.

A simple word.

One syllable.

Something everyone does on a daily basis.

Try to be successful.

Try to push harder.

Try to smile more.

Try not to break.

Try not to allow hurt to win.

Try not to die.

There are many things that propel others to change. The problem with change is you have to choose to take the actions necessary to be better. You can't do the same thing and expect it to work. You can hope for the best and not actually put forth the effort.

You have to want to make a difference. You have to actually fight and not give up.

It's simple to give in to the easiness. Take a bottle, chug it, fuck some random woman, be the mistake because it's something you're used to being. That's what I did. My dad beat me, and I allowed myself to be the mistake from that point on. Every problem I've had leads back to that excuse. My childhood sucked, so why can't I suck too?

Seeing my wife break beneath my fingertips isn't something I ever want to experience again. Not unless she's breaking for me in a way that brings her pleasure. We're bonded through our hatred; it's something that tethers us together. That hatred we've both clung to kept us here and continues to thrust us together. No matter how volatile or desperate our actions may be, it's us that always ends with one another.

"Mr. Hayes?" the doctor interrupts my chasm of mindlessness. I'm sitting on the lounger in the living room, holding a bottle of Jameson, wondering if he'd make today easier or just push me further down a hole of no return.

"Yes?" I ask, looking up. He watches me as I stare at the bottle.

"Addiction isn't something you can just throw away."

"Didn't ask you, now did I?"

He nods, pursing his lips. "No, but I'm a doctor who made an oath. Whether or not you want to hear it, I'll tell you." A sardonic laugh leaves me. *This motherfucker.*

"That anger rising inside you from me just offering you some advise only further proves my point."

"And pray tell, Doc, what might that be."

"You need help, Mr. Hayes. Not the kind you think that bottle brings, but the kind that takes the bottle out of the equation."

My nostrils flare as I barely contain the unnatural rage inside me. It feels like a tea kettle whistling, barely a breath away from explosion. It's not healthy, but I can't seem to wish it away.

"Is that what you came out here to say?" I avoid his caring tactics. I'll win this by myself.

I will.

"No, but it's not something I can avoid." I stare up at him and the pensive expression he's toting. He pulls out his wallet and a card. "This is Natalie, my sponsor." *His sponsor.* It dawns on me that whether he was a doctor or not, he'd spot me from a mile away. Broken people find broken people. They heal and help, or they tarnish and torture. Toxicity can go one of two ways. It can burn and fester, bringing you to your knees. Or, it can be a blessing in disguise, making your low go even lower than you imagined possible and, in that sense, brings you light, enough to get you detoxified.

Detox.

That's what I need.

A detox of pain. Of alcohol. My self-pity.

Take it all.

"I have a sponsor," I respond, peering into his icy eyes that remind me of my wife's when she's frigid and unfeeling. "She's probably done with me by now. A few months ago, she stopped reaching out."

"That's the thing about addicts, whether they're sponsors or not, it's hard to give up. Our vices own us, but it's up to us to choose to alter our lifestyle to soothe that. Your sponsor, is she a recovering addict?"

I nod, thinking of Bobbie, wondering how she's doing and

if I've driven her to madness. Her love for Lo's little brother always brought me a sense of peace, knowing it was more than a job to her. That *I* mattered, not just my progress. And that's why she and I connected.

"She doesn't struggle like many of us."

He shakes his head immediately. "I'm sure, like me, that's untrue. You'll always be an addict, just as I will. It's ingrained. An addictive personality that clings to something. She has her own struggles, but she just hides them well from others. Since you have a sponsor, I hope you'll do what's right for you and your wife and take that first step."

With a sad acceptance, I take the card and wait for him to tell me why he came here.

"Lianna needs to be moved to a facility. At first, I didn't know if she was battling the detox or what, but she's going to need to be admitted soon. There's something off with her mind, altering her behaviors, and until a psychiatric physician looks over her, I'm going to need to do this the hard way."

"Whatever needs to be done, let me know."

"You're too good for helping her while struggling with your own vices," he praises. But I'm not a good man. A very selfish one is more like it.

"Anything else?" I ask, trying to shoo him away. Understanding flickers over his features, and then he's turning away to leave.

Now, it's my turn. To change. To try. To fix my wife and our marriage.

"Let me fix you, Sous. I hate that you're hurting and never want you to be forced to hurt yourself. I can't imagine a life without you in it."

"Toby," she cries, tears slipping down her cheeks. Gripping her wrist, I feather my fingers over her cuts and see two new ones.

"What's making you hurt, Josephine? Tell me. Let me fix it."

Her eyes shine with tears, ones that are heavy and burdened by pain. She's so sad at this moment, broken and damaged, just trying to live.

And that fucking hurts.

Pain isn't an easy emotion to tamper, it's one as invasive as a disease, it spreads and consumes, killing its host once its destination is reached.

"I want a baby." Her admission is soft and bereft. It's so tender and filled with desperation. It's a plea all while being hopeless in the dark.

During this moment, I love her even more if that's possible. I'm feeling an intense need to save her, protect her, be whatever she needs just so she'll never hurt herself again.

Rubbing the fresh red marks, ruddy crimson smears with the action. The hurt in her solemn eyes begs me to stop and pretend they're not there. The shame she's experiencing is as present as the moon tonight. It's so true and frail. Leaning down as the pain leaks from her eyes, My lips touch the vermilion slices. I kiss and soothe. I love and conquer. I'm here and always will be.

"It'll happen, Sous. I fucking promise it will," I swear. Whether we have to go to every doctor across the world, every clinic that specializes in fertile care, I'll do it.

Not a fucking dime will be spared.

"It won't, Toby. It won't happen. I'm broken. So goddamn damaged and hideous." I let her wrist and arm go, pressing into her.

Her skin feels even more fragile beneath my rough palms.

Rubbing circles across her cheeks, I try and convey the emotions in me. Heavy ache burrows itself inside me, seeing and feeling every agonizing sensation she's feeling.

How can I love the pain away from you?

How can I love you enough?

How can I love your scars if you pretend they don't matter?

Her sodden gaze pierces mine. Sad and lonely, her quivering lips cause the inner turmoil to boil over and beat all the happiness out of me.

Kissing her nose, I breathe her in. Her sunshine scent mixed with the spicy aftermath of Fireball whiskey infiltrates my senses.

Unlike a year ago, my vices aren't controlling me.

Except her. She's one of them now, and I'll never let her go.

Those sad ambers close, and I kiss them too. My lips trace every inch of her face, pushing all my love into her, giving her everything I have.

"You are so goddamn beautiful, Sous."

Her shoulders shake. Stiff agony washes over her as it rumbles and has this protective growl releasing from me. When the world is cruel, who punishes it? Does it pay comeuppance for the torture it ensues? How can we overcome our hardships when it holds our head under water? While we thrash beneath the surface, so close to happiness and reprieve, it takes and takes and continues to force us beneath into the nothingness.

"I'm not, Toby. I'm so ugly. My scars show that, they convey my disgusting insides. They're the revelation." I rub her face before gripping it tighter, forcing her gaze to connect with mine.

"You're the most fucking beautiful person in this entire world. Your scars don't make you any less; they prove your strength, they reveal your fight, and they explain that while you may be the most stunning woman I've ever met, you're also one surrounded by pain that surmounts the ease in your life. You're a goddamn fighter, Sous. A fucking warrior. No one on this godforsaken earth can take that from you."

I kiss her, silently promising her that each word is my oath. It's my truth. Heady whimpers escape her as she wraps herself around me. Rearranging us on the bed, I prop her head on top of my chest, holding her, loving her, wanting every good thing for her.

We'll have a baby.

Fighting heaven or hell won't be an issue because she's worth it all.

"I love you, Sous."

She shudders from the words, then moves to where my heart rests. Warmth from her ear shocks me as she places it flat against the base of my ribcage. Her fingers trace lazy swirls around the light smattering of hair. Love bleeds into me with each pass of her touch, feeling everything words cannot convey.

"I love you too, old man. Don't give up on me," she nearly begs. Halting her hand, she lifts her chin toward me. Then she's moving to kiss me.

When she pulls back with heavy vexation, it's then that I see her fear.

"Never, Josephine. Not even for a second. I'll never leave your side, and I'll always fight for you."

My body shakes with acute suffering, feeling so much at this moment. Then she's tucking herself back into me.

I love her.

She's worth it.

She's mine.

CHAPTER 44

PRESENT

JOEY

HE WANTS TO TRY.

I don't.

It's all I've ever wanted, but as he brought it up three weeks ago when he slipped into our bed, holding me like no time had passed, I changed my mind.

For the past few weeks, we've been eating dinner every night, talking more, becoming friends all over again. But that's all I'll offer. My heart isn't his to hold anymore.

Heading down the elevator to leave and see Gray, I am stopped on the fortieth floor. My stomach clenches. It's not news to me that this is the floor where Toby fucks his women. He thinks I'm stupid, but in reality, I've seen the invoices, the card charges, everything. I know what he does in there and the names of the women he does it with.

It took every ounce of control not to search and stalk them. See what makes them so goddamn special. I bet they don't know how he likes his cock sucked, or how he likes being ridden while I bend backward. No, they couldn't know anything because they aren't *me*.

I groan as the doors open, and a brunette walks in. It wouldn't be anything suspect until my eyes land on the tattoo showing on her arm. A butterfly.

My eyes go to that night almost a month ago.

It goes to the image he sent me.

The woman beneath him.

The one he fucked.

The one he chose over me that night.

My stomach flip flops in a nauseating way.

"Up or down?" I squeak, unsure of how to keep my emotions at bay. Tears don't spring, but hot-filled rage does, it overflows, making me shake.

"Down. Only came for a quickie," she simpers, smirking at me. My blood runs cold.

He wouldn't. There's no way he'd ask me to try again if he was still fucking his whores on the side, right? *There wasn't a stipulation, Josephine. He can fuck whomever he wants.*

"Oh, nice," I grind out, trying not to sound as aggravated.

"He's super rich and hot. His body… my God. The abs on that

man…" she trails off, her eyes glittering in a memory. "He fucks me like a dream, and if he wasn't married, we'd be together."

I swallow the bile rising. Shutting my eyes on the imagery, I feel my body near collapsing.

He wouldn't do this all over again.

No.

He… can't.

"There's no feelings involved, Sous. I only want to hurt you."

"God, and that cock," she continues. I'm going to gag. "Not only is it huge, but he knows how to use every inch." The elevator beeps then, stopping at the main floor. I'm booking it while the woman stares at me as if I've grown two heads.

My heart—or what was left of it—is gone.

With those parting words, I know there's no going back. It's one thing to know about his affairs that happened while we were separated, but seeing them in the flesh, knowing he's trying to get back into my good graces and is still fucking around? No. I practically book it to *Mi Casa*.

When I see Sanje, it's like he knows something is wrong. "Chef?"

"I'm quitting. I know this is the worst timing, but don't tell Toby for at least an hour."

"I can't not tell him. That's—"

"My last act as your managing chef, don't tell him for an hour. I need that. An hour, Sanje."

"But—"

"Please," I implore, my emotions must be trickling through

because he nods solemnly.

After I give him and my favorite staff members hugs, I practically bolt. Adrenaline rides me up the elevator. It pushes me to pursue this issue and not be a lost cause.

He can't fix himself if he's still screwing other people. I can't fix myself with him around. Maybe this was the push we both needed. Me, leaving.

Hitting the sixtieth floor, my heart aches. Not in the physical sense but more psychosomatic. It's painful, but only because my mind knows how much it hurts.

After scanning my card, I grab the handle and freeze inside my door. Closing it behind me, I allow myself to soak in my only home. The foyer is elegant and huge. White upon white with black upon black accents. It's perfectly modern and clean. The walls are filled with selfies from across the world with Toby. That's who we were. That couple. The one who took selfies during every adventure, but instead of uploading them on social media, we cherished each memory for our eyes alone.

I stop at my favorite one, unable to keep the smile at bay. It was our first anniversary. We decided to go to Italy. He took me to go wine tasting. The problem was, I couldn't be with him for the tasting. It was the first time we ever really sexted, and God, it was so hot. He came back to our hotel and fucked me for hours.

My body warms at the memory. The photo is of us wrapped in each other. We're naked, but it's so sensual and tactful that you can't tell it's us. It's beautiful in a tasteful way.

It's my favorite photo of us.

Toby always had an exhibition streak, and it turned me on to no avail. That is, until that night he sent me a photo of himself with the woman in the elevator. With that in mind, I check my watch and see it's already been twenty-three minutes. Grabbing the photo off the wall, I carry it with me to our walk-in closet. Inside, it's a mess. A metaphor for our relationship.

We don't have a side each; we're intertwined. It used to bring me happiness. Now, looking at it with jaded eyes, all I see is madness.

Grabbing the first few things I can see, I take them and look for my luggage bag. Not wanting to overpack, I grab all my favorite undies, socks, shoes, and dresses. He won't even notice anything missing immediately.

Shoving all the items in my bag, I grab my favorite make-up kit with all the essentials and my straightener. Forgetting all my other shit that's replaceable, I rush out of my room and don't even bother telling my mom as I trail to the front door. She's been recovering here, but isn't allowed to leave her room unless she is accompanied by someone. I've kept my distance, and after the doctor gave the go-ahead for her home recovery, she was back here for detox.

I stop at the counter that I fell in love with when we bought this place and take off my ring. The one on my finger belonged to Toby's Mom's. Only then when I'm leaving my finger naked, after it being so heavy for years, do I let the emotions slip from my eyes. The wetness smacks my chest, letting me know it isn't going to be easy to end this.

"Goodbye," I whisper to no one, shutting the door behind me. With a renewed sense of purpose, I head to the elevator, making sure not to enter the one the woman was in earlier.

As it trails down, my only prayer is that he doesn't come up. It'd ruin this easy break for me. It wouldn't take much for him to convince me to stay. He has so much power over me and this treacherous heart of mine.

When I finally hit the ground floor, I hit up the valet.

"Mrs. Hayes, so nice seeing you." I nearly laugh and crawl out of my skin at the same time. Wouldn't it be convenient for someone to say it's nice to see me when mascara streaks my cheeks? I didn't bother to clean up before rushing out.

"My car, Adam," I rush. "And please hurry." He must see the urgency in my eyes because his widen in response, and before I know it, he's running toward the parking garage. I have my own spot, but parking in Hollow Ridge is hell. Their stalls are miserable to reverse out of, so I always use the valet service here.

When he comes back with my Lexus series, I smile and nearly cry. Toby bought me this car for Christmas, saying my Avalon needed to go. It's the most beautiful vehicle I've ever owned, and it's fast as hell too.

He exits the car and smiles at me, but it doesn't meet his eyes. I reach into my purse and pull out a hundred, making sure he makes eye contact.

Handing it to him, I hold his hand a moment. "Please, don't say anything to my husband."

Understanding licks his features, but I can tell he's getting the wrong ideas. Toby doesn't beat me, I just need to leave. He nods at me. "Your secret is safe with me, Mrs. Hayes. Safe trip."

More tears surface as I cry, and when I get into my car, the time on the radio shows my hour is up. *Fuck.* Connecting my Bluetooth, I set up my *Heartbreak playlist* waiting for my heart to literally break. Will I feel it? Will it make a sound? Will I even care?

NF's "Time" blares from the speakers, and the waterworks come pouring out. This man always knows how to brutalize my vital organs with his vocals and emotive performances. And as the lyrics belt out, I press on my gas pedal and leave. *Hollow Ridge has never been my home.*

Being raised here, then moving back with Toby, it was never set in my soul as a place to stay forever. It wasn't until Toby told me how much he wanted me to settle here with him that I did.

It's amazing that in the years we've been here, not once has our paths crossed with his brother and Lo. It's like they all avoided areas that they knew each other frequented. They don't call him or reach out. It's almost as if he disappeared, and they don't care.

Even now, only five minutes from my favorite beach, I feel myself leaving like a death toll. It wracks my body with solidarity, making a pact with my soul that we're damaged and done.

Now, I can move forward.

That's what we both wanted.

The difference between then and now is it won't be together.

Maybe it was never meant to be.

CHAPTER 45

PRESENT

TOBY

"WHAT IS IT, SANJE?" I ASK, WONDERING WHY he's calling me and not talking to Joey. She works all day today. She wanted the extra time away from her mom, not that I blame her. She's being tortured by memories that are all lies.

It's not surprising she's diving in deep.

"Remember when you told me not to waste your time three years ago?" he mutters dumbly. Either this guy is stupid, wasting my time, or thinks I care about that far into the past.

"Look, I don't have—"

"Joey quit," he interrupts me, sending my brain to

skyrocket. I'm at the office on the main floor. Why didn't she come to me? What happened? I've been in meetings all day; we're opening a new store in Las Vegas, and it's taking all of my spare time. Is she okay?

"Is she okay? Did something happen? Is she hurt?" I mutter quickly, spitting the words like I'm a rapper in a battle of life and death.

"She chose to leave, sir. Forced me to give her an hour of time or she'd fire me."

I laugh sardonically. There's no way she did that. Joey isn't rash or cruel. She says what she means and means every word she says.

Shit.

"How did she seem?"

"Erratic. She had mascara stains and red eyes. She had to have been crying. She was a mess." His voice seems far away now. What the fuck happened?

"I have to go. Take over for her."

"But, sir—"

"No buts, Sanje. Get it done."

"Of course," he says before I hang up. Not even taking the time to shut down my computer, I rush out of my office and run to the elevators. People glance at me as if I've lost my mind, but I'm beyond caring. The only thing that runs through my mind is fear. What if her dad did something? What if Marsha did? What if her mom... my mind trails to the woman fighting for her life in our home. She has a full staff watching her, keeping her alive as she purges her plague.

The elevator is too slow, but I wait as it rises, hoping it goes faster. It doesn't. When it finally hits our floor and beeps, I run out, heading straight for the door.

Why ask for an hour? Who was she running from?

I make it to our room and see nothing is missing. I head to the guest room, our shared bathroom, then our closet. I can't really tell what's different—

My mind stops as I peer at my side of the closet. She ensures it's not my side. That there are no sides, but there is. It's where I put all of our favorite clothes. Hers and mine. And that's where I notice all the missing items.

But what really catches my attention is my Green Bay Packer shirt. It's long-sleeved, charcoal gray, and something Joey stole when we first started living together. She wore it all the time.

It's so big on her tiny body that it's practically a dress. But it's definitely something I couldn't miss. That's when I realize her leaving wasn't a fear tactic. It was a choice. Her choice.

My heart sinks and hammers in tandem, like it simultaneously keeps me alive and promises me death. I choose the latter.

She left.

Abandoned me.

Something finally made her leave.

That alone hurts like a motherfucker.

I stare at my shaking hands and go to my liquor cabinet.

Three weeks is nothing, right? Three weeks doesn't matter. Three weeks means I'm not even that far into sobriety. I can cheat. I can indulge. I can rip out what's left of my soul.

An unopened bottle of Jameson rests in my palm. The glass cools my heated skin. You'd think with realization would come doom and heartache and a bitter coolness like my wife's heart, but that's not true. It's heated. Anger beats faster, rushing through your system with emotions on repeat. Almost like it's heating you from the inside out, just like alcohol.

I take off the plastic wrapping and open the lid.

Bringing it to my lips, I scrunch my nose, inhaling way too deep. It smells like bad decisions and wrongness. Like my next fix, next overdose, next end.

Maybe I'll die with my companion in my hands.

Maybe I'll not live to see this outcome.

Maybe I'll exhaust every organ inside me and won't have to feel this kind of agony again.

It's my fault.

All my fault.

I stare down at the bottle, bringing it to my lips once more, but then it hits me. What if she left so I'd change? Isn't that why she said no to trying when I asked? Isn't that why she played hard to get?

A newfound energy surges through me, and I cap the bottle and place it back inside my cabinet. And as I head toward the door to leave, I notice two things.

One, my wife took our favorite picture. She says it's her

favorite, but what she doesn't know is that it's my favorite too. I took that image while she rode my cock. That was the first night of our sexting. The first night I fucked her so hard that we were both exhausted the next day.

Two, her ring.

Ten feet to my right on our black marble counters sits her ring. Well, my mom's ring. It's rose gold, antique, and entwined with vines. It felt so fitting for us. It was the first time I asked Gene for anything. Ma stopped wearing it when Brant died. It was a ring his mother gave to him to give to my mom. Gene was happy to give it to me.

He's the only one who knew of my marriage.

He came to our small redo ceremony.

He's more of a dad than mine ever was.

Holding the dainty little band in my hands, it dawns on me... she left and she *isn't* coming back. With this newfound information, I do something I never thought I would.

I call my brother.

CHAPTER 46

JASE

LIFE TAKES MANY TURNS, BUT SINCE DEDICATING myself to my wife and family, everything has changed for the better. Between counseling and my constant groveling, Peaches and I have come out stronger.

My heart aches when she's gone, and nothing stops me from pursuing her as if we were just newly dating again.

She's mine.

Again.

I fight for that right every day.

She deserves the entire fucking world.

To be worshiped. Adored over. Praised.

And fuck, do I praise her. Whether with words or on my knees as I eat her from behind, I fucking praise her. She doesn't cease to amaze me day in and day out.

I'm at my corporate building, handling some things Sally and the team are unable to deal with. Since I'm still the owner of Collins & Co, it's something I tend to do on occasion, even if I don't do the usual day-to-day.

Flipping through the final files for expansion on Hollow Hills in Vegas, a smile takes over my face. Fuck. It feels good, knowing I chose the right man—or in this case, woman—for this job. Sally makes sure to get shit done, and in turn, my retiring feels less like a loss.

My phone vibrates in my pocket, the buzzing barely registering in my otherwise silent office. Today is one of those days when hardly anyone is in the office, which leaves me pretty much alone, sans Sally's assistant.

"Hello?" I ask, not recognizing the number. Usually, I'd use the scan-call feature, opting to avoid speaking with a random caller. Most of the time, it's a scammer or telemarketer. Either way, I'm not a fan.

"Jase," Toby's voice rasps. It's not usual for him to call. Hell, it's been five years of silence. Just like Lo and I asked. Hearing his voice now, the strain in it, makes me believe something is wrong and reminds me how much missing him has become an inexorable ache. "I fucked up." His voice strains, and that hollowness he left in my chest by his actions and my choices makes itself known, reminding me of simpler times.

"Jase, I messed up bad," Toby grouses. His eyebrows are drawn in, his hair in disarray, and his busted lip and black eye stare at me like a crime scene.

It's violent, the reminder of Dad and what he does to me and not Toby. God. I'll protect him no matter what, though, because he's my baby brother.

"What happened?" I ask, tipping his head back to peer at the shiner. It's bad. Possibly did more damage than broken blood vessels. My brother is prone to fighting, it's a reactionary thing for him. Someone will say shit and make him mad, and instead of being understanding or blowing it off like I do, he beats them.

This time, though, it seems like he went for someone too big.

"I-I," he stutters, his eyes glossing. My brother may only be fourteen, but the little shit causes so much mayhem you'd think he was five.

"Spit it out, Tobes. Let me fix this." Something is eating him up inside, and it has my body shifting uncomfortably. He's not shy by any means, but he's cowering into himself, hiding. It's not something I'm used to seeing with him.

Running a hand through his hair, he frowns and grips the back of his neck, avoiding my gaze. It's embarrassment and fear wrapped into one, and I hate every moment of his discomfort. Did someone attack him? Did—

"Dad caught me in the whiskey cabinet," he mutters, stopping my train of thought. Dad did this? Hit him? My chest aches, rising with hatred and power, my mantra of "don't react" not holding itself well inside me.

"What did he do?" I practically spit, the unabated vehemence *spreading through the air with each word. Brant is a piece of shit, and even that is a kind descriptor for the waste of air that brought me my brother.*

"You're not going to ask why I was in the cabinet?" he deters the question, but I know it's because he doesn't want to talk about the fact that Brant hit him. While Brant used to be bigger than me, like he is with Tobes, it's different now. I fight back. It gets me beat more, but it's worth it.

"No. Doesn't fucking matter. What. Did. He. Do?" My voice brooks no argument as I grip my brother's shoulders. I stare into his fearful eyes, the ones that haven't had that boyish glint in years.

He doesn't realize I know his secrets.

He drinks.

Like a goddamn sailor.

Just like me, except my vice of choice is weed and Molly because booze barely does anything for me. Finally reaching my gaze, Tobes bites the inside of his cheek.

"I can't stop, Jase. I've fucking tried." I bring him to my chest, feeling him relax and breathe. His chest rises and falls as if the world finally let up on weighing him down.

"Let me help. Anything, Toby. I'll do anything you need."

And I will.

Even if Brant kills me.

I'll save him.

Always.

I'm brought back from the memory when Toby's voice is in my ear.

"Jase? You there?" He sounds so fucking broken, showing me the lost fourteen-year-old kid is still in there. Broken. Scathed. Damaged.

"Yeah, yeah. What's wrong?"

He lets out a heavy exhale, and fuck if that doesn't make me feel like a shitty brother. "Can we meet?" The fact that he wants to see me face-to-face scares me far more than it should.

Does he want to ruin my life?

Does he need help?

Is he still my brother?

"Yeah, I'm at C&C for the day. Stop by."

"That didn't go so well the last time," he mutters. Toby came here five years ago, causing havoc amongst my employees. It wasn't pretty, and that asshole can throw a punch.

"That's all I can give. Lo's super busy at home," I lie. Not wanting to admit the fact that we have a son and Toby has no fucking clue every secret bridled there.

"Be there in ten," he finally responds, his exasperated breath only offers me more confusion.

Twelve minutes later, I'm opening the door to my brother, and he looks worse for wear. His eyes are bloodshot, his skin sallow, and the fucking haunted expression on his face isn't one I recognize. The only time he ever agonized like this was when Lo tried committing suicide.

"You look like shit," I offer.

"No shit, Sherlock. Got anymore compliments?"

"Still a fucking brat, it seems." We both laugh at that. The familiarity wraps around me, but with that, memories do too. The rose vines wrapping around my heart, needling the appendage with pain and hatred. Why does this exist? Why does this ache still hit me?

"I'm sorry for coming out of nowhere." Our eyes meet, his full of remorse. The surprise on my face must show since he's grimacing in the next moment. "I'm a shit brother, a fuck-up. I mean, it's not news, Jase. Since we were kids, you were perfect, and I was the troubled child."

"You said it," I return, walking back to my desk. Instead of sitting behind it, I lean against it, feeling the way Tobe watches me with heated anger. But unlike five years ago, it isn't leveled at me, it's elsewhere, somewhere I'm not privy to. Makes sense since we've been apart for so long.

"I'm married," he shoots out, scratching his stubbly chin. Closing his eyes, he grips his forehead and starts rubbing it as if it's throbbing.

"No shit?" I question, not believing my own ears. Hearing that he moved on from my life is the best news I've had since Lev was born.

"Such surprise, brother," he complains. "Fuck you very much."

"Going to explain why you're here?" I ignore his baiting. He better not want anything to do with my son. He just fucking better not.

"Were you ever going to tell me?"

And there it is.

"No."

"Why the fuck not?" he bites out, gripping his hair, tugging like the thought is blasphemous. Is it really? To think he fucked everything up—no matter our relation—and doesn't feel bad? To believe he'd have any right to *my* child? Fuck that.

"He's not yours."

"DNA doesn't lie, fucker."

"DNA doesn't make a father, dick. Just ask Gene."

He rushes me, his fists gripping my shirt. I ball up my own, preparing to fight if need be. This is my family. Lev is mine. Lo is mine. They're all mine.

Letting go and pushing off my chest, he lets out a strangled noise. Then his eyes are wet. "That's not why I'm here," he says raggedly. My eyes wander over his face, trying to detect lies.

"You said you fucked up. What happened?" Just like being a sixteen-year-old protecting his little brother, I watch as he crumples in front of me. The cocky son of a bitch who always had this front of confidence and edge is nowhere to be found. But this Toby? This is the little kid who drank to wash away his sins. The one who nearly killed himself to be happier. The one who made choices that ruined both of us forever.

"I married someone, and she changed my fucking life," he moans, his voice sad and strangled. The way the mood has vastly changed has me shaking with adrenaline and anger, yet very aware that the man on the chair across from me is anything but challenging right now.

"Keep going," I push, wanting to know what he's done and

what I need to do to fix this. That's what I am, after all—the fixer. Whether he sees it that way or not, it's what he's always reduced me to.

"Her name is Joey. Joey Moore-Hayes."

"Moore... like Mayor Moore?" I nearly choke. If I had water, I'd be a comical commercial, spitting it everywhere. Leaning against my desk once more, I grip the table, not knowing what to make of this information.

"We got wasted in Vegas five years ago. Tied the knot. Then when we finally found out, instead of annulling it like Joey deserved, her father convinced her to stay for her inheritance." He sputters this information out so fast that when he takes in a sharp breath, I'm stuck on the fact that this wasn't a choice marriage. "Before he convinced her, he threatened me. To ruin my life. He knew about my alcoholism and how finicky my business handlings have been."

"What a piece of shit," slips out from my mouth without me acknowledging it.

"Yeah, but that's not the worst part."

"There's more?"

He laughs bitterly, the jaded front present on his features. "Much more. Might need to sit for this, brother." Letting out a heavy breath, I nod, heading to my chair.

"Joey and I fell in love," he admits, wiping his thumb across his lip as contemplation festers above the surface. "She was bright and perfect. Fierce. So fucking fierce," he rambles. "She changed my life. I got sober. We had everything, Jase. Every-fucking-thing."

I stare at him as I recognize the lost soul leaking from his pores. Something happened. A damaged moment that tethered them was somehow severed, and the foreboding present in my veins only has me on edge. Whether our hatred runs deep from past memories, seeing my brother on the brink of throwing in the towel has me on edge.

"We got pregnant." The tears leaving his eyes make my throat feel sticky, and I try swallowing back the emotion, thinking of Lilac. "We lost it."

My chest pinches at that. The barren look in my brother's eyes is one I know all too well. He's hurting, resigned to the fact that pain is his routine.

"What did you do?" I whisper, wanting to know if he fucked up as I did or if he truly became a better man than the one I allowed myself to be.

"She pushed me away and found herself with Francis."

"Fuck," I hiss.

"Sound like a fucking sob story?" He lets out a self-deprecating laugh, and it takes all my strength to stay seated and not hug him. Not too long ago, he was Francis.

"I was wrong," he angrily adds. "About everything."

"What do you mean?" I ask hesitantly, not sure if I want to know.

"Well, I saw them. Hugging, he kissed her face and shit."

"He's French," I offer.

"Don't act like you weren't always on edge when I'd kiss

Lo's forehead."

"You were in love with her," I bite, grinding my molars, feeling my nails dig into my flesh. God, the fact that the resentment rides me this hard isn't pleasant at all.

"Francis and Joey have history."

Rubbing a palm down my face, I pinch the bridge of my nose. The fact that his story somehow mirrors mine is fucking astounding.

"They didn't do anything, according to both of them."

"Do you believe them?"

"Starting to," he admits. "That didn't stop me from telling her to sleep with who she wants and I'd do the same."

"Please don't say—"

"I fucked other people," he spits. "In spite of her and hating myself every fucking time, I did it. Didn't enjoy it or fall in love, but to hurt her, I fucked other women."

"What the fuck is wrong with you?" I hiss, suddenly not feeling as bad for him. He's goddamn toxic, always has been.

"I don't know, bro. How much time you got?"

"Seriously, why wouldn't you try?"

"And repeat the same actions? She had more power than Lo did to break me. Albeit, I broke us apart and felt like shit the past two years, I felt I had control."

"You started drinking again, didn't you?"

He nods, his face scrunched. He stands, pacing back and forth. Then he's at my desk, palms flat, his gaze hitting mine. "She's gone, Jase. That's why I'm here. She fucking left, and I don't know why."

"What do you think I can do?" He stares at me, his expression imploring all while he seems visibly shaken.

"We own the top floor of Hollow Hills."

"So that was *you*," I mock. "Couldn't just find somewhere not relative to me and everyone else?"

"Where's the fun in that?" he taunts. "Glad I did now because you have access to the database, no?"

I nod, hating that he knows this. If anyone knew outside of us, I could be facing lawsuits.

"Find out what happened," he begs, straightening himself and backing away.

So, I do.

After combing through the time frames Toby supplied, I find his wife in the elevator with some woman.

"That fucking cunt," he growls. I'm so surprised I almost punch him for calling his wife that. "Whatever she said to Joey set her off."

Turning the audio on, we both listen to that lady say, in explicit detail, what she wanted and planned on doing with a married man's dick.

Apparently, that man is my brother.

"I didn't love her. I'd never leave Joey, and I'd just cut things off with her. Fuck."

He grips his head and bites his fist. I understand his helplessness. It's something that I used to feel often. Even now, there are moments when the distrust haunts Lo. Even with therapy, that little niggling at the back of her mind doesn't fully disappear.

"I have to go find her," he says a moment later. He's a mess. A goddamn tornado terrorizing his own mind.

"How about we give her some time, and you come see Lo and the kids?" I offer out of nowhere. It stops Toby in his tracks, and he gawks at me as if I'm mad.

Maybe I'm crazy. Either way, this meet, it's fate. Has to be.

"I can't!" He raises his voice. "She's a cutter, Jase. She fucking cuts when she's a mess." The strain in his eyes has me worried. Lo was suicidal, but her self-harm tended to reside in her own mind. A personal hell of her own making.

"Then talk to me about her. Settle your mind so I can help and maybe we can come up with some viable options."

He nods and starts from the beginning.

His spitfire reminds me of my own.

And once again, I finally feel like we're brothers and not enemies.

CHAPTER 47

PRESENT

JOEY

I DON'T KNOW WHAT BROUGHT ME HERE, BUT I'M here. Hell, I don't even know why. I was halfway to the cove before turning around, heading right to where I am now.

The house is massive but so white picket. It's something that I've never cared for. I'm not an extravagant wife, by any means, but this is too mundane for even me. It looks like my dad's place, and that's exactly what I avoided my entire life.

Him.

Repetition.

Hatred.

I stare at the three-story home, seeing the way it seems too peaceful. From everything Francis told me, this is anything but a happy home.

It's been five years.

Sitting in my car for another five minutes, I don't even notice my passenger door opening, but when it does, a little shriek escapes me. The teenager from Gray's house sits next to me, a scowl darker than ever covers his face. If I thought the world made me bitter, this little psychopath is something else entirely.

"The fuck are you staring at my house for?" a gravelly voice barks at me.

My eyes connect with the figure inside my car, and chills break across my flesh like little pinpricks of unease.

His dark hair is jagged and unruly like he runs his hands through it in an attempt to make it look as fucked up as his soul.

His eyes, so heady with hatred and filled to the brim with experience and death, burns me.

He makes his own marks, and I find it has me shriveling into myself.

It's not something I'm used to.

Little punk kids don't evoke these reactions in me, but this one does. He digs deep with his nearly black eyes, his pupils dilated with agitation. He makes sure I'm aware that he doesn't have a single fuck to spare the likes of me.

"Well?" he pushes, baring his teeth like an animal. He reminds me so much of Toby with that expression. The disgust and repulsion. It's all too familiar.

"Needed to talk to Lo," I offer.

"If you're another one of Jase's whores, you can back the fuck away." He grips my wrist, as if he has power over me, his eyes—razor-sharp and hateful—bore into mine. "My mom doesn't need your shit, and he's done with you all. I'll fucking make it happen myself." His hand tightens, squeezing me as if he has a single right. Are people really scared of this asshole?

I scoff. "First of all, tweener... gross. Second, I'm here for your mother. Third of all, extra gross. He's not my type."

He laughs emphatically, no traces of humor present. "Wallets don't have to look good to get pussy. They just have to be big."

My eyes narrow at the little shit, seeing how much he probably gets away with. If I wasn't used to dickish behavior, I'd probably be more scared. He's huge in comparison to me. But I've been through it all, and I'm only twenty-two. I've lost a child, a husband, my innocence, and my home. This dude—no matter how big of an asshole he is—won't deter me from my mission.

"How about *fuck you*?" I scold. "You're only two years younger than me, and you act like some big badass. News flash, dickweed, I'm not—" He places a hand over my mouth.

"No. You listen. In the past five years, my mom has been through so much that I'm lucky she's still alive and kicking. My piece of shit father destroyed her, and though he claims to be a changed man, we all know people relapse and break themselves. Look at my uncle Nate for that matter. He did so well, but one slip up and he's back to being an addict. You see, Red. You're not much different. You have this desperate, almost feral gleam in your eyes. That's a look I want nowhere near my mom. She's grown, changed, and fuck, she came out strong. One thing could tip her over the edge, and I'll kill any motherfucker who dares to risk her life again. Whether you're here for her or some hush money, it's not happening."

He stares at me for my reaction, but I don't know what the fuck he's talking about.

"I'll remove my hand if you don't scream. If you do, well, I have a knife in my pocket I'm not afraid to acquaint you with." Raising his calloused palm, I stare at him in incredulity.

How can someone so young be so bitter?

"I'm Toby's wife," I mutter, finally letting that information out. Technically, as of two hours ago, I'm his no one, but on paper, he's definitely still mine.

He doesn't show his shock, but I'm sure it's there. His eyes aren't as narrowed and his anger isn't as deep. It's almost lighter. Like he realizes I'm not a threat.

"You're *the* Joey?"

"You've heard of me?" I mumble, feeling emotions bubble inside me. How would he possibly know? Toby hasn't kept in contact with Lo or Jase. I'd know. I've tried getting him to reach out often enough.

"Uncle Tobes always calls me. We haven't lost touch. He keeps me sane when my father is around. I've nearly killed him several times."

He jokes about murdering his dad like it's nothing, but I

see the rabid look in his eyes. He's not even joking right now, and that awareness scares me shitless.

"I had no clue," I let out. "We got into a fight over your mom, and I wanted to ask her what to do. She's my idol." The words slip out, and I nearly regret them before seeing his rapacious smile.

"Toby says you're a top chef. There's no one better to admire than my mom. She's fucking glorious." The pride in his eyes and voice has me tearing up again.

Fuck.

My heart aches with nostalgia. Would my child have been as loving and fiercely loyal to me as this kid? Would they have loved me endlessly?

This kid has my heart in a vise, and he's not even mine.

"You're a great son," I cry softly, the words as broken as I feel.

"Why are you getting so emotional?" he asks, looking at me like I'm an alien.

"No reason," I bite out, wiping my already fucked eyes.

"You already look like a goddamn misfit from a Tim Burton movie, might as well just go with it," he mocks. It must be his personality, but he's a serious dick. Except when it involves his mother.

"You're a real asshole, you know that?"

He smiles. It's not really a smile, just a slight tilt to his lips. Almost boyish, almost homicidal, but all him. "Everyone is going to hate you," he snarks. "Everyone except me, and I don't even like you."

"Fuck off," I hiss.

"Let's go inside. Meet the dear ole fam." He hops out of my car before I can respond and is trailing to the house. He doesn't wait for me, so I'm stumbling over myself to keep up. He must find me amusing because in the next instance, a dark chuckle escapes the Satan spawn.

When we reach the door, he doesn't hesitate to swing it open. His eyes are haunted when he walks inside. He must have memories here he doesn't like to relive. Honestly, I know the feeling.

"I'm not usually here, but I heard a little storm is visiting for spring break, and I couldn't resist." His euphemism is lost on me for only breaths before that scene comes to mind, the one I walked into. He calls Gray his storm. It's not a bad name, but it definitely isn't in kind either.

"Why do you hate her?" I ask without thinking twice about my life.

"She fucked up, and I intend to make her pay." Shaking my head and knowing better than to meddle, I follow him through the foyer to a living room. It's vast, the ceilings are vaulted, and I can here dishes rattling. He looks back at me and points his head in the direction of the sound.

Walking the distance to the kitchen, I see my idol. She's holding a huge baking sheet of asparagus and onions. It smells divine in here. Like olive oil, oregano, and parmesan cheese.

"Mom," Ace calls out, scaring Lo. She startles a moment

before setting the hot pan down.

"Jesus, Ace. Be less invasive next time, huh?"

Her voice is as soft as I remember it. She has this kind way of speaking, like she's a goddess who has more emotions inside her than a psychiatrist's office.

"Oh! Josephine?" she asks, almost like her mom brain is a permanent fixture. I wouldn't know. "I was so worried about you!"

"Yes?" I mutter confused.

"Honey, why do you look so distraught?"

"Mom, this is Josephine Hayes."

As he says my last name, Lo's face hardens in a sad way. Like memories flow into her, hitting her where it hurts more. She's so soft around the edges, so seeing this much pain on the surface seems unnatural.

"Hayes," she repeats softly, bereft, and almost faraway.

"Toby is my husband," I mutter. It sounds like a thousand light bulbs bursting, until I'm met with only silence. It's like being buried six feet deep and the only noise is the breath leaving your body as you suffocate slowly.

It's a painful pause.

Stifled and stagnant.

I hate it.

"You didn't mention that when we met," she mutters poignantly. In her eyes, I see a deep-seated emotion. I'm not sure what that is because I don't know her well enough to tell one from the other, but it's not a kind one. Is she jealous? Was

I wrong in thinking she was over my husband? Does she still love him?

My heart feels like it's on a spindle, being spun by Rumpelstiltskin, not made into gold though—made into deadly strands of hopelessness.

If she still loves him, that means he could go back to her.

Why does it matter? You left him...

Even walking away, I don't want him with her or anyone else. The thought spears me, hurting me deeply.

"I didn't want you to refuse to see me. Regardless of how it looks, I really did want to ask you for advice. It was cut a little short by Toby."

"He was there?" she hisses, gripping her chest. I turn to Ace, his face blank and expressionless. Smart kid. Holding it close to the vest.

"He was about to yell. I could see it on his face, but I didn't think it was a good time. Being you were with *his* child in that coffee shop."

Her eyes narrow into slits. They are deathly like this.

Ace clears his throat from behind me. "I think you should go," he states, his softer tone from earlier vacant in the words.

"No, she can stay. Seems like your uncle has been up to a lot. And Josephine here has been digging a little *too* deep."

"Is Lev really Toby's?" Ace asks. The smallness in his voice is one of a son getting news he wasn't expecting. News that's unsettling and turbulent, throwing him out of orbit. I've really fucked them both tonight. All for some goddamn reason that makes zero sense.

"Ace, please go make sure Jazzy bear and Lev are washed up."

Shut down.

His face darkens as he grinds his molars. His hands ball into fists, and I just know he's on the verge of an explosion. So much like his uncle in that way.

"No one in this household but my husband and I know that information," she scolds, washing her hands and leading me into the dining area. "When Toby and I had our affair, we were stupid."

I want to cry, seeing as she has a child with my husband and not even I—his *wife*—get that kind of blessing. It shouldn't hurt because this was before we met, but fuck, it hurts so badly.

Tears prick my eyes.

"I didn't intend to discover that information. It fell on my lap," I explain. "It broke me. I-I..." Tears flow freely, and the deadness inside me leaks out all over. It's painful. "We miscarried almost two years ago, and it's just... I needed something to bring us back together."

Her features soften, and she's reaching for my hands. "You're a strong woman, Josephine. There's nothing like losing a child."

As she says the words, I can see the honesty, the pain, the reality of that simple statement. She lost a child, and she still hurts.

A strangled noise leaves my throat as I break down. "I'm sorry for coming here. I don't know why I did or what led me, but I couldn't stop. I just couldn't stay there with him... not after what he's done."

She pulls me into her arms like I'm her child. She holds me, shushing me, rocking me and loving me in a way my mother never has. I cry and cry, feeling my body shake with agony.

"It hurts so much," I sob. "Why me? Why us? Why is this happening?" My heart hammers inside my chest, bleeding as my soul is letting loose all its burden in this woman's arms.

"Let it out," she coos, holding me. "Cry all you need, sweetheart. This kind of weight isn't meant to be held in."

As I start hiccupping, she lays a gentle kiss to my forehead, just like Francis, just like Toby.

"How is Toby handling this? He's really good at soothing heartache," she admits with a bit of nostalgia. Even that hurts, and I'm sobbing more.

"H-He hates me. He's never around. Instead of being here, he cheated," I bawl, feeling my body lock up from lack of oxygen.

"Sweetie, I need you to calm down. You're having a panic attack." I try breathing. I try to stop the rapid rising of my chest, and I try not to feel the onslaught of emotions.

"C-Can't."

"Inhale," she instructs gently, and I do. "Exhale." I let out the most ragged breath. "Now, breathe." I do it again. "Just keep doing that, just like that. Deep breaths."

It takes a couple of minutes, but I'm finally calming down.

"I'm sorry," I apologize with guilt riding me. "I had no

intention of unloading on you."

"Don't apologize, honey. Broken people find broken people. It's a matter of fate."

I stare at her in awe. She could be so angry right now, but she's not. She's looking at me with love and understanding, and it doesn't make any sense.

"Why are you being so nice to me?"

"Because my broken sees and recognizes yours. You're my family now. Family soothes family. We're meant to be there for one another and make sure to heal where we can."

"I wish I didn't lie to you. It feels so wrong."

She eyes me with understanding. "If I was in your situation, I'm not sure the outcome would be different. When I lost my daughter, I'd have done anything for a connection and answers, but I shut down. It's taken years, but I'm finally healing. Therapy helps a lot, and medication for my suicidal tendencies and depression. It's slowly fixing the damaged pieces."

"I don't think I'll ever feel whole again." She rubs my arm softly, squeezing. It's such a motherly thing to do, and I feel myself warming up to this woman even more.

"You will. You'll feel complete, even if the child isn't one you give birth to."

Adoption.

What Toby and I had originally agreed upon before everything went to shit. I nod, knowing what she means. "I just want to be a mom."

The pain in my voice scares even me. It's on the verge of

full desolation. When I stand, she holds my arm. For the first time in ages, my arms are visible.

Scars upon scars.

Blood upon blood.

Sadness upon sadness.

Hopelessness upon hopelessness.

"This isn't the answer." Her voice is far off. "It may ease some pain at first, feel good even, but it's a short-term remedy, and it fuels the destruction. Next time, when the need arises, draw on your skin. Every place you want to bleed, write things. Words, objects, hell, song lyrics work. Just don't use the blade anymore."

I nod at her, absorbing her advice.

"I'm a little broken," I whisper.

"All the best people are."

As soon as those words leave her, a very tall, very attractive, and very intimidating man walks in. His eyes land on his wife, and he must see something there. Because in the next second, he's rushing to her, cupping her jaw, looking at her as if she stole all the stars and put them in her eyes so he'd never have to look elsewhere again.

I want that.

I miss that.

Fucking Toby.

They kiss passionately. The grip he has on her jaw reminds me so much of my husband that longing hits me between the ribs. I miss him. His touch, his love.

Fuck me.

It's impossible to look away as they make love with their mouths. I should, but I can't.

"Could you not?" Ace barks from the same area his dad came in. I stare at him as he rolls his eyes slowly. It's apparent there's more than the normal amount of bad blood between him and his dad.

"This is—" Lo starts introducing me.

"Joey, Toby's wife," he answers for her. His darkened expression rakes over me. "Guess we've found you without actually trying."

"What are you talking about?" I say at the same time Lo says, "How did you know?"

He turns to her. "You'd be amazed, but after a really big argument where we barely stopped ourselves from hitting each other, we discussed the past five years of his life."

I balk.

Lo's jaw drops.

Ace grimaces.

"Please don't tell him I'm here," I cry, to which Jase narrows his eyes.

"Whether you want me to tell him or not, he's already on his way."

"What?" Lo and I both hiss at the same time.

"He wants closure," he explains to the both of us. "I decided to give an inch and invited him over."

"But I'm not ready. Don't put me in that position—" Lo

frantically denies, shaking her head, her face paling.

"You're more than ready, Peaches. You both need this. Plus, he already knows about Lev."

"Jason," she whimpers in a way that's so sad and desperate.

"Lo baby," he soothes. "You're so much stronger than before. You both need closure."

She cries now. Those soft brown eyes glisten, and it hurts to see. Never in my life has a woman looked so troubled and sad while crying.

"I believe in you, Peaches. Now get your ass changed before I spank it."

The stark contrast in his words now from ten seconds ago makes me blush like I'm a child of theirs.

"Jason!" She hits his chest, attempting to wipe her eyes at the next moment. He smacks her ass loudly, and I cover my eyes, walking backward.

"Shower. I'll be there in two."

Rushing out of the room before I see them paw at each other, I see Ace with a teenage girl and Lev. He's unamused, but his eyes, whenever his siblings look at him, softens. He's a mystery to me.

"Nauseating, huh?"

I'm thrown off by his words but nod. "I'm not even their kid, and that made me feel like a child."

"Yeah, they're gross. Meet Jazzy bear." He points at his sister. Her long blonde hair cascades in waves past her hips. She reminds me of Rapunzel, her hair thick and curly.

"Hi," her meek voice sounds out.

"And this is Lev." He points at the little boy who looks so much like my husband it hurts. "But it seems you already have."

I nod sadly.

Right as I'm about to make a comment, the doorbell rings out, silencing my voice, thoughts, and heart.

CHAPTER 48

TOBY

MY HEART FEELS HEAVY AS IF I'VE LOST SOMEONE.
The only pain that compares is the loss of my unborn child. Even then, it doesn't feel as vital to me as my love for this woman.

Why did her leaving force my hand? Why did it take this long for me to come to terms with my stupidity? I called Jase, and we had it out. I asked about the little boy and he told me to fuck off because it wasn't my child.

I'll be asking Lo tonight, but he doesn't need to know that.

The car ride feels a lot shorter than it should. It's too soon. The hammering of my pulse sets me in motion. I'm parking my car at the house that both ruined and freed me. This home has so many memories—mostly sad—but there are those few that I keep close to my heart with a woman who was never meant to be mine.

My brother doesn't seem to hold as much of a grudge as I suspected. Whether it's because it's been five years, he's a new father again, or they're doing great, I'm not sure. But it was his bright idea for me to come here. He said maybe closure would set me free. Maybe it'd ease my addictions, but we all know afflictions are lifelong battles. Mine is and always has been.

It doesn't help that my childhood is nowhere near perfect or that my brother always won.

At least, he did.

But he doesn't have a Joey. My Joey.

No one knows what that's like.

Or so I believe.

Did she leave me for Francis? He's been ignoring my calls, setting my trust issues off even more so than normal. I walk the pathway to the door, remembering all the times I popped in. For *Dirty Dancing*, coffee dates, runs, and just to spend time with the woman who held my heart like a gunman holds a hostage.

My palms are clammy as I'm about to knock. Sweat beads my forehead and lines my back despite the cool spring day.

Ringing the doorbell, I let the fear settle inside. It's never been an issue before, but the last time I was at this door, my brother told me to leave and give Lo and him a chance to make up.

It was one of the hardest days of my life. After that, I went on a five-month bender, which ultimately led me to the woman I'm madly in love with.

When the door opens, my stomach squeezes.

Lo.

In the flesh.

Her black hair is long like I saw at the coffee shop months ago. She's vibrant, but her eyes are puffy. Has she been crying?

"Tobes," she mutters. It's so soft and so caressing. I hate that she still has this way of connecting with me. Her tone always dug deep, ever since we were fifteen and didn't know what to do with our lives. Back then, it was an obsession, and now it's just an admiration kind of love that seems entirely platonic.

I stare at her pleased expression, and I feel elated in a way that's insane. It's not with the love I was scared I still held for her. It's not with a panic that she was the only one ever for me.

No, it's with this kind of closure.

She's vibrant, and it's for all the right reasons.

None including me.

And that's exactly what I needed to see.

Her happiness.

"Going to stand out here all day?"

"Looks like your snark is back, Sparkle." Her eyes shine at that, a little emotion bleeding through. It's nice to see she still cares.

"Huh, seems like you haven't left your charm either."

"Charm?" I feign disappointment. "I'm the goddamn king."

She chuckles and waves me in. It takes all of five seconds for my smile to fall from my face. Because right beside this door, ten feet to my left, is my wife.

Her eyes are glistening with pain. It's not only visible, but it's graspable. An attainable thing that I never want to see again.

I'd do anything to take that look off her face.

Instead of saying hi to the clan, I stalk directly toward Joey, my mind made up before my body could catch up. My feet are silent but hers tap as she retreats. No one exists at this moment. Maybe they all should, but they don't matter.

Only she matters.

The woman who's owned me since Lo broke me.

My destiny.

My fate.

The woman meant to be mine and only mine.

I stare at her heartbroken expression and want to wipe it away, to swipe it along with her tears and heal everything I've broken in the past year.

Why did I hurt her so much?

We continue this war between us, a battle of wills. She's running out of space to run, and that's exactly what I need. For her to lose. To give in. To love me back.

She shakes her head at me like a wounded animal, but it doesn't stop me.

"You can't run anymore, Sous. I won't let you." It's dark and low, so goddamn low that I'm almost shocked at how deep I sound.

She's like a frightened animal, and I'm going to catch her and soothe her back to good health.

"Stop," she whispers, her voice small. "I left you." The words are barren of emotion, almost like she's trying to ice over. It's too late for that, sweetheart. I've already melted those walls. You just forgot.

"I'll never stop. We're inevitable."

Her eyes glaze, and her back hits the wall, making several pictures wiggle above her. She looks up, and by the time she's looking back down, I have her boxed in. It reminds me of all the times I've taken her body against a solid surface. To dig in deeper, thrust harder, taking what's mine without plushy cushioning. She loves it, and as a tiny whimper escapes her lips, she's loving it now too.

"You broke me."

"You destroyed me," I counter, feeling the pain surge. "You chose *him*."

She scrunches her lips in displeasure, her face morphing into that hatred that scorches me alive. "I didn't fuck Francis, you idiot." She pushes at my chest. "I'd never do that to Gray, let alone you." It's as if she's smacked me. I look over every inch of her face and don't see a trace of mistruth.

"Since we've been together, it's only ever been your stupid ass."

With that, I take her smart-ass mouth with mine. She moans, and I take that too, swallowing it with every ounce of oxygen she can spare. Gripping her throat, I need that connection, to feel her heart, to have every part of her for myself, and I groan.

Tears leak from her eyes as we battle with our tongues, not knowing what to do. It's been a year of turmoil, a year of agony, a year of missing her every fucking second.

I pull back and kiss her tears, taking each one with my lips, hoping to soothe them and never make her hurt like this ever again.

She looks at me with so much love, but the brokenness is more apparent. This is far from over, far from happiness, far from anything other than the beginning.

A throat clears behind us, and I see Ace assessing the situation. He's such a little dick.

"This is nice and all, but take your emotional baggage somewhere private. Some of us have souls to keep away."

"One day, you're going to change, Ace. And when that day comes, you're going to realize love comes in many weird forms."

"So, if it's anything like you or Jase's, I'm fucked, right? Since you both can't seem to keep your dicks to yourselves."

I'm about to rush him and give him a good talking-to when Joey's hand clutches mine. "He's hurting, and you just ruined the good image he had of you."

"Fuck," I mutter.

"No, he didn't ruin shit. He's as worthless as Jase. You deserve better."

"Don't do this," I growl, seeing the hope die from his eyes.

"I honestly thought you were better than him. Guess we're all wrong at some point." It's his parting words before he walks out the door. I've tried to keep him somewhat humane over the years, but it seems no matter what I do, he's not a fan.

"He's hurting," Joey repeats. "It'll all change one day."

I nod before bringing her lips to mine again.

She breaks away from my kiss, pushing me back as her eyes trail my entire face like a facial recognition scanner from some cringy sci-fi show.

"What were you doing today around noon?" she asks, her face giving nothing away. Sanje called at one. He said she made him wait an hour.

"Filing payroll in the office," I respond immediately. It's what I was doing. Even when Sanje called, he interrupted. Now that it isn't filed on time, everyone's going to be pissed when they receive their paychecks late.

"That's *all* you were doing?" she pushes, and I can see how much she's trying to keep calm. Her eyes are glossing over. It's a tell for most people when they're upset. People give more away than they think. Usually it's a twitch or a smirk, but for those who have the best poker faces, it's in the eyes.

Joey's eyes whisper all the truths to me while her mouth tells all the lies.

I want to be angry at her for questioning me, but how can I? I've cheated. Slept around. Broken every sliver of trust she ever gave me.

"I swear, I was only doing payroll. When I woke up this morning, I gave you a kiss, told you I'd miss you, and checked on your mom. After drinking several cups of coffee and reading the *Hollow Ridge Post*, I headed downstairs. I was a little late to the office, having to handle a few loose ends."

Her face falls, a little horrified, as if everything she worked to ice over has melted, and she's showing every expression she wished to hide from me.

"Loose ends?" she strains, pulling her lip between her teeth. At this rate, she's going to chap it. It's her biggest tell. She's beyond upset and on the verge of breaking.

I scratch my head uncomfortably. How do you tell your wife that you cancelled the room you kept for your affairs? Or that you told the women you used to fuck that it wasn't going to work out and that you loved your wife?

Would she understand?

Would she berate me?

Would I drown because the deep-seated hatred I have for myself overwhelms my very existence?

"That room," I start. Biting the inside of my cheek, I nearly drawing blood at the pressure. I hate admitting I had my very own sex pad. It's not exactly something you boast about.

"Yes, your sex dungeon," she gripes, folding her arms and forcing distance between our bodies.

"I canceled the room today. Called the women to meet up there and told them it wouldn't be happening again." Tears spill from her. I want to taste them, see if her pain matches my own.

"Did you fuck anyone of them goodbye?" Her tone is filled to the brim with bitterness. Trying to keep my face neutral instead of bursting like I want to, I cup her chin.

She jerks it away, needing an answer from me.

"I haven't fucked anyone since that night, Sous. No one."

Her pained expression is enough to make me hate myself even more. The acrid taste of bile rises, and I'd do anything to ease the distress she's showing me. I've absolutely ruined every shred of trust we had. She can't even bury that expression from her face, but she shouldn't have to.

"I don't believe you," she says in a broken hushed whisper. Her chest heaves harshly, reminding me of Lo and her panic attacks.

"Joey," I gently murmur. I need her to look at me, brand me with those eyes of hers, tear me to bits if that helps her, but no matter what, I need her to breathe. "Look at me, sweetheart." She does. Her forehead scrunched in displeasure. "I told her today that it was over. I didn't touch her, didn't say more, and I sure as hell didn't fuck her."

She grimaces at the word. How will I ever fix this? What have I done to us?

"Why do I hate you and love you?"

The question throws me off. *She still loves me?*

"How do I love the hate out of you?"

CHAPTER 49

JOEY

"I FUCKING HATE YOU. YOU'RE SUCH A PRICK,"
I seethe, practically spitting the words at him as we
make it to the kitchen. I don't dare to think of the maids
overhearing us because I don't fucking care who knows
how big of a piece of shit he is.

Even if I still love him.

"Do you fuck your husband with that mouth?" he sneers,
callous and bastardly as usual.

"Hard to do when he's dead to me."

"Are you sure you're not just jealous that he's shared his
body like you've shared yours?" I want to correct him, to yell

at him and tell him that I haven't shared a thing and that he's the fucking cheat, but I don't. I think half of it is knowing I deserve this pain since our child died before it got to live. The other part—while small and meager—tells me that if he knew, maybe he'd treat me right.

Maybe this is what we were supposed to be all along— hormones, lust, and simple fucks.

"I'd be jealous, but your cock isn't anything special," I fire back, biting his throat where his heart beats. He growls and pins me to the wall. He forces my legs open, and I only fight him to let the fire back in that I've missed. He's such a fucking dick, but he has the best dick, which means he's *my* dick.

"You keep challenging me like that, and you'll bruise my cock's ego."

"That's okay, *husband*. Your head has enough ego for the both of you." He hisses as I sink my claws into him, wanting to dig deep and leave my brand. So, when he's fucking those bimbos, it's me that has him marked all over.

"Is your cunt wet for me, Sous? Is it dripping with the knowledge that your husband's cock has been inside so many cunts it has lost count?" I whimper, hating him more, wanting to fucking stab his heart over and over again, just to see if he even dies. There's no way something beats beneath those ribs.

He smirks when I push at him.

"Hit a nerve?" he condescends, biting the inside of my thigh. I scream as he keeps sucking and biting back and forth in spite of our mutual hatred. "Sounds like my wife can't keep her husband satisfied. Such a shame she has to share."

"Fuck you," I hiss.

"Plan to, Sous. Plan to fuck you so good that your toes curl, and you cry out with only my name on your tongue. Then when you're begging me to stop because you're shaking with satisfaction, I won't. Because until I'm done marking every goddamn inch of your body so the entire fucking male population knows you're mine, I won't stop."

"Toby," I moan as he swirls his tongue across my goose bumps.

"The world must know this cunt is mine, even while it rents itself out. It'll learn. It'll know its home and beg for me to remind it."

"Fuck," I hiss as his teeth bite my folds.

"If bruises and bites don't work, Sous, and if all else fails, when someone looks at your body, your cunt will tell them it's mine. I'll brand you here," he growls, tracing the juncture between my thighs. "I'll put my goddamn name here as a permanent fixture, so whenever you spread your thighs for someone, they'll know they're *nothing*."

I bow into him as he licks that spot, showing me where he'll place his name. I want that so much, for him to trace his tongue there, making sure he's just as much mine as I am his. I'd do anything for him to stop fucking those other women. Anything.

"Fuck me," I demand as his tongue teases everywhere but my clit. He makes me go through hell as he nibbles and dives into my hole.

"Bet Francis hasn't come inside my pretty pussy, has he?" I groan at his words.

"What if he has?" I challenge, wanting more of his hate, letting it fill me to the brim. Just having his lust confuses me. If hate isn't included, my heart betrays me and seeks him out. If I were upright, I'd be falling to my knees in worship, just to have something of his to fill me and make me whole again.

"He hasn't," he barks with a sureness that doesn't make sense. "No one has but me. This is mine, isn't it?" His hand cups me, gripping me as if it'll make all his dreams come true.

"Say it, Sous. Tell me it's mine."

I glare at him, wanting him to feel even an ounce of the desperation he makes me feel every day. Shaking my head, I'm surprised when he thrusts three fingers in me with no warning.

"You're saying this tight hot tunnel isn't only for me? That it doesn't know the master of its pleasure?" I shake my head again, biting my lip as the sensations zip up my spine. He's wrecking me, absolutely destroying my control.

"You're wrong, Sous. This cunt only gets wet for me, it only leaks in my mouth and hands. It only pleasures my cock."

"Could've fooled me," I nearly hiss, feeling him pull my barbell.

"Don't worry. I'm about to show you." As soon as the words have hit my ears, he's grinding his mouth against my pussy, licking, biting, and rimming my ass. He grips my thighs, pulling me to the edge of the counter and dives even deeper.

The pressure is too much, so ravenous and languid. He's making me moan unabashedly.

He fucks me with hate.

I love him with the same.

Our bodies connect. The grunt he releases is like every other lie he offers. Fake. He hates me. He wants me. He can't stand me. Lie after lie after lie after lie. I let him degrade me with them because, masochist or not, we all know I deserve it.

"You wilt under my fingertips like a dying flower, Sous. Just for me," he breathes. "Just for me."

CHAPTER 50

PRESENT

JOEY

"HOW DO I LOVE THE HATE OUT OF YOU?"

He whispered it so low, I'm almost certain he didn't mean for the words to escape him. I love so much about this man. His lips that are plush but not pillowy, his strong and sharp jaw that could slice glass, his eyes that are haunting while sad and darker than the starless sky when angry, and his body that is a goddamn wonderland.

But with love, hate follows.

The things I hate about this man are too many to list. But if I can't understand and love the flaws, am I supposed to be allowed to love the perfect parts?

His heart is fractured. Way before I came along, it was broken and tattered, bruised in a never-healing kind of way. It was deep, the pain, and it never had a chance to heal.

His alcoholism. It's the bitterest pill to swallow and he's never actually admitted it to me. Yes, I know he's an addict. I see it in his tells, how he goes to AA meetings but never mentions them, and how he looks at liquor as if it'd feed the unending loneliness inside.

That's the biggest lie of any addiction.

They don't fix or fulfill the emptiness.

They only grow the small hole into a massive cavern, then slowly, it tunnels into a wide systematic threat, and by then, it's too late.

Toby's damage speaks to mine. Maybe that's how we found each other. Bound and destined by our troubles and thrown together in hopes we could fix and not further ruin each other.

He's my disease.

I'm his addiction.

We're a catastrophe, but in the chaos, it's always him.

I love him more than I hate him.

But it's not enough.

Not now when we've lost so much. Not when he took the easy way out. And definitely not when he walked out on me.

"You can't," I finally answer. It's been a pause too long, but I needed that extra breath to think it through. He can't love the hate out of me.

We all have choices in life. They are the make-up to what ends up happening. A domino, ready to tip the rest, even the ones we didn't realize we stacked.

My choice for now is me.

"What are you saying?" His voice is small. Soft and kind, but so goddamn bereft of hope. I can't be his fixer, and he can't be my livelihood.

In all my life, I've always depended on someone to love me and me them. What if I took love out of the equation and wrote my own story? One where happiness isn't a result of what someone could offer me, but in what I could offer myself?

"I'm saying, I need time. We were in this marriage for all the wrong reasons, Toby." For the first time in our relationship, I see emotional build-up in his eyes. They're wet and heavy, and it pains me not to kiss him better.

"We fell in love," he tries, his voice cracking with the words. My husband's biggest weakness isn't alcohol and escaping. His biggest fault is abandonment issues. He's never done well with people leaving him. Even now, as someone who is unable to fix this and us, I want to kiss his worries away.

"You weren't supposed to fall in love, old man. Guess we both fucked up."

"*We* fell in love," he repeats, emphasizing the *we* part.

"We. did. So deeply that our pain can't be fixed with an apology. You breathe life into me, Tobias. You breathe love. You breathe hope. But when that's gone, when you're hurting, when you hate me because of your own pig-headedness, you steal those very things away from me. You don't offer anything but malice and heartache."

Emotions bleed from me as I cry to him. My voice, along with my lips, warble because admitting these words are painful in the most visceral way.

"You hurt me in more ways than I can count," I finally let out on a sigh. "I never knew what pain was until you were the one behind the blows."

He bites his bottom lip as tears of anguish flow freely down his cheeks. His eyes are devastating right now. A pale green that just hurts my heart.

"I never meant to hurt you… at first. I mean, I know what I was doing after I thought you broke us, but before that, my intentions were never set out on making you hurt."

"Then why did you do it?" I wonder aloud.

"You closed yourself off." He grips his head, twining his fingers through his hair and pulling. "You reminded me of Lo when she'd shut down and nothing mattered. It scared the fuck out of me."

He's pacing now, his body full of something—adrenaline, maybe fear, something that's keeping him from being still.

"I couldn't be him. Not him. I couldn't ruin you like he ruined her. I couldn't," he mutters, pain lacing his words. They're not cohesive, almost garbled, and he keeps repeating, *I couldn't*. The pain inside him, the demons he holds and shelters, they're eating him alive.

His actions were terrible, but who doesn't fuck up at least

a hundred times in any marriage?

"Who? Who are you talking about?" I ask, trying to calm him. He hasn't stopped shuffling. I reach for his face, the contact making him shiver. His wild expression meets mine, it's harried and desperate. He comes closer to me again, pinning me against the wall.

"My dad. I can't be him. I won't. I couldn't," he rushes out, the words short and sharp. As he brings his face to mine, I hope he sees the honesty in my words.

"You're not your father, Toby. You're my husband. A loving man. Someone who fixed all my jagged pieces, putting them together to make something beautiful. You are such a wonderful man."

"I've fucked up, Joey. I've fucked it all up."

"No, you haven't. We both made decisions that damaged us. We. We're a team. When one makes a choice, it affects us both."

"I fucked other people," he hisses, moving away. "I fucked other women, and all while you stayed home and cried. I cheated when you were suffering. It wasn't a team effort or a choice you made, Joey. It. Was. Me. I picked everyone but you."

A choked sob leaves my mouth, and I cover it with my palm, hoping to hide how much those words physically strike me.

He comes closer, seeing my pain.

"It's better that you left. I'd have just fucked up even more. Probably slipped inside another hot cunt and got them pregnant."

I smack him. It's a gut reaction, but I do. I slap him so hard that there's a red mark forming on his cheek. He doesn't mean these things. He can't. He wouldn't do this to me. He's always hurt me when he's upset, but this?

"You know it's true, baby." A strangled noise escapes me at that word. I fucking hate that word, and he knows it. "It's inevitable. Me fucking you over."

"Fuck you, Toby. Fuck you."

His eyes darken, but I see the chip in his armor. He's saying these things to make me leave. And the thing about choices is I'm not scared to make the one that finally saves my heart.

"Goodbye, Toby."

He shuts his eyes as if he's both miserable and elated that I finally said it. How can he go from trying to win me back to what he's doing right now? It's not right.

Not fucking okay.

He reaches for me, but when I flinch, he drops his hand. After saying goodbye to Lo, Jase, and their kids, I leave. I rush out of the house and to my car, knowing that from now on, I'd be selfish.

I'm choosing me.

We were the consequence of circumstance.

That's all we were. Everything else was lost.

He was mine.

Until he wasn't.

I stayed for so long because fighting for him over a misunderstanding mattered to me. I love him; he hates me. Everything fell apart with one simple mistake—a miscommunication. With honesty, a little trust, and understanding, we could have lasted. We could have conquered. We could have loved.

But he chooses hate.

I think it's easier for him. Rather than accepting that he messed up—didn't trust me—he threw us away. It's fair. I met *Lo*. I know what she did to him. What she held over his head. What kept him with her.

Guilt.

Such a cunty little emotion.

CHAPTER 51

PAST

JOEY

HE PUSHES ME AGAINST THE SURFACE OF THE
elevator we've used for years. His mouth hovers my lips as he
breathes as raggedly as me. "Are you wet, Sous?"

"For you? Never."

He chuckles darkly, his face masked with anger and
hatred. It's always one or the other, but tonight, it's both. It
sends chills up my spine, tingly, and zapping each inch of me
like a little 9-volt battery.

He hates as strongly as he fucks.

Endless.

Brutal.

With every inch of him.

"If I lifted your little dress, would your cunt tell me otherwise?" I stare at him and his dirty mouth, hating him so much at this moment. How can he be so cruel and make me weak for him to the point I throw all my needs out the window? My pride doesn't seem to be an issue. If anything, people see a spineless woman, but the pain feels too good to let it win. I use it instead, letting it breathe fire back into me with every pulse.

I'm not weak. I know the stakes and the rules. I'm just strong enough to fight him instead of give in to every demand.

"No. It's wet for Francis."

With those words, he flips me against the wall and raises my dress. The lace panties I picked cover next to nothing, but he growls anyway. A resounding slap hits my ears before I feel the sting against my ass. It's harsh and brutal, but it has me clenching my thighs.

"He's not here," Toby barks.

"He's right here," I taunt, tapping my head, waiting for an explosion. Because with my husband, there's always an explosion.

"Fuck him, you're here. With me. Wet and soaked for *me*."

It's like he's barely holding onto his humanity as he spits the words. They're barely strung together as a proper sentence. His hatred brews in the air, suffocating me.

"Prove it."

With those parting words, another slap echoes within the

confines of the small box.

"Oh, wife, I will. I'm going to fuck you until your cunt knows nothing but the length of my cock. Spread your fucking thighs," he demands, gripping the back of my neck and forcing my face against the glass.

That's the hot part about exhibitionism, not knowing if you'll get caught, not knowing if some freak is watching us from the little camera in the corner, or if we'll get arrest for fucking each other without a goddamn care.

I try turning to him, and when I do, we're face-to-face as I let out my next words.

"Right here in a dirty elevator?" I question, my voice breathy, revealing how much it turns me on to be degraded by him. It shouldn't appeal to me—or anyone, for that matter—especially since he's such a prick, but it's an urge neither of us deny. His taut body boxes me in, the weight of his built chest pressing me into the wall. The glass clings to my skin like a film. Filthy, cold, and barren, heated only by my body. Just like this man's heart. He presses his thick cock against me, leaving no room for me to move.

"Do you think you deserve better?" he hisses harshly, his mouth hovers over mine, taunting me like a snake does its meal.

I shake my head, even if it's a lie. He'll never stop punishing me, and I'll never stop loving him. Seconds pass as his eyes scan mine. Heat flickers there, desire swirls, and that goddamn tongue licks his bottom lip. As fast as it's there, it's gone. His face morphs back into one of hatred and distaste, in an attempt to hide the lust that had oozed out only moments ago, reminding me his loathing always comes before my orgasms.

"Then turn the fuck around and show me that pretty pussy."

This time, I flip of my own accord, making sure he sees every inch of my ass before spreading my thighs. The way the moisture is pooling between them lets me know he's getting to me. He always does.

His finger dips between my folds, and when he brings it up to his face, I watch him suck it clean in the mirror.

"Just as delicious as always, sweetheart."

My body shivers at those words, hearing their hidden meaning. He's going to fuck me with his mouth. He's never been able to resist after his first taste.

Gripping the lace, he slides them down my legs, sending chills all over me. I wiggle as he takes his time removing them.

He scrunches them up and takes a sniff, forcing me to watch, releasing a husky little groan that has my nipples poking through my dress from how hard and stimulated they are. Fuck. He's so raw when we're like this. We can lie all we want, but this passion we've always had hasn't waned. If anything, it's stronger with each hate-filled session of pure fucking.

I'm about to say something when he puts a finger to my lips. "Open."

I do.

He smirks callously and shoves my panties in my mouth. It's like he needed to degrade me in every way.

"Now when you scream, only I'll hear you."

Fuck.

He's such a prick.

"Now widen and bend a little, I have dessert to eat." I groan and adhere to his commands. We went from nothing to married, from being married to lovers, to lovers who hate each other's guts. He hates me, and I return the fervor.

He fucks other people; I let him believe I do too.

We're so fucking twisted; it's going to kill us both.

I hate him.

He hates me.

We fuck anyway.

When I'm finally spread for him, he falls to his knees. "Your cunt is the only one I'll ever worship, Sous. It's mine to devour and taste and fuck. Just mine."

He flattens his tongue and swipes from my clit to my asshole. It's so hot and dirty. If anyone were to call the elevator, we'd be fucked. They'd see my husband kneeling behind me, eating my pussy and ass like it's his career of choice. Devouring, slurping, and making noises that have me flushed and wanton.

I'm desperate for these moments, and they're all mine. I don't have to share them with anyone.

"You're my favorite meal of the day, Josephine. Every time you bend for me, I never want to leave your thighs." He grips both of my cheeks and spreads them, rimming me and biting on each cheek for good measure.

"So fucking delicious. So fucking mine," he grunts and dives back in. I wiggle against him, wanting more friction, more pain, just more. He slaps my ass, hard. The sound making me wetter.

"Fucking greedy little pussy, isn't it?" I moan around the fabric and watch in the mirror as he smiles devilishly. I feel his fingers slide from my ankles all the way up to my thighs. He rubs the spot he bit and sucked earlier.

"Marked up, imprinted, all mine," he coos. It's so tender and baritone. Like he's a proud lover, making me come over and over again.

His fingers glide upward, finally hitting my sweet spot. He doesn't enter me, just toys with the sensitive flesh around my hole, teasing, making me desperate. When I groan, complaining in the only way I can, he sinks it in and hooks it upward, making me see stars. I shake from the pleasure of his fingers and mouth.

He never ceases to bring me pleasure. It's like he's made it his mission to get me off as much as he can before he's finally allowed to explode.

His one finger turns into two, and as he laps at my asshole, he starts stretching me there too. He's such a dirty bastard, and I love it. I moan so loudly, not even my undies can silence the noise.

He stops all movement before making himself visible in the mirror.

"You were always a slut for ass play," he taunts, and I whimper as he removes his finger.

"Has Francis been inside this tight little hole, Sous?" I

shake my head vehemently. Knowing if he believes otherwise, he'll plow into me.

"But he's had my cunt. Maybe I need to reclaim both tonight. Good thing you don't work tomorrow. After I'm done fucking him out of your system, you won't be able to walk."

I moan as he removes all his fingers, and the loss makes me clench. I want every goddamn part of me filled by him. He rises and leans toward me, removing the fabric from my mouth.

"On your fucking knees. We need to start here," he says while tapping my lips. They have drool on the sides, wet with desire and desperation.

I lick my lips without hesitation, wanting to taste him. While Toby is a giver, he doesn't let me suck him off often. He always tells me my pussy wants his cum more than my mouth, but I think it's fair to say, I don't care where it's at, as long as it's all mine.

He traces my mouth with his cock, spreading his bead of precum across them. I can't help but lick my lips again and taste him.

He's salty and sweet and all him.

I lick up his shaft, making sure to tease him just like he does me. He hates it, but when he fights my mouth for his release, I know he loves it all the same.

"Open," he hisses, and I stare at him, seeing his disheveled appearance. It has me grinning, hot and needy for him. I widen my mouth and watch in fervor as he sinks his cock inside with a grunt.

He's so huge. There has never been a time where he's fucked my mouth without me choking, drooling, and nearly combusting as he shoots down my throat.

He peers down at me, the strain visible has a smile begging to break free. He grips my hair, fisting it tight, all while pumping into me.

Relaxing my throat, I take his punishment, begging for his seed, wanting to have that power over him. But Toby rarely loses his will; he doesn't give over to his pleasure until he's ready, and I envy that power.

It's not like he can't fuck me five minutes later. His stamina is astounding, but he likes to wait it out until his balls physically ache.

It's admirable.

It's sexy.

He bucks his hips and drool sweeps down my face. I love that he does this. I think he loves it, too.

CHAPTER 52

PAST

TOBY

I FUCK HER MOUTH LIKE IT'S MY DUTY, LOVING HOW tears paint her cheeks and drool pools down her face. She's a sight for sore eyes on her knees. I nearly lost it when she told me Francis was the one to make her wet. I saw red.

I can rarely get off when I'm with other women, and even then, it's with our porn stash replaying in my mind that gets me there. When I fuck other women, it's my wife's cunt I'm imagining. I can't even keep my eyes open when I'm away from her.

It's always her.

It'll never be anyone else.

They mean nothing.

I thrust into her throat, wanting to explode and choke her out, then paint her lips with the remnants of my cum, but I need to be inside her, remind her cunt that it's my cock that pleases her.

She's always moody and sad. Francis is obviously not doing his job. Never thought the passionate Frenchman would be so displeasing.

My wife needs to be forced into pleasure.

She needs her will taken.

She needs *me*.

I pull out and watch as drool drenches her throat. Fuck. I want to come there too. Bathe her in me in every way possible.

I help her up and push her against the mirror. Without preamble, I thrust inside her wet channel and fuck her harshly.

"I can't fuck them like I fuck you, Sous."

"W-What?" she stutters, her eyes fluttering at the jackhammering of my hips.

"They don't please me like you do," I grunt and pound into her. She cries out when I pinch her clit, then rub slow, methodical circles the way she likes.

I know her body inside and out. What she likes, what she craves, even what she's scared to admit.

"Stop talking," she grumbles.

"Jealous, Sous?"

"Fuck you."

"You must be. Knowing that even though I hardly even come with them, they're still who I pick."

"Get the fuck off me," she berates.

I stop inside her. "Is that what you want?" Her eyes hit mine in the mirror, and she shakes her head. That's all the answer I need before I pull out and slam back into her as she screams.

"It'll always be you, Josephine. No matter how much I hate you," I grind out. She clenches around my cock, moaning out her release. I thrust into her with abandon, unable to stop the manic thrusting of my hips, and when I'm finally yelling out my own release, coating her walls and barely able to stand, the elevator beeps. I hurry and leave her body, shoving my dick in my pants as she tries adjusting her dress. The doors open, and a maid comes into the elevator. Scanning our home badge, the light shines, and we rise.

When the woman gets off two floors below us, we both burst out laughing before Joey's face turns sour.

"Never talk about fucking other women in front of me again."

I smirk, and she leaves me in the elevator.

She acts like I won't be fucking every hole of hers tonight.

She will bend for me.

She will come for me.

She will be mine and mine alone.

CHAPTER 53

PRESENT

TOBY

"YOU'RE UNBELIEVABLY STUPID," I HEAR JASE before seeing him. "I figured after all the shit I put Peaches through, you would have learned and not be a piece of shit like I was. But here you are, being just as bad."

"Fuck off," I growl.

Hurting Joey once more and forcing her to leave was my parting gift. I'm only going to destroy her. In the midst of our discussion, when she broke me, I realized she needed better. And that wasn't me.

Not yet, at least.

I can't be better without change. I need change. She

deserves someone who can say they've worked to better themselves before expecting her to try.

"You really haven't changed," he bites out. It's like all the hostility from earlier that he kept at bay is oozing through. "You're still an entitled little shit who thinks he deserves everything he damn well pleases."

I glare at him, not something he's unused to, but fuck him and his hoity-toity bullshit routine. It's not my fault he didn't treat his wife well. It's not even my fault that she loved me. Most of all, if he didn't decide Ellie was what he wanted when he was hurting, Lo would never have slept with me.

"You're just pissed because I fucked your wife," I bark, feeling all the resentment slowly seep into my words. "You're mad that I got her pregnant and gave her a baby. You're so desperate to hide that fact from me that I didn't even know she had a child!"

He rushes me, bunching my shirt between his fists. If anger was a person, my brother, with all his pent-up rage, would be it.

"Lev is *my* son. Not yours."

"Why? Because you raised him without bothering to tell me? He has my blood, Jason. *My* blood. He *is* mine."

"No, he fucking isn't," he barks, spittle leaving his mouth.

"How does it feel knowing my cock gave your wife what she wanted most?"

Those words do it. He swings back and hits me right in the eye. I stumble back and then charge, tackling him to the ground. The whoosh of air that leaves me from the impact doesn't stop my assault. He ruined everything. By fucking some slut and making me love his wife, all the way to him not telling me I had a child. My own fucking flesh and blood.

"Stop!" Lo screeches. "Stop it!" I hear her, but I don't. The muddied way my mind is set on hurting my brother and making him feel my absolute agony is stronger than her pleas.

It isn't until someone pulls us apart that I notice how badly we've wrecked each other. Ace glares at us both, and I'm shocked to see the kid is the same height as us and even a little bulkier. He must've had one hell of a growth spurt in the past few years.

We kept in touch, but I hadn't seen him at all in that time. He's unamused at the predicament I've found myself in.

"You two are such little bitches," he curses. His expressionless mask doesn't hide the contempt coming off him in waves. "Both of you cheat and fuck other women. For what? Why don't you leave?"

When neither of us have an answer, he scoffs.

"You're both dipshits. My mom deserves better, and Joey sure as hell does too."

I'm nodding at him because he's right. I've fucked up so many times that I've lost count.

"You need to get this off your chest," he says as he points at me. "Talk to Mom and get this shit over with." When Jase goes to protest, Ace narrows his eyes into slits.

"And you need to fucking let it go. You fucked up while he swooped in and raised your kids."

438

"You little—"

"Stop," Lo hisses. "Toby, let's talk. Ace, behave."

Ace rolls his eyes at his mom as I walk past him, following Lo to wherever she decides to take me. This'll be fun.

As soon as we enter her old guest room, the words bleed out of me.

"Do you realize how hard it was to watch you fall apart?"

"T-Toby," she tries, but I stop her, needing her silence. Never thought I'd want that, her nothingness, the non-existence of words, apologies, and feelings… but I do.

"Please, I need to say this."

She nods, her eyes sadder than I've seen in a long time. You see, when she went into her numbness, a lot of the grief disappeared entirely.

Right now, it's shining brightly, illuminating as a Zippo flickered to life during a power cut

Now, her pain is as vibrant as a double rainbow, giving twice the hope, doubling the chances of happiness. *It's change.*

"When you fell apart all those times, so did I. Along with you, I died."

Slowly. Withering. Desperately.

"That connection I'd held so dear since high school, it was there. I knew it. Whether buried deep or at the surface trying to claw out, it was there, and I needed it. I didn't know how to achieve it. I only knew I needed to. I thought, maybe if I loved you more than living, I'd deserve you and finally not feel alone."

Understanding stirs in her eyes, it wells up over her eyelids like a promise. And they are. Promising healing, sanctuary, and hope.

That's the problem with hope, though. You fool yourself into thinking you're meant to be, but reality has a harsh way of showing you how wrong you are.

"You fixed me."

"Tobe—"

"No, let me talk, Sparkle. Please," I implore, watching as her face blotches with emotion. "That day, when we were in the hospital, you stood up to Brant. It was the first day I felt more scared for you than myself. It was a day-to-day fear. *Death.* Not knowing if he'd kick too high or into a narrow crevasse where my heart would decide to give out and it'd be more than my body could endure..." I pause, the pain rushing out of my eyes like pinpricks, ebbing away the shield I've slowly grown.

I stare at her, the woman I believed to be the owner of every part of me—and she was at one time—but now as her face morphs into so much pain, it's not her who I worry about and have at the forefront of my mind. *It's Joey.*

"I didn't know if you'd survive him. He terrified me shitless, Lo. He abused the fuck out of me for years, and besides you, I learned the only escape I could find was booze."

She shakes her head in disagreement, but she didn't know. She had Jase. Jase had her. *I only had scraps.*

Morsels are enough to feed the hungry, but I was starving—

famished—diminished by the light and guided by the dark.

"It numbed me, eased a broken and pitiful part of me. Or, at least, I thought it did. It consumed me in a new way, giving me a comfort I sought in you. Then before I knew it, it was my only friend, my only sustenance, my only excuse. But again, I asked for it. I reached for it instead of help, knowing it'd make me forget for a little while. It hurt me as much as I let it. Now… now that I'm aware and sure of what it truly did, I can move forward."

She closes the distance, hugging me to her chest.

Once, this would have been everything.

Once, it would have changed my world.

Once, I would have loved her more.

Not anymore.

It means closure.

It's *the end*.

The closing.

Our ever after, not happy nor sad, it just *is*.

"Thank you for giving me life, Lo. You were the life I was missing, the closure I needed, the push to be the best me… you were that. So, thank you."

I pull back as I watch every emotion and memory flutter in her angst-sodden lashes. Lo was circumstance, but Joey is my destiny.

"I love you, Toby," she finally says. Hugging her closer for a moment, I pull away for the last time.

"I love you too, Sparkle. Till the end of time." I kiss her forehead softly for the last time, cherishing the sweet smell of peaches, love, and resolution.

As I walk away, I hear her break down. This wasn't about her or us. It was entirely about Joey and the future I'm not risking ever again.

LO

THERE'S SO MUCH I WANT AND NEED TO SAY. So much. He rushed out the door before I got the chance to say a single thing. It only takes seconds to run after him. So I run after him, chasing him like how he used to chase me for years.

That's it, isn't it?

He chased. I let him.

He put in effort. I used him.

He loved me unconditionally. I loved him limitedly.

"Toby!"

His head swivels to mine, his face forlorn and full of emotion. Our conversation is burned into my heart, searing the flesh to record a new meaning, a heartbeat that means calm and tranquility.

Peace.

A fresh start.

I want him to be a part of our child's life. Always have, especially after finding out Lev is his too. It's a burning sensation that hasn't ebbed. If anything, this conversation confirms his growth as a man. Maybe life can change, and everything will work out.

He deserves it.

Lev, too.

"Please, I need to say some things." I'm next to him now. His hand is on his car door, his eyes are shiny with emotion, and his face is full of fear.

"I want you to be a part of Lev's life. I need that."

He nods, almost like he can't believe the words escaping my mouth. "Why now?"

"Seeing you, knowing you fell for someone. Understanding that she loves you the way I never could," I release shakily, my heart ping-ponging inside my chest. "She's good for you."

"Too late now," he bites, his voice teetering on unhinged.

"What did you do?"

"Did you not notice she left? Ran, really... she hates me."

"I repeat, Tobias, what did you do?"

"Sent her away," he admits, his voice strained. "Told her the things she feared most. That's what I do. I'm fucking toxic, Sparkle." He touches my face, and I flinch. Not because he's not comforting, but because he's using me as a way to convey emotions that he wants to give his wife. Just as Jase did with Ellie.

Pulling away, I glare at him. "You fix this." It's a command. "You fix your marriage and love that girl. You've both lost so much already."

With my words, his eyes gloss over. "Be a good husband and not a piece of shit."

It comes out with resentment, and I hate that. Hate that it slipped out. We have so much to work out. If we want to

443

be a family again, that's what needs to happen. He needs to realize we can't fix everything and moving forward is our only option.

"After you fix yourself and win that girl's heart, then we can talk about you being a part of Lev's life. You ruined me, and I ruined you, Toby. Let's stop the vicious cycle and fix this."

He nods but doesn't say anything.

"We were good once. Let's be that again?"

"I'm not good for anyone in this state," he says solemnly.

"Then get sober, call Bobbie, and fucking make amends."

His eyes connect with mine

"You're right."

"Aren't I always?"

"So modest," he chides. Then I'm hugging him, feeling the barrier I've constructed between us break in his hold. It's familiar. Not love. Not forbidden. Just what it was meant to be.

Us.

"I love you, Toby," I whisper.

"I love you too, Sparkle."

"Now go be the man you were with me for her. But this time," I say, pulling back, "be better. She deserves nothing less than your best."

He nods, kissing my forehead. The heat swims through me in a comfortable way. It's crazy to think how five years ago, it brought me mixed emotions. Now, it brings me nothing but closure.

When he releases me and drives away, I don't feel any more pain or resentment. All that's left is happiness.

CHAPTER 54

JOEY

WHO KNEW GETTING YOUR HEART BROKEN WOULD feel like a loss worse than death? I've been living at Treasure Cove—a hotel—hoping my life won't end with the many times I've taken a blade to it.

I know it's wrong.

I know it's detrimental.

I can't seem to care anyway.

Blood bubbles at the newest site. The makeshift razor I made from a broken knife blade is my only tool. This cut is deep. So deep that the bubbles are forming into a huge stream.

Fuck.

I'm usually careful. Use the pressure as a release, stop crying, allow myself a new pain to make me forget about the true culprit.

Not this time.

No matter how many strikes against my bumpy flesh, I can't stop. It's not abating anything. It's worsening my hatred and absolutely wrecking me.

I need to breathe.

Just fucking let me breathe.

Instead of getting a rag for the crimson leakage, I just rest against the door of my temporary bathroom and let the red drip.

Everyone says red is an indicator of negative behavior. Whether anger or rage, it describes a feeling that isn't pleasant.

It always made me wonder why blood was red. It's not an angry liquid. It's a solemn and desolate one. Where your body hates itself so much that the blood wants to leak as tears do. It's such a fluorescent color too, bright and thick. It's so beautiful.

Blood travels down my pale arms to my open palm, and I watch as it paints me. Not in anger, no. It's something else. It reminds me of hopelessness, but there was never any hope, was there?

I set aside my new blade and stand. The red smears the carpet and drips as I walk. I must've hit a muscle or something because I'm getting a little woozy.

Maybe it's the sight of blood. I've never been a fan, even if cutting is my ritual.

I find the bottle of Jameson I stole from Toby before

leaving three weeks ago. He thinks I don't know he has one in every room of our place. I'm stupid, just not *that* stupid.

When I grab the green bottle, it feels heavy in my palm. I pop the cap and take a swig. A cough leaves me, because shit, this stuff is potent. After drinking a ton of wine, this almost seems like gasoline in comparison.

How the hell did he gulp this like water? Grabbing my phone, I take it with me to the bathroom, grab my blade, and sit in the bathtub.

I take a swig; I strike my skin.

I take a gulp; I dig into my flesh.

I choke back a sob, and repeat.

My arms are vermilion and dark, but I don't care.

Nothing matters anymore.

I have no life. No child. No husband.

I have desolation and emptiness. If only my ice didn't melt...

My head fogs, my stomach clenches, and my body aches. I take the blade and put it to my thigh.

With as much strength as I can muster, I carve a little heart, and before I know it, blackness is welcoming me.

What took you so long?

CHAPTER 55

PRESENT

TOBY

SHE ISN'T ANSWERING HER PHONE. AVOIDING CALLS from me. Her father. Lo. Jase. I even asked Francis. It's been three weeks of searching. She's gone.

Something is wrong. I went too far. After talking to Lo, it all made sense. I fucked up and hurt my wife. My words were too strong, too hurtful.

She's struggling.

Lo mentioned Joey's arms when I asked if they heard from her.

How had I not noticed she started cutting again?

How did she hide the marks?

Why am I such a fucking loser?

My heart races as I stalk our accounts. Then, as if a siren is blaring, I see that our card was used at a fry shop. The one right by the cove she used to love to surf at. I get in my car and break every law known to man to get there.

"What can I do—"

"I need to find my wife. She's not responding, and she's suicidal," I practically yell at the older woman before showing her a picture of Joey.

"You have to help me, please. The cops are on their way."

And they are, I called them before driving here.

"She came in a few weeks ago, sad little poppet. She had smears of make-up and tears so fresh my flowers bloomed from them."

"Please, ma'am. I need to find her."

"She's in room twenty-one. The middle tower."

"Where's that?" I question, feeling a deep-seated need to save her rush through me. She points and then hands me a key. I'm running, faster than I've ever done, and I head up the stairs. She's only two floors up, and the elevator won't be quick enough.

This gnawing in my stomach is telling me something is god-awfully wrong, and I can't stand worrying anymore. I haven't felt this way since Lo overdosed. And even then, I didn't feel this much of a foreboding, so it only solidifies my belief that Joey and I are soulmates. Inevitable.

Fate.

Not circumstance.

I find her room and scan through. It's silent. Not even her favorite heartbreak playlist is playing. She does that, goes on music binges to convey how she's feeling. As soon as I see the hallway, I see red spots on the ground. My stomach heaves with a rush of nausea.

Rushing into the bathroom, I see my wife. Jameson in hand. A knife on the floor, covered in blood. Her eyes closed.

Her skin is covered in blood, red and sliced up.

"Why would you do this?" I yell, unable to calm the frantic pulse of my heart. "Why, Josephine? Why!" I scream and feel my chest heaving with pressure. I cry, my fucking eyes burn with the tears and their rampant need to escape. It hurts feeling them bleed from me, and I lift my wife as I sob. She's cold and as white as a sheet. I don't know if she's breathing, but I can't seem to settle enough to check. I place my head at her throat and hear wheezing. She's still breathing. But why is she so white? So cold? So numb?

I bawl as I hold her to my chest, not knowing the protocol for this situation. Lo wasn't a serial cutter. How do I prepare for this kind of depression?

I barely survived when Loren went through it, but someone as vital to me as breathing? There's no way I'll survive if I lose her. The door bursts open, and I yell, "In here!" My voice cracks with the strain and worry.

"Name, sir?"

"I'm Toby, this is my wife Joey." He checks her body and

puts a pump mask to her mouth. "What happened?"

"We got into an argument a few weeks ago while at my brother's. His wife said Joey started cutting again, and it took me all this time to find her."

They nod.

"She's been drinking. There's a bottle in the other room." The words just keep rushing out of me, bleeding like my wife does.

They lift her, taking her outside the room.

"The police will want to get a statement."

"Can't they do that at the hospital? I'm not leaving her side," I nearly bite his head off. I'm not leaving her like this.

He nods, and I follow.

The entire way to Hollow Ridge General, I sob and wait for her eyes to open.

CHAPTER 56

JOEY

MY EYES FEEL HEAVY, AND THE SMELL OF antiseptic sends me into a spin of nausea. It isn't until I hear beeping that I realize what I've done.

Shit.

Shit.

Shit.

"Joey?" Toby's timid voice speaks, and my eyes entirely open. He's kneeling, holding my palm and looking as if he died.

Did he?

Did I?

Is this hell?

I try to talk, but my mouth is too parched. He reaches for the water and helps me take a drink.

"I love you," he promises, his tone deeper and surer, but mostly sad. "Don't ever try to take my girl away from me." It's a threat, but the kind that are endearing and harmless. I try to smile, but my body aches. Instead, he gets a grimace.

"Pain?"

I nod.

He grabs a little remote, and it lets us know a nurse is on their way. I can't believe I'm in the hospital. I really fucked up this time.

Toby stares at me in wonder, like he can't believe I'm alive. Did I die? I only remember sadness and pain and alcohol.

"You scared me," Toby sounds out, gripping my wrist harder. "I think I died waiting for you to open those eyes." Tears prick at the corners of said eyes, and I'm barely holding them in as he kisses my hand. "Living a life without you is impossible, Sous. I can't do it."

"Then don't," I whisper, my voice hoarse and broken.

"Why did you run? That's my forte," he says, his face sunken with stress and fear.

"Because as soon as I walked out of that house, I died. Even with everything you put me through and what we struggled with, I already forgave you. It made me hate myself more."

CHAPTER 57

JOEY

"YOU'RE THE MOST BEAUTIFUL WOMAN I'VE EVER laid eyes on.

"You say that now," she whispers, her face filled to the brim with emotions. She's been like this for days. I practically hired a new manager for my job, taking care of Joey since she left the hospital. We sit here in the front room of our home. She still doesn't wear her ring, and I know it's my doing.

I watched my brother destroy his wife with words and actions.

And I've followed his lead.

Annihilated my wife's trust, her heart, all because I

couldn't be a decent human.

She stares outside, but I can see her pain, feel it as if it's my own.

"I'll always say you're beautiful. Even when I'm stupid."

She doesn't respond, just hugs herself and nods.

"They never kissed me," I admit, needing to get this off my chest. Needing her to know. "I never kissed them either."

Tears slip past her eyes, and I know it's because of pain, not relief. She needs to know how much I hated myself. At least, so that she can have the full picture.

"It's not really something I thought I'd ever be explaining, but we always wore protection. I never went down on them."

She shakes her head, closing her eyes as they pool with tears. My stomach seizes at the sight. I don't want her to hurt, I hate seeing her hurt, but I need her to know.

"I'd watch our videos before… every time." I cough around the words, not wanting to say what they blatantly are. Sex. Fucking. Cheating.

"You mean to say, instead of staying in our room and fucking me, you allowed yourself to watch our times together and fuck someone else instead?" she spits. "How is that okay, Tobias? How does that make a fucking lick of sense?"

I flinch at her words. She was never one for formalities.

"Yes," I admit, feeling that absolute despicable hate for myself rise.

"It doesn't matter that you never licked their pussies or that you never let your lips touch theirs. It's the fact that you fucked them instead of me," she all but hisses. "Was I not enough for you?"

Her body shakes with her question, and I move to be closer to her. She doesn't stop me as I lift her onto my lap. I'd never call my wife frail, she's anything but. Right now, though, with her sobbing in my lap, looking at me with the utmost sadness, she feels so small.

"You are enough, more than fucking enough." I sound angry but it's not directed at her. It's directed toward myself. "And you're right. I shouldn't have fucked them in spite of you. But you agreed. That day when I saw you with Francis, you said okay. You accepted my deal."

"I thought it was a joke!" she sobs. "Who the fuck tells their wife that?"

"I figured you wanted him. We signed a contract with your dad, so it's not like we had much of a choice to stay. I spent my entire life being the second choice. Seeing you with Francis. His hands all around you... comforting you when we had just lost our child... I lost it. Absolutely and entirely. I couldn't breathe realizing you were going to break me just like Lo did."

She vehemently shakes her head, her face full of pain. "I went there for Gray," she explains, her face scrunches at the memory. "She was with your nephew, and they were fighting. When I went to talk to her, she ran after him." I look at her, wondering when Ace drove all the way to Hawthorn when Hollow Ridge wasn't close by any means. "Then I turned to enter the house and wait for her, but Francis found me."

I nod, knowing this part. I witnessed this part.

"He held me and told me he was sorry that I lost our child. He wished he could fix it for me and you. He was worried about you, but mostly he wanted to know how I was handling everything."

I'm staring at her, not seeing the situation like she did.

"He hugged me and told me I'd be a mom eventually. I cried a lot while he just held me. Then he said you'd be here for me and make me feel better. You just needed time."

"I was there," I mutter, hating that she went elsewhere for comfort.

"I know, but you weren't. You were there in all the right ways except for the most important one." She hiccups, her chest rising and falling with pain. "You didn't grieve with me. It was like I was the only one who hurt. Our child was gone… dead. And you were working and being a doting husband without feeling a single ounce of pain."

"I felt everything," I say in exasperation, not wanting to yell. She's going through enough as it is. "I cried every fucking night. When you went to bed, work, or to Gray, I allowed myself to break down."

She stares at me dumbfounded, as if I'm a mystery to her. "You cried?"

"Yes, Sous. I did. Every single day."

Her eyes shut as fresh tears leave her. "I thought you were a robot and didn't care that we just lost our only chance at having a baby."

I grip her chin, adjusting her on my lap. "It's not our last chance, Sous. Not by a long shot. We won't stop trying." With her pain-filled nod, I pull her face to mine and lay a soft kiss on her forehead, wanting to bleed emotion into her with every second our skin connects.

"I cared about our child. When we got the news, it took everything in me not to break down with you. After watching my brother and his wife go through this, I knew one thing. My pain couldn't possibly compare to your pain. You lost a child that grew inside you. You lost a life. Yes, I did too, but not like you did. How could I allow you to experience my hurt when you experienced it so much worse?"

Our gazes meet, both of them wet with intense sentiment and pain. So much fucking pain. She leans forward and takes my lips with hers. She's not soft but not aggressive. She's pouring every ounce of her sadness into me, telling me we are meant to experience this together.

She's right.

I grip her jaw and hold her to my mouth, worshipping her as best as I can. She moans when my hand slips into her fiery hair, massaging her scalp as I swipe my tongue between her lips.

She starts rotating on my lap, making me hard as a fucking rock, but I won't take advantage. She's in a bad headspace, one that's fueled by desperation and sadness. It's not like she'd be into this otherwise. Not after what I've done and what she's seen with her own eyes.

"I need you," she whispers against my lips. Pulling back

enough to see her face and make sure it's not the grief riding her, I wait for her to show anything akin to not wanting me.

"You're hurting," I offer. She has to want this. I've fucked up too much to ever break that trust.

"Make it stop hurting, Toby. I need this," she promises, fusing our mouths together. She bites my lip, digging hard and nearly piercing my skin. "Please."

With that plea, I'm lifting us both off the couch. She wraps her thighs around me. We don't break our kiss. Not even for air.

When we make it to our bedroom, I lay her on the bed. Her eyes are filled with lust and something I feel too—the need to reclaim what's mine.

She's so beautiful. Her eyes, those lips, and that fucking throat that makes me want to mark her for everyone to see. She's tarnished perfection. I'll spend the rest of my life fixing us. I'll do anything. Love her harder. Love her deeper. Love her more than anyone else ever has.

"Fucking breathtaking," I breathe, pulling down her night shorts. Underneath, she's wearing cotton panties. Something else I've always found absolutely intoxicating about my wife? Her sexiness when she's comfortable. She doesn't have to wear lace and satin. Not garters and nighties. She's fucking sexy without all the added touches. It's her. She does it for me. Every goddamn time.

Tracing her pale legs and the little scabbed over heart on her thigh, I moan. She's my reckoning, and I didn't even know it when we met.

Leaning down, I kiss her heart, making sure she knows it's beautiful too. It's a bearer of pain, an appendage of love lost; it's strength when she could've been weak.

She's unravelling me, and we haven't even started.

She pulls my head away from the heart and shakes her head. "It's ugly," she whispers, embarrassment and fear tickling her features like a feather to the wind. "All of them are." The way her voice breaks with those four words has me trailing kisses until I reach her mouth. She folds into herself. The long sweaters she's been wearing for the past few weeks covering every inch of her upper body.

"You're absolutely beautiful, Josephine. You fucking kill me with your beauty every single day. If I wasn't already absolutely gone for you, I'd fall to my fucking knees with your presence alone."

She shakes her head at me, her lips trembling with sadness. It's tragic, really, that she can't see how beautiful she is by simply existing. I kiss each of her closed eyes, her nose, her cheeks, and finally, when she's breathing heavily, I take her mouth.

She bends into me, her body molding to mine. It's something I've wanted for months. Her entire body, pressed against mine, loving mine, being mine and only mine.

I pull back, but only so she doesn't deflect what I'm about to say. When I help her to sit, she hides her face. I tip her chin up, and she shuts her eyes.

"What'd I say about those eyes, Sous? They're meant to watch."

She lets out a deep exhale, shivering in my embrace. I know it's not from the cold. Not offering me those pretty amber eyes of hers, I start to undress her anyway.

She wiggles, trying to keep the sweater on. "Can't I leave it on while you fuck me?" Letting out a little scoff, I continue to wrestle the sweater off her small frame.

"And waste the perfect opportunity to both ogle and grope your tits? Fat chance."

She smiles at me, fully smiles, and I know I've hit my mark. My girl is competitive, and brash, and so goddamn sassy. It's her confidence I've always loved. From the second our eyes met across that room to the moment we woke up next to each other the following morning. We're meant to be. It's us. She battles me, and I fight her tooth and nail. We clash, yes, but when we both bend for each other, our resilience snaps like a fucking rubber band about to burst.

We aren't opposites at all.

We're the same.

She hates, and I hate.

She loves, and I love.

She fucks, and I fuck right back.

Not listening to her groaning as I lift the material, I see her tattoo. The one I still haven't asked her about. We've been together for nearly three years now, and I still don't know what this vital quote means. One that had to matter enough for her to mark her skin.

Tracing my fingers over the simple line, I decide right

now is a good enough time as any. "Be free, not still," I recite, thumbing her ribs. She shivers, goose bumps rising to the surface of her perfectly pale skin. I love them on her. "I've never asked what it means to you."

She bites her plush lip, grinding her top teeth over it like it'll divulge her secrets so she doesn't have to. "When I was attacked in Paris, I lost all hope to be free. Exploring was the one thing that brought me all my hope and desire to become a chef. It drove me to want to taste weird things and experience all the bad just in case good came along."

I smile at that. This is the first time she's spoken about Paris without crying. It's progress. It's hope.

"When I came home and had to go back to school, I felt empty. There was this hole in my chest that was ripped open by a man who had zero morals. I felt stilted. My growth and freedom halted in that alleyway in France. He took from me. Not just my innocence, but my hope, my will to explore, my desire for the unknown."

As I watch her like this, her eyes glossy with the memory but shining with strength and voracity, it's breathtaking.

"I met Wesley then."

I grimace, thinking of the loser surfer douche who thought he could win my wife back. He can fuck right off.

"Yes, him." She laughs, and it's so melodical and light. It's perfect and sweet. It's tender and loving.

"He helped me not feel so lost. Made me want to take risks and win. He changed the game for me. Even if he was an absolute waste of time."

"I disagree. Without him, we wouldn't have met," I joke and wink. It's true, even if it seems unlikely.

"You're right. He fixed the meek part of me. When I came home and Dad didn't see the change in me, I didn't tell him any of it. Not about the miscarriage, the rape, or the disease, and he didn't care to ask."

I hug her to me then, hoping to love all the sadness away. Imagine if a hug could do that? Love every bad thing away and only offer hope and peace? We'd have a new cure for all of life's hardships.

"Meeting Wes was purely fateful. Dad was doing a rally, and he was there to surf on the same beach. When he spilled his beer near my dad and Daddy dearest hated him immediately, I felt a fire I thought I lost in that alley. One that hadn't rose or erupted for anything. Plus, Wes was cute."

I growl, nipping her throat.

"Jealousy looks hot on you," she teases. "Wesley was *hot*," she clarifies, and I'm sucking her flesh between my lips in hopes I leave a mark. "Okay, beast man. I'll lay off. Let me finish my story so you can get back to touching me."

I smirk, knowing that I make her wet and horny whenever I'm rough in a caveman sort of way. She'll never admit it, but she loves when I'm possessive. She has since that night at Francis's house when I showed her exactly whose cock would be filling her for the rest of her life.

"He was checking me out…" I bite her again and pinch her

nipple for good measure. "Oh, come on!" she grunts. I chuckle at her flushed face.

"Smart man, knows a hot piece of ass when he sees one."

"You're a perv, Tobias."

"Yet you still like riding my cock." Her face reddens, and she bites her lip.

"As I was saying," she deflects. "We hit it off, and he reminded me of why I'd never be still ever again. I'd always seek freedom and peace, even if it meant sticking it out to the shitty times no one could plan for."

When she says those words, she looks away from me. But I won't have it. Not today, not when we're making progress, not when she thinks she'll hurt me.

It hurts, but it's my fault not hers.

"I'm sorry I fucked up."

"Those words don't mean what you want them to," she whispers.

"They do," I argue. "Because I'll never fucking make the mistake of hurting you again."

"How can you be so sure?" she questions, finally looking back at me. Her trust is broken, but I'll work endlessly, even if I never get it back.

"Believe me, Sous," I swear, holding her jaw and rubbing it softly. "If there's anything in life I'll ever promise you, it's that I'll never betray you again. If you're mad or hugging other men, I won't assume and accuse." She stares at me in open-mouthed shock.

"If they get too handsy, though, I'll fucking string them up by their balls myself."

A giggle escapes her, making me feel so warm inside it's unreal.

"Love me even when I'm a mess, Sous."

Her gaze locks with mine, and she doesn't waver when she responds. "I do. Pretty sure I have since we scowled at each other in that event room."

"It was foreplay, Sous. All fucking foreplay."

"I love you, Toby. More than cooking."

A smile breaks free from my mouth. "I love you too, little chef."

I waste no time to pin her to the bed, watching as her mouth opens in a moan. This is my fucking wife, and it's about time I remind her.

CHAPTER 58

JOEY

I WANT TO SAY MORE, TO TELL HIM HE CHANGED ME more than Wes ever could. That I hated him as much as I loved him for so long that giving in to just the love freaks me out.

But he has different plans.

He splits my thighs and resides between them, rubbing against me slow and torturously. Fighting him with my sweater wasn't supposed to end with him winning. My scars are still fresh and scabbed over. They're ugly and treacherous, reminding me of my weakest moments.

They always paint suicidal people as the bad guy.

Committing suicide is selfish.

I've heard those words on so many occasions that they're painted in my mind like a memoir of what not to say to someone who debates living on a daily basis.

Not debating death, nor debating whether to live another day.

Suicide isn't selfish.

At the time, when the pain is too much, where it overrides every single fiber of your being to where nothing else matters, it's freedom.

It's spreading your wings and shedding the weight of what the world has toppled upon you. It's escaping that constant pain that burrows into your flesh whether you want it to or not. It's feeling nothing when life has only given you everything in heavy doses.

So no, it's not selfish. Living is selfish.

Living with a burden of pain that refuses to ebb or ease, that's not fair. We can only live for others for so long before even that becomes too much.

Staying, now, that's also selfless. Not to ourselves, the ones experiencing endless torture, but to the ones who surround us. We're only breathing because you wish it. We're only staying because you'd be empty without us. We're only here because letting go would leave us with guilt as our final thought.

Suicide isn't simple.

It's not.

It's hard and full of never-ending pain.

It's not something someone who has never experienced its

thrall can explain or allude to. Because until you're at the end of your story, the last chapter, last page, and last sentence, you couldn't understand.

Yeah, you may have an idea of what it means and that a person must be hurting, but you couldn't possibly feel what a person at the cusp of ending their lives is feeling.

Me wanting death wasn't Toby's fault. It wasn't mine. It wasn't one thing here or there. It was a build-up, something that started young and carried itself on my back through life. It was a burdensome weight that suffocated me if I got too comfortable, one that drowned me when I floated too close to the sun, and one that would bleed me dry if I thought for even a second that life was a little too much.

And as Toby kisses my throat and shoulders, trailing his lips across my arms, I want nothing more than to hide that truth.

"Not there," I whimper as his face hovers over my forearms. His eyes peer directly into mine, digging deep, making sure I see what he's seeing.

"Yes, here," he murmurs, placing his lips on the tender flesh. "And here." He kisses the juncture of my elbow. "Right here, too." His mouth touches my largest scar. The jagged one that's the most tender. "Because these scars, Joey," he reiterates, hovering his face over mine. "They're fucking breathtaking. A reminder of what you've been through, how much I've hurt you, and that I'll do every fucking thing in life to make sure no new ones join these."

Through the tears, I see and feel him kissing the same path

on my other arm.

"You're sexy, Josephine. So fucking sexy, scars and all." He finishes at my wrist and then starts all over again, kissing, caressing, touching. When all my tears are gone, he's moving up my body to take my mouth, silencing my demons once and for all.

"Now spread your thighs and let me kiss the wet cunt that belongs to me."

I push my legs apart and his mouth hovers over my pussy. He stares at me with intent, and as he lowers, my eyes shut of their own accord. Before he even touches my clit, he stops.

Opening my eyes to see him smirking devilishly, I realize my mistake. He wants me to watch. Forcing myself not to become consumed with pleasure is a feat in itself, but he always wants to be seen.

"That's a good little chef. Keep those pretty amber eyes on me." Watching him lick my pussy is so much hotter than closing my eyes to feel each tongue-lashing, but fuck, sometimes the pleasure overwhelms me, and I can't breathe without feeling it all instead of watching.

His tongue flattens and swipes slowly. He wants me to feel every sensation. He's torturing me. His eyes are hot and ravenous on mine as his tongue flicks over me slowly. I moan as I watch him wrap his lips around my clit. He groans, and I'm already on the fucking edge. We haven't had sex in ages, and the only orgasms I've had are with my hand or BOB.

Unlike most men, Toby knows where my clit is, so he

makes sure to only focus on it unless he's taunting me. He drags his teeth over the swollen nub, and I'm crying out.

"Count." I know immediately what he's demanding of me. He wants me to count all my orgasms. Internal and external. Full body shakes and all.

"One," I hiss as he sticks two fingers inside me, trailing the wetness across and licking it clean. He's such a ravenous bastard. Always taking his fill and nothing less.

He thrusts into me, curling his fingers, wanting me to scream. He eventually gets what he wants when I can no longer hold in my pleasure. It's too much.

My clit throbs, and my legs shake. Knowing I won't be able to handle much more if he doesn't spread the stimulation, Toby rises and takes my mouth with his. My flavor bursts all over my tongue, swirling, and branding me with memories.

We're soulmates.

Toxic but perfect.

Bad but so good.

He groans when my hands wrap around his steel length. It's harder than I've felt in a long time. After our conversation, I keep thinking of all the times we've fucked, and how he tortured me with the details of his sexcapades. He'd always fuck me, and it was after he had them. He'd use me, and I'd let him.

"Stop."

He stills, freezing above me, removing his mouth.

It's not what he thinks, but I just need to know.

"Did they ever suck you off?" I ask, my heart hammering.

He doesn't smirk or make light of the words. I figured he'd come out with an *are you jealous, Sous?* But he just seems disappointed in himself all over again.

"Yes," he mutters. "That's all it was at first. It was an easy way for me to not see their faces…" he trails off, almost like he doesn't want to explain it.

"To pretend they were me?"

"Yeah," he says softly, guilt eating him up.

"Then I need to start there. Reclaiming what's mine."

His eyes gleam with ferocity. He doesn't waver as I push him off me, only lifts and assists. I lie at the edge of the bed on my back. "Is this how they did it? Where you couldn't see anything but their throats?"

He growls, fisting his length as if recreating every past sexual experience, replacing them with me.

"Yes," he growls.

"Then fuck my throat, husband. And show me how you wished it was me all along."

His eyes simmer. His cock twitches. He's going to choke me with that cock, and I'm going to come because of it. He steps to the end of the bed where my head hangs off. He bends a little to place himself at my lips, and I take him in one go.

In no time, he's fucking my face deep and hard. I keep my throat relaxed. He pulls out, and I peer up to see if something is wrong and realize he's not just watching me, he's recording me.

"New memories," he husks.

Then no more words are shared as he pushes back inside

my mouth, recording his cock choking me out. He thrusts and thrusts, and I'm drooling everywhere. Before he's about to release, he pulls out of me, stroking my throat, then kneeling to lick and nip my pulse point.

He bites and sucks and I just know he's leaving marks and branding me once again. He traces every inch of me all while holding his phone, recording it.

Grabbing my ankles, he drags me up the bed with no phone in sight.

"No more recording?"

"Oh, it's recording, sweetheart. But the only thing it'll have is your moans as I bury my cock inside your tight cunt."

"Toby," I moan as he grabs my throat and slams inside me. I'm so full of him, being stretched. It's so good to feel him rip me in half with his monster cock. It's so thick and rigid. I'm coming within ten seconds of him rotating his hips.

"Two," I sound out, and he kisses me on the lips.

"Good little chef."

He thrusts and thrusts, and when I'm about to combust again, he's pinching my clit and my back bows off the bed.

"Three," I barely whisper, not recognizing my hoarse voice.

My body trembles from head to toe as he drills into me. He's such a beast when it comes to reclaiming my body. Every time he thought I'd fucked Francis, he'd fuck me after. Punishing me with his cock, his mouth, and his hands.

"Fuck," he growls, pistoning his hips. I watch his taut

skin flex, licking my lips as I see the veins leading to his steely length inside me. He's huge and so fulfilling.

"Harder," I complain, trying to thrust up as he goes down. I need the pain. He lets my throat go, trailing his fingers down to my breasts. He pinches my barbell nipple, and I scream.

"Four." It comes out half hiss, half moan. He's pulling out of me in the next breath and lowering his face to my abused heat.

"I'm going to keep making you come, Sous. I'm going to own every fucking hole."

"You talk too much," I grumble.

"I've heard that before."

"Then you know... you talk too much."

He bites my clit and then soothes it with his tongue, eliciting a cry that turns into a moan. I shake as he eats me out, his tongue spearing inside me in tandem of his hands gripping my tits like they're his last hope.

"So fucking delicious, Sous. Are you going to squirt for me? Come on my tongue?"

His hand snakes down, spreading my folds wide as his other finger enters me. He's gathering my juices before he's trailing them to my asshole. His finger presses in, and I moan, wanting more. His mouth is between my legs, slurping and sucking my clit while he spears into my ass. I'm a mess of whimpers and near sobs as the sensitivity takes over. I'm about to combust.

He grinds down on my clit, and that's all it takes before I'm screaming his name and releasing all over his face. I can feel my body squirt, it comes out of me with my heartbeat as its tempo, yet he's not done with his assault of my clit.

"Five."

When he *finally* lets up, he's wiping his mouth with the back of his hand, smirking.

"We should add your cunt to the menu," he grunts as he works his way into me. "Scratch that, they don't deserve to taste heaven, and this is all *mine*."

"If it's yours, then why is it not filled with cum?" I challenge, seeing as his face morphs from teasing to desperate. That's all it takes to get him going again. He takes my wrists, pinning them on the bed, and then he's jackhammering inside me as I scream his name.

"I don't hear you counting, Sous," he husks.

"Six," I hiss, feeling my body wanting to shut down. He's definitely not stopping until he hits a number he's happy with.

"That's right. Keep counting." He kisses my sweat-lined forehead before flipping us over so I'm riding him. This is my favorite position. Not just because he's beneath me, but because he hits higher and makes it pinch with every thrust.

"Want me to claim your cock, husband?"

"Yes," he grumbles. "But we both know it's always been yours."

I bounce up and down on him, proving just that. He groans as I use his abs for leverage, wanting to rise as much as I can before I come down harder. After he's gripping my thighs as if I'm going to break his balls, I rise off and turn around, taking his cock while my ass is the only thing he'll see. When I slide down, the noise he makes is almost inhuman.

"Josephine." It's a bite. I can feel it as if it's digging into my flesh, leaving a brash red mark. I slide up and down his rigid length, and it's not even twenty seconds in that we're both finding our release.

"Seven," I whimper, barely pulling myself off him. His seed spills from me, escaping me in strings of white. It's warm and there's so much. He never comes this much; this must be a build-up.

"Fuck, Joey," he murmurs, pulling me to his chest. He holds me, and I rub up on him, nestling, feeling him cocoon me with love and warmth. It's everything I've wanted for months, and now that I'm getting it, it'll never be enough. I'll always want more. Always want him. Always want this.

I breathe in deeply, kissing where his heart is nestled beneath his ribs.

"Love the hate out of me, Toby." He shifts us so we're eye to eye.

"Love me more than I hate myself, Sous."

When his lips touch mine this time, it's with finality and promise. It's with love and lust and everything in between. It's with hate and sadness and heartbreak.

It's everything.

We are everything.

When life gets impossible, take a moment. And don't forget to breathe.

THE END

EPILOGUE 1

JOEY

"I WANT TO ADOPT," I TELL TOBY OUT OF THE BLUE. "I've been thinking about it, and that's what I want."

He nods happily.

"I've been thinking the same."

Heaving out a sigh of relief, I seek out his eyes. "I'm glad you say that," I let out. My breathing coming in short, panicked waves. "Because I already found a little boy."

"Already?" he questions, as if the idea is absurd.

"Yes." I'm nodding spastically now. There was a baby boy who was born early, nearly a year ago, and is barely leaving the NICU. He's so sweet and adorable. They haven't named him because when the teenage mother gave birth, she gave him up.

His story broke my heart, but it also reminded me of Toby and I. Abandoned. Loveless. Broken.

We'd love him so much, give him everything, and be the best parents he'll ever need. Already, I love him. I haven't even brought him home or met him in real life, but I'm absolutely enamored.

"I may have been researching before mentioning it to you." He kisses my nose, my cheeks, then my forehead.

"Who is he?"

"Nameless," I whisper, almost too emotional to think of how hard and lonely his life must have been. "He's in the care of the hospital. His little body has struggled so much. I want him, Toby."

He looks at me with care, scanning my face for my every need, before kissing the tears I didn't realize were spilling. "Then let's make it happen. We'll have to—"

"Get a case worker? Done."

"We're going to—"

"Need a home that's not attached to a hotel? I know."

"We are—"

"Going to need to work this out and figure out all the details? I'm on top—"

"No, now stop interrupting me." I laugh at the widening of his eyes. It's almost comical. "We're going to have to pick a name because once we bring him home, there's no going back."

I cry as he says those words. We've come a long way since

our short time apart. We're so much stronger now.

"Jasper," I say on a hushed whisper. "Jasper Tobias Hayes."

"JT," he muses. "I love it."

"I love you," I murmur, bringing his mouth to mine. "More than hate."

"I love you, enough that the hate leaves you too."

EPILOGUE 2

JOEY

AFTER BATTLING FOR JASPER, WE ARE FINALLY bringing him home. With his soft red mane, that nearly matches mine, and his olive skin, he makes these little noises. I'm obsessed. Barely able to put him down for naps and tummy time. He's so sweet when he smiles up at me.

And those eyes. They're an odd shade of brown. Almost like there's a battle between the red and orange hues surrounding his irises. They're like little sunsets, beautiful and vast and so breathtaking.

"I love you, Jasper. Your mommy loves you so much."

Our adoption was finalized, and we finally got our baby boy home. He's so perfect. The most precious thing I have. I kiss his little nose and hand him over to Toby.

"What's wrong, Gumby?"

"I'm feeling a bit nauseous," I mutter, the icky feeling overwhelming each breath. It's worse than bile; it's this overpowering need to purge my body of every sensation.

"You okay?" he asks, his eyes crinkling in kind.

"I'm sure it's nothing," I offer, but as I walk to our new bathroom, looking into the mirror, I notice how swollen my face seems.

Then it occurs to me.

I haven't had a period in two months.

Fuck.

"Hey, I need to run to the store." Toby looks at me with an odd expression.

"You alright?"

"Oh, yeah. Just need to pick up some things for our trip to Loren's. She insists we bring Jasper to meet his brother." A smile takes over Toby's face. He hasn't been outwardly about it, but he wants to raise Lev with them. He wants Lev to know he has two dads and a mom. And that while Jase isn't biologically his dad, he's no less Lev's father than Toby is. We had a big talk two months ago when we decided that we wanted to be a larger part of that boy's life.

Jase didn't want to hear it at first, but after the discussions progressed, and with help from Lo, he decided he wouldn't want to take the opportunity away from Toby since it's his son too.

"Can you get me some Skittles?"

I laugh. This man rarely eats anything with his strict diet, but lately, now that he's in AA again, he's addicted to sweets. It's easing him off the cravings—the alcoholic kind. Even I don't drink anymore. We're in this together. I'm in intensive therapy for my self-harm, depression, and miscarriage. I'm growing, and he's growing with me.

We're in this together.

Finally.

AFTER I USE THE STORE'S RESTROOM TO PEE ON A

stick, I'm in shock when a positive sign is staring me blatantly in the face. It's pink and pink and pink. It's real. I cry for a moment as I stare at it. Do I tell him? Do I wait?

Definitely need to tell him. We promised no more secrets. I purchase another three packs and take them home with me, crying the entire way.

When I'm inside, Toby is passed out with our baby boy nestled within his embrace. It's now, with him holding our child, that he's never looked sexier.

We've been going at it like rabbits since we mended our relationship. Nothing has stopped us from making constant love with our mouths and bodies.

It's no wonder I'm pregnant.

Me.

Pregnant.

I whimper, fresh tears falling down my face. Fucking hormones. Toby's eyes shoot open and a look of panic hits him. He lifts Jasper slowly, placing him into his bassinet, and rushes to where I'm standing at the doorway. "What happened? Are you okay? Who do I need to fuck up?"

At his words, the tears continue to flow freely, bleeding from me as my wrists once did from my pain. He cups my jaw. "Tell me what's wrong, sweetheart? Please. I can't fix it if I don't know the cause."

Handing him the little brown paper bag, he opens it to a box of tests and the one I peed on. His eyes widen. Fear rests in his dark gaze, bleeding into me like it's his only function. His face doesn't pale, but sweat is starting to form on his brows.

Pulling the little stick out, he eyes it, tears spilling down his cheeks. "I'm so scared, Toby," I sob.

He holds me to his chest, rubbing circles into my back. He peppers kisses all over my face, holding me as if I'm fragile and will break in his arms. I just might. "I'm scared too, Sous. But guess what?"

"What?" I gripe.

"We're in this together," he confirms my biggest fear. "I'll cry through this entire process with you. I'll hold you, hug you, cherish you, and I'll take care of you and our children. Because unlike last time? We're stronger, and nothing will come between us. We're a family, Josephine. And nothing will take any of you away from me."

He peels off my clothes in the next few minutes, laying me

on the floor. When he thrusts into me slow and surely, I have to silence my moans of completion. As he makes gentle love to me, worshipping my body, I know this is fate. We're destiny. Our battles were circumstance, and together, we're forever.

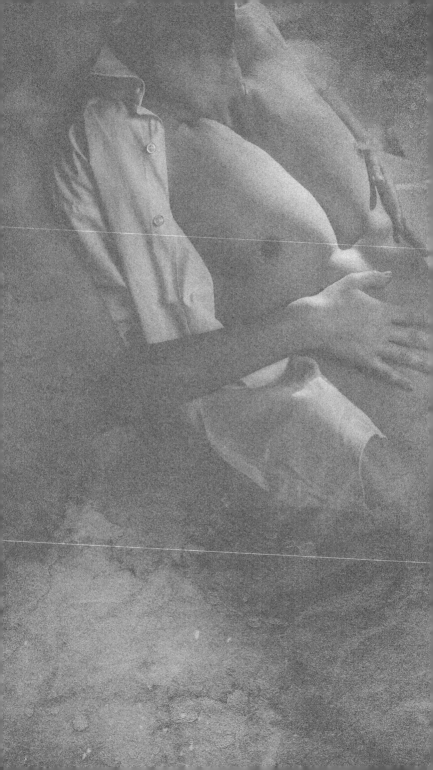

ACKNOWLEDGEMENTS

And they say blurb writing is hard.

Ha.

Joke is on me.

Matthew, my love, my other half, my light. I'm so grateful that you continually support me and love the brokenness from me. The fact that you watch me bawl my eyes out and comfort me whenever I write this sad stuff, it means everything.

Dimples. My British-buddy-who-doesn't-know-what-a-real-taco-is, thank you. Like, honest to the taco gods, I'm grateful AF for your guidance, support, and shoulder for me to scream on. Literally, this book would not have been finished without you. This book is here because you never gave up on me or it. Love you, bro.

Alexiss, lil sis. I'm so honored to help mold you into the woman you are, but I have to thank you for molding me into the woman I am today. And for helping me plot this book three times, you're the real mvp. YEET.

Selena, my writing bae, my ho, one of my bestest friends. I love you, dude bro. Whether it's four hour phone conversations, ten minute voice messages that are impossible to remember by the end, or the texts of your support, I appreciate them and you. You're a fucking gem and I don't know how I was lucky enough to have you be a part of my life, but I am.

Safae, Rukaiya, Geynar, and Cat. My Betas. You guys rocked it. Without your suggestions, your adamant need to make Toby and Joey their best, and TLC, I wouldn't have been able to bring these loves to life.

Cali, you will always be my twin. Love without hugs, ho.

Michelle, my Milkshake, life without you wouldn't have meaning. I adore you, love that we've grown so much, and am grateful to have such an amazing and close confidant that never stops supporting me. I love you.

Rina. I just adore you, bro. Thank you for coming into my life and never giving up on me. I appreciate you more than words and love you more than tacos.

MCG, my satanic smiling friend. You look so sweet, but in reality, a devil lurks. And I'm not joking! Fine, I am, but whatevs. Without you and our weird ass adventures, I'm sure I wouldn't have survived the torture I put myself through for this book. I love you, dude. Even if you destroy me with your books.

Mel, you found me, but I'mma say I found you too. Because why the hell not? You're a champ, going through all my sad episodes, trying to make me laugh, and sharing parts of yourself that I'm honored to hold near to my heart. Love you, girl.

To my editor, Jenny, thank you so much for helping me on this one! I appreciate you fitting me in!

There are so many authors I want to thank who may never even see this, but they always fight for me, cheer me on, and keep me going. You know who you are! I love and appreciate you all.

To my readers, for sticking around and championing me on this, for having patience and excitement, for just being you and loving my writing, thank you. I couldn't have accomplished this without you.

To all the bloggers who have spread the word, for helping me and being awesome, thank you!

And finally to you, if this is your first book of mine, hello! If it's not, welcome back, and I hope you can forgive me for toxic relationships I bring into fruition, and understand that no love is easy, but in the end, I always hope it's worth it.

But as always, love, no hugs, and a lot of tacos!

OTHER WORKS BY C.L. MATTHEWS

Inhale, Exhale. (Hollow Ridge #1)

Here Lives a Corpse (Here Lies #1)

Firsts (Cape Hill #1)

Lasts (Cape Hill #2)

Always (Cape Hill #3)

The Dating Games: Author Edition

Welcome to Cape Hill (Cape Hill Vipers #1)

COMING SOON

Dernier Souffle (Hollow Ridge #3)

Stagger (Driven World Novel)

Turbulent (Salvation Society Novel)

Everything You Heard is True (Standalone NA Romance)

Forevers (Cape Hill #4)

AND AS ALWAYS, IF YOU WANT TO FOLLOW ME, I WELCOME Y'ALL WITH OPEN ARMS!

Website: clmatthewsbooks.com

Facebook: www.facebook.com/clmatthewsauthor/

Instagram: www.instagram.com/clmatthewsauthor/

Twitter: www.twitter.com/clmatthews121

Books + Main: www.bookandmainbites.com/clmatthewsauthor

Join CL's Book Bitches: www.facebook.com/groups/858074374226482/

491

C.L. MATTHEWS

MA*C/L*THEWS

ABOUT THE AUTHOR

C.L. Matthews lives in lala-landia with her husband and invisible friends. She wants to riot the lack thereof authentic Mexican food in her state, but she's an introvert at heart. She enjoys tacos, Red Bull, and warm water, because she's crazy. She's an oddball, and realizes it's been mentioned before, just go with it. Her joys in life consist of writing unconventional romances, making book covers, causing havoc to her reader's hearts, and genre hopping when she needs a change of scenery. She's a special kind of weird and enjoys every moment of it.

Made in the USA
Middletown, DE
26 October 2023